The Gosey Series

Dan Bomkamp

Lovstad Publishing
www.Lovstadpublishing.com

ISBN: 0692533303
ISBN-13: 978-0692533307

Printed in the United States of America

Cover design by Lovstad Publishing

DEDICATION

This book is dedicated to our parents. Teenagers don't realize how much their lives are influenced not only by their own parents, but by the parents of their friends, too. As a kid, not only did I have the best friends in the world, I also had the benefit of knowing their parents and learning from them. This book is dedicated to Chick's mom, Bertha, who always had time for a game of Canasta with a bunch of teenagers. It's dedicated to Wayne and Darlene who put up with Doug's and my animals, and always had time for a few extra kids around the place. It's dedicated to Duane's mom and dad, Isabel and Orville. It's a wonder their restaurant was able to stay in business with all the food the four of us ate there for free. And of course, it's dedicated to my mom, Elaine. When my dad died unexpectedly when I was only 13, she took over and raised my brothers and me and made a wonderful home for us. And she always opened her heart—and her kitchen—to my famished friends, too.

The four of us, Dewey, Dougie, Chick and I have all turned out pretty good… thanks to *all of our great parents.*

The Gosey Series

The Gosey

Prolog

St-Sauvin, Bordeaux region of France, Autumn 1839:

Henri Albert Gauthier was perched on the stone fence that surrounded his family garden. Beside him was his best friend, Philippe De Luc. The two boys were lifelong friends, born two days apart and living on farms that bordered each other. But this evening, Henri was daydreaming of a life far away. He watched the sun setting over the vineyards to the west of the family farm and thought of the life that he was planning in America.

"Are you sure you will go to America?" Philippe asked. "There is nothing to keep me here," Henri said. "America is a new land that has many opportunities. You should come, too."

"Henri! Come to supper," his mother called from the house. "I must go," he said to Philippe. "See you tomorrow." He jumped down from the stone wall and went to the house where his four brothers, three sisters, and parents were sitting around the large, wooden table, waiting for him.

Henri had finished school that spring and had been helping on the farm during the summer. Now he would harvest grapes and assist with wine making on neighboring farms. After the long winter, he would head to America. He had informed his parents of his dream and-while not overjoyed at his decision to leave home-they supported him and hoped he would find a good life in the New World. Henri and Philippe worked the grape-harvest duties together. Henri was not able to convince his friend to accompany him to America because Philippe was sweet on the neighbor's daughter and had his mind made up to make her his wife and settle down to a life of farming.

The following spring Henri boarded a ship in Calais, in Pasde-Calais, and soon he was sailing for his new life in America. He shared a stateroom with three other young French lads who were also looking for fame and wealth, and desiring to escape the farm and the poor conditions in their country. The ocean miles passed quickly and soon they were steaming into New York Harbor. Henri was amazed at the immense buildings and the throngs of scurrying people. The city was full of noise and smoke and aromas from food vendors. There were dozens of languages being spoken as people from all over the world lived in this wonderful, new place. He made his way through Immigration and soon found himself on a busy street in downtown New York City. One of his ship bunkmates who had a cousin living in Brooklyn invited Henri to accompany him to see this individual who could help them get a start in this new city.

The fellows located the cousin, who operated a bakery.

Cousin Charles was overjoyed to see the two young men and invited them to stay with his family until they could find jobs and lodging. Henri and Emile helped in the bakery each morning, getting up at 3 AM, and after the bread was baked, they went searching for work. Emile soon found employment at a butcher shop but Henri was not as lucky. In time he felt he was imposing on Charles and decided to look for his own place to live. But rent was too expensive.

One day a billboard caught his attention. A man named Col. William S. Hamilton of Wiota was searching for workers for lead mines and smelters in a place called Wisconsin. He offered "top dollar" to anyone answering his ad. The idea of going to a frontier town appealed to Henri who was tiring of the big city. So he signed up, and a few days later, he boarded a train to Chicago. When he arrived at the train station, he was met by an employee of Col. Hamilton who put him on a buckboard wagon, along with a dozen other workers, and they headed north-to Wisconsin.

They arrived in an area called Mineral Point. They were given sleeping quarters and were taught how to work in the lead mines. It was hard, dirty work but the pay was good, the food was adequate, and when the men had time off, they delighted in the wonders of this new land. It was a beautiful part of the country with amazing wildlife, steep hills, and lush green valleys.

One day Col. Hamilton came to the mining camp recruiting workers for a new smelter in the north, in English Prairie. (Later English Prairie would be called Muscoda.) Henri and three of his fellow-miner friends volunteered to go, thinking that working at the smelter would be better than slaving in the dark, dirty mines.

They climbed on a wagon and, after a half day of traveling, found themselves in a small village along the Wisconsin River. The place was breathtaking! Tree-covered bluffs bordered the wide, clear river. Deer, squirrels, rabbits, ducks, and other game could be seen in abundance. The river was alive with fish of every kind. Col. Hamilton had built the smelter on the riverbank north of the village. They had constructed a large timber dock that flatboats could tie up to while they took on their loads of blocks of purified lead, called pigs. The flatboats were huge, thirty-feet wide and nearly seventy-feet long.

A small structure with open walls was built over the smelter to keep the rain out and behind was a bunkhouse for the workers. This place and the job were great improvements over Henri's former situation. He was happier than he had ever been.

In a few months he had saved a sum of money to send to his family in France. He included a letter telling them about this remarkable place, his work, and new friends. All in all, things could not have been better. The summer passed and the work carried on. Henri and his fellow workers reveled in their new environment.

Then the fall rains began and the weather turned cool. There was plenty of lead ore and Henri and his fellow workers labored on, thankful for the more moderate weather. Henri had made friends with the other three miners and they became like brothers. Two of them were from Cornwall, England, and one was from Bohemia. Their place of national origin did not matter, however, for now they were Americans. His fellow workers called Henri, Gosey, the Frenchman. Gauthier was pronounced Goay, but they thought Gosey was easier to pronounce. Henri didn't mind; in fact, he rather liked the nickname he had been given.

As the rains continued, the river began to rise and soon the gentle current in the river channel became a rushing torrent. The flatboats were now riding high in the water and instead of walking horizontally on the gangplank to load the boats, Henri and his workers had to walk uphill to access the boats. The gangplank was slick with rain and the turbulent channel caused the boat to rise and fall, making the job dangerous.

Henri had a canvas sling filled with lead pigs over his shoulders. Just as he got to the edge of the longboat, the current caused the boat to lurch, the gangplank jerked, and Henri tumbled into the water.

The sling was over his shoulders and the weighty lead pigs pulled him to the bottom of the river. He struggled and was able to free himself from the sling. He tried to swim to the surface, but the current pushed him under the flatboat. His head crashed into the bottom of the boat and he tried desperately to escape, but the current was so powerful that it pushed him farther under. He wasn't able to reach the bank side because the boat was tight against it.

Henri was panicking. He was desperate for air. His ears began to ring and he saw bright flashes of light in his eyes. He clawed the underside of the boat in a frantic attempt to break free. It was no use. The current was carrying him deeper. Finally he could hold his breath no longer. His lungs filled with water. He became calm and resigned himself to his fate. A picture of his mother, father, and family flashed in his mind. He felt no fear or pain; he just drifted off. Everything went black.

Henri's co-workers found his body two days later about a mile down river. Colonel Hamilton and Henri's friends gave him a funeral. They buried him on the riverbank near the site of the smelter. His friends planted a maple tree at his grave as a memorial. The tree had a large branch that pointed out over Henri's beloved river. As the years went by, the lead business underwent changes as more efficient smelters were built. Eventually the smelter on the banks of the Wisconsin River was abandoned. The smelter house and the bunkhouse burned down during a lightning storm. The rock foundations still sit on the riverbank and Henri's burial site has been preserved. The maple tree, with its branches stretching over the water, stands as a sentinel on the riverbank. To this day, the place is called the Gosey Hole.

School Daze

The summer I turned thirteen years old looked to be pretty much like all the other summers of my life, with one exception. I was finally going to be a teenager. No more little grade-school kid stuff for me. My friends and I were about to join the brotherhood of teenagers. But, first we had to finish seventh grade at St. John the Baptist Catholic School.

St. John the Baptist School; the kingdom of Sister Henry. She was principal, warden, and Reverend Mother of all the nuns, and she ruled like a czar. Sister Henry was a stern woman with a thin face that looked like it had never smiled. We called her "Hank" when she was safely out of earshot. She was the supreme ruler, the commander-in-chief, the sheriff, and she answered only to Father Lewandowski. Hank was the principal and taught seventh and eighth grades. When Hank was on patrol in the hallways, everyone was on best behavior. When school started in the morning, Hank stood at the end of the hall, watching. When the lunch bell rang, Hank stood at the end of the hall, watching. When school finished at the end of the day, Hank was right there again, watching for any misdeed, ready to grab the miscreant by the ear and haul him to the office. She was all-seeing, all-knowing, all-hearing.

Next in command was Sister Loratella. She was a heavy-set woman with a round face that was set in a permanent scowl. She was rumored to be a prison guard during World War II but we never found proof of this. There was no fooling around in Sister Loratella's classroom. If she caught you goofing off, she cracked you over the knuckles with her pointer. Now this was no ordinary pointer; not a little wisp of a stick used to point out words and numbers on the blackboard. No! This was a pointer made of many strips of wood laminated together in an intricate pattern with a diameter of about three- quarters of an inch. It looked like a work of art but it was really for cracking the knuckles of kids who whispered or made unacceptable noises in Sister Loratella's classroom. It was sturdy enough to use on the baseball diamond as a replacement for our bat if it ever came up missing. You didn't want to get a crack on the knuckles from Sister Loratella's pointer. Sister Loratella was fondly called, behind her back, Sister Tubatallow. Of course, no one, but no one, uttered her nickname loud enough to take a chance of getting a whack from the pointer.

Next in line was Sister Arsenia. She taught first, second, and third grades. Sister Arsenia, or Arsenic, as we called her, was a clone of Sister Loratella. In fact, there were those who said that they were cousins. Same shape, same face, same sunny disposition. The only thing missing was a pointer like her twin had. In its place was a heavy-duty yardstick, a complimentary gift from Krouskop's Lumber Yard on the occasion of their 20th anniversary. Arsenic was also the "lunch" sister. She rode herd over the kids in the lunch line and saw to it that no food was left on plates. If you tried to sneak carrots or broccoli into the wastebasket, she would whirl around like a radar antenna and stop you and insist that you eat the offending vegetable. "Just think of the starving children in China and how grateful they would be to have this food you're wasting," was her favorite saying. We often wanted to suggest that she get an envelope and we'd mail a few pounds of carrots to China, but, of course, we never were brave enough to recommend such a thing.

Then there was Sister Avonne. Why she became a nun, I'll never know. She was young, she was pretty, and she was nice. She was our music teacher. Being twelve years old at the time, I thought she was the most beautiful woman in the world. Of course, I could only see her face and hands. The rest of her was covered by her habit, which made her look like a penguin with a Dixie cup on top of her head. But she was attractive. And she smiled, and laughed, and taught us to sing. Sister Avonne was my first crush; probably not the best choice of a girlfriend, but I was young and didn't know any better.

The lord and master of the school was Father Lewandowski. The nuns were "boss" when he wasn't around, but when he came to the school to visit or to see the nuns about parish business, they cowered in his presence. "Yes, Father! No, Father!" What Father wanted, Father got.

He was a nice man and we all were in awe of him, mostly because he struck such fear and obedience into the nuns. Anyone who could do that had to be powerful. Anyone who could make Tubatallow or Arsenic grovel was quite a guy in our eyes. Even Hank would wring her hands and follow him like a lost puppy when he was giving instructions about something he wanted done this way, or that way. And, he had a "hot" housekeeper.

The priests at St. John's always had a live-in housekeeper. They were usually old, rather frumpy ladies who cooked and cleaned for the priest and lived in the rectory with him. Father Lewandowski's housekeeper was Polly. She looked like Jayne Mansfield. Her dresses were bright red, tight, and sexy looking. She had blonde hair piled up high in a big hairdo. She smoked long cigarettes and held them in a holder that she carried like the wand of a fairy princess. She smelled like lilacs and roses and candy all mixed together. She was a babe! Of course, the boys at St. John's took every possible opportunity to check her out. There was never a shortage of volunteers when one of the nuns needed someone to run to the priest's house with a message for Father. Polly would answer the door and usually give the messenger a cookie or another treat. We could have cared less about the cookie. We wanted to see Polly and be close to her. She "stood out" in our little town and turned the heads of much of the male populace.

Of course the wives of the town were very nice to Polly, but I'm sure they had a lot of things to say about her among themselves. If the women had their way, Polly would have been run out of town. But as long as she was Father's housekeeper, she was able to do as she pleased. It was fun to see Father and Polly attend a school play or music recital. Parishioners would sit on uncomfortable folding chairs in the school gym. Just before the curtain went up, Father and Polly would make their grand entrance and march down to the front and sit in plush, padded chairs that were put there especially for them. The only thing lacking was a trumpet fanfare-heralding the entrance of royalty, and flower girls scattering rose petals on the floor. It was good to be a priest. You were treated like a king.

We were nearing the end of the school year and my friends and I could hardly wait for summer vacation. There were fish to be caught; and there was swimming, baseball, and other adventures that we hadn't dreamed up yet. But first we had to endure that final week of school.

The days dragged on as if the whole world was in slow motion. The week seemed to last a year. The weather had warmed and it was torture sitting in a classroom. So, when Sister Henry asked for a volunteer to rake and clean up the playground in preparation for our school picnic, there was no shortage of offers. Anything was better than staying inside; even doing yard work.

Two of my best friends, Dewey and Chick, and I were assigned this task. That was good news for us because there was a chance that Polly would make an appearance and we were always glad to see her.

The three of us went over to Father's house which was on the corner of the school playground. We had two rakes and a galvanized washtub for hauling the leaves to the leaf pile on the other corner of the playground where they would be set afire and burned. Of course, first we had to bicker as to who would rake and who would haul the leaves. Not that it made a difference. We would end up taking turns but it seemed important to decide who was assigned what job.

Dewey wanted to rake. He didn't want to lug a washtub of leaves all the way across the playground. He liked jobs that took little effort and offered many breaks. Now, I'm not saying that Dewey was lazy, but he was definitely not overly ambitious. His world ran on a slower time clock than ours.

Dewey was of average height but he was on the "husky" side. He wasn't fat; just "chunky," as he always told us. "I'm big-boned," he said. Dewey never got excited, was never in a hurry, and was always hungry. He also had a little gas problem. "I have gastric distress in the lower tract," he would say just before he let one go. Of course, teenage boys thought that Dewey's talent was hilarious so he always received many laughs.

In all the years I had known Dewey, he had never once been on time for anything, except school; and he was late for that, too-about three times a week. No matter what it was-fishing, baseball, movies-Dewey was late. He even talked slowly. One time we had made plans to go fishing early on Saturday morning. Dewey's parents owned a steak house where they served food and beverages. They lived above the restaurant. I was up at dawn and had my fishing gear ready. I ate a quick breakfast and rode my bike to Dewey's. I climbed the stairs and knocked quietly on the door since I did not want to awaken his parents. No answer. I knocked again, a little louder, and I could hear someone walking in the apartment. Finally Dewey came to the door. He was in his underwear, scratching, and yawning.

"I thought you were gonna be ready!" I said.

Then, the standard answer from Dewey: "My alarm clock didn't go off."

Dewey had an alarm clock that managed to malfunction almost every day. I often suggested that he throw it in the river and buy a new one, but he insisted that it was just a little glitch and he thought he had it figured out. So, there I stood, in the living room of the apartment, waiting for Dewey.

"Hurry up! I'm ready to go," I said.

"I'll be ready in a couple of minutes," he mumbled as he waddled off scratching his behind.

I waited. I was dressed for fishing with my heavy jacket to keep off the morning chill. I also had my hip boots on, and I was getting hot standing in the warm apartment. Sweat began to form on my forehead, and I could feel a trickle running down the middle of my back. Suddenly, I could smell bacon! As much as I hated to walk into Dewey's apartment in my hip boots, I moved carefully toward the kitchen. There sat Dewey, still in his underwear, eating bacon and eggs, reading the morning newspaper. "What are you doing?" I asked, ready to blow a gasket.

He looked up at me like it was the most natural thing in the world and said, "Eating my breakfast! What does it look like?"

That was Dewey: never in a hurry, never on time, and always the last to arrive. You would have thought I'd be used to his habits.

Chick, on the other hand, was always on the go; rather like a shrew. Hurry up, and do this; then hurry up, and do that. Between Chick, moving at light speed, and Dewey, moving like a snail, I settled into the middle.

Chick was an import. He had moved to town a few years earlier from a big city. I met him at school the previous fall and we just sort of hit it off He didn't have a lot of friends at first but we quickly became good buddies. Coming from the city, it took him a while to get used to our small town. He was always full of ideas for things to do. And, most of them usually got us into trouble. Not that he was a bad influence; he just had ideas that frequently turned into disasters. He would come up with some hair-brained scheme and it usually didn't take much to get Dewey and me to go along with it.

We became friends because of something that we both loved: fishing.

The first time I met him, he asked me if I fished. Fished? I lived to fish! I knew immediately I had a new friend. The following weekend, I took Chick to one of my favorite fishing spots in the river bottoms. It was a little river slough we called "The Little Cat." There was a spot where you could catch big bullheads and I showed it to him. You had to cast to an opening in the weeds about halfway across the slough. I cast to the spot and my bobber disappeared instantly and I reeled in a lunker bullhead. My next cast went to the same spot and I caught a second fish. Chick saw that the spot was vacant as I was taking the bullhead off and he reeled in his line to cast to my hotspot. He was in a big hurry and as I bent over to take my fish off, he swung his pole back and hooked me in the top of the head. I began yelling before he cast forward and tore my head off. His night crawler was hanging over my forehead between my eyes. Of course, he was regretful about hooking me, but he was also in a hurry to dislodge his hook so he could catch a fish. He had his priorities in the right place, according to my thinking.

Back to the clean-up job at the Father's house ... we went behind the house. We rounded the corner and there, sitting where we had left it about two months earlier, was what was left of the Giant Snowball. Actually, now it was a Giant Slushpile.

"Wow!" said Dewey, "Can you believe that?"

"No way! I thought it would be gone by now," Chick said. I just stood there with my mouth hanging open.

The Giant Snowball was one of those once-in-a-lifetime things. About two months earlier, we had a spring snowstorm that dumped nearly a foot of the most wonderful packing snow we had ever seen. School was called off for the day but Dewey and Chick and I had gone to the playground and built a snow fort. First, we went to the grocery store and asked Mr. Kalsher for several cardboard boxes that we took to the playground and filled with snow. We packed them tightly; then turned them over to create a rectangular slab of snow. We stacked these big white bricks until we had the best snow fort we had ever seen. Then, for an unknown reason, we started rolling a snowball. We went back and forth across the playground and the snowball grew bigger and bigger. Soon it was as tall as we were and, not long after, it far surpassed our height. We were barely able to move it. But, we didn't want to leave it behind, so we tried to roll it to my house two blocks away. We figured that if we left it on the playground, someone would steal it, and it was the biggest snowball we had ever seen; probably a world record. Well, we got to the back of Father's house and the Giant Snowball stopped, and we couldn't move it any farther. We tried to figure out what to do, finally deciding that the snowball would be safe in Father's yard, so we left it there. Who would steal a giant snowball from the yard of a priest? By the next day it no longer seemed important, so we just forgot about it. Now it was a pile of snow and slush, nothing like it had been.

"Well, we'll have to rake around it," I said. It was rather sad to see the Giant Snowball in such a pitiful state. It had been the biggest and best creation we had ever made, and we didn't know a snowball could last so long. We began raking and soon had enough leaves for Chick to haul to the burning pile. Dewey wanted to take a break while Chick transported the leaves but I kept raking. Next it was Dewey's turn to take the leaves and Chick took over on his rake. We worked around the yard, raking and hauling leaves, taking turns with the jobs. After an hour, we were finishing the job and it was my turn to haul. We had the washtub filled and I stepped inside and jumped up and down to mash the leaves so we could squeeze in a few more. At this time, Dewey decided that he needed to rest again. He dropped his rake and sat down in the grass. I squashed the leaves down as best I could and then I jumped out of the tub. My feet landed square on the up-pointed teeth of Dewey's rake. When my feet hit the rake teeth, the handle came up like a striking cobra and hit me between the eyes. I remember hearing a cracking sound, but nothing else.

The next thing I knew, I could smell this wonderful smell like lilacs and sweet candy. Then I could feel something cold on my forehead and soft hands stroking my hair. I struggled to get my eyes open and when I did, I thought I was in heaven and an angel was hovering over me.

"How do you feel?" the angel said.

"I'm good," I said. "Am I dead?"

The angel laughed. "No, you're not dead, but you have a nasty knot on your forehead. Does it hurt badly?"

"No, I'm good," I said. "Are you an angel?"

The angel laughed again and then I knew it was Polly! "No, not quite. Are you able to sit up?"

I tried to sit up, and Polly put her hands under my shoulders and helped me. She was kneeling next to me and began rubbing my back as I sat there.

"Just sit for a minute and get your bearings," she cooed.

I looked up and Dewey and Chick were standing there with their eyes about popping out of their heads. Polly put her arm around my shoulder and helped me up.

"There. Now how do you feel?" she asked. "I'm good."

"Do you want to come in and have a glass of milk?"

"Uh, yeah. That would be good." I was such a smooth conversationalist.

She took me inside, sat me at the kitchen table, poured a big glass of milk, and put several cookies on a plate for me.

"These will make you feel better. I've never seen a boy yet who didn't like cookies."

"Thank you, uh," I said. I had no idea what to call her. She wasn't "Mrs." and I didn't know her last name.

"Polly. Just call me, Polly," she said.

Polly. I could call her Polly! I took as long as I dared to eat the cookies and drink the milk. I wanted to make this last as long as possible. It was incredible watching Polly glide across the kitchen, working at her cooking chores. Finally I could stretch the cookies and milk no farther and, when I finished, I thanked her and she walked me to the door. "You be careful, now," she said, and kissed me on top of the head. I almost fell down the steps!

Dewey and Chick were still standing in the yard with their mouths hanging open like a couple of bungling rattlebrains. When they saw her kissing my head, they almost had juvenile strokes. I walked down the steps and strutted over to my friends. "Boy, she makes good cookies," I said.

"Cookies? You got cookies?" Dewey asked.

"Yup, and a cold glass of milk, too. Polly's real nice."

"Polly? Nice?"

My status among the seventh grade boys at St. John the Baptist School had just risen to "super stud."

The School Picnic

Our school year culminated in a school picnic. It was a day of fun and games and lots of food. Instead of being inside and eating lunch in the cafeteria-which usually consisted of something very healthy, which we hated-we went outside, played games, and cooked hot dogs and marshmallows over an open fire. Not only did we like hot dogs and marshmallows much more than cafeteria food, we were also able to play with fire!

The sisters organized games for each age group. There were prizes and we had lots of fun. Of course, the older boys-like my buddies and me-weren't interested in those kiddy-games. Even if prizes were offered, we didn't participate. The prizes consisted of religious bookmarks or medals that had been blessed. If they had given packages of fishing hooks or baseball cards, we might have joined in. But, for holy stuff, we weren't interested and we went off to play either softball or "Bloody Murder." Now, as awful as the name sounds, "Bloody Murder" wasn't a terrible game about death and killing. A soccer ball was tossed on the playground. One boy, who was either extremely brave or stupid, would grab the ball and run with it. The rest of the players would chase him, screaming like wild savages, and when they caught him, they would pig-pile him. Eventually the ball would eject from the mass of screaming boys and someone would pick it up and take off running. That was our favorite game. It wasn't complicated. It involved running and shouting, dust and dirt, and the mayhem seemed to please everyone.

We played "Bloody Murder" for a couple of hours and then decided it was time to eat. We were covered in dust and sweat and there were generally a couple of bleeding elbows by that time, but nobody was injured enough to turn down hotdogs cooked over an open fire. Sister Arsenia was in charge of the food and she made us go to the school and wash up before cooking. Of course, that involved a lot of shouting and splashing water all over the restroom and, when we emerged, we were free of dust and dirt, but dripping wet. Then we each took a weenie stick-a branch from a lilac bush at Father's house that had been sharpened on one end-and inserted it into a weenie and held it over the fire. Not only was it great to be out of school and to be in the sunshine, but we also got to horse around with fire.

There were about a dozen of us at the fire-pit cooking and eating hot dogs and potato chips and drinking Kool-Aid. There was no limit so, of course, we tried to surpass each other in the number of hot dogs consumed. Dewey was leading the pack with his eighth "dog" and there were no close contenders. Then Sister brought out a bag of marshmallows for roasting for dessert. There was only one thing that I liked more than roasted marshmallows, and that was s'mores: roasted marshmallows between two pieces of Hershey Bar and two graham crackers. Unfortunately, the nuns' budget didn't allow for Hershey Bars so we had to eat plain marshmallows.

I was roasting a marshmallow, and it was almost perfect. The trick was to hold it to the side of the flame so it became golden brown and gooey inside without turning black on the outside. If you didn't get it close enough to the fire, it stayed solid in the middle. If you got it too close, it turned black, and sometimes it caught on fire. It was a very delicate operation.

Anyway, my marshmallow was turning the most beautiful, golden-brown color, and Dewey was next to me, roasting one. He was always in a hurry to get it cooked so he could get another, so he held his directly in the fire. Of course, it burst into flames and turned black instantly. As he retrieved it, it touched my perfect specimen and ignited it. I quickly pulled my marshmallow out of the fire pit and blew on it attempting to salvage it.

Then I thought, rather than blow, I'd fan it, so as to not take the chance of burning myself I whipped my stick back and forth to extinguish the flames and, at that same second, David Kite ran past, chasing Chick, who had swiped his potato chips. The flaming marshmallow hit David behind his right ear and stuck to the side of his head! Of course, it was still on fire so it burned off a large patch of his hair.

When the flaming marshmallow hit him, David did exactly what we were taught not to do in safety class. He took off running, screaming like a banshee. Of course, everyone knows he should have stopped, dropped, and rolled. It happened quickly and I wasn't sure what had happened to my marshmallow. Then I saw David running across the playground with smoke coming from the side of his head. He was headed toward Sister Arsenia!

Dewey looked at me and said, "You're dead."

David got to Sister Arsenia. She grabbed him and put her denim apron, covering her habit, over his head to snuff out the fire. He was bawling and screaming. Somewhere, in all the confusion, I heard him mention my name and Sister glanced at me with a death-sentence look. I wanted to take off running for home I but knew she would get me in the end so I just reached for another marshmallow and tried to look innocent.

Sister Arsenia took David to the school and a few minutes later, Hank came out of the door, looking at me. I wanted to crawl under a rock; I even thought of running for the church and asking for sanctuary, but I couldn't move. I was so scared. Hank marched up to me and told me to follow her to the school.

It was the longest walk of my life. I had never been in Hank's office before. It was small with painted cement block walls. There was a bookcase and a file cabinet against the right wall and a picture of Pope Pius on the left wall. Behind the desk were two windows. And there sat David. His eyes were red; his nose was running, and he was blubbering. The hair on the right side of his head was gone and the office smelled like burnt chicken feathers. There was a big, red blister-about the size of a large marshmallow-behind his ear. Sister Arsenia had treated it with a gob of ointment that made David's head look greasy and nasty. Sister Arsenia was standing behind David who was sitting in one of two wooden chairs in front of Hank's desk. Her apron was smeared with marshmallow and soot from David's burning head. Hank sat at her desk, put her hands together, and looked at me.

"Do you see what you did to poor David?" Hank asked.

"Yes, Sister."

"Do you feel badly for doing it?"

"Yes, Sister."

"What are you going to do about it?"

I didn't have the faintest idea of what she was asking. What did she expect me to do? Throw myself in front of a train; jump off a bridge? Maybe she wanted me to stick a flaming marshmallow on the side of my head. I had nothing to say, so I thought it would be best to rely on Hank's wisdom. "Um ... what do you think I should do, Sister?"

"You need to tell David that you're sorry and then go to the church and ask God's forgiveness."

Whew! That was easy. I didn't expect such a light sentence. I thought maybe my entire eighth-grade year would be spent in detention or I'd suffer another punishment; but an apology and a few "Hail Marys" weren't bad at all.

"David, I'm sorry. Please forgive me," I said, with all the earnestness I could muster. David blubbered something that must have been okay.

Hank motioned for me to follow her and we walked into the hallway. "You run over to the church and say a little prayer for David, and then go back to the picnic." And then she smiled at me. I had never seen Hank smile before! "I know you didn't do that on purpose, and I know you're a good boy, so let's just let it go at a little prayer, okay?"

"Yes, Sister Henry! Thank you." I ran as fast as I could to the church and said a little prayer for David, and then I threw in "thanks" for the good luck I had in the past few days with Polly, and now with Sister Henry. The summer was looking good.

Fishing

Ever since I was old enough to ride a two-wheel bike, I fished. Summer was for fishing and baseball. Nothing else was important, and fishing was my first love. Our house was about a mile from the Wisconsin River, but the river was off-limits. My mom insisted that I do my fishing in the sloughs where there weren't currents or whirlpools.

For some reason, my mother was an expert on currents and whirlpools. I doubt that she had ever even gotten her big toe wet in the river but she always warned me not to go there because a whirlpool would suck me under and drown me. I was required to fish in one of the river bottom sloughs where the water was shallow and the current was so slow that you could barely see it move.

There were many sloughs within bike-riding range so my friends and I had many places to fish. If it was a day when we only had a couple hours before a baseball game, we would go to the Cat. Actually there were two Cats; the Big Cat and the Little Cat. Both of the Cats were small sloughs and were close to town. We sat on the bank and fished mainly for bluegills and bullheads. Once in a while we caught a bass or a northern, or an ugly dogfish, but generally, just bluegills. We didn't care. As long as we were fishing, it didn't matter what we caught, how many, or how big. We were happy just to be fishing.

On the days we didn't play baseball, we went to Gutweiler's Lake. Now this was a real lake; not a little slough like the Cat. Gutweiler's was about three-quarters of a mile long and about a hundred yards across at its widest point. At the upper end, there was a small creek running into the lake, and at the lower end, the lake became a creek again. The creek meandered for a while through the woods and then emptied into the Wisconsin River. The water moved slowly from one slough to the next and eventually ended up back in the big river.

Gutweiler's was our favorite place to fish. There were lots of good-sized northern pike and bass, and the bluegills were much bigger than in the Cat. We could ride our bikes to the lower end and then cross the creek on a beaver dam if we wanted to fish on the marsh side of the lake. Otherwise we would fish on the high bank that bordered the woods. Often we would take our lunch and spend the whole day at the lake. If the fish weren't biting, we could look for frogs or wade around in the shallow water. Additionally, the woods had cool stuff for us to poke around in and we always found lots of interesting critters.

Standard attire for the summer was a short-sleeved cotton shirt, or a tee shirt-usually white-and cut-off blue jeans and tennis shoes. Even though our moms would buy us jeans each fall that were about four inches too long, we seemed to outgrow them fast enough to have a good supply of cut-offs for summer wear. Everyone had the same shoes. There was only one choice for tennis shoes. They were all high-top, black, and made of canvas. During the summer we wore them without socks, so after a few fishing trips-which included wading in the mud and a few innings of baseball in the hot sun-they became a bit aromatic. Of course, made of canvas, they were easy to wash, and most moms kept them from getting too rank.

While fishing, we generally took off our shirts so, after a while, we all looked like south-sea islanders. Everyone was the same. It was the standard uniform of the day. It made us all equal; all on the same team.

Not all my friends were from my class at St. John the Baptist School. In the summer, I also enjoyed the company of friends from the public school. Although the nuns would probably not have thought well of this, my friends and I associated freely with kids from the public school in the summertime. After all, if we were limited to only our friends from St. John's, there would not be enough players for a proper baseball game, so we had to include other kids, one of which became one of my best buddies.

His name was Dougie and he was an import kid. His family had moved to our town the previous summer. His dad was a bigwig in the public school system. The family lived a short distance from my house and they had four boys. Dougie was my age and he had younger brothers the same age as my younger brothers, so my brothers and I got new friends.

One day that summer I was riding my bike down to the Cat for a couple of hours of fishing, and I rode past their house. Dougie was sitting on the front porch steps doing something with a fishing pole. Of course I noticed him immediately. Fishing poles always caught my attention. I had my pole and tackle box and a can of worms in my bike basket and, as I rode by, he looked up and waved at me. I wanted to get a better look at his fishing pole so I made a V-turn and pulled up in front of his house.

"Goin' fishin?" I asked.

"Naw. I don't know where the good spots are. I just moved here," he said.

I got off my bike and parked it and walked up to him. "Nice pole! Is it new?"

"Yeah. My grandma gave it to me for my birthday. Want to see it?"

Wow! Did I!! It was a spinning rod with a Mitchell 300 reel!

"Wow! This is cool. I've never used one of these reels," I said. I had always had the push-button reels and this was something new and wonderful-looking to me.

"Give it a throw," Dougie said.

He showed me how to open the bail and hold the line in my finger and then throw it. It cast like a dream, clear across the street.

"Whoa! This is really cool!" I said, reeling the line back up.

"You wanna go fishin' with me?"

"Sure."

He ran into the house and asked his mom if he could go. She came out and I told her about the Cat and how it was safe and she gave Dougie permission to go. She told us to wait a minute and soon she returned with a sack of homemade cookies. This was getting better all the time.

Well, Dougie and I went to the Cat. We fished, talked, and got to know each other and became friends, even if he was a public school kid.

From then on, Dewey, Chick, and Dougie were my constant companions. We fished, played baseball, swam, slept out, and spent the summer together. The four musketeers: one for all, and all for one.

One evening, when we were fishing at the Cat, the discussion turned to the book The Three Musketeers.

"I wonder why that Dumas guy didn't call it The Four Musketeers," Chick said.

"The first three guys were already Musketeers, and the D' Artagnan guy was a new recruit," I said.

"Kinda like Dougie; he's new in town and goes to the public school," Chick said.

"Yup! Just call me Dougie 'Tagnan," Dougie said. We all laughed at Dougie's joke.

A short time after our first experience fishing at the Cat, Dougie and I were fishing on the marsh side of Gutweiler's. Dewey and Chick had been required by their moms to do chores. Dougie and I decided it was not a good idea to hang around and take the chance that our moms would get wind of our friends doing home stuff, so we headed to the lake. The lower end of Gutweiler's narrowed before it reached the beaver dam where it became a stream that flowed into the river. Many trees had been blown down by summer storms and were lying in the water. We often caught fine fish around the downed trees, but on this day we were sitting, watching our bobbers, and there was no action. Dougie was always interested in poking around in the swamp, looking for creepy, slimy critters, and he had found a frog. He was attempting to get the frog to sit in the palm of his hand and soon he had the critter calmed down and it stayed put. Just as he began to brag about what a great frog-tamer he was, the frog took a mighty leap and landed in the lake, about six feet from shore.

"Oh, yeah! The great frog-tamer," I laughed.

The frog decided it was a good idea to escape and just as he took a couple strokes, a huge large-mouth bass came up and gulped him off the surface.

"Wow! Look at that!" Dougie yelled. We both got the idea at the same time and took off running for the marsh. It didn't take us long to each capture a frog. We put them in our shorts pockets, reeled in our lines, removed our sinkers and bobbers and tied on our biggest hooks. Then we hooked the frogs through the lips and cast them into the lake, about ten feet apart. Neither frog had time to take a stroke because the water erupted and both of them were gulped down by two bass. We waited a couple of seconds and then set the hook. We both had a big bass on our lines at the same time. We fought the fish, back and forth, and finally landed them. We took them off quickly, put them on a stringer-which we tied to a tree branch-and then we ran off to look for more frogs. Dougie found one first and raced back to the lake. I could hear him yelling that he had another fish while I was still looking for a frog. I finally found one and caught it, and while I was racing for the lake, Dougie met me on his way back to go frog hunting again.

I don't know how long this procedure lasted, but finally we realized no more fish were biting. We waited and waited, and reeled in our frogs and cast them to another area, but the fish were gone; or we had caught them all.

"Wow!" Dougie panted. "I've never seen fishing like that in my whole life."

"Me, either," I said. We finally gave up and reeled in our frogs. They were both still in good shape so we carefully unhooked them and turned them loose. Then we lifted a stringer of six huge bass!

"I've never seen so many big fish on one stringer in my life," I said, admiring the fish.

"Me, either. Let's go show Dewey and Chick. They'll be so mad they had to stay home." Catching the fish was fun, but showing them off to our envious friends was almost better.

"Hey, let's take them to the newspaper office and see if they want a picture of this," Dougie said.

That sounded like a dandy idea to me, so we loaded up our gear and walked across the beaver dam to our bikes. Dougie had one basket on the front of his bike and I had double baskets on the back of mine, so we put all the fishing gear in my baskets and he took the fish. We rode our bikes as fast as we could to the local newspaper office-as if there were other groups of boys on their way at the same time and only one group would be featured in the paper. When we arrived, a newspaper reporter assessed our catch. He thought this would make a good story. He instructed us to lay them on the sidewalk and kneel behind them. He snapped our picture and asked us questions about our unbelievable success.

Of course his first question was, "Where did you catch them?"

I looked at Dougie and he was obviously trying to think of an answer that wouldn't give our hot-spot away.

"In the river bottoms," he said.

"I see. What did you use for bait?"

Again, our bait was something that we wanted to keep a secret, so I said, "Top-water baits."

"Top-water baits? Care to be more specific?"

"Nope."

He grinned and said that would be okay, and we took off for Dewey's and Chick's houses to show them what they had missed by working at home. Of course they were angry at us for catching fish without them, but if they had been there, it probably wouldn't have happened. Dewey would never have been quick enough to catch a frog and Chick would have been in such a hurry to get his frog into the water that he would have fallen in and scared the fish away.

We were on the front page of the newspaper the following Thursday. We had a smug look on our faces and the accompanying story was that we were tight-lipped about the place and method of catching our fish but, suffice it to say, it must have been a secret weapon and we were probably the envy of the other fishermen in the area. We expected a contract from a fishing company to serve as spokesmen. Surely someone would want two expert fishermen to endorse their products, but sadly that didn't happen. We had to be satisfied with the glory of being two of the best and most famous fishermen among our gang of friends.

We never managed to get into the middle of a feeding frenzy like that again, but, for Dougie and me, it was an experience we would never forget.

Adventures in Chicago

During our seventh-grade year, we had endless bake sales, car washes, dances, lotteries, bingo nights, raffles, and candy sales to raise money for our class trip to Chicago. It had been in the planning for a year and now we were at the train station, standing in the morning darkness, waiting for the train to pick us up to take us to the big city.

There were kids and moms huddled in little groups on the train platform and in the depot. Every kid was receiving last minute instructions as to how to behave and orders to mind the sisters. Mom was making sure I had our phone number tucked safely into my shirt pocket and she was fussing over the way my hair was sticking up in the back. Just then we heard the sound of the approaching train and everyone began moving toward the platform. The boys were trying to put distance between them and their moms so they wouldn't have to suffer the indignity of a kiss in front of the other guys. Chick and Dewey were, likewise, getting their final instructions, but their moms might as well have been speaking Flemish to them as they weren't paying a bit of attention. They were struggling to get to the front of the line to board the train.

The lumbering locomotive came clanging into the station, great clouds of steam billowing out from the belly with a loud hissing sound as the engineer applied the brakes. The sisters were trying to get everyone in line so a head count could be taken and slowly, one by one, we were checked off the list on Sister Henry's clipboard. Dewey, Chick, and I passed by her, climbed on the train, and ran smack into Sister Arsenia. She was herding kids to seats and told us to go to the other end of the car, take a seat, and be quiet.

Soon everyone was on board and the train pulled away from the platform, heading for Chicago, so far away from our little town. Our moms waved and mouthed good- bye as we set off into the darkness. We were excited and chattering like a bunch of squirrels when a porter came through the car. He was a huge, black man, wearing a bright blue uniform with gold trim and a blue and gold cap that looked like a policeman's cap. He smiled at us as he passed and we smiled back, somewhat apprehensively. We had never seen a black man close up before and especially one that was so big. For most of us, the only black men we had ever seen were in the movies since there were none living in our town.

"Wow!" Dewey said. "I have never seen such a large, black man."

"You have never seen a black man before, period!" Chick said. "Well, I guess you're right," Dewey said.

"He seemed nice," I said. We were all a bit in awe of the big man, not only because of his color, but because of his size. He was at least six and a half feet tall, had huge hands, and looked like a giant to a bunch of grade-school kids.

Soon the man returned to our car and said in a loud voice, "Ladies and gentlemen, your breakfast is served in the dining

Dewey looked at me. "Wow! This is great. We get food on the train, too." We took off, on the run, to be first to reach the dining car. There was a platform outside our car that butted up to a platform on the next car. The wind was howling between the cars and you could peer down and see track whizzing by. You had to step across the small gap between the two platforms to get to the next car. We crossed through three crowded cars in this manner before reaching the dining car. It was like a long narrow restaurant with booths on each side. Each booth had a table with a white tablecloth and a vase in the middle with a flower.

Dewey, Chick, another kid, Mike and I slid into a booth and a young, black man in a white waiter's jacket approached us and asked what we wanted to drink with breakfast. He was much younger than the other man and was about the size of most people we knew. He looked at us and held a little pad in his hand waiting for our drink orders.

"Whatcha got?" Dewey asked.

"We have milk, chocolate milk, orange juice, grapefruit juice,
and soda," the man said.

"I'll have soda."

"Me, too," I said.

"Me, three," said Chick. We all burst out laughing at the joke, and the man in the white jacket laughed, too.

"And you, sir?" he asked Mike.

"Me, four," said Mike. And then ... raucous laughter, again.

The man smiled as he walked toward the kitchen and soon returned with four sodas, four glasses, and four straws.

Soon the car was full of chattering and laughing kids and then a number of waiters wheeled in carts piled with plates of food, each covered with a silver lid. Our waiter pulled the cart to our table and set a plate in front of each of us and then lifted the lids to expose our breakfast. Each plate contained two eggs, two pieces of bacon, two pieces of toast, and a little paper cup filled with jelly. The eggs were what they called sunny side up but they looked almost raw as they jiggled around on the plate with the motion of the train.

"Cripes, these eggs are raw!" Dewey bellowed.

The waiter's smile vanished and he looked worried.

"Dewey, shut up! They're okay," I said.

"I'm not eatin' raw eggs," he said.

The waiter said, "I can take them back and have them cooked more.

Dewey handed his plate to him. He looked at the rest of us.

"Uh, could you cook ours a little longer, too?" Chick said, and we all handed him our plates. He smiled and took them to the kitchen and in a few minutes he returned; eggs were cooked through, alright! Hard as rocks, but that was the way we liked them.

"Thanks," Dewey said, and we all echoed words of gratitude.

The man grinned and served the others.

We finished our breakfast, went back to our car, and began watching the scenery go by. Soon the hills and woods, common to our part of the world, began to disappear and big buildings and cities were appearing. The landscape became flatter as we traveled into Illinois and approached Chicago. There were buildings and skyscrapers all over the place-quite a change from our town where the tallest building was the hotel which stretched up three stories. We pulled into the train station and the sisters herded us off the train and down the aisles between the loud locomotives coming and going. There must have been 50 trains in the station and diesel fumes, steam, and noise. We hustled out of the station and into the terminal where the sisters ushered us onto a waiting bus.

We had our noses pressed to the glass as we went through downtown Chicago, craning our necks to see the tops of the huge skyscrapers.

"Wow! Holy Cow! Look! Look!" We were awestruck. We drove through streets that weaved around hundreds of impressive buildings until the bus pulled up to the Shedd Aquarium. Sister Henry stood in the front of the bus and gave instructions as to our behavior inside the building. She might as well have been talking in Latin, like Father Lewandowski did in mass, because we weren't listening. We piled off the bus and began our tour of the aquarium. It was an immense building and there were tanks and tanks of fish, from little, brightly-colored ones to huge sharks; even some small whales. Dewey and I were looking at the sharks and he put his mouth against the glass and blew so his mouth got real big and his lips stretched out. I was laughing at him and saw Chick get a worried look as Sister Arsenia came up behind him and whacked him on the back of the head. "Hey, you dummy," he said, as he turned. "Oops! Sorry, Sister." Sister Arsenia made him get paper towels from the washroom to clean off the glass. After she walked away, Dewey was grumbling that there was surely an aquarium employee who was in charge of cleaning the glass, and he didn't think it was fair that he be made to do it. In fact, he said, he might be taking away some guy's job, causing him to be fired because he didn't have any work to do. Only Dewey could think of something like that.

We spent a couple of hours in the aquarium and then we headed to the Museum of Science and Industry. This place was full of cool things-like real airplanes hanging from the ceiling, and a mock coal mine that seemed like a real mine. Sister Henry told us that we were free to explore but we must be on the bus at two o'clock to go to the next museum. Chick, Dewey, and I made our way through miles of the place and had a great time discovering many extraordinary things. Of course, Dewey found a snack bar and we had to stop for ice cream and soda so he would have energy to keep looking. We kept a close watch on the time and were back at the bus with a few minutes to spare.

Off we went down the canyons between the tall buildings again and we stopped in front of the huge Museum of Natural History. It took up a whole city block and there were busses parked all around it. Sister said we had to tour this museum as a group because it was so large so we followed her like a string of baby ducks. Upon entering the building, we were captivated by the huge dinosaur skeletons. Dewey stood there, gaping at them, and he blocked the door until Sister Arsenia smacked him on the head.

We walked up to a mammoth set of bones and stood there without talking. It seemed that the skeleton would come alive if it heard us.

"Do you think there is anything like that around our home?" Dewey whispered.

"Yeah, Dewey. I saw one down at Gutweiler's the other day; did I forget to tell you?" I whispered. Chick burst out laughing and Sister gave us the kind of look we usually got for fooling around in church.

"Come along, children, and don't stray behind or you'll get lost," Sister Henry said, as she waved us toward her.

"Come along, children; don't get lost," Dewey mimicked. We went for miles through the museum and soon I had no idea which way was which. We were in a display area with stuffed fish and whale exhibits that made them look as if they were swimming. I was fascinated by a gigantic blue whale as big as a school bus and I stood there mesmerized, imagining it alive in the ocean. It was the biggest swimming creature I had ever seen.

"Do you think that crappy fishing pole of yours would land this one, Dewey?" I said. I turned to verify that my insult to his fishing tackle had been duly-noted and found that I was alone! I checked both ways in the big room and there was no one there but me. I took off running for the door, peered into the hall, but I saw no one I recognized. But, this was the door through which we had entered, so I ran to the other end of the room and went out that door. Nobody was there! Now I panicked. I had no idea where the rest of the kids and the sisters had gone, so I began running up the halls, looking for somebody I knew. All I saw were strangers who looked at me like I was lost. I was lost! I ran and ran and began sweating and panting like a dog in August.

Suddenly I was in the big room with the dinosaur skeletons.

There were four entrances and I had no idea which door we had entered by, so I ran for the closest one and flew through it. There was no one from my school anywhere to be seen, and there were at least a hundred busses parked end to end as far as I could see around the block. They all looked the same to me so I ran across the sidewalk to the closest one and looked in. It was full of kids I didn't know; so I ran to the next one.

It was empty, so I ran to the next, and the next.

I was about half way down the second street of buses when, just as I got to the bus door, Sister Henry stepped out on the sidewalk. I stopped in my tracks, trying to decide if I wanted to make a break for it through traffic and become a homeless kid in Chicago, or face her wrath. Her face was tightly pinched and she grabbed me by the T-shirt.

"Do you realize that everyone else is on the bus?"

"Yes, Sister."

"Do you know how long we have been waiting for you?"

"No, Sister."

"Do you think it's proper for you to keep the whole bus waiting for you?"

"No, Sister."

"Why is it that everyone except you is on the bus and you are out here fooling around?"

I thought for a second on that one. I wanted to say that if they had mentioned to me that they were leaving the whale room, I probably would have been on the darn bus, but they slipped out and ditched me, so that was why I was late. But, my better sense told me to plead for mercy. "I'm very sorry, Sister. I must have been too interested in learning about whales and I didn't see you leave the area."

She looked me up and down and apparently bought my answer because she said, "Get on the bus, and try to behave for the rest of the trip."

"Yes, Sister!"

I was never so glad to see Chick and Dewey, even though they made fun of me for getting lost for the rest of the day. We toured the city a while longer and the bus driver, using a loud speaker, told us about the sites we saw as we traveled. Suddenly, Chick, Dewey, and I were spellbound as we approached Wrigley Field. This was like the most famous place we had ever heard of, and there it was-the home of an actual major league baseball team. We watched it go by like it was a shrine to the Virgin Mary. There were probably live baseball players behind those walls; the guys whose baseball cards we collected, traded, and guarded like gold. And here we were-so close to them. We watched as the stadium disappeared behind the bus, gazing until we could no longer see it.

Our next stop was China Town. Actually, it was just a part of Chicago that was full of Chinese people and lots of little tourist shops. We had two hours for walking and shopping, so Chick, Dewey, and I looked for souvenirs. I found a fancy tea cup and saucer for mom and chopsticks for my brothers. Chick chose an elaborate silk fan for his mom, and Dewey bought a Chinese straw hat that looked like an upside down funnel. "This will make a cool fishing hat," he said. Chick and I just shook our heads; poor Dewey had finally lost his mind. Then we went to a Chinese restaurant for our meal. We did not know what we were eating but the food was tasty and there was plenty of it for not much money. Then we met up with the bus again and loaded up for our last pass through the city.

We finally arrived at the train station and we piled on the train for the trip home. Soon it was dark and the lights of the city faded away into the night and the distance. Lights of farms and small towns began to dot the landscape and the car quieted down as, one by one, kids drifted off to sleep. Dewey, Chick, and I, still awake, were talking about Wrigley Field. Even Sister Henry and Sister Arsenia had fallen asleep. Arsenia was slumped over with her mouth hanging open and drool was running out while she snored away. We gingerly stepped through the car to the back door, crossed to the next car, and then to the next. We reached the caboose and found it empty. We stepped out onto the little plat- form and noticed an electric light hanging on it, like a taillight. We breathed in the night air as the wind swirled around us and we watched the tracks disappear behind us. Home was just ahead and the big city was farther and farther behind us.

"Would you like to live in Chicago?" Chick said.

"Naw! Not me," Dewey said.

"Me, either," I said. "I didn't see any place to fish except Lake Michigan, and that looks like a place where we would really get into trouble." The three of us laughed and then we just stood there, getting closer and closer to home, where we didn't have to worry about getting lost. It was a good feeling to know our moms would be waiting for us, and we knew our beds would feel good that night. It had been a great adventure to visit the big city, but we were small town boys, satisfied with what we had at home. Once we were home, I barely made it from the car to my bed before I was sound asleep.

Play Ball!

There were two home-made baseball fields in town; one on the west side of town, where we played, and one on the east side of town, where the east-side kids played. There was a ball field at the city park where the big kids played but we avoided that one. Our field was on the same block as my house. There were two vacant lots next to my neighbor's house that we had converted into a baseball field the previous year. The area was about a hundred and fifty-feet square and it made a perfect ball field for us. My neighbors, Fred and Mary, mowed the grass when it got too tall for playing ball. They didn't mind us yelling and playing; in fact, they often sat in the shade and watched us. We laid out our bases, home plate, and a pitcher's mound in the back corner of the field near the alley. Then we hauled in dirt, dumped it on the pitcher's mound, and placed a piece of rubber doormat on it for the pitcher's foot. Our bases were seat cushions off old kitchen chairs that we had come across behind the furniture store. They worked well even though they were covered in red vinyl instead of white canvas like you'd see in the major league parks. Home plate was a converted rubber car mat from a car we had found in the junkyard. We used a tin snips to cut it to the shape of an actual home plate. It did the trick, even if it was light blue-not exactly the color of a manufactured one.

There was a sand pit in right field and a couple dozen small pine trees so it made a long-ball hard to field. Fred had planted the trees several years before so we couldn't think of clearing them out. We had to make do by jumping through them to catch fly balls, or by crawling through them, as fast as we could go, to intercept the grounders. There were also sandburs growing in right field and it wasn't uncommon for a base runner passing first base, on his way to second, to get a strip of them thrown at him as he sped by. The street was the home run line, and the Methodist church was across the street in deep right field. The church, with its stained glass windows, was something we thought about whenever a long ball was hit in that direction. Thankfully, few of us could hit well enough to come close to it on the first bounce.

Left field was flat and grassy and well suited for the outfielders. But, it was the worst direction for a long ball to go. Across the street lived the meanest man in town, Verlin Berkamer. He kept an eye on us and whenever we hit a ball into his yard, he picked it up and kept it. Of course, we would yell and scream, but he didn't care. We tried to play during the day when he was at work so we wouldn't have to constantly replace the ball.

Our biggest problem was our backstops. Fred's garage was behind the right side of home plate. Fred's garage had two four paned windows on the ball field side. During the course of the summer, we managed to break every one of them; and some, several times. Then it was necessary to take a time-out to replace them. Fred kept a supply of windowpanes and a can of window putty in his garage and, by summer's end, we were experts at window repair. Chick and I could take out the old pane, clean off the old putty, and install a new one before the other players could get a drink from Fred's water hose.

The backstop on the left side of home plate was also a garage. The door, which faced the ball field, had six small windows in a line. These panes were also replaced frequently and these neighbors, Henry and Mary, likewise kept a supply of panes and putty for us. Mary, or Grandma Stadele, as we called her, often treated us to cookies during the game. We took special care to do a good job on their window repairs. Fortunately, for the most part, we had pleasant neighbors with a good sense of humor who enjoyed our games, except for old Verlin.

Dewey was in right field because he was our slowest guy and there generally wasn't much business in right field. Chick was our second baseman, and Dougie played shortstop. My neighbor, Charlie, was our pitcher. He had a fastball that would whiz by so quickly that you could barely see it. We figured he would be a professional baseball player someday. "Sticks" was the center fielder. He was the tallest kid on the team, weighed the least, and had arms and legs that looked like sticks; hence, the nickname. "Rocket" was our left fielder. Next to Dewey, he was the slowest guy on the team; so, of course, he was "Rocket." Dennis was our third baseman, but we called him "Hounee," for no reason other than everyone had a nickname and he seemed to be a "Hounee." Fred's grandson, Tommy, was catcher, and I was first baseman. If someone was missing, we usually moved Dewey into the spot, leaving right field undefended. That was most of the time—even if Dewey was there. He lost interest in the game easily and would lie down in the shade next to a little pine tree and take a nap if things were a little slow. Sometimes he would collect a supply of sandburs for an attack on a poor base runner.

Sandburs grew in abundance in our town. The ground was sandy and they were tough little plants, surviving where nothing else could. The plant looks like a clump of grass, but it sends up a shoot with seeds, or in this case, burrs. The seed shoot is a stiff spike with pea-size burrs that bear about a thousand sharp, protruding, tiny barbs. I suppose Mother Nature designed them that way so they would attach to the fur coats of animals and be distributed across the landscape where they would produce new plants. It was a very clever idea. But we used them as weapons. If the spike was broken off when the sandburs were green, they adhered to the stem and you could throw the works at a passerby and the burrs would stick in the hide like a row of daggers. If you threw them with force, they would become buried and most difficult to remove. Individual little burrs had to be pulled out and they stuck in the fingers of the victim, causing even more pain and discomfort. All in all, they made a delightfully effective weapon. And they were plentiful, and free.

We played baseball almost every day, taking turns batting and having infield practice. About three days a week, we played against the east-side team. Their field was an entire vacant block. They had a real backstop, made of poles and chicken wire, which worked much better than the garages we used. But they didn't have a street for a home run fence, so they used flags tied to sticks for home run lines; a crumby setup compared to ours. Somehow, they had acquired real bases and a home plate, and their pitcher's mound was a little better than ours. Still, we were proud of our field, despite the sandbur patch in right field.

Most of the kids on the east-side team were from St. John's but they had some public school kids, too. A couple of them were eighth-graders and pretty good ball players. They even had one ninth-grader who was almost a professional compared to the rest of us. We met at one of the ball fields about every other day in the summer and we played a game that just kept going, from day to day, and week to week. We never kept score, but we played and played until we got tired of it, or until the sun became too hot. Then we headed to the Gosey for a swim.

Most of us weren't allowed to swim in the river, but the Gosey technically wasn't the river. Where the stream from Gutweiler's Lake emptied into the river, there was a protruding finger of land that made a small lagoon. That was the Gosey. We felt it was safe to swim there as long as we didn't stray past the finger of land into the main river.

It was a great life in the summer. Sleep late, go fishing, go swimming, or play ball-every day. Some days we had a full team; other days we were a few players short, depending on how well the bluegills happened to be biting.

A few days after our trip to Chicago, the east-side guys came to our field for a game. Of course, there were the usual insults to our red bases and floor-mat home plate, but the game started and soon we were enjoying a good afternoon of baseball. One of the east-side eighth-graders was up to bat and he hit a long fly ball into deep right field. As usual, Dewey didn't even come close to catching it and the ball cruised over his head, bounced on the pavement, and sailed through one of the basement windows of the Methodist church. The game was brought to a halt and we hurried to the church to assess the damage. We peered into the church basement through the broken window and saw our ball resting on one of the tables in the church kitchen; sitting in the little basket on the center of the table where the napkins were kept.

"Well, that ball's gone for today," Dewey said. "Let's go swimming."

"We've got another ball," said one of the east-side team members, so we ran back and resumed the game. On the next pitch, their batter hit a line drive out of the park and into mean, old Verlin's yard.

"Holy cow!" Chick said. "There goes our other ball."

"I'll get it," said one of the east-side kids who didn't know about old Verlin. He took off across the street, entered Verlin's yard, and grabbed the ball. Verlin came flying out of his house, yelling at him as he hurried back to the ball field. Of course, we had to shout back, and soon there was a major melee going on between a mean old man and a dozen and a half kids. He was standing on the curb, threatening to call the police and we told him, well—we told him a lot of places he could go, and things he could do, that were not particularly pleasant.

Next we mounted our bikes and rode back and forth in front of his house, yelling at him and calling him names. He stood there, shaking his fist at us, using the word jail. I don't know how long the racket kept up. Suddenly he retreated to his garage and came out swinging a long pole at us as we passed by. Now we were having a great time dodging the pole and yelling insults at him until Chick got too close and Verlin stuck his pole into Chick's front wheel spokes. Chick's bike came to an abrupt stop and he flew over the handlebars and landed on his head, in the street. That did it! We piled off our bikes and headed toward Verlin. He backed up and ran into his house. We were attempting to remove the pole from Chick's wheel spokes when Mr. Audetta, the town policeman, drove up.

"You boys picking on Mr. Berkamer?" he asked.

"No, sir. We were minding our own business and he came out here yelling at us and he tossed this pole into Chick's bike wheel," Dewey said.

"And why was he yelling at you?"

"Don't know. We were just playing ball," Dewey said, as innocently as possible.

Just then, Verlin came out, bellowing that he wanted us arrested and thrown in jail.

"Hold on, there," Mr. Audetta said. "These boys said you started it."

Verlin came unglued, complaining that we play ball and make a lot of noise and trespass on his property. Mr. Audetta looked at me, questioning if that was true.

"Well, we just play ball. Kids need to yell when they play ball.

We only go over there to retrieve our ball if it's hit across the road. Besides, he has kept about a dozen balls of ours."

Mr. Audetta became interested. "You have baseballs that belong to these boys?" he asked old Verlin.

"If they come into my yard, they're mine," Verlin said.

"And what are you going to do with them?" Mr. Audetta asked.

"Keep 'em."

"What for?"

"So they can't play ball."

Well, Mr. Audetta didn't like that answer and you could see he was getting irritated with old Verlin.

"Well, Mr. Berkamer, here's what we're going to do. You get the baseballs that belong to these boys and give them back. Then, go into your house and stay there. Furthermore, when these boys play ball, you stay in your house, and don't come out. When I drive by, if I see the boys playing ball, and if you are in your yard, I'll take YOU to jail for harassing them. You got that?"

Verlin stood there looking rather stupid. He went to his garage and came out with a pail of baseballs and dumped them on the ground. Then he opened his mouth as if to address Mr. Audetta but he must have changed his mind, so he turned and went into his house. We let out a huge cheer and scrambled to pick up the baseballs.

"Now, you guys listen up, too," Mr. Audetta said. We stopped dead in our tracks and listened. "You boys play as quietly as you can, and if a ball goes into Verlin's yard, get it, and get back as fast as you can. Don't tramp in his garden or step on his flowers, or anything else, for that matter. Okay?"

"Yes, Sir! Thanks, Sir," we said, almost in unison. Mr. Audetta smiled and climbed into his car.

"Now you have balls to last you all summer," he said. "Have fun, boys." And he drove away.

We picked up our bikes and one of the guys took care of Chick's bike since he was injured. We headed back to the ball field and continued the game. Old Verlin must have been scared off because he never bothered us again. We had a supply of balls that would last us for years to come. After that, we always went out of our way to wave and say hi to Mr. Audetta as he went by. Sometimes he would park his car on the street by the Methodist church and watch us play. He must have liked watching baseball.

War Games

During the summer, we occasionally took time out from fishing and baseball to play Cowboys and Indians or GI's and Germans. Not that we had anything against either one of our make-believe enemies, but someone had to be the bad guys. We took turns taking sides.

A few of the guys had toy guns, or bows and arrows, but generally we used a stick for a gun, and a dirt clod for a hand grenade. This arrangement worked well along with the sound effects we made as we attacked. After a few weeks of make-believe, Chick showed up one day with a water pistol. Of course, we each began a campaign of pestering our moms for money to buy a water gun, too. It didn't take long until we were all sporting water pistols of one sort or another which made the game more fun since you could see that you had scored a hit by the wet spots on shirts and pants.

Then Dewey came up with the idea of water balloons and the game took a new twist. Now we could not only shoot at each other, but we could hurl water grenades at the enemy. The possibilities were endless and the water made the game gloriously wet and muddy. The water balloons were also tossed at unsuspecting friends as they stood in their yards, or up town on the sidewalk, minding their own business. We would ride by on our bikes and pelt them before they knew what had hit them.

By the middle of the summer, the water weapons had become old, but the sandburs were peaking, and they became the weapon of choice. Sandburs grew everywhere. At least they grew wherever the area was not mowed. Vacant pieces of land always had a few sandbur plants; they grew in the right-field area of our ball park, along the roadsides, and in other neglected places. One block from my house was a wooded area with a fairly steep hill that we used for sleigh riding in the winter. The wooded area was also great for our mock battles in the summer. We would divide into teams. One team would hide near the hill and the other team would come in for the attack. Each person, armed with a bouquet of sandbur stems, would run at his opponent, throw the stalk at him, and then retreat as quickly as possible. The sandburs would become buried in the flesh and hurt like heck. This was fun, unless you were on the receiving end. The sandbur season didn't last long because the plants dried out, the burrs fell off, and they became useless for warfare.

Luckily, Chick came up with a solution for a new weapon when he went to the A & W. He ordered a thick malt. Special plastic straws were provided because regular paper straws collapsed with the extra sucking effort required to draw the malt up to the mouth. Chick happened to keep his straw one day, and when he got home, he noticed that a dry navy bean would fit in it perfectly, and if you blew through the straw, the bean shot out like a bullet. We were sitting in the shade near the ball field when he rode up on his bike. His cheeks were stuffed, like a chipmunk's, and a straw was dangling out of his mouth. We looked up, reprimanded him for being late again just as he aimed the straw at us and delivered a volley of wet beans. We were taken by surprise, and by the time we had figured out what had happened, he was reloading and gave us a second round. It was a delightful new weapon and we couldn't get to the A & W fast enough to buy a malt and obtain our own shooters. The bean shelf at Kalscher's Market was empty in a day. We had a new and wonderful weapon for our war games.

One day we decided it would be a great joke to launch a sneak attack on the east-side baseball team members with the bean shooters. We filled our pockets with beans, grabbed our ball gloves and caps, and pedaled to their field. They had just begun their practice. This wasn't a game day so they were wondering why we showed up and they came over to us. As they got within range, Dewey yelled, "Attack!!!!" and we rallied together and hit them with mouthfuls of beans. They were bombarded mercilessly with beans and fell to the ground in a heap, yelling like madmen. We sped out of there, feeling proud of ourselves for our successful surprise mission.

We heard nothing from the east-side guys for several days so we decided they were afraid to attack us. It was a super hot day. We had knocked off baseball practice early and rode our bikes to the Gosey for a swim. It was far enough from the main road that no one ever ventured down there except us, so we usually felt safe skinny-dipping. It took but a moment to pull everything off and jump into the water. No one was shy, and no one cared if we were swimming naked, so we did it all the time. Additionally, we didn't have to go home with wet shorts or a wet swimming suit and explain to our mothers why we were wet. The river was off limits, and the Gosey was pushing it, as far as the rule went. It was almost part of the river, but we reasoned somehow that as long as water from Gutweiler's Lake flowed in there, it was part of the lake and not the river. I know, it was a stretch, but we managed to convince ourselves and that made it our favorite swimming hole.

We were swimming and screaming and laughing. Then Dougie shouted, "Hey, look! Those guys took our clothes!" And sure enough, there were a couple of east-side kids running down the trail toward town with their arms full of shorts, T-shirts, and shoes. We swam in and took off after them, calling them names and hollering threats. When we were halfway down the trail, the rest of the east-side guys jumped out from behind the bushes and pounded us with beans from their newly-purchased bean shooters. We were in a fix: no bean shooters, no beans, and no clothes! We turned and ran for the water and swam out of bean range. The east-side guys were swollen with pride as they shot beans at us from the bank. We used our only defense-our mouths-and shouted useless threats at them. Finally they ran out of beans and left.

"Now, what we gonna do?" Dewey questioned. "How are we gonna get home, naked?"

"It looks like they left our underwear," Chick said. So we left the water, and sure enough, our underwear was there, in a muddy pile. We sorted through, finding our own, and then we mounted our bikes for the long and humiliating ride through town. It must have been quite a sight-nine almost-naked boys riding down the street in mud-streaked underwear. We arrived at the ball field and found our shoes and clothes in a pile on the pitcher's mound. We jumped off our bikes, picked through the stuff, and dressed, thankful that they hadn't thrown our clothes in the river, or something worse.

Now, we had to retaliate, or suffer the indignity of being the joke of the town for the rest of the summer.

"We have to really make them pay," said Chick. "Let's think of something we can do that they'll never forget."

We agreed the payback had to be something catastrophic, and it had to be delivered quickly. We went home to think and to find ammunition.

The next day we congregated at the ball field and we each brought something for the attack. Chick had the ultimate bean shooter. He had cut off the ends of his mom's fly swatter and the result was a plastic tube, about two feet long, capable of delivering a speeding kidney bean. It was like a grenade launcher instead of a bean shooter. Kidney beans were twice the size of regular beans and would hurt twice as badly. Dougie had a pail of overripe tomatoes that he had "borrowed" from a neighbor's garden. I had water balloons but, instead of water, I had filled them with pickle juice and vinegar. The others had contributed such things as ripe cucumbers, squash, and other nasty stuff. We were ready for the attack. Dewey rode in, late as usual, and he had a big grin on his face. He was handling a sack very carefully. When he approached us, he smiled, and opened the bag to reveal his treasure. It was full of eggs. "They're rotten," he said. "I got them from behind the grocery store. They're the ones that don't sell."

Mr. Kalscher bought eggs from farmers and checked each one with a light to see if it was okay before he sold it. Eggs that weren't clear were thrown away, sometimes remaining for a while in the hot sun before they were collected by the trash men. They got very stinky and nasty in a short time. We were proud of Dewey!

We sent Dougie on a scouting mission. When he returned, he reported that the east-side guys were practicing and all were accounted for. That meant they didn't have spies out. We hopped on our bikes, rode to their side of town, and parked in an alley about a block away. We hid our bikes by a lilac bush behind a garage and worked out our plan. The idea was for Dougie to ride by the ball field and call them names and shoot a few beans at them; then take off as fast as possible. In this way, he would lead them into a dead-end alley. As they passed us, we would attack from behind and they would be at our mercy. It was a good plan.

We divided up the produce and eggs and stink bombs and we hid behind bushes and trash cans and Dougie took off to initiate the attack. Soon we heard screaming and cussing coming closer and closer as Dougie flew by on his bike.

"Ha! He rode into a dead end!" somebody shouted.

"Get him! Make him pay!" The east-side guys came flying by, dust billowing; then, tires screeching to a halt.

Dougie was off his bike, running across the yard when, suddenly, a stink bomb hit one of their guys in the head. That was the signal to attack.

"Yiiieeee!! Attack! Attack!" We threw everything we had at them. They were still on their bikes, trying to ride back to safety, but we pelted them with eggs and stink bombs and beans. Soon they abandoned their bikes and tried to hide behind each other, using their bikes as shields. We kept up the attack until the ammunition ran low and they were pretty well beaten. As the attack slowed, they ran down the alley toward the street, and we let them go. They were plastered with tomato juice, vinegar, rotten eggs, and red welts from kidney beans shot at close range. "High fives" were traded among us. Then we got on our bikes, each one picking up one of the abandoned bikes of the east-side guys. We rode slowly, holding the handlebars of the confiscated bikes, and headed toward the river. When we got to the Gosey, we took off our shoes and clothes and we each took one of the eastside guys' bikes and dragged it into the water, across the Gosey, parking them on the opposite side.

We waded back, put on our clothes, and returned to town. The guys had seen us going in the direction of the river with their bikes so we knew they would eventually head there. We rode around behind them and inched up to the riverbank just as they were emerging from the water on the other side of the Gosey. Chick and Dougie crawled out, gathered up their clothes, and crept back. Then we melted into the woods and found our parked bikes.

Suddenly, you could hear a lot of yelling and shouting as they realized their clothes were missing. "Let's get out of here," Dougie said. We rode to their ball field, piled their stuff neatly on the pitcher's mound and left a note for them: How about a game tomorrow; our field, two o'clock: truce?

Soon there came nine naked boys riding as fast as they could pedal toward the ball field. We hadn't been as charitable as they had been since we had taken everything-even their underwear! They dressed, and then they gathered around to read the note. We saw them talking and then one of their guys waved and made the "okay" sign. All was well.

We had proven that we were not easily outdone. I guess that's why we never kept score in the ball games. Had we done so, we would have taken it too seriously, and that would have taken the fun out of it. At any rate, it had been an exciting few days.

The Haunted House

My friends and I received weekly allowances. The amount varied from kid to kid but it always seemed that the other guys got more money than I did for doing less work. We all complained about our pocket money, but, in reality, we each received about the same amount. The trouble was it never seemed to last the week. Allowance was to cover movies, candy, and summer entertainment. But if we bought soda, ice cream, and baseball cards, there wasn't anything left for movies and popcorn. We had to find ways to supplement our income.

Dewey came up with the perfect enterprise. His dad owned a bar and supper club and if patrons bought beer and soda to take home, there was an additional charge for the bottle. When bottles were returned, the deposit was returned to the customer. It was called cooperage. All bars and grocery stores charged this fee and many bottles went home with customers each week. Often people would consume the beer or soda on the way home and toss the bottles into the ditch. That became the source of our extra spending money. We would ride our bikes toward a neighboring town and collect the strewn bottles. When we got as far as we wanted to travel, we returned on the other side of the road, still searching for bottles. On a good day there would be two or three dollars worth of bottles which helped our finances immensely. Small pop bottles and beer bottles were worth three cents each. Large quart bottles were worth a nickel but they were not as plentiful, probably because more people saved them, and because they broke more easily when tossed from car windows.

We had wire bike baskets on our bikes and, on a good day, we could fill them up. Then we hauled them to Dewey's dad's bar. He counted them and we collected the money. We shared the profit evenly unless we were buying something for the ball field or an overnight camping trip. There were five main roads coming into town and if we alternated between them, leaving a week or so between passes, we would generally fare well.

One particular day, we were riding to Blue River, a town about five miles away. We usually went halfway but on this occasion we intended to go the entire distance because we were planning a weekend camping trip and we needed a good supply of pop and chips for the outing. Dewey and Chick were ahead of Dougie and me, loading up a good find of bottles they had located in a ditch. Dougie and I passed them. Then I spotted a quart beer bottle and stopped to pick it up. Dougie rode on. Soon the three of us caught up with him. He was waiting for us.

"Do you know where this sandy road goes?" he asked, as he pointed to an overgrown path that disappeared into the woods.

"Nope. I've never been down this far before," I said.

"Let's take a look," said Dewey, who was always looking for a loophole when it came to work.

"Yeah, let's," said Chick who was always looking for something to explore.

"Okay, here we go!"

We snaked down the wooded, winding road. Hot and dry conditions caused the dust to billow behind us as we moved farther from the highway. Suddenly we came to a clearing and an old house. It had once been white but the paint had faded to gray. The siding was buckled and dried out. Windows were broken and the front door was standing open. The rusty tin on the roof was buckled. Weeds and brush had grown up around the house and the place looked like it had been abandoned years before.

There was a small shed and an outhouse behind the house, but the strangest thing of all was the fence. It had been constructed of sticks and branches that were piled and woven together. It surrounded the entire yard and ended in front with a wooden gate. The fence was about four feet tall and it reminded me of movies about Africa where people built fences around their villages to keep out lions.

"What the heck kind of animals did they have in here?"

Dougie asked.

"Maybe pigs or something," said Chick.

"Or, maybe spooky people like you see on Twilight Zone, or a monster of some sort," Dewey said. "I saw a show that had a house like this that was full of nasty-looking people who were from outer space or somewhere."

"Oh! Sure! Those weird people on the Twilight Zone are real and are running loose these days," I said. We all laughed at Dewey and his big imagination.

"You never know. They could be real and maybe this is a place where they were kept in pens, like animals," lamented Dewey. ''And I suppose this happens to be one of those places?" I asked.

"Could be! You don't know," Dewey said.

We laughed at him and decided to take a look. There was a dead tree, standing like a scarecrow with its naked branches stretched toward the sky, in the front yard. A worn out tire was attached to a rope hanging from one of the big branches. There was a bare spot in the dirt where swinging feet had made a depression. We walked behind the house and jarred open the door of a shed that was full of trash, tin cans, broken furniture, and tattered clothes. Dewey took a stick and began digging in the trash, searching for pop or beer bottles, and the rest of us turned to go. Suddenly, Dewey let out a scream and plowed into us as he flew from the shed. "A dead baby! Oh, no! There's a dead baby in there!" He was blubbering and shaking. We mustered up the courage to peek into the shed. Chick started laughing, went to the trash pile, and picked up the head of an old doll.

"Dewey, you dummy!" he said. It's a doll."

"A what?"

"A doll. It's a toy doll's head." Chick tossed the head at Dewey who dodged it and then carefully looked it over on the ground.

"It looked like the real thing when I uncovered it."

We laughed at Dewey. Now it was time to check out the house. Perhaps the Twilight Zone people were big pop drinkers, leaving us a fortune in bottles. The boards on the front porch creaked and groaned as we stepped on them.

"Dewey, you go first. If they hold you, we're safe," said Chick.

Dewey stuck out his tongue at Chick.

The house was empty, except for the worn curtains hanging on the windows and the strewn-about magazines and papers. Out-of-date wallpaper had peeled off the walls and the ceiling was marred with brown, water-stained spots. As we passed through the house, room after room, I noticed that it was getting dark outside. I looked at the sky and spotted an approaching ominous black storm cloud.

"Uh, oh! We're gonna get wet," I said. "We either gotta make a run for home or stay here till the storm passes."

"Let's stay here," Chick said. "Yeah. This is cool," said Dougie.

"I think we should go. There might be the ghosts of Twilight Zone characters lurking here and they might not want us hangging out in their house," said Dewey. We chuckled and decided to ride out the storm in the old house.

As the wind picked up, the curtains fluttered and billowed.

The papers that were lying on the floor were stirred as the lightning crashed and the thunder rumbled. It was scary. The first drops of rain made a loud thumping sound on the tin roof. Soon there was a cloudburst and the sound changed to a constant drumming. Then it became very dark. Dewey was terrified so Chick, taking advantage of this, sneaked up behind him, grabbed him, and scared him half to death.

Meanwhile Dougie was exploring the house and called out, "Hey! Come here. I found something."

"Oh, no," Dewey said, "I'm not going anywhere. You guys are trying to scare me."

Chick and I went to Dougie. Dewey stayed put for about half a minute and then joined us. "You guys wait up. Don't leave me alone," he said.

"Check this out," Dougie said, pointing toward the ceiling in the bedroom. There was a rope dangling from a trap door. "I'll bet that's where the last of the Twilight Zone folks were kept," he said, winking at Chick and me.

"Come on, you guys. Let's go. I've seen enough," Dewey said.

"It's pouring rain, Dewey! Let's see what's up there," Chick said.

Chick got on his hands and knees and Dougie climbed on his back, reached up, and grabbed the rope. Then he jumped down, pulling the rope with him. As he hit the floor, the trap door popped open and a set of stairs slid part way down.

"Wow! Stairs," Dougie said. "Pull them down." We gave a yank and a set of stairs slid down a little track, accompanied by a cloud of dust. It looked as black as night behind the opening.

"Who's first?" I said.

"I'll go," Dougie said. He climbed up and cautiously peered into the attic. Then, a scream! "Ah! No!" He frantically backed down the ladder. Dewey turned and ran into the front yard, into the pouring rain, as the three of us stood laughing in the doorway. "Psycho!" Dougie said.

"That wasn't nice!" Dewey said, as he ran back into the house. "You scared me again!"

We had another good laugh on Dewey. Dougie climbed the stairs again. "Wow! There's an ancient rocking chair up here."

"Anything else?" Dewey whispered.

"Nothing but a lot of dust," Dougie said.

"Let me see," I said, and Dougie came down and I took my turn.

There was a lone rocking chair in the middle of the attic. It looked strange to me and I was trying to figure out what was wrong when Chick pulled on my leg and motioned for me to come down so he could climb up. When he came down, Dewey reluctantly climbed up. Chick gave the ladder a shake.

"Oh, you guys are so immature," he said. He looked at the chair for a few minutes and then said, "Hey, guys. Why isn't there dust on the chair?" Then I knew why the chair had looked funny. The attic and contents were layered in dust, but the chair was shiny and clean, as if it had been dusted, or rocked in recently.

Dewey descended as fast as his legs would go. "I think there's a ghost up there and it rocks in that chair; that would explain the absence of dust," he said. We were contemplating that thought when we heard a creaking sound coming from the attic. It was a steady creak, creak that sounded like someone was rocking in the chair. We looked at each other and had the same idea. We bolted out the front door at lightning speed. Once on our bikes, we peddled down the dark road toward the highway as fast as our legs could pump.

"Hurry up! It could be coming after us," Dewey shouted.

Our tires were throwing mud and the bottles in our baskets were rattling and clanking as we rode faster than the wind traveled.

The storm had passed by the time we hit the highway. We slid to a stop and gazed down the dark road that weaved through the pine trees.

"I ain't going down there again," said Dewey.

"Oh, come on Dewey. You aren't really scared, are you?" Dougie said.

"I didn't see you waiting behind to take another look," Dewey retorted.

"Let's go. We have a great bunch of bottles. We don't need to go all the way to Blue River today. Let's head back on the other side and finish up," I said.

"Yeah! And let's go to the A & W for a chocolate sundae. I think I need one after that!" said Dewey. Good, old Dewey. No matter how bad things were, ice cream made him feel better. But then, a sundae did sound like a good idea.

We Build a Boat, or Two

Dougie and I were fishing at Gutweiler's Lake one day when we came up with a new idea. We thought if we got away from the usual fishing holes, we would attract fish that hadn't seen our baits and, of course, we'd have better luck. Only part of the shoreline was good for fishing because the beaver dams caused the low places to flood and become swampy. In other words, if you kept to the hard ground, you missed out on much of the lake. We figured the big ones were surely in the places we couldn't get to. One day we wore boots and were able to wade along the edges of the lake, casting to new and unexplored waters.

"This is great," Dougie said, as he reeled in a nice bass.

"Yeah! We should have thought of this a long time ago. We could be the best fishermen in town," I said.

Dougie unhooked the bass and let it go since we had previously decided to throw back all fish. Then he cast toward the weed bed. I had directed my trusty, red and white *BassOReno* into a patch of lily pads and I was cranking it back. This was probably the luckiest *Bass 0 Reno* in the whole world. The paint was almost worn off from the teeth of the many northern pike that had taken it. If you cranked slowly, the *Bass 0 Reno* stayed on top and moved along with an enticing wiggle, like a sick, struggling fish; just the right-size meal for a big bass or northern pike. It was about half way back when a huge fish made a swipe at it, but missed. "Whoa! Dougie, there is a huge northern after my bait," I said. I kept reeling, had about three feet of line still out and I was just about to lift my *Bass 0 Reno* out of the water and cast again, when a northern pike, the size of Moby Dick, came out of the weeds open-mouthed and grabbed it. The fish's mouth appeared to be the size of an ice cream bucket and it was lined with long, spike-like teeth. The northern grabbed it with such momentum that he kept coming at me as if he wanted to eat me, too! I let out a yell and ran backwards in the weeds and water while the fish thrashed on top of the water with my lure in his mouth. Then it slapped its tail on the water as it dove back into the weeds. I was standing there, dripping wet, with my fishing pole and a limp line dangling in the water.

"Holy cow! That was a huge one!" Dougie yelled from down the shore.

"He got my favorite *Bass 0 Reno!"* I was furious because the lure cost almost two dollars and this one, particularly, brought good luck, and now it was gone. "Let's go home. I'm tired of fishing," I said.

Dougie knew how special that *Bass 0 Reno* was and he felt sorry for me so he didn't make any jokes about it. "We gotta get a boat so we can get out to those places where the big fish live without being in the water with them," I said. Dougie agreed.

We rode the dirt road back to town and I was feeling pretty miserable. Now I'd have to save up allowance and bottle money to replace the lure, and who knows if the new one would work as well. We were riding past Mr. Schwingle's hardware store when Dougie yelled, "Whoa! Stop! Look at that."

There was a large, empty, wooden crate sitting on the sidewalk behind the store. It was about ten feet long, three feet wide, and three feet deep. "We could make that into a boat," I said, as I looked at Dougie who nodded in agreement.

"No kidding! Let's ask Mr. Schwingle if we can have it," he said.

We parked our bikes, went into the store, and Mr. Schwingle came to greet us. We were regular customers, buying our hooks and sinkers and stuff from him, and we were often there when he uncrated refrigerators. If we helped him, he would give us the boxes for forts and stuff. We asked him if he planned to throw away the wooden crate. He said yes and went on to offer it to us--and to haul it to my house after store hours. We were happy, thanked him, and went to Chick and Dewey's houses to report the good news. We had a boat!

That evening we began working. We decided the box was too tall so we got saws, hammers, and nails, and lopped about one foot from the top of the box. Then we used the wood we cut off to make seats in the boat. It resembled an old-fashioned casket and was slightly odd looking, being square on each end, but we didn't care.

The next day we decided to pool our money to buy putty or caulk to seal up the cracks so the boat wouldn't leak. We soon realized we needed a method of moving the boat through the water. We found a few straight small trees, cut them down, and stripped off the branches. These became our pushing poles. Then we encountered our biggest problem-getting the boat to the lake. We were sitting in the shade, trying to figure it out, when

Mr. Schwingle drove up in his pickup truck.

"I thought I'd see how your project is coming," he said. We showed him our handiwork and he seemed very impressed. "How are you going to get it to the lake?" he asked.

"Don't know," Dewey said.

"Nope, don't know," we all chimed in, looking at the back of his pickup.

"Maybe I can give you a lift," he said, smiling. We gave a hearty cheer and grabbed the corners of the boat and lifted it into Mr. Schwingle's truck. Then we piled our bikes on top for the ride to the lake.

When we arrived, we unloaded the stuff and thanked Mr. Schwingle for his help. "You guys try that thing out in the shallow end of the lake."

"Okay, we will," we said, and we started to drag the boat to the bank. Mr. Schwingle drove away, chuckling to himself

The boat settled into the water with about a foot and a half of boat sticking up. "That's good," Dougie said. "Doesn't look like the water will come over the side."

"I wanna ride in the front," said Chick, and he crawled in. "Me, next," Dewey said, and he walked to the other end next to Chick. Then Dougie got in and I pushed the boat away from the bank and jumped in the back of the boat. Now there was only about half a foot of boat sticking above the water.

"Whew, we better sit still, or we'll take in water," Dougie said, leaning over to see how close we were to the water surface.

"Row! Row!" Dewey said. "Push those poles; swab that deck!"

Suddenly Dewey had become Captain Hook. Dougie and I began pushing with the poles and the boat moved slowly toward the middle of the lake. It wasn't a pretty thing, but we made it to the center of the lake where we never had a chance to fish before and it was great.

"Let's head to the other end," Chick said. So Dougie and I began poling toward the deep end of the lake. We were moving along well when Dewey yelled, "Hey, guys! Water is seeping in!" We looked down and, sure enough, lake water was coming in through the caulked seams!

"That's not so bad," Dougie said. "We can add caulk when we get it back to shore." Dougie had no more than said that when a big crack opened up on the side of the boat and more water began squirting in.

"Uh, oh! That can't be good," Dewey said. And another crack opened on the other side! Now, more water was coming in, like a geyser.

"Head for shore!" yelled Chick.

"Hurry up! We're gonna sink," Dewey said, and he stood on top of the seat. Well, that about did it. When Dewey stepped up, the boat tipped to the side and we took in a few more gallons.

"Dewey--you bonehead! Get down. You're gonna sink us," Dougie yelled.

"I'll get my new tennis shoes wet," Dewey whined.

"You're gonna get more than that wet if we sink," Chick added.

Dougie and I tried to turn the boat toward shore but we were having a difficult time accomplishing that because the boat was filling with water.

"Give me a pole," Chick said, and I handed him my pole and he was able to turn us. Just as we were pointed in the new direction, the boat tipped again, and another flood of water came in on us! The boat was now about three-fourths under water and the shore was a long way off.

"We're not gonna make it," I said. "Pole fast, guys, or our boat is going down."

About a minute later, the boat sank downward and we found ourselves swimming. As soon as we were out of the boat, it bobbed at the surface momentarily; then it turned over and plunged out of sight. Luckily, we were all good swimmers, so we made it to shore. We climbed on the bank and gazed at the bubbles coming to the surface of the water as our boat settled into the mud.

"Well, that was a good idea," Dewey said. "And my new tennies are all full of mud. My mom will kill me."

Dougie and I shook our heads at Dewey, and Chick threw a mud ball at him.

"Well, it was a good idea as long as it lasted," Dougie said. "Yeah, it was fun," Chick said.

"We need a boat, one way, or another," I said. I had that unforgettable northern pike on my mind with my *Bass 0 Reno* in its mouth.

We rode our bikes back to town. By the time we arrived, we were coated with road dust that had adhered to our wet bodies. Chick and Dewey turned toward their houses and Dougie and I went the other way to his house. We were sitting in his backyard feeling glum when he suddenly looked up. "You know, I've got an old telephone pole out back that was once a basketball backboard pole. My dad wanted it out of the way so he took it down and the pole is lying behind the garage."

"I don't want to get up in the air," I said. "I want to get to the middle of the lake."

"I know, but listen. We'll cut the telephone pole in half; then, we'll lay the two halves about six feet apart and nail a few boards between them. The inner tubes we use at the swimming hole can be attached to the under side and we'll have a raft. It'll be even better than a boat because it'll be bigger and we'll be higher off the water." I knew right then that I had made a good choice when I made friends with Dougie. He was a genius.

The next day I called Chick and Dewey and told them to meet me at Dougie's house with their tools. We got there about a half hour later and we had a good assortment of saws, hammers, and drills, along with nails and screws that we had borrowed from our dads' workshops. Dougie explained the plan and Dewey and Chick became as excited as I had been.

First, we had to cut the telephone pole in half. We measured it and then began cutting with Dewey's saw. Dewey sawed and sawed and he had barely put a scratch in the pole when he turned the saw over to Chick. Again, a lot of sawing happened but not much pole was cut. I took over; then Dougie took his turn, and we were barely halfway through. "Whew! This is harder than I thought it would be," Dougie panted. "A saw with longer teeth would cut faster." He left and returned with his dad's meat saw that he used to cut up deer. It had long teeth and it worked much better. "We just gotta clean it up and put it back, and he'll never know," Dougie said.

The pole was finally cut in half. We laid the two pieces across from each other and placed a number of boards across them horizontally. We nailed the boards down, making one end even but the other end was jagged because of the varying board lengths. Then, with the meat saw, we trimmed the uneven edge, and our raft was finished. Dougie and I were on one side and Dewey and Chick were on the other and we lifted the raft to check its stability. As we lifted it, one board came loose, Chick dropped his end, then Dewey dropped his end, and in a couple of seconds, the whole thing was coming apart.

"We gotta put it together better," Dougie said. "I have a few 4 x 4 posts that could be nailed to the telephone posts, and then the boards could be nailed to the 4 x 4's. That would give added strength." Dougie was such a good engineer that we all agreed and we tore the boards from the posts.

Then we got the 4 x 4's and, since they were already about six or seven feet long, we decided that it would be easier to make the raft longer than to cut them off. We put them in place and drilled a hole in each one. We pooled our money and sent Dewey to Mr. Schwingle's store to buy four long bolts and nuts for connecting the 4 x 4's to the posts. It took much drilling but we finally completed the job and we nailed the boards to the 4 x 4's. We had to use additional boards since the raft's dimensions had grown. Soon, we had our finished product.

"Let's see how strong it is now," I said. Each one lifted a corner and, with a lot of grunting and groaning, we managed to raise it off the ground.

"Wow! This thing weighs a ton," Dewey said.

"No kidding! We're gonna need a lot of inner tubes to keep it afloat," Dougie said.

We also had another problem. How would we get the raft to the lake? We decided to visit Mr. Schwingle and ask if he had an idea since he had helped us with the boat first time around.

We walked into his store and he came to meet us. "How's the boat working?"

"Um ... not so good. It sunk," Dewey said.

"Really? Were you able to get it out of the lake? You were in the shallow end, right?"

"Um ... not exactly. We started in the shallow end but then we went to the deep end and that's where it sank."

"So, where is it now?" he questioned.

"On the bottom of the lake," Dewey said, as if he had asked a stupid question.

"You guys were in it when it went down, I suppose."

"Yeah, but not for long. We had to swim to shore."

Mr. Schwingle just shook his head and chuckled. "I'm glad you guys are good swimmers. So, what are you up to now?" Mr. Schwingle asked.

"Well, you know the bolts Dewey bought a while ago? We made a raft and we want to take it to the lake and get back to fishing," Dougie said.

"A raft? Do you think it'll last longer than the boat?" Mr. Schwingle wondered.

"Yeah. It's much better than the boat and we're gonna put inner tubes under it to keep it floating."

"I see. Well, I hope you have good luck with it."

"Well, we ... well, we kinda wondered if maybe, later, when you close the store, if--maybe, could you help us haul it to the lake?" Chick said.

"Need a lift? Sure. I guess I can do that," he said. "Where is it?"

"In my backyard," Dougie said.

"Okay! You guys be ready at about six-thirty, and I'll help you."

We thanked Mr. Schwingle; then we rode to our homes to eat supper and get the inner tubes. We planned to meet again at Dougie's house.

When Mr. Schwingle pulled up in the alley behind Dougie's house, he looked surprised when he saw our raft. "That's a pretty big raft. I don't think it'll fit in my pickup. I'll go home and pick up my trailer. I'll be right back." We were in such a hurry to launch our raft that we were becoming impatient waiting for him to return. Finally he pulled up with his trailer. With two of us on each side, we were able to lift it up and slide it on the trailer. Then we tossed our pushing poles and inner tubes on the trailer, followed by our bikes, and then we piled on. Mr. Schwingle drove slowly. When we arrived at the lake, he backed the trailer close to the high bank. We removed our bikes and other stuff. Then we edged the raft off the trailer and down the bank. At the shore, we attached the inner tubes and shoved it into the water. Six inner tubes seemed to keep it nicely afloat. Then we climbed aboard what seemed to be a perfect and stable raft. It rode high in the water and gave us much room for fishing and moving around. "Wow! This is great!" Dougie said, as he proudly surveyed his creation. We all congratulated Dougie and thanked Mr. Schwingle for his help.

"You boys be careful, and have fun," he said, as he drove off. We could hardly wait for the maiden voyage but it was already rather late so we decided to tie it up at shore and return early the next morning.

We were extremely happy as we journeyed home. We sang "Row, row, row your boat ... " and "Take me out to the ball game ... " as we rode our bikes. We sang the baseball song because we got tired of "Row, row, row ... " and we didn't know any other lively song. When we got back to town, we separated. Dewey and Chick headed toward their houses and Dougie and I went toward ours. We stopped for a minute at Dougie's house and he said, "I can't wait until tomorrow."

"Me, either! That must be the best raft in the whole world.

We're gonna catch so many fish that we'll easily be the best fishermen that ever lived in this town," I said. We "high-fived" and I went home, dreading the thought of trying to go to sleep, barely able to wait until morning when we would launch the raft.

The next morning, I was up with the sun and got my stuff together for a day of fishing on our new raft. I made peanut butter and jam sandwiches and put them in a plastic bag along with a banana and an apple. Then I grabbed my fishing pole and bait, placing the bait in an old cigar box that usually held my baseball cards. I didn't want to take my tackle box on the raft in case it sank, or in the event that Dewey would manage to kick it overboard.

I arrived at Dougie's house and he and Chick were waiting. They were carrying lunches, tackle, and their fishing poles. Dougie also had a canteen of water so we would have something to drink. Of course, Dewey was late. In about half an hour, Dewey rode up with his pole, already tied with a lure, and a huge grocery sack full of food.

"Jeez, Dewey! Are you going for a week?" Dougie said.

"I know I'll be hungry and I don't want to run the risk of going without food," he said. We got on our bikes and headed for the lake.

Our raft was where we had left it. We loaded up the food and gear, then took off our tennis shoes and shirts and left them on the bank. Dougie and I wore Milwaukee Braves baseball caps and Chick had a Philadelphia Phillies cap. He always had to be different. Dewey sported a "grandpa-like" straw hat.

"It's my Huck Finn hat," he said proudly. "If we're gonna be on a raft, I'm gonna be Huck."

"Right, Dewey. But you look more like Aunt Polly," said Chick. We laughed at poor Dewey.

Dougie and I poled and soon we were on the lake with many square yards of new water available to us. "I'll bet nobody has ever thrown a lure in this water before," I said, as I flung my new *Bass o Reno* toward an opening in the lily pads.

"Good shot," Dougie said.

My lure hit the water and it looked like I had thrown a bomb into the lily pads. The water exploded and a huge northern pike shot up like a dolphin in a movie. Then it hit the water and made a huge splash and burrowed back in the weeds.

"Holy smokes!" Dewey said. "Jeez, you got a whale."

"Hang on!" Dougie yelled.

I was holding on for dear life and suddenly the raft began to move across the lake.

"Holy cow! That fish is pulling us!" Chick yelled.

Everyone was talking at once and Dewey was swinging one of the poles, trying to figure out how to stop the raft.

"Dewey, let him pull it. He'll get tired faster that way," Dougie said.

"Get out of my way. Get back! Give me room!" I said, as I tightened the drag on my reel.

We were moving along at a good clip when suddenly the fish turned and came back at the raft.

"He's charging us!" Dewey yelled. The fish came at us and I was reeling up line as fast as I could. He went under the raft and across the lake in the opposite direction. My rod was pulled into the water and I was trying desperately to get it to round the side of the raft.

"Turn us! Hurry! He's gonna break the line!"

Chick was poling and got us about halfway around when the line gave a noisy snap. The raft came to a stop and the four of us stood there, looking at the water.

"That was the biggest northern in the world," Dewey said. "Probably a world record," Chick said.

"Man! That was a huge fish," Dougie said.

I couldn't talk.

"I only got to throw that *Bass O Reno* one time," I said. "That was the biggest fish I've ever had on a line."

"Here," Dougie said, handing me one of his *Bass O Reno* lures. Good, old Dougie. He was always there to make you feel better. Chick patted me on the back and Dewey offered me one of his sandwiches, and soon we were casting again and having a great time.

We fished all day, consumed all the food and water, and caught a dozen fish. We poled our raft from one end of the lake to the other, believing we had conquered the world. It was one of the best fishing days ever.

As we neared the shore, we were chattering about the good times and what we would do the next time we took the raft out. We rode toward town just as the sun was setting. By the time we got to our homes, it was dusk, and after a bath, we headed to bed--with northern pike in our dreams.

The next day we had a game planned with the east-side guys so we didn't go fishing. But we made plans to do so on the following day. We met at Dougie's house with food and beverage and headed to the lake. We parked our bikes and shoved our shirts and shoes in the baskets and walked over the high bank. The raft was gone!

"What the heck?"

"Not No way! How could anyone have stolen it from this spot?" We were all talking at the same time.

"Look here," Dougie said. The rope that we had used to secure the raft was still around the tree.

"Someone dragged it up the bank," Chick said, pointing to scratch marks in the sand. Sure enough, there were tracks where somebody had lugged the raft up the hill and then the telltale marks that indicated that it had been loaded on a truck or trailer.

"Some thief took our raft!" Dewey said. We stood there, looking down the road as if it had to be there, somewhere! But, it was gone.

"Well," I said, "I hope when they use it, it sinks."

"And may a big whale eat them when they're swimming back," Dewey added. We laughed at Dewey and his ideas.

"Well, it was a lot of fun while it lasted," I said.

"Yeah, we had two boats, each for one day and now we're stuck on the bank again," Chick said.

Well, it had been a couple of enjoyable days with exciting adventures, so what the heck.

"Well, I guess we should hunt bottles and see if we can find more wood for another raft," I said.

"Yeah, and we'll be sure to buy a chain and a padlock next time," Dewey said. We all laughed; Dewey could always say something to make us laugh. Good, old Dewey.

We never did get around to building another raft, and we never found out who stole ours, but that one glorious day of fishing was never forgotten.

Refrigerator Boxes

It started one afternoon when Dougie and I happened by Mr. Schwingle's hardware store as he was taking a new refrigerator out of the cardboard shipping box. Refrigerator boxes were in great demand by all the kids in town. We kept a close eye on the store, trying hard to be on the scene whenever new refrigerators arrived. On this particular day, Mr. Schwingle gladly passed one on to us, and we towed it behind our bicycles to my backyard.

Refrigerator boxes weren't as much a box as a tall, square tube; like a skyscraper without a top or bottom. The bottom of the box was attached to a pallet that was bolted to the refrigerator so it could be moved with a forklift. The metal band, used for securing the load, stayed on the pallet when the refrigerator was removed. The top was the same as the bottom except it was made of cardboard and it also had a metal band. The box was about six feet tall and about three feet square. It had many great uses for kids who had imaginations.

In the winter, a bunch of kids could get inside a box and slide and roll down the sleighing hill. On cold days, the box would last all day; but if it was warm, the cardboard became wet and soggy and useless, but it was great fun as long as it held together.

In the summer we used the discarded boxes for forts and tanks. We would take one box, lay it on its side and bend the sides up to make a big tube. Then we would crawl inside, pretend it was a tank, and we would advance toward the enemy. We played "Soldier." One side was a tank division; the other, a dug-in enemy. The tank guys would roll toward the infantry guys and, invariably, we would roll over them with much screaming and shouting. The infantry guys would be crushed beneath the unstoppable tank. Imagining was great fun. Sometimes we would "crawl" all over town--even crossing streets.

The plan for this particular box involved transforming it into a fort for use in my backyard. Dougie and I laid the box on its side so that one open end was against the end of our picnic table. We built a door for the other end out of laths, beach towels, and blankets, giving it an opening like a tent. More blankets and an old painting tarp were used to incorporate the picnic table into the structure. When it was finished, it looked like a patchwork square igloo instead of a smooth and rounded one. Inside, was a comfortable area with two rooms; one being the box, and the other, the area under the picnic table. Chick and Dewey arrived and we played army all day, inside and outside the new fort.

"Let's sleep here tonight," Chick said.

"Yeah! Let's!" chimed in Dewey. We thought that was a good idea, so everyone went home to get permission and to find food and blankets. I went in to check the plan out with my mom. We all got the "okay" to sleep outside, and soon we were preparing the fort for the overnight adventure. There was room under the picnic table for two to sleep, and two could fit in the refrigerator box. We spread out our blankets, pooled our food, and soon we were having a great time telling jokes and stories, and eating lots of good junk.

"Anybody know a good ghost story?" Dougie asked.

"Did you hear the one about the guy with the hook?" Chick said.

"Yeah, Chick. You've told that one about a hundred times," I said.

"My dad told me about a ghost in this town," Dewey said.

"Oh, sure, Dewey."

"No foolin'. It's a true story. It's about the Gosey."

"What about it?"

"Didn't you guys ever wonder why the Gosey is called the Gosey?" We had to admit that it had never crossed our minds, so we asked Dewey to tell the story. "Well, once upon a time, long ago, there was a kid who lived in France. His name was something like Gosee."

"Something that sounds like a French name," Chick laughed.

"It was a French name. I just can't remember it, dummy: anyway, this kid decided to move to the United States. He left his family, boarded a boat, and arrived in New York City. He couldn't find a decent job so he moved west, finally stopping in Wisconsin. Back in the old days, there was a big dock down where the Gosey is; they loaded ore onto big boats for the trip down the river to the Mississippi. "

"Is there a ghost in this story?" Dougie said.

"I'm getting to that; just wait. This Frenchman gets a job at this dock loading the heavy ore onto the boats. The local guys couldn't pronounce his name properly so they called him Gosey, the Frenchman. One day, while carrying a load of ore, he fell into the river and was not able to escape so he went down to the bottom and drowned. They found his body and buried him there on the riverbank. So, from then on, it was called the Gosey Hole, and they say his ghost is still there, haunting the Gosey."

We were sitting open-mouthed when Dewey finished his story.

"No foolin', Dewey?" I said. "Did you just make that up, or is it for real?"

"My dad told me that's how the Gosey got its name. I don't know why he'd say that if it wasn't so," Dewey said.

"Let's go down to the Gosey and see if he's there," Chick said.

"Yeah, let's," Dougie said.

"When? Now?" Dewey questioned.

"Yeah. Our moms think we're sleeping here. They won't know," Chick said.

We discussed it and decided that if we rode our bikes on the back streets, then cut across the main street at the bridge, no one would see us and we could get to the Gosey undetected. Dewey was the only one who was hesitant.

We slipped out of the fort, got our bikes, and sneaked our way through town toward the river. It was late so there weren't people walking or driving around and we arrived without a problem. We took the sand road to the Gosey and jumped off our bikes at the swimming hole. "Come over here. This is where he drowned," Dewey said, walking toward the high bank. We walked to a bunch of rocks cemented together to form a structure as large as the foundation of a house.

"This is where the dock was, my dad said." Dewey pointed to the foundation.

"I always wondered why this was here," said Chick.

We peered at the block of cement above the riverbank and we could imagine a wooden dock attached to it, projecting out into the river. It would be a good place for a boat to dock to be loaded with ore.

"It's very deep here, too," Dougie said. "Yeah. The deepest part of the Gosey," I said. "Let's go swimming," Chick said.

"What? Now?" Dewey said.

"Yeah. Why not?"

"You afraid the ghost will get you, Dewey?" Chick teased. "Well, no. I don't believe there is really a ghost, but it's dark."

"So what? Come on. Let's go."

We ran to the swimming hole, stripped off our clothes, and hit the water. It was cool at first, but, after we were in for a few minutes, we began to have a great time splashing and dunking one another. Earlier in the summer we had tied a thick, hay rope to a tree branch that hung over the water. We used the rope for a swinging ride over the water, letting go, then splashing down into the water. Dougie and I took off for the swing. Dougie stopped part way to catch a firefly. The air was full of glowing green lights that went off, then back on to a spooky green color. Dougie took the firefly and squished it across his forehead, making it glow.

“Wow! That’s cool. You’re green,” I said. “Put on more.”

We both caught fireflies and smeared them on our arms and legs, and on our bellies and faces. Soon we were gleaming like two giant fireflies.

"Let's hide and scare the other guys," Dougie said. "Dewey, come here," we yelled.

"Hey, Chick. See what we got." They came running up the bank, sand and water flying, as Dougie and I hid in the bushes. After they passed us, we stood up quietly and tiptoed behind them. Dougie slipped up behind Dewey, and tapped him on the shoulder. Dewey turned to see two glowing figures. He took off yelling and running for town. Chick knew it was us and laughed as Dewey sped down the road, yelling that a ghost was on his trail.

"Dewey, you numskull! You're naked! Come back!" we yelled.

Dewey almost got to the main street before he realized he was in the nude, stopped, and covered himself with his hands.

"Look at him; he thinks no one will notice him." We were laughing like crazy as Dewey turned and came back.

"Geez, you guys! You're really funny! What if someone would have seen me?"

"They wouldn't have seen much, Dewey," Dougie said, and we laughed again.

The green glow began to fade so we dipped ourselves in the water and scrubbed off the bug juice. Then we sat on the grass to air-dry before putting on our clothes. "That was a good story, Dewey; and it does make sense. Otherwise, why would this place have such a strange name?" Dewey was proud of himself and his fine story.

We dressed and rode our bikes home and settled down in the fort. We ate the last of our food and drank the last pops and then turned in for the night. Then we heard thunder rumbling in the west and soon there were streaks of lightning.

"It's gonna rain," I said to Dougie.

"Yeah. I wonder how long this box will protect us from the rain?" he asked.

"There is a tarp over this part," Dewey said, smugly, from under the picnic table.

A drop or two of rain hit the top of the refrigerator box.

Then-harder and harder--it began to pound and became a downpour. The cardboard part of the fort began to leak and collapse. "Time to abandon the fort!" I shouted to Dougie over the roar of the rain and thunder. We grabbed our blankets and crawled under the picnic table with Chick and Dewey where it was dry. Four boys attempted to be comfortable in a space made for two. Soon the ground was no longer able to absorb the rain, and water trickled in under the edges of the tarp.

"I'm getting wet!" Chick said. "Me, too," said Dougie.

"We better run for my house," I said, and we crawled out through the remains of our ruined fort, ran across the yard in our underwear, and into my house. My mom heard us stomping and banging around in the hallway and got up to see four nearly naked boys fighting over one towel.

"Here," she said, as she handed us dry towels. "I'll get a few blankets and pillows, too." Soon we were bedded down on the living room floor.

"Good night, boys," she said. "Good night, Mom," I said.

"Good night, Mom," Dewey, Dougie and Chick said, chuckling. Mom shook her head and headed back to bed.

"Well, this was a fun night," Chick said, as we laid and listened to the raging storm.

"Yeah, this was pretty cool," I said.

"You know, if we had a real tent, we could sleep out every night," Dougie said.

And, with that idea in our heads, and the storm howling outside, we drifted off.

The Elephant Boys

It had been the subject of conversation for two weeks. The circus was coming to town and we could hardly wait. We had gone on extra bottle-hunting trips, scouring the land until there wasn't a bottle to be found anywhere. We had mowed the lawns in the neighborhood until the yards looked like manicured golf courses, and we had taken other odd jobs to earn extra cash to spend when the circus rolled into town. We didn't want to worry about running out of money, thereby missing something at the circus.

Finally, on Wednesday, the big trucks arrived. Chick flew in on the wind on his bike to inform Dougie and me. We were in my backyard, talking about the death-defying acts we would surely see as well as the wild animals trained by daredevil circus performers that we could watch. We jumped on our bikes to pick up Dewey and then we were off, as fast as we could go, to the vacant lots on the edge of town where the circus was to be set up.

There were dozens of big trucks painted bright red, white, and blue. Some of them held caged animals. There were four elephants, three lions, three tigers, numerous horses, and cages with monkeys and dogs.

"Wow! This is the biggest circus I've ever seen," Dewey exclaimed.

"This is the only circus you've ever seen, Dewey," Chick corrected. We all laughed at Dewey.

The men began to unload the gear from the trucks and to set up tents and, excited as we were, we could barely discipline ourselves to stay out of the way. Soon the guys from the east-side arrived and we sat on our bikes in the shade, watching the spectacle of the circus unfold before our eyes. After the gear was unloaded, the circus workers set up the small tents. The east-side guys became bored and left for swimming, but we stayed, not wanting to miss a thing.

The circus workers knew exactly what they were doing. They set up the tents for the animal cages. They led the enormous, gray elephants, one by one, off the truck and chained them to posts that had been pounded into the ground. Then a man threw leather harnesses on the biggest ones, attached harnesses to the wagons which were stored on a truck, and the strong beasts pulled the wagons off the truck. The man directed them where to go. "Wow! He's got them trained!" I said. We were most impressed. Our training efforts were aimed at our dogs and it was limited to "sit" or "shake a paw." This guy had the ability to make these large critters to do the work of a tractor.

Dougie had had pretty good luck training his beagle, Cookie. He was an overweight beagle who was born hungry. Dougie would take a wiener and make Cookie sit with his paws up. Then he would lay the wiener across his nose. Poor Cookie would sit there, like a nail keg with feet, looking cross-eyed at the wiener. Sometimes he would hold that pose for an hour before Dougie would tell him it was okay to eat the wiener. Then Cookie would flip it into the air, catch it, and "down" it-in two bites. It seemed like a lot of work and patience for such a minimal reward, but Cookie was always ready to do it again and again.

We watched for most of the day as the trucks were unloaded and the vacant lots were transformed into a circus. The men rolled out the big canvas tent that would house the show and soon the elephants were pulling on ropes and raising the tent on big poles. It was almost suppertime when the two worker elephants were led back and chained to their posts. The attendant fed them hay, lettuce, carrots, apples, and oranges. The elephants were extremely hungry and they squealed and stomped when they saw the food. The man called them by name as he fed them and they seemed to like him a lot. "Here, Naomi. Good girl. Here, Shirley," he said to them. "Some for you, Zelda. Come here, Alma." He spoke to each one of them as he fed them, and they wiggled their ears and ran their trunks over him, smelling and feeling him.

"Wow, Mister! Those elephants are really cool," Dougie said. "Yeah! They're my babies," he replied. "I've raised them since they were young so they know me very well."

We were awestruck that someone could have an elephant for a pet. It made our dogs and pigeons and stuff seem puny.

"You guys want to pet them?" he asked. DID we?? Does a one-legged duck swim in a circle?

"Yeah! We sure do," I said.

"Well, come quietly and talk softly to them." We crept forward, slowly approaching the elephants. When we were close, they raised their trunks to sniff and touch us.

"Oh! Oh! I think I'm gonna pee," confessed Dewey.

"Dewey, you dope. Shut up. You'll scare' em," Chick warned. Naomi was sniffing me and Shirley was snuffling Dougie. He reached up with his hand and touched her trunk and she didn't mind. If Dougie could do it, so could I. I touched Naomi's trunk. She looked at me with those elephant eyes and I rubbed her trunk again and she seemed to like it. "Hey guys. Look at this! She likes me," I said.

Chick was petting Zelda and Dewey was watching Alma check out his pants pockets. "She thinks I've got food in here," he said.

"You probably do. Your pockets are likely crawling with crumbs," Chick teased.

It was an incredible experience. All four of us were petting elephants!

"Take some fruit and feed them, if you'd like," the man said, pointing to pails of oranges, apples, and bananas. We each held up a piece of fruit for our elephant and, sure enough, they took it in their trunks and stuck it in their mouths, gave a couple crunchy bites, and then looked for more.

"Oh, my gosh! This is the greatest thing I've ever done," Chick giggled.

"Me, too," Dewey said. Dougie and I were speechless.

We fed the elephants a lot of fruit and then the man said it was time to bed them down for the day, so we thanked him, got on our bikes, and headed home for supper. When we passed the bank, we noticed the time. It was seven-fifty! Dewey said, "It's almost eight o'clock! My mom will kill me for being so late for supper." Eight o'clock! We had been fooling around with the elephants for two hours. We would get killed, but we figured it was worth it.

When I got home, I acted like it was perfectly normal to eat supper at eight-thirty in the evening, but my mom didn't buy it.

"Where have you been?" she scolded.

"I was at the circus grounds and the man attending the elephants invited us to feed them," I replied, as if it was a typical afternoon event.

"You were what? You stay away from those elephants. One of them will grab you and stomp you to mush," she said. Moms could always find terrifying and terrible things to worry about.

"Mom, they're very gentle. They like us." I was just about to explain everything when the phone rang. It was Dougie.

"Hey, can you come out for a little while?" he questioned.

"I don't know. Mom's rather irritated that I was late for supper. Why? What's up?"

"You know that watermelon patch by our worm-digging place? Let's "borrow" a few ripe ones to give to the elephants in the morning." That sounded like a great idea to me, so I asked Dougie to wait a minute and I pestered my mom about giving permission to go to Dougie's for a while. It didn't take much convincing and she gave in. I told Dougie I'd be right there.

Dougie was waiting for me and we rode toward the east side of town, then followed a gravel road that went of town to a dry creek bed running through a rich, black-dirt valley. That was where we harvested our fish worms. We knew a farmer, who lived adjacently, who had about an acre of watermelons growing in the middle of his cornfield. We wouldn't have known about the watermelon patch except that, one day, we had walked up the ditch looking for bigger worms and we spotted it.

It was almost dark, so we rode quietly, stopped at the bridge, and parked our bikes in the tall grass. Then we crept into the creek bed and headed toward the watermelons. We bent over so as not to be noticed and soon we were in the patch, surrounded by watermelons.

"Let's each take two so we can share with Dewey and Chick," I whispered. Dougie nodded and we slinked into the field and began thumping watermelons.

Thumping was how we knew if a melon was ripe. You took your middle finger and tapped it on the side of the melon, in the middle. If it was ripe, it sounded hollow. Dougie and I crawled through the field and thumped until we each found two choice melons. We picked them, putting one under each arm, and headed back to our bikes. We put the melons in our baskets and set off for town.

We took the back streets toward the river and rode down to the Gosey, hiding the melons there in the tall grass. The Gosey was close to the circus so we figured we'd retrieve the melons in the morning. We rode home, feeling quite smug about our evening's work. We never thought it was stealing to take a few melons since the farmer had hundreds of them and he wouldn't miss one or two; or, in this case, four. Besides, it was for a good cause: the elephants.

The next morning we met at Dougie's house and we told Chick and

Dewey about our evening's work. Chick thought it was a great idea but Dewey was annoyed that we hadn't invited him.

"Dewey, we'd still be waiting for you to get ready; and besides, if we took you, you would have made so much noise that someone would have discovered us," Dougie reasoned. Dewey stayed irritated but he was also thankful that we had a melon for him, so he recovered.

We collected our melons from the Gosey and set off for the circus. The man who worked the elephants was dragging a hose toward them to water them.

"Hey, Mister," I said. "Do you think your elephants would like fresh watermelon?"

He turned and smiled at us. ''And where did you get them?"

"Well, uh ... we just got them," Dougie said. The man grinned and said he thought the animals would love a watermelon treat and he invited us to help him, if we wanted to.

IF we wanted to! What a silly thing to say. We parked our bikes and again tucked the melons under our arms. The elephants seemed delighted to see us and began rocking back and forth, swinging their trunks. We could detect a low rumbling sound coming from their bellies. "Guess that is the hungry sound," Dewey announced.

The man laughed. "That's how they communicate. They're probably saying, "Those fine boys brought us watermelon," the man chuckled.

"Break the melon into pieces and feed it to them piece by piece," he instructed. We each went to "our" elephant, held the pieces up, and watched it grab the food with its trunk, stuffing it into the mouth. There was crunching and slurping and they stuck out their trunks for more. "This is the coolest thing we've ever done," marveled Dewey. We all agreed.

"I wish the east-side guys could see this! They'd be so jealous," Chick bragged.

It would have made the whole thing really cool to be seen by our friends, but we were having such an amazing time, we didn't really care if we were seen or not.

The melon was soon gone and the elephants squealed for more. "Sorry, it's all gone," Dougie told Shirley. The elephant man then asked if we wanted to help him bathe the animals. Bathe an elephant!! Of course we did!! He returned with long-handled brushes and pails and he showed us how to wash an elephant.

First we took off our shirts and shoes and then we filled the buckets with water and added soap. We wetted the elephants down with the hose. They loved it, and so did we. (We squirted water at each other, too, and soon the eight of us were soaked). Then we dipped the brushes in the soapy water and began scrubbing. Suds covered everything and soon the elephants looked like immense, gray piles of snow. We were having a ball and so were our new friends. When they were squeaky clean, we hosed them down.

"You did a great job," the man praised. "You want to exercise them?" This whole thing was getting better and better.

"Sure! What do we do?" Dougie inquired.

He took hold of Naomi's trunk and said, "Naomi, Hup!" And she began walking forward. "Naomi, Back!" The elephant stopped and backed up. "That's how you speak to them. They know you so they'll follow you. Take them to the field and walk them."

The man unchained the elephants and we each chose our favorite one and began to give commands.

"Alma, Hup!"

"Zelda, Hup!"

"Shirley, Hup!"

"Naomi, Hup!"

The elephants walked with us to the vacant field. I don't think our feet touched the ground. It was like we were walking on air. It had to be the most exhilarating thing we had ever done and we all were grinning like the Cheshire Cat as we exercised our mammoth friends around and around the field.

"I'm walking an elephant," Dewey uttered, with a most astonished look. We were four of the happiest boys in our town, if not the whole state; or the whole country, for that matter.

About thirty minutes later, the man asked us to return the elephants to the pen where he chained them. We thanked him for giving us such a neat job and he invited us to return to exercise them again in the afternoon. We promised to return and off we rode to the Gosey for a swim.

We were relaxing in the shallow water, enjoying the coolness, and being very quiet. The experience of being in charge of four elephants had mellowed us. We looked at each other and smiled. If someone had looked in on us, they may have thought we were drunk or stupid. It wasn't typical for us to be so calm.

Finally we recovered from the euphoria of the encounter with the elephants and we resumed our normal behavior of swinging from our diving rope and dunking each other.

We fed and exercised the elephants in the afternoon, as promised. Now, when they saw us coming, they raised their trunks and squealed at us, as if we were long-lost friends.

Meanwhile, the circus people had been setting up the tents and carnival stuff. There were popcorn stands, cotton candy, candy apples, and heaps of other great foods to sample. Plus there were games with teddy bears and other wonderful toys to win. There was a sign on a tent that advertised an incredible monster inside-the strangest animal ever found: a cross between many animals, a freak of nature.

"We gotta see that!" I blurted. Dougie agreed, but Dewey and Chick weren't too interested.

"I'm gonna spend my money on that game and win a teddy bear," Chick announced, pointing at a booth.

"I'm gonna spend my money on food," Dewey added.

Dougie and I were the animal lovers in the gang so we wanted to see the one-of-a-kind freak animal. We would be there first in line in the morning to see everything. It would be a long night as we waited for the circus to get underway.

Next morning we rode to the circus and asked the elephant man if he needed our help. He smiled as we rode up and told us to get to work because the girls were waiting for us. We knew what to do and we fetched the buckets, brushes, and hoses and began scrubbing the elephants. Then we exercised them, just like professional elephant handlers. We were putting on our shoes and shirts when the elephant man said, "Here, you guys have been a lot of help to me. Take these free passes to the big show this afternoon." He handed us four tickets.

"That's great! Thanks, Mister," we said in unison. What super luck! Now we could spend our own money on candy and junk.

We went home to clean up and were back, in line, at noon when the games and stands opened for business as advertised. We made our way around the entire grounds, checking out everything, looking for the best places to spend our money. Chick wanted to playa game with a BB gun because he thought the prize was a big teddy bear-but he only won a Chinese Finger Trap. We made fun of him and his "impressive" prize. Dougie and I were still fascinated by the strange animal so we approached the tent where a man with a microphone was addressing the people who had gathered. He was talking in a dramatic, deep voice. "It was found on the banks of the Missouri River and is thought to be a cross between four or five different animals. It's the strangest animal ever found; one of a kind. No one has ever seen anything so horrible or terrifying before. You'll be amazed!" Dougie and I were standing there with our mouths open, sucking it all in.

"We've gotta see that," I said. Dougie agreed, but Chick and Dewey didn't want to spend the quarter, so they headed to the hotdog stand. Dougie and I paid the man and entered the tent. We were expecting a huge monster in a cage, but all we could see was a tiny wooden crate, with a chicken-wire top, sitting in the middle of the tent. We walked up cautiously and peered over the top. Inside was a bunch of straw, a dish of water, and a little critter that looked much like a raccoon. Its face looked like a coon, but its nose was longer and the tail stood straight up. "Cripes, this is no monster," I said, disappointedly.

"What a gyp!! This is just a freak-looking coon," Dougie complained.

I took a closer look and suddenly it dawned on me. "Hey, I've seen a picture of this in the encyclopedia at school. It's a relative of our coon. But, I can't think of its name."

"That guy was lying to us. He said it was some kind of freak," Dougie fumed.

"No way! I've seen pictures of it. It's from South America, but what is it?" Dougie and I loved animals and were always collecting critters for our home zoos and I knew this was something I had read about. Then it came to me.

"It's a Coati Mundie, and it's from South America," I explained, proud of myself for remembering. "I'm gonna tell the guy what he's got."

We set out to find him. He was talking low and spooky about the strangest creature in the world.

"Hey, Mister! That's not a freak! It's a Coati Mundie from South

America," I bragged, thinking the man would be grateful for the information.

"Beat it, kid!"

"But, Mister ... it's not a freak cross. It is a normal animal; a South American coon."

"I said, beat it! Get out of here!" he hissed.

I looked at Dougie and we knew the man was a fraud, making a lot of money with this fake freak.

"Hey, Mister!" He looked down at us. "Either we get our money back or we're gonna squeal the truth to everybody who walks up."

"I told you to beat it!" he exploded.

That did it! Dougie and I stood in front of the tent and yelled out to people that the animal was a Coati Mundie from South America, that the man was a faker, and to save their money. We hollered that out about twice when he motioned for us to come.

"Here, take your quarters, and get out of here!" he said, tossing two quarters at us. We picked up our quarters and shoved them in our pockets.

"Thanks, Mister," we said, smiling smugly. We walked off and quietly spread the information anyway. In an hour, the tent was closed and the man was nowhere to be seen. We saw him later, cleaning cages behind the big tent, and he gave us a nasty look. We smiled and waved to him. We didn't appreciate getting cheated in our hometown.

The afternoon performance of the big show was to start at two o'clock, so we made our way to the big tent, presented our passes, and got good seats in the front row. There were swings and high wires stretched across the top, and festive circus music was coming from a big calliope at the end of the big ring. Soon the bleachers were packed with spectators and the ringmaster came out and greeted us with a booming "Ladies and gentlemen, children of all ages: Welcome to the circus." It was all very exciting and we could hardly wait for the show to begin. The man announced that the first act, directly from Africa, was a quartet of trained elephants. We were just about busting when Naomi, Shirley, Alma, and Zelda lumbered out, decked in bright red harnesses with little plumes of feathers in bonnets on top of their heads. They looked beautiful and were obviously excited to show their tricks. Our friend, the elephant man, was dressed in a bright red suit and as he gave commands, the girls did their tricks while the calliope played circus music. We could hardly contain ourselves! Our elephant friends doing such marvelous stunts! Just as they finished an act where they all stood on top of big round platforms and twirled around, Dewey yelled, "Good girl, Zelda! Way to go." Zelda turned and started to walk toward us. She had recognized Dewey's voice.

"Dewey, shut up! You'll get us in trouble," I raged. But when Zelda saw us, the other elephants also looked our way and suddenly the whole group moved toward us and stuck their trunks in our hands.

"Oh, no! Now we're in for it," Dougie assumed.

"Back, Zelda; Back, Alma; Back, Shirley; Back, Naomi!" the elephant man commanded. The elephants obeyed and he whispered something to them. Then he turned and said to the audience, "Sorry, folks. Those boys have been helping me with the elephants--washing, feeding, and exercising them. That is why the animals responded to them." All eyes turned to us. We about busted with pride. We were now the most important thirteen-year-old boys in town, if not the county. We were elephant boys.

The show continued with high-wire walkers, jugglers, and lions, and so much fun stuff that we could hardly contain ourselves. The clowns had a funny act that ended with them chasing each other with a bucket of water, finally throwing it into the crowd. Luckily the water turned out to be confetti. We were in the perfect position to get covered with the stuff, much to our delight. What a day!

When the show was over, we ambled back through the crowded midway and many people stopped to talk to us about being elephant boys. We loved the attention. Even the east-side guys passed by and congratulated us on our good fortune.

Finally we went by the elephants. They squealed and swept over us with their trunks.

"The elephants really like you guys," the elephant man grinned.

"We like them, too," Dougie echoed. "Sorry that we interfered with your show."

"Oh, that was nothing! Don't worry about it," he reassured us.

It was time for their walk, so we each took our special elephant to the vacant lot. The elephants held our hands, followed us, and we commanded them with "Hup" and "Back" just to prove to our friends that we really were elephant boys. Soon a crowd had gathered. Then it was time to return them to their pens for feeding and watering.

We were walking mighty tall when we went back to the midway. "How much money do you have?" I inquired.

"I've got two dollars and fifty cents," Dougie said.

"Two dollars and a quarter," Chick said.

"I've got eighty-five cents," Dewey reported.

"I've got a dollar and ninety cents," I said. "That's enough for four tickets to the evening show--or we could eat it all up."

"Show," said Dougie.

"Yup, show," said Chick.

"Well, there will be enough money left for popcorn and stuff, so I vote show, too," Dewey chimed in.

Good! That was settled. We bought tickets for the second show and then proceeded to buy as much food as we could with the money left over.

When the second show was over, we were stuffed with junk food and just about worn out from clapping and laughing so hard. We strolled down the midway, soaking up the final moments of circus bliss. "Wow, this has been the best day we ever had," Dewey said.

"Yeah! No foolin'," sighed Dougie.

The circus was shutting down so we got our bikes and rode past the elephant pen and said good night to our friends and then rode home, exhausted.

The next morning we gathered at Dougie's and picked a few tomatoes and cucumbers from his mom's garden to take to the elephants. When back at the circus grounds, we couldn't believe our eyes. Almost everything was down and loaded on the trucks. There were a few men carrying the last boxes and things so we walked to the elephant truck. The girls spotted us through the bars on the windows and began to squeal when they saw us. "Come to say goodbye?" asked the elephant man.

"Yeah! We didn't think you'd be going so soon," I lamented. "Gotta move on! We have a show tomorrow night in Iowa, so it's time to hit the road," he replied.

"We brought the girls a snack. Okay if we feed them?" "Sure! Go ahead," he said with a smile. We crawled up and fed these last treats to our friends; then we patted them on their heads and said goodbye. They rubbed us with their trunks and it seemed that they were sad to leave us.

"You made friends with them," the man said. "They usually don't like strangers. Thanks for the help and kindness to the girls."

We swallowed hard, and blinked a little, but we managed to say that we had had a stupendous time; that his elephants were special to us and we thanked him for allowing us to make friends with them. Soon the trucks were pulling out, leaving big clouds of dust behind. The elephants squealed as they pulled away; we waved.

We watched until they were out of sight.

"Well," Dougie sighed, "what should we do now?"

"I'm ready for a swim," I said.

"Yeah! Me, too," replied Chick.

"Let's go! Last one in is a booger," Dewey said, as he jumped on his bike and headed for the Gosey.

The circus was an experience that we would relive for years. We would reminisce while sitting by a campfire, or when lying under the stars on a summer night, about the moments we spent with the great, gray beasts that were as gentle and loving as kittens. We would never forget Naomi, Shirley, Alma, and Zelda and the days when we were the elephant boys.

Dog Days

The four of us were lounging in the water at the Gosey. It was hot. It was so hot that we were hardly able to leave the water to swing on our tree rope.

"I'm getting cooked in this water," Dewey said.

"Yeah. It's like a bathtub," Chick said.

"I know, but what can we do about it?" I asked.

"These are the dog days of summer," Chick said. "My mom mentioned it this morning."

"I know what it feels like to be boiled like a hot dog," Dewey said. We all laughed at Dewey.

"The river would be cooler because there is a current," Dougie said.

"Yeah, but our moms will kill us if we swim in the river," I said.

"How they gonna know?" Chick said.

"My mom says there are whirlpools that will suck you down, and deep drop-offs you could fall from, never to come up again," Dewey said.

"Dewey, how many times has your mom been swimming in the river?" Dougie asked.

"Well, I don't know, but she said it's dangerous, so... well, I ... "

"Right, just as I said, she probably hasn't ever been in the river; any of our moms, for that matter, so how do they know?" Dougie had a good point. "Do you ever remember anybody drowning in the river?" he questioned. We thought about that, but we couldn't come up with anyone except the French guy who drowned in the Gosey a long time ago.

"Yeah, how do our moms know?" Chick said.

It didn't take too much talking for us to decide to wade to the end of the

Gosey where it met the river. When we arrived, we could see the swirling current, but we stepped in.

"Wow! This is cool and comfortable," remarked Dougie. "Yeah! Much better than back there," I said. We swam a short distance in the river to a sandbar. We found a decent-sized drop-off and soon we were screaming, running, and jumping into the deep water, having a ball. We played on the sandbar all afternoon and then waded back, got our clothes, and headed home.

We stopped at Dougie's house.

"Let's go back tomorrow with our fishing poles," suggested Dougie.

"Yeah! Let's! Then we can swim and fish," Dewey said. Chick thought it sounded like a good plan so we agreed to meet at Dougie's the next morning for a day of fishing and swimming. I asked my mom to make me a lunch to take fishing. I met the guys at Dougie's house. We had our poles, lunches, and canteens of water for our day at the river.

We rode to the Gosey, stripped down, waded into the river, and swam to the sandbar with our lunches and fishing poles held high over our heads. Once on the sandbar, we fooled around for a while and then we decided to get serious about fishing. Dougie had his jackknife with him so he swam to the closest wooded area and cut four pole holders for each of us. We put worms on our hooks and cast into the deep water below the sandbar. We sat in the sand, waiting for a bite.

"It is cool to fish here. Maybe we will catch real fish; not those useless little bluegills we usually end up with," Chick remarked.

"Yeah! A real monster! A big catfish would be great," Dewey said. It was true. There were rumors of catfish, the size of a small boy, in the river and we all hoped to tangle with one someday.

Soon Dougie had a bite that turned out to be a walleye.

"Wow! We don't find these in the river bottoms," he said. He put the fish on a stringer and put it in the water. A few minutes later Chick caught a catfish and I caught a small-mouth bass.

"Jeepers! This is much better than fishing in the Gosey," I said. Just then Dewey got a bite, set his hook, and watched his pole bend over. He got to his feet and backed onto the sandbar just as a huge fish stripped offline from his reel. "It's one of those monster catfish," he yelled as he fought the fish. We reeled up our poles and gave him space to battle his fish. He managed to bring the fish close to the sandbar where it came to the surface of the water. When we realized it was a huge gar, about three feet long, with a mouthful of sharp teeth and an evil look on its face, we took a step backward.

"Unbelievable! Dewey, it's a big gar," Dougie said. "Somebody grab him and take the hook out," Dewey said. "Yeah, right! Have you seen those teeth, Dewey?" objected Chick.

"C'mon guys, take him off for me," begged Dewey.

"No way, Dewey. You caught him. You take him off," instructed Dougie.

Dewey dragged the fish to the shore and walked over warily to inspect it. "Jeez, it's ugly. It looks like a crocodile," he said. He handled the fish with care in order to position the hook between his fingers and then he attempted to remove it from the jaw of the fish. Just as he did, the fish began to thrash and snap its jaws. Dewey dropped it and ran for cover. "You better be careful, Dewey. You'll loose your weenie," Chick said. We all laughed at that, except Dewey.

"You guys are a lot of help. I'm gonna cut the line and give him the hook," he announced. We thought that was a good idea so Dougie gave Dewey his knife. He released the fish and pushed it into the water with his foot. The gar delayed for a minute. Then, little by little, it swam off into the deep water.

"Whooie! I hate to think of swimming here with those big things," Dougie said. "One might come along and make you a sit-down pee'er." We thought that was hilarious and laughed at Dougie's joke.

We ate our lunch under a hot sun. "Wow! I'm cookin'!"

Dougie said. "I'm gonna sit in the water and fish." That was a super suggestion so we sat down and the water came up to our necks. We held our poles in one hand and watched for bites.

"This is great," Chick said. It was cool looking, too: four heads, and four hands holding fishing poles, sticking out of the water. Soon we were catching catfish and bass and walleyes, and the day slipped by. When we caught a fish, we crawled to our stringer, attached the fish, and returned to our sitting position in the water. By late afternoon, all the stringers were nicely filled with fish and we decided to call it quits. We waded back to our clothes and bikes.

"Now, don't tell anyone we were in the river," Dougie said.

"Then we can return without getting into trouble." We agreed to keep this place a secret. Off we went to our homes to clean our fish and have supper. As I worked on my fish in the backyard, my mom strolled up to check out my catch.

"Where did you get those?" she asked. "What?"

"The bass, catfish, and walleyes," she said.

"Uh, down at the, by Gutweiler's stream," I stammered.

"Gutweiler's stream? Where is that?"

"Well, it's where the water in Gutweiler's Lake comes out. It's like a little river," I said.

"Since when does Gutweiler's Lake, or its stream, have catfish, walleyes, and smallmouth bass?"

My mouth was hanging open like I was a simpleton. First of all, how did mom know what a catfish or a walleye or a smallmouth was in the first place; and secondly, how did she know they weren't in Gutweiler's Lake?

"Well, I'm waiting for an answer." I didn't have one.

"Have you been at the river?" She knew without me answering so there was no point in telling a lie.

"Yeah, we went to the river because the Gosey was too hot." "The Gosey? You've been in the Gosey, too?" She must be in the FBI! Where was she getting all this information? "I thought you were fishing in the sloughs."

"You know where the Gosey is?" I asked.

"Of course, I do. Do you think I've never been near the river?" Yeah. That was exactly what I thought.

"Your dad and I used to fish at the river before we had you kids."

"Fish? You fished?"

"Of course, and I'm a pretty darn good fisherman, too."

You could have knocked me over with a puff of wind. My mom was a fisherman!

"Do the other mothers know you guys hang around the river?"

"Oh c'mon, Mom. Don't tell. They'll kill me for getting caught."

"Okay, I won't tell. But, you boys be careful and stay out of the water. Just fish; don't swim."

I nodded my head; somehow thinking I was agreeing with the fishing part and ignoring the swimming part. "Okay, we'll be careful. Wouldn't want to fall into any whirlpools or something," I grinned.

"You won't think it's funny if you fall in and drown," she said. When I finished cleaning the fish, I called Dougie and told him what had happened. "My dad saw my fish and he knew I didn't get them in the bottoms," he said. Well, I didn't feel so badly after all. Dougie also got caught. Chick phoned later to say he got busted, too. Then, after supper, Dewey called and said he had gotten the third degree from his dad and had also spilled the beans. We all were discovered. Who would have thought that adults knew one fish from another? Fortunately our parents did not forbid us to go to the river but we were each told to be safe and to stay out of the water. Well, it was too late so, until we got caught, we planned to stay quiet.

It was amusing that our parents were so educated on the kinds of fish. We never imagined they knew anything about fish. You'd have thought they were once young, and learned what we knew, and somehow never forgot. Maybe they recalled all the fun times they had enjoyed at the river so they allowed us to go. Who knows? From then on, we had a greater respect for their knowledge of the outdoors. We enjoyed swimming in the river hundreds of times that summer, and for that matter, for many summers following. And, surprisingly, we never once saw one of those deadly whirlpools.

Take Me Out to the Ball Game

Chick, Dewey, and I were sitting in my backyard, waiting for Dougie and the rest of the guys to come over for a game of baseball. We had practice a couple days each week and we usually played a game with the east-side boys once or twice a week on the off days.

Dougie was riding in as fast as his bike would carry him and he slid to a screeching halt, throwing up a cloud of dust from the alley.

"Hey, guys! You wanna go to a Braves game?" "Braves? Milwaukee Braves?" I exclaimed. "Yeah, The Milwaukee Braves!"

"How? When?" We were on our feet asking Dougie questions all at once.

"One of the teachers at my school organized this trip. He calls it "The Knot-Hole Club." It costs two dollars for the game and a dollar for the bus ride. It's a great deal," Dougie reported.

"But, it's through the public school," Dewey cautioned. "We can't go. We go to St. John's."

"That doesn't matter. It's for any kid in town," Dougie reassured.

"No foo1in'? Dougie, you wouldn't fool us," Chick said.

"No foolin'! Look! Here is the form your parents can sign to give their permission for you to go," he said, as he pulled folded, crumpled forms from his pocket. We each took one of the wrinkled sheets and read it over. It was true! The following week, a bus trip to attend a Braves game!! We wanted to jump up and down.

We had to come up with three dollars, get our parents' permission, and return the form to the school. We raced home to start in on our parents. Practice was cancelled for the day.

"I'll give you money for the game and bus ride and an extra two dollars," Mom said after I explained this great opportunity to her. I couldn't believe my ears. I expected an uphill battle in persuading her to let me go and then a ton of pestering for the money part of it. The surprise was written all over my face.

"What? Didn't you think I'd agree?" she asked.

"I just didn't expect you to say yes so quickly," I confessed. She smiled, signed the form, and handed over three dollars.

"Sometimes moms and dads are human, too," she reminded me. I decided there and then that she was a pretty darn good mom.

I raced to Dougie's house on my bike and found that he had his form signed, too. Soon Chick and Dewey arrived with the required signature and we headed for the school office. It was the first time I had ever been in the public school and, actually, it was quite nice. I expected it to be like a prison or something because that was the idea we got when the sisters talked about it. Somehow it didn't seem to be a terrible place after all. The teacher, who had organized the trip, was helpful and seemed delighted that Dougie had invited us. Dougie was proud of himself, too.

Well, for the next week, we were on a high! The trip was all we talked about, and no matter what we were doing-baseball, swimming or fishing-the conversation always came back to the upcoming trip.

The morning of the trip arrived and we assembled at the bus garage an hour before departure. Every kid in town was there and we could hardly wait for the bus door to open. Everyone was wearing a baseball cap and most of us were extra prepared by carrying our baseball gloves-in the event a ball should come our way. We were like a bunch of chattering monkeys, all trying to get on the bus at the same time. The teacher called our names, we yelled here, and climbed on. Our four names were called first so we got to sit in the choice seats in the back of the bus. The rest of our team and the east-side guys were also aboard, as well as many kids from the public school. It was fantastic.

The bus pulled out of town and the noise was almost deafening. Everyone was chattering at the same time. If the energy in that bus could have been harnessed, the city could have been lit for a week. After an hour, things quieted down and someone started singing A Hundred Bottles if Beer on the Wall Everyone joined in and sang until we got down to one bottle if beer. The bus driver and the adults must have been relieved when the song was over. To this day, I can't figure out why the bottles of beer were "on" the wall. Why weren't they in the refrigerator? Oh, well. It was a fun song.

The miles swept by and we were nearing Milwaukee County Stadium, the home of the Milwaukee Braves. We became super excited and the noise level went through the roof again. The teacher had planned it so we would arrive at the stadium in time to watch batting practice. Of course, we planned on catching a fly ball and getting it autographed. We figured the Braves surely knew we were coming and players would be waiting for us, eager to give their autographs.

The scenery had changed from trees and grass to buildings as we approached the big city. The buildings were of greater dimensions than anything at home, for sure. At home, the hotel, at three stories, was the tallest building. In Milwaukee, there were massive structures, stretching up twenty or thirty stories. We were very impressed. Then we came to the freeway exit to the stadium. There it was: Milwaukee County Stadium. It was like Mecca or the Vatican. It was the home of the Braves. How many times had we listened to games being broadcast on the radio from this place? How many legendary baseball heroes had stood at home plate, tapping the dirt from their spikes? It was like a religious experience. We couldn't wait to get off the bus and get inside.

We stood in line and handed our tickets to a man in a blue uniform. He tore them in half, giving us a torn half back. We went through a turnstile thing and then up the stairs to the field. We were running through a tunnel toward the sunlight and suddenly we emerged in-Milwaukee County Stadium. We stopped and drank in the moment. The field was amazing. The grass was green-green and it had been mowed back and forth in a manner that gave it diamond patterns. The infield was as smooth as brown silk and chalked with lines running to the bases. The stadium towered above us with row upon row of green seats. There were thousands of them. Pennants flew from the upper deck railing and the scoreboard was lit up like a Christmas tree. It was totally amazing to us.

"Wow! This place is huge," Dougie marveled. "And look at all the seats," Chick said, gapingly. "Look! A hot-dog guy," Dewey said.

"Dewey, only you would think of your stomach at a time like this," I teased. We all laughed at Dewey.

"Hey, hot-dog guy!" Dewey said, breaking the effect of the moment.

"Dewey, don't you ever get full?" Chick asked.

"It's been a long time since breakfast," Dewey said as he waved at the guy who came over and Dewey bought a hot dog. They smelled pretty good so we each bought one, too.

"See, I knew you guys were hungry," Dewey said, licking the mustard off his lip.

We were hanging over the railing in the right-field bleachers when several Braves team members ran to the field to take batting practice.

There they were, for real; the guys we listened to on the radio; the ones we read about in the newspaper; the guys whose baseball cards we collected. They were our heroes: Eddie Mathews, Johnny Logan, and Joe Adcock. Soon outfielders appeared and began to catch fly balls. "Hey, there's Hammerin' Hank," Dougie said, pointing to Henry Aaron. Henry was only in his second year at Milwaukee and he was a great hitter.

"I bet he'll hit a homer today," Chick said.

"Yeah, he might," I said. "He's a pretty good long-ball hitter." "Hey, Hank!" Dewey yelled. Hank turned, smiled, and waved.

"Wow! That was cool," Dewey said. We were leaning on the railing, watching, and soon a long ball was coming straight at us. Hammerin' Hank shot over and caught it at the wall below us.

"Nice catch, Hank," Dougie cheered. "Hi, guys," Hank replied.

"Hi, Hank," we yelled in unison.

"I see you guys have your baseball gloves. Do you play a lot?"

Henry Aaron was actually talking with us!

"Uh, yeah! We play almost every day," Dougie stammered. "Yeah! We got our own field and everything," Chick added. "We're all big Braves fans," I said.

"That's great! Enjoy the game," Hank said, and he trotted off to center field.

"That was the coolest!" Dewey murmured.

"Yeah, no foolin'! Hank's a good guy. I hope he makes it in the big leagues," I said.

"Me, too. If he always hits like he does now, he'll turn into a great player," Chick said. We all wanted Hank to make it big.

The stands were filling up so we picked our seats in the bleachers and got ready for the game. We were wearing our ball gloves in case a homer came our way so we'd be ready. Vendors were coming by with hot dogs, peanuts, ice cream bars, popcorn, and soda, so we were kept busy eating almost everything that passed by.

Finally the game began and the Braves took the field first. Warren Spahn was pitching. He was one of our favorites so we yelled and cheered at every pitch. It was a good game. After the seventh-inning stretch, we sang Take Me Out to the Ballgame with the announcer. When the Braves came up to bat in the eighth, Hank was up, and on the third pitch he blasted a long ball toward us. We were yelling and had our gloves in the air to catch the ball. On it came. It cleared the railing and hit the bleachers about ten rows below us. It bounced into the air and was coming our way when a guy, sitting two rows down, jumped up and caught it in his bare hands. We just sat there with our mouths open in disbelief: how close we had come to catching a stadium ball!

"Crap! That guy intercepted our ball," Dougie pouted.

"We should pound knots on his head," Chick said.

"I dropped my pop when I stood up to catch it," Dewey said. "Hey, Mister! That ball was coming to us," I said. He turned around and smiled but he didn't offer to give us the ball. We were very disappointed. If Hank ever turned out to be a famous player, we would have had a notable trophy.

All too soon, the game was over. The Braves won and we were as delighted as a bunch of boys could be. We made our way out of the stadium and back to the bus. When a head count was taken, every body was accounted for so we were able to take off for home. The bus was packed with excited kids carrying home souvenirs. Some had pennants; others had ball caps, or Braves jerseys. None of us had money for anything expensive so we cherished our programs and the memories of almost catching a home run ball and talking to Henry Aaron. It didn't take long for A Hundred Bottles of Beer ... to start again and by the time we got to the twentieth bottle of beer we were in Madison. The driver took us to a new restaurant called McDonald's. Supposedly we could buy fifteen-cent hamburgers and ten-cent French fries. We piled out of the bus and went in. Instead of sitting and waiting for a waitress, we walked up to a counter and gave our order to an employee behind the counter. The food was ready and came down slides from the kitchen. The employee picked up the order and stuffed it in a sack. We each had enough money to order three hamburgers, two fries, and a chocolate shake, so we handed the guy a dollar and got a dime back! It was such a good deal that we decided to buy another bag of fries. Back to the bus we went, with our bags of food. "This is cool," Dewey said. "You get a lot of stuff for a dollar."

"No foolin'! This is a good place," Dougie chimed in.

"I hope they stay in business. How can they sell food so cheaply and make money?" Chick wondered.

"Enjoy it while we can. It won't be around long," I said.

The bus quieted because we were involved with our meals and then many of the kids slid down in their seats and dozed off I t was getting dark and we had all gotten up early so everyone was tired. The next thing we knew the bus was pulling into the public school parking lot and the bus lights came on. "Time to wake up, sleepy heads," our chaperone announced. We yawned and groaned and made our way to the front of the bus. "Thanks for the swell trip," we all said.

"You're welcome. I hope you had a wonderful time."

"It was the best ever," we said.

We got our bikes and said goodbye to each other and made plans for a ball game the next day. "Let's start at two o'clock," Dougie said. "I think I'll sleep till at least noon." No fooling! That sounded good.

As tired as I was, it was difficult to sleep. Every time I closed my eyes, I could see Milwaukee County Stadium. I could see the grass, the seats, and I heard the crowd cheering. I could smell the hotdogs and popcorn. From now on, when we listened to ball games on the radio, it would be different. We could close our eyes and see it happening. And I thought about Henry Aaron. Gosh, I hoped he would make it in the big leagues. It would be impressive to tell people that I had talked to him once.

The Menagerie

Dougie and I were critter collectors. We loved animals and we each had a private zoo in our backyard. Dougie's critter house had once been a woodshed. It had an outside chicken-wire pen with partitions and it made a great home for his pets. His pride and joy was his rabbit, Zsa Zsa. She was a beautiful, white rabbit; she was tame and loved to be petted. Dougie also had homing pigeons as well as regular pigeons. There was an older kid in town that raised homers so we each had bought a pair of them from him. Dougie also had his dog, Cookie, who was good at his one trick of sitting up and begging for food; a trick, but nothing spectacular.

My dog, Butch, had been rescued by my dad from the dog pound. He was a friendly guy so my dad felt sorry for him and brought him home. Butch was fairly old when he came to live with us so he didn't know cool tricks. He liked to play ball and sleep; mainly he slept. He was a great friend.

My zoo consisted of a collection of little sheds that I had built myself About a year earlier, before Dougie had moved to town, I had been at Walsh's grocery store and was checking out the live chickens in the storage yard. They had a shed for the chickens that the farmers sold or traded for food, while they waited for the butcher to prepare them for sale in the store. I always liked to look for eggs in the pens. Eggs came in handy for one thing or another, especially if we were having a war with the east-side guys. One day I went to Walsh's and I saw strange looking chickens in the pens. They were small and pretty. Instead of being plain white, they were shades of red, black, and gold. I had never seen chickens like that, so I went in and asked the butcher about them. "Those are bantams, or ban ties, for short," he said.

"Why are they so puny?" I asked.

"That's their size. They lay small eggs, too," he said. Hmm, they were cute, so I asked him for a price and he quoted me a quarter apiece. What a bargain! I paid up and asked if I could leave them there until I got a chicken house built.

My neighbor, Fred, had a pile of used lumber behind his garage and I asked him if! could borrow some of it. He gave me the go-ahead. He suggested that I attach my chicken house to the side of his garage that bordered our backyard. That way I'd only have to build three walls and the pen would be extra sturdy. Fred was a smart guy and a good neighbor.

I began work on my chicken house and I completed it in a few days. It looked like a long outhouse, about six feet tall and ten feet long. I used chicken wire to make a pen on the front. Then I cut a little door in the wall and made small boxes for nests and set a few poles for the chickens to roost on. Fred gave it the inspection and said I had done a good job.

I went to the feed mill for a bag of chopped-up corncobs for the floor. Then I went to Walsh's and picked up my chickens. There were three hens and one rooster. I took them home, turned them loose in the pen, and they seemed to like it real well. I guess anything was nicer than the shed at Walsh's and getting your head lopped off. They looked around, then went inside to check out their new home. They were pretty cool chickens and the next morning I found a little egg in one of the boxes. The rooster crowed every morning.

It didn't take long until I had collected a few more hens and then I let one of them sit on a batch of eggs and soon I had about a dozen banty chickens. Then I met Dougie and saw his pigeons, so I decided to raise pigeons, too. That meant an addition to my chicken house and another outside pen, so-back to Fred's for more lumber. After the pigeon business, I decided I wanted a rabbit. I bought a black one from a kid in town and I named her Snowball. After that, I got a free squirrel from a kid that had raised two of them. My zoo was growing.

One day I was riding my bike past the salvage yard on the outside of town and I spotted a large tub on the ground. It looked like it would be the perfect thing for making a turtle farm. The man who owned it said I could have it. I went back, taking Dougie with me, and we rolled the tub to my house. We filled it halfway with sand and buried an old dish pan in the sand. Then we put water in the dish pan. Now we needed turtles, so we went to Gutweiler's Lake and fished until we caught a couple and then took them to their new home. We caught insects and dug worms for them. After that, whenever we caught a turtle while we were fishing, we added it to the turtle exhibit. I had a great zoo!

There was a partially burned factory on the edge of town that was home to lots of pigeons. We decided to go there after dark when the pigeons were sleeping and catch a few for our pigeon collections. Dewey and Chick wanted to help so one night we rode our bikes to the old factory. Dewey didn't have a place for a zoo and his mom wouldn't let him have anything except a little turtle in a plastic dish with a little plastic palm tree in it. Chick's mom had a cat and wouldn't let him add other critters to his backyard so they both enjoyed coming with us, helping us develop our zoos.

"This place is creepy," Dewey said, as we went through a creaky door.

"Shhh! Dewey. Don't talk so loudly. You'll wake up the pigeons," Dougie instructed.

We walked upstairs to the second floor and shined our flashlights toward the ceiling, expecting to see a ton of pigeons. There weren't any to be seen.

"Where are the pigeons?" I whispered.

"Hey, look," Chick said, pointing his light toward a trap door in the ceiling. "I'll bet this is the attic."

"The pigeons are probably up there," Dougie said. We shined our lights around and located an old desk and a few wooden crates which we stacked below the attic opening.

"I'll go up and take a look," said Chick.

He crawled up and stuck his head into the attic. Soon he lifted himself up and disappeared into the black hole. We all stood there, staring up, and suddenly Chick's face appeared out of the blackness, "Millions of pigeons up here."

"No foolin'?" Dougie remarked.

"They're sitting on beams all over the place."

The three of us climbed up and turned on our flashlights to reveal pigeons-everywhere!

"Guess we've got all the pigeons we'd ever want," exclaimed Dougie.

"Let's try to catch a few real pretty ones," I said. "Spread out and try not to spook them."

We crept through the rafters and the pigeons began cooing and fluttering around.

"They're getting nervous," Chick said.

"Let's try to each catch two and then we can come back later and take a few more," I suggested.

Just then I spotted a rare white one and I reached up to get it. As my hand touched the pigeon, it took off. When that pigeon flew, so did the rest of them. There were pigeons taking off and flying everywhere and the quiet turned into chaos. The beating of the pigeon's wings made a lot of wind, like a hurricane. Soon there were pigeon feathers, pigeon poop, and dust everywhere.

"Jeepers! They're attacking," Dewey hollered. "Just grab a couple, Dewey," Dougie shouted.

Chick and I each had two pigeons. Dougie had a pretty one and was trying to catch another. Dewey was still attempting to make his first capture. A nice one landed above him and he reached up and caught it.

"Hey! I got one!" he boasted, as he turned to show me. He took one step forward and suddenly there was a huge crashing sound and Dewey disappeared. One second, I was looking at Dewey; the next second, he was gone. I shined my light where he had been and I saw a big hole in the floor--which was actually the ceiling of the room below. I peered down and there was Dewey, on his back.

"Dewey, are you okay?"

"Yeah! I still have my pigeon, too," he said, holding it up for us to see.

"Let's get out of here," Chick said. "These pigeons are riled up. We can come back another night."

It sounded like a good idea. I took one of Dougie's pigeons and Chick took the other and he climbed down. Then we passed the pigeons down to him and he put them in the little cage we had brought. Chick and I climbed down. Dewey was still sitting on the floor petting his pigeon. "He's a nice one, huh?"

"Yeah, Dewey. He's a beauty." We put Dewey's pigeon in the cage and made our way outside.

"Whew, that was fun!" Dewey declared.

"Gosh, Dewey, I thought you'd be complaining about falling through the ceiling," Chick responded.

"I got a pigeon, though," Dewey said. Dewey was mighty proud of his pigeon. Of course, he didn't have a place to keep his pigeon so he decided to keep it at my house.

"I think I'll name it Frank," he said.

Since Dougie and I were the only ones with pigeon pens, we inherited all the pigeons. It appeared that they liked their new homes and we took good care of them, feeding them well. We made more raids on the old factory until the pigeons caught on to what we were doing and they became so nervous when we showed up that they would fly around, making a terrible mess, so we left them be. We had plenty of pigeons, anyway.

One day, when Dougie and I were by Walsh's storage shed, we saw a pigeon fly into a hole in the eaves. "Hey, did you see that?" Dougie asked.

"Yeah, let's see if we can catch him," I said. We parked our bikes and looked up at the hole in the eave. You could see the pigeon sitting inside looking out at us. "See that pipe on the side of the building?" I asked. "One of us could shinny up that pipe, reach around the side of the eave, and grab the pigeon."

"I'll do it," Dougie offered. "You be ready to take him in case there are others inside."

The pipe coming through the wall was attached to a rod that came up from the bottom of the building. Dougie began to climb it. When he was halfway up, the pipe detached from the rod at the bottom and came crashing to the ground. When it hit, the end broke off and black stuff came gushing out, covering me.

Dougie had fallen off the pipe when it hit the ground and he rolled into the black stuff.

"What the heck is it?" Dougie asked because he was covered.

He stuck his finger into the substance and smelled it.

"It smells sweet, like pancake syrup."

I sniffed it and tasted it. "It does. What should we do with this broken pipe?" I inquired.

"I don't know, but I think we best get out of here," Dougie insisted, and we hopped on our bikes and beat it toward his house.

"We can't go to my house covered in this stuff," Dougie blurted. "Let's wash it off at the Gosey," he suggested. We removed our syrup-soaked clothes, waded into the water, and scrubbed the sticky stuff off. It came out easily enough and then we hung the clothes in the trees to dry. Meanwhile, we took a nice swim and then we relaxed in the shallow water. "I wonder how much of that stuff squirted out of the pipe?" I mused.

"Probably, not much. Someone likely noticed and turned it off at the source," he said. At least, that was what we hoped.

An hour or so later our clothes were dry so we dressed and rode our bikes to Dougie's house. We were in his pigeon pen when his dad came into the yard. "You guys been at Walsh's today?"

"Why?"

"Someone broke their sorghum pipe and about a hundred gallons of the stuff poured out on the ground," relayed Dougie's father.

"Sorghum? What's sorghum?" His dad looked at us; then walked over to Dougie and pointed at his tennis shoe.

"That's sorghum! The black stuff all over your shoes!" he scolded.

Busted!

We knew better than to try to lie our way out of this one so we admitted that we had broken the pipe but that it had been one huge accident.

"And, just what were you doing on that pipe?" he wanted to know.

"We saw a pigeon and tried to catch it," Dougie said.

"Pigeon? How many pigeons do you have?" We had no idea. "How did they know we did it?" I finally asked.

"A worker saw you riding past the store, drenched in sorghum. Didn't take a genius to figure that one out," he added.

"Well, I must head to the store to pay for the sorghum that you two Einsteins spilled. Stay here until I get back."

Dougie's dad was gone for about fifteen minutes but it seemed like fifteen hours. When he returned, he looked peeved. "Well, your little pigeon raid cost me forty-seven dollars," he said. Forty-seven dollars! We wouldn't see an allowance again until college! Dougie's dad must have realized how badly we felt. "I know you guys weren't trying to break it, and that it was an accident. I'll pay for it but you two stay out of trouble for the rest of the summer." We couldn't believe our ears!

"Thanks, Dad!" Dougie said, and he hugged his father. "Yeah, thanks," I said. Then I hugged him, too. He grinned and told us to go take care of our zoos.

"Wow! Your dad is a cool guy," I said.

"Yeah! No kidding. I thought we were dead," Dougie stated, very relieved.

"Let's see what the other guys are doing," I said.

We hopped on our bikes and rode to Chick's house, then to Dewey's. The four of us rode to the river for a couple of hours of fishing. We were sitting side by side on the riverbank fishing. "You know," Dougie said to me, "a long time from now, when we have our own kids, maybe we'll think back to this and give them a break if they do something stupid." Yeah, that sounded fair, but at that time, we didn't even LIKE girls, so that would be a long time off!

A Found Lure

If you ever look my way and don't see me, come over, and you'll find a puddle," Dewey whined from right field.

"Yeah! It's so hot, my glove won't stay on my sweaty hand," Dougie said.

It was hot. It was probably the hottest day of the summer, and we were playing ball with the east-side guys. It was just past noon and the sun was beating down, turning our outfield into the Sahara Desert. Sweat was trickling into our eyes and our shirts were soaked and sticking to our backs.

"Hey, let's call the game, and go for a swim!" Johnny Deagan said. Everyone agreed that it was way too hot to play ball, so we picked up the bases, put them in my neighbor Fred's garage, hopped on our bikes, and headed for the Gosey.

Usually we kept the Gosey to ourselves, but today the east-side guys were joining us. Both teams were short a few players, so instead of a group of eighteen kids, there were about a dozen of us. Some kids were on vacation and some had stayed home because of the heat.

Johnny Deagan was the leader of the east-side guys. He was going to be in ninth grade in the fall, so he was the oldest and probably the coolest. He was tall and good-looking, and instead of being skinny like the rest of us, he had muscles. His clothes were clean and nicely fit. His hair was always perfect, and he stood out as someone you wanted to have as a friend. The girls followed him around like a litter of puppies and he even LIKED girls. Most of us were still repulsed by girls and their silly, giggly ways. Johnny always told us that some day we'd change our minds. Right now it was too hot to think about anything but getting our clothes off and getting into the water.

We threw up a massive cloud of dust as we sped down the dirt road to the Gosey. When we arrived, we parked our bikes, stripped, and jumped into the cool water. It didn't take long for the quiet pool to turn into a wild, thrashing cauldron of screaming boys, dunking each other, and having a great time.

Our rope swing was mounted so that it hung out over the Gosey. Long ago, someone had planted a maple tree by an old rock foundation by the riverbank. A thick hay rope was tied to one of its sturdy branches. A hefty knot was tied at the end to support the feet while swinging. We also tied a long string to the end of the rope so we could easily grab the rope when we wanted to swing. Johnny swam to the string and side-armed it to the bank. Then he pulled on the string and the rope and climbed on the tree branch to swing out across the water. "Banzai!" he yelled as he swung out, doing a cannonball into the water, making an impressive splash. We appreciated his stunt and soon we were imitating him, seeing who could make the biggest splash.

It was Johnny's turn again and this time he put his feet on the knot, but when he got to the top of the arc, he held on with his feet and then let go with his hands, did a back flip, and landed in the water, feet first. "Wow, Johnny! That was awesome!" we exclaimed. Johnny was good at everything he did.

Then we played tag. It didn't take long until Chick tagged Dewey and Dewey became IT. Dewey wasn't the fastest swimmer, so when he was IT, we had a lot of fun taunting him, trying to get him to chase us. Johnny was yelling at Dewey, allowing him to get close before ducking underwater and swimming away. Dewey was behind him when he came up for air and he almost tagged him, but Johnny dove again, and swam across the Gosey underwater.

"Hey, Dewey! Over here," Johnny yelled, from the other side of the Gosey.

"No way! I'm not going over there," Dewey said.

"C'mon, Dewey. I'll stay here till you make it over."

Dewey must have had a sudden burst of ambition because he began swimming across the Gosey toward Johnny.

"Here I am, Dewey," Johnny taunted. Dewey was close to him and Johnny was darting back and forth, waiting for Dewey to commit to one direction or the other.

"Hey, look! A Daredevil," Dewey said, pointing to the lower branch of a tree just behind Johnny.

"I'm not stupid, Dewey. You can't fool me with that old trick." "No, look. It's hanging in the tree," Dewey said, and he started swimming toward the tree. Johnny took a quick look over his shoulder and then he, too, saw the Daredevil. He spun around and grabbed the lure just before Dewey got to it.

"Hey, that's mine!" Dewey said. "I saw it first."

"Tough, Dewey! I got to it first," Johnny jeered.

"Well, I'm gonna tag you, at least," Dewey said, and he took a quick swipe at Johnny. Of course, Johnny was quicker than Dewey and he dove underwater. He was under for a long period of time when he emerged about halfway across the Gosey, screaming, "Oh, God! Help me! Help me!"

We all laughed as Johnny thrashed around in the water pretending to be in trouble. We figured he was fooling Dewey and would wait for him to get close and then take off swimming again.

"I'm hooked. Help me!" he choked.

Dougie looked at me. "Do you suppose he's really hurt?"

"We better check," I said. Dougie and I swam to Johnny.

When we got there, Johnny was doubled over, barely able to stay afloat.

"What's wrong?" Dougie questioned.

"I got hooked on that Daredevil," Johnny said, through clenched teeth.

By then Dewey had swum over to us and was yelling that he had Johnny and tagged him.

"Where is it?" I said, looking at his hands, thinking he had a hook in his finger.

"It's in my bag," he said.

Dewey, Dougie, and I looked at each other, not understanding what Johnny had meant.

"Your bag? What do you mean?" I asked.

Suddenly, Dewey, Dougie, and I all got it at the same time. Johnny was hooked in his crotch!

"No way!" I said. Johnny nodded his head and rolled on his back. Dougie and I almost fainted.

"Oh, no! Johnny's got the Daredevil hooked in his sack! Dewey shouted.

There, hanging from his most tender part, was the red and white Daredevil!

"Oh man, I'm gonna puke," Dougie said.

"You guys gotta help me to shore. I can't swim," Johnny said, weakly.

Dougie and I each took one of Johnny's arms. He rolled to his back and we towed him to shore. By now all the rest of the guys knew something was really wrong, and when we got to shallow water, they helped us get Johnny to the shore. "Oh, my gosh!" Chick said. "He's got that hook in his bag."

Everyone was grimacing and trying not to look but was fascinated by the lure hanging from Johnny--in a terribly wrong place.

The spoon was about four inches long with a treble hook.

One of the three hooks was through Johnny's scrotum.

"Well, it's good it's there, and not higher," one of the east-side guys said, trying to cheer Johnny up. Johnny just looked at him with a look of murder in his eyes.

"You think it's funny?" he asked.

"No, Johnny. I'm sorry," the kid said.

One guy lived just a few blocks from the Gosey. "Philip, ride home and get a wire cutter so we can cut the barb off the hook," Johnny said. Philip slipped on his shorts, jumped on his bike, and rode off in a cloud of dust. We stood there staring at Johnny who tried to remain very still.

"Does it hurt a lot?" Dewey said.

"Yeah, Dewey. It hurts a lot," Johnny said.

"I'm glad you got that lure now," Dewey said, smiling.

"Dewey, shut up, you idiot! Johnny's in pain," Chick said. Even in his situation, Johnny managed to smile at Dewey.

"It's okay, Dewey. I know you didn't mean any harm. I wish I had let you take the lure, but I wouldn't wish this on anyone." Dewey smiled, and nodded at Johnny.

It seemed like hours until Philip returned. He screeched to a halt, throwing up a huge cloud of dust. He dropped his bike in the sand and came running to the edge of the water where we were surrounding Johnny.

"Here, I couldn't find a wire cutter, so I brought this," he said, holding out a big hunting knife.

"Cripes, get that thing away from me!" Johnny said, rolling on his side to protect his crotch. "You're not gonna cut it out!" Philip looked disappointed, thinking he had done a good thing, and now he was getting yelled at.

"I'll go get a wire cutter," Chick said. "We've got one." He picked up his bike and rode off, and while he was gone, we just stood there, feeling sorry for poor Johnny. A few minutes later, Chick rode back with a huge pair of bolt cutters. "This'll do it," he said, as he ran down the bank to the water's edge. The bolt cutters were bright red with handles about two feet long and with jaws like a piranha's from South America. Johnny looked at the cutter and then at Chick.

"You be careful with that thing. Don't cut anything but the hook," he said, with a nervous laugh. We all laughed, too. We needed something to lighten things up.

"Somebody take hold of the hook and lift it up so I can get at the end of it with the cutter," Chick said.

Everyone looked at everyone else.

"Well, come on. Someone, take hold of it," Johnny ordered.

Nobody wanted to be messing around in that area of a friend's anatomy, but finally Dougie, good, old, cool-headed Dougie, stepped forward and took hold of the hook, and carefully lifted it upward so Chick could remove the barb. Chick put the jaws of the bolt cutter on the hook and pulled the handles together and the hook snapped off like a wet noodle. Then Dougie freed the hook from Johnny's crotch. We were watching open-mouthed as Johnny inspected himself. It seemed that he was in pretty good shape with just a tiny spot of blood. "Looks like I'll live," he said, smiling.

"You better put some iodine on that," Dewey suggested.

We all felt better now. "I think I'll just sit out for a while. You guys go ahead and swim." We waded back into the water but the mood had changed. We swam for a few minutes, then we decided to quit for the day. Johnny slid into his underwear and shorts with a gentle motion and ran his hands through his hair and every hair fell into place. It was perfect again. He tied his T-shirt to his handlebars and put on his shoes and carefully mounted his bike. He was just as cool as ever. The coolest kid in town, tall, tanned, good looking, with a hole in his bag! Anyone that cool, who could handle something like that, deserved our respect.

"Johnny, don't forget this," Dougie said, as Johnny was about to ride off. He tossed the two-hooked Daredevil up the bank to Johnny who caught it and hooked it onto his handlebar.

"Yeah, thanks! After all I went through to get this, it better catch a fish or two for me," he said, laughing.

"It better catch you a world record," I said. Johnny laughed, waved goodbye, and rode off, still the coolest guy in town.

The Pool

It was finally finished. The town had begun construction on a public swimming pool in the early spring and the day of the grand opening arrived. We had been monitoring the progress since the time the hole was dug. We sat on our bikes and watched as they poured concrete into big forms. We looked on as they installed pipes and drains, and then built the changing houses and the office where pool employees would collect money and hand out wire baskets for clothes. When it was finished, they put a fence around the whole complex. It had taken many months to complete the project. Everyone was excited to have a pool in town.

We gathered together as the mayor and other important townsfolk made speeches about the pool and the advantages of having kids swim there instead of in the river. Then they opened the doors and treated everyone to a free swim. We got in line, with about every other kid in town, and received a wire basket with a number on it. We went to the boys' changing room, peeled off our clothes, and put them into the basket. There was a metal safety pin with a number that we removed from the basket and pinned to our swimming suits. The changing room was wall-to-wall boys, all scrambling to get changed and into the pool. Before you could enter the water, you had to pass through a shower room, then through a shallow tank filled with a whitish liquid designed to kill anything that was growing on your feet. Finally, we handed in our baskets at another window and we were ready to swim.

The pool was great. There was a shallow end for the little kids, sectioned off by a rope with plastic floats. The other end was deep and it was equipped with two diving boards. We ran to the diving boards and climbed the ladder to the high board for our first plunge into the pool. "Hey, you guys get back on the other side of the rope!" We turned to see who was being yelled at. The lifeguard was looking at us.

"Who? Us?" Dougie objected.

"Yeah, you! Get back to the little kids' side until you pass your swimming test."

What indignity! We, with the exception of Dewey, could probably swim circles around this guy. He was a college guy hired by the town as head lifeguard. His name was Bob Mick and it seemed that he took his job very seriously.

We walked over to him. "What do we have to do to pass the swimming test?"

"You have to swim the length of the pool and back without stopping." We looked at each other and grinned.

"I'll go first," Dougie volunteered.

"Okay, hotshot. Give it a try," Mr. Mick said.

Dougie walked to the deep end of the pool, dove in, and swam part way underwater, then surfaced and swam the rest of the way doing a crawl. Then he turned at the wall and did the backstroke part of the way back; then side-stroked to the end. "Anything else I can do for you?" he asked, looking up at Mr. Mick.

"Don't be a wise guy," the lifeguard barked. "Who's next?"

"I'll go," said Chick, who copied Dougie's performance. Then Dewey went. He wasn't as graceful as Dougie or Chick but he managed to make it down and back. Then it was my turn, so I dove in and swam the first length with a crawl, turned, swam on my back to the rope, then dove underwater and swam about a foot off the bottom toward the twelve-foot deep end. Underwater, you could hear the sound of the pumps and see the drains that sucked in the water. I stayed on the bottom until I reached the wall, came up the side of the wall like a porpoise, and shot up out of the water. When at the top, I blew a mouthful of water into the air; indeed, a very dramatic move. The water hit Mr. Mick in the face and chest.

"Hey! Watch where you're splashing that water!"

I was hanging onto the side of the pool with a grin on my face and the other guys were laughing at my joke.

"You passed the test, but you have one-half hour out of the pool for splashing."

What? I had just passed my swimming test, but I was being punished. I didn't think I liked this pool very much.

The other guys got in the water and I had to sit on my towel by the fence. It wasn't long until Dewey grabbed Dougie from behind and dunked him. Mr. Mick's whistle made a shrill noise and he pointed at Dewey.

"You! Out for a half hour for dunking!"

Dewey looked around and realized he was the one being corrected this time.

"Who? Me?" he questioned.

"Out of the pool!" The lifeguard was getting spiteful now. Dewey joined me on the concrete and soon the whistle shrieked again and Chick was targeted for running along the side the pool and jumping in. "No running! Out for a half hour," bellowed the lifeguard. Chick joined Dewey and me. Dougie was the only one of our group still in the water. He looked at us, grinned, and then swam to the side of the pool and climbed the ladder to the high diving board. The lifeguard was sitting on a high chair by the diving board, watching the pool. He wore a round hat like you would see in a movie about Africa, hard and shiny. He had wiped off the water I had splashed on him and then he applied tanning lotion. Dougie walked to the end of the diving board and did a can opener into the pool.

A can opener was like a cannon ball, except that the foot was placed against the opposite leg, making a kind of a P-shape. When the diver hit the water, a column of water shot into the air in the direction the P pointed. A cannon ball was just a big splash, but the can opener directed the spray of water.

Well, Dougie did one doozie of a can opener. He hit the water and the splash shot up about fifteen feet and hit the lifeguard in the face, blowing off his African hat. He just about toppled off his chair! He blew his whistle so forcefully that his eyes about popped out of his head. "Out! Out! You're out for the whole day. Get out!" Dougie smiled and picked up his towel. We grabbed our towels and followed him to the changing room.

"You guys, get back here. You haven't put your time in yet."

We stopped. Chick, Dewey, and I looked at each other. Chick nodded and we ran to the deep end of the pool and jumped in. We all did can openers that pointed at the lifeguard. There was such a splash that everything on that end of the pool got wet, including the lifeguard's towel, and his tanning lotion was sent onto the grass under the fence by the wave.

"You guys are all out of here! Get out, now!"

We laughed as we ran toward the changing house. Dougie was waiting for us. We dressed and turned in our empty baskets.

We had been in the new swimming pool for less than a half hour.

"That place is a bummer," Chick grumbled.

"Yeah, all you can do is swim. You can't do anything without getting in trouble," complained Dougie.

"Let's go to the Gosey," I said, and we jumped on our bikes and rode to our old swimming hole. Once there, we stripped off our clothes and piled them on the ground. We didn't need any stupid basket here, or a swimming suit, for that matter. We plunged into the water, splashed and dunked, and did can openers as much as we wanted. And no one blew a dumb whistle at us.

About a week later, we went back to the pool because a free swim day had been organized. In about twenty minutes we were sitting on the concrete, so we gave up and left. We were just not the kind of guys to survive in a pool. There was nothing to do but swim. What fun was that?

Later that week, we were spending the night in a tent, but it was one of those sweltering nights when it never got cool enough to sleep.

"Whew, I'm roasting," Dewey whined.

"No kidding. Let's go swimming," Chick said. We quietly left the tent and wheeled our bikes out of Dougie's backyard until we reached the street. We mounted them and headed toward the river.

"Hey, why don't we try the pool?" Chick suggested.

"How we gonna get in with that barbed wire fence?" I asked. "Well, I noticed the other day that the doors in the changing rooms have locks that can be unlocked from the inside. There is no roof over the changing rooms, so if we boost one guy over the wall, he can go in and unlock the door from the inside." Chick was a criminal genius.

We parked our bikes nearby in a vacant brush-filled lot and gingerly inched our way to the pool area. When we got to the changing house,

Dougie and I held our hands together to make a step for Chick. He lifted himself to the top of the wall and grinned as he disappeared over the top. We ran around the corner to the door and heard a click as the door opened. We were giggling like girls as we stripped off our clothes and ran to the pool. Now, this was a treat! You could hear the sound of the water running into the gutters on the sides of the pool as the filter system cycled the water. We jumped in the pool and began having a great time. We played tag and jumped off the diving board and dunked and splashed. The pool was pretty cool without the lifeguard from hell.

We finally decided it was time to return to the tent so we put on our shorts, carried the rest of our clothes, and locked the doors of the changing house. We were cooled off and we smelled like chlorine, but it didn't take long to fall asleep.

A few nights later, when we were sleeping out, we decided to visit the pool again. We proceeded in the same manner and soon we were in the water having great fun. It started to rain but we didn't care because we were wet already. Unexpectedly we heard the lifeguard whistle. We looked up and there was Chick, sitting naked, with the African hat on his head and the whistle around his neck. "You! Out for ten years! Hey, you! Out for the rest of your life!" He was acting big, blowing the whistle, and yelling at us. It was 3 o'clock in the morning.

We were screaming and laughing and making nasty gestures at Chick, having a great time, when Dougie yelled. "Hey, look! The cop!" Sure enough, Mr. Audetta, the town cop, was driving up. We didn't have time to run to the changing house so we huddled in the water against the wall on the side of the pool where he would park. Chick threw the African hat and the whistle on the concrete and jumped into the pool. Mr. Audetta pulled up and shined his lights on the water. We were tight against the side with just our faces out of the water, so he didn't see us. He sat in the car for several minutes with his lights aimed at the pool. Then he drove away. We watched until he was out of sight.

"I bet someone heard Chick playing lifeguard," I said.

"No foolin'! You think so?" Dougie asked.

"That was a close call! Let's get out of here in case he comes back," Dewey said. We dressed and headed on bikes to Chick's house where we were spending the night. As we were settling down, we noticed a car. A spotlight shined on the tent but we stayed motionless. The light went off and Chick peeked out.

"It's him," he said.

"Mr. Audetta?" someone asked in a whisper.

"Yup," replied Chick.

We didn't risk a midnight swim again for a while, giving things time to cool down, but we made it a point to swim in the pool occasionally, and always after hours. The Gosey remained our favorite swimming place. We had a rope swing. Diving was allowed off the big branch. Dunking and splashing were okay. We could scream and make all the noise we wanted and we didn't even have to wear swimming suits. But the best part was no whistle, and no one yelling at us. Later that summer, the town fired Mr. Mick. Parents complained about him being too mean to kids, but we never went back much to swim at the pool, even though he was gone. We had the Gosey, and the only rule there was, "There are no rules."

Gassed

Sleeping out had become a regu1ar thing for Dougie, Dewey, Chick, and me. Dougie and I each had a tent in our backyard that stayed up. After our first disastrous experience with our makeshift "picnic table and refrigerator box" tent, Dougie talked his dad into allowing us to set up their camping tent. We used it repeatedly. My pestering resulted in my parents purchasing a tent for me. I came home from fishing one day and there it was, set up in the backyard. Dewey didn't have a backyard but he was always good for the food detail. His family owned a restaurant and he managed to talk them out of leftovers appropriate for sleep-outs. He would contribute cold French fries or leftover baked potatoes, ham, and chicken. Once he brought prime rib. His mom was pretty mad at him for taking that but we thought it made wonderful sandwiches. Chick had a small tent that was not big enough, so we usually slept in my backyard, or at Dougie's.

Dewey had a gas problem. No matter what he ate, he seemed to end up with gas. It never failed; we would settle in and Dewey would let one go.

"Whoops," he would apologize.

Of course, we would moan and groan and hit Dewey with pillows or tennis shoes and have a great laugh over it. Then we'd settle down again and he'd let another one go.

"Whoops," again.

The rest of us had our days, but Dewey was consistent. He could fart on demand. If we were at a movie, one of us would whisper to Dewey, "Hey, Dewey, let one rip," and he would smile, raise a leg, and let one go. He had one lined up ready for launching just for the asking.

In school, he'd wait until we were working on a group project and then he would rip a loud one. Sister would give us all a dirty look, but Dewey would take on that "offended" look and gaze at one of us, as if he wasn't the culprit. And, in church, he could stop a mass. He would wait until there was a quiet part, when no one was singing or praying, then he'd let it go. Dewey had a real talent.

One night we decided to take Chick's tent to a sandbar not far out in the river. We put the tent, our sleeping bags, clothes, and food into garbage bags and held them over our heads as we swam to the sandbar. On the next trip, we took fishing poles, fry pans, and a metal grate. We set up the tent, gathered firewood, made a fire pit, and placed the grate over it. We had a sack of cooked potatoes to fry, four cans of beans, cooking oil, salt, pepper, and flour for breading the fresh fish fillets.

The plan was to catch fish, clean them, and fry them and the potatoes, heat up the beans, and have supper. We always caught fish so supper would not be a problem.

We fished and fished. At first we had no bites. Just before dark, we got a few bites but we only caught shiners, carp, and red horse suckers.

"We can't eat these things," Dewey wailed. "I'm starved." "Just fish, Dewey. We'll get walleye or catfish soon," I said.

Famous last words!! It was dark and we didn't have a single fish.

"Well," Dougie said, "it looks like we're gonna have potatoes and beans for supper." Well, potatoes and beans were better than nothing, so we began cutting up the potatoes and frying them. Then we opened the beans and dumped them into a pan. Soon the meal was ready and we scooped up the food and ate. The potatoes were gone in a minute and the first batch of beans disappeared quickly, too. Chick opened another can of beans and soon there was a second helping for each of us. What remained, Dewey ate directly out of the pan.

"I'm still hungry," Dewey moaned.

"That's it, Dewey," I said.

"Unless you've got something stashed away, we're done eating for the night," Dougie said.

Dewey moaned and groaned for a while but it did no good.

We sat around the campfire and talked about the stuff thirteen year-old boys talk about. We covered baseball, fishing, and the movies we liked. Finally we were yawning.

"I'm going to bed," I said.

"Yeah! Me, too," Dougie and Chick said. "I'm still hungry," Dewey repeated.

"Go to sleep, Dewey. Then you won't be hungry anymore," Dougie said.

One by one, we undressed and piled our clothes on a log.

We were barefooted, so I cleaned the sand off my feet and climbed into the tent first to my sleeping bag on the far side. Chick followed and crawled into his bag. Then Dewey climbed in. Dougie stripped down to his underwear and put a plastic tarp over our clothes to protect them from possible rain or morning fog. He was the smallest, so he came in last and wiggled into his sleeping bag in the middle. It was a tight squeeze and we were packed in like sardines.

"This tent isn't gonna be big enough for us next summer if we keep growing," Chick said.

"Yeah, Dewey, did you hear that? If you keep growing, we'll have to get a bigger tent," Dougie said.

"FFFFFRRRRRRRRRRTTTT!!" was Dewey's answer. "Dewey! You pig!" We burst out laughing at Dewey's loud fart. "Does that answer your question, Douglas?" Dewey laughed.

We all chuckled and giggled and finally settled down.

"FFFFFFFFRRRRRTTTTTTTT!!" The tent rocked with laughter again.

"Dewey, you animal," chided Dougie.

"Dang, Dewey! Put a cork in it," echoed Chick.

"Cripes, Dewey! That one stinks like something you ate a week ago," I blurted.

"You guys are just jealous of my talent," Dewey boasted, and then let another one go. FFFFFFFFFRRRRTTTTT!! We were laughing so hard that tears filled our eyes. And then the odor of the last one hit us.

"Dewey, knock it off. That one was bad," Dougie coughed. FFFFFFFFFFRRRRRRRRRRTTTTTTTTTTT!! It was a champion! I had never heard one of such long duration in my whole life. We laughed so hard, the tent almost came down. And the smell was unbearable! We took refuge in our sleeping bags, trying to escape, while Dewey basked in total delight.

"C'mon, you guys! Come out for a courtesy sniff," Dewey invited.

The tent smelled like a sewer and Chick was the first to abandon it. "I can't take it," he said, and crawled over Dougie to get fresh air.

"Me, either," chimed in Dougie. I wasn't far behind. We were standing in the cool, night air, shivering in our underwear. Dewey laid there like an old sow, enjoying his stink.

"Dewey, you better go to the other end of the sandbar and make a donation," I said.

"I'm okay now. It's all gone," declared Dewey.

"Oh, sure! We believe that," Dougie said, as he waved the tent flap back and forth in an attempt to air it out.

"C'mon, Dewey! Get out and do your business so we can sleep," ordered

Chick.

"I don't gotta go," Dewey announced. "I'm fine now. Come back in. I'll be good."

We didn't have much choice. We surely didn't want to sleep outside so we brushed the sand off our feet and crawled in.

"Now, you be good," Dougie said.

"I will," promised Dewey.

It was quiet for several minutes and then I smelled something nasty again.

"Dewey!" I bellowed.

"Whoops!" Dewey said. "That one was an orphan."

We bawled out Dewey but he just laughed and gave us another blast. He knew we weren't really mad and he always livened up even the dullest time with his talent. I don't know how many times he said "whoops" the rest of the night, but we endured them, laughing and threatening him until we were exhausted and, one by one, we drifted off to sleep.

The next morning, right on cue, Dewey gave us a wake-up blast.

"Next time, no beans for you, Dewey," Dougie said.

"That doesn't make any difference," I said. "He does that on white bread and water."

Dewey laughed, lifted his leg, and another one ripped.

"Whoops."

The Mill Dam

We fished almost daily during the summer. The Gosey was one of our favorite spots, but we also liked fishing in the sloughs, like Gutweiler's and the Cat. Since we had finally convinced our mothers that we could fish in the river and get back alive, we often fished there. And we had another spot that was good for just catching fish if we didn't care what they were.

The Mill Dam was about two miles north of town. It was an easy bike ride that ended with a fast ride down a steep hill and then across a bridge. The hill was the scariest part of the trip. You had to hang on tightly to control the bike so it didn't careen into the ditch.

The Mill Dam had been built long ago to generate electricity. It held back the Mill Creek, making a small lake above the dam. Over the years, the lake had filled in with mud and now there was more mud than water. The lake had a few bluegills, but mostly it had bullheads and carp. Carp fishing was good below the dam. We would dig worms, ride to the dam, and fish opposite the electrical plant. A spring ran over a cement platform, making a little pond. We would make our own small dam with rocks and mud and put our carp there while we continued to fish. At the end of the day we would open our dam, releasing the water and the carp into Mill Creek. We would count the carp as they slid by. On good days, we would catch over two hundred. Since they weren't good to eat, we had no reason to keep them so we did the catch and release thing, over and over. Occasionally, we would catch a catfish or a walleye at this spot.

Sometimes we fished above the dam where we caught bullheads but they weren't as much fun and they had stingers that usually ended up giving one of us a sore hand.

About three inches of water passed over the dam so it was a challenge to walk across it without falling in. Moss and algae made the concrete slippery and we crossed it like tightrope walkers in a circus. At least one of us would generally slide off and go over the edge, but it was an easy swim to the shore if that happened.

One day we found a kayak that somebody had left on the shore above the dam.

"Well, let's take this for a spin," Chick said.

"It's not ours. We better not take it," Dewey replied.

"We won't hurt it; we'll just take it for a ride," Chick said. We finally decided to give it a try and to be very careful.

Chick and Dougie got in and paddled to the pond. It was a fine kayak with waterproofed canvas stretched over a wooden frame. I t flew across the water. Dewey and I watched as they went to the other end of the pond and scared up a few geese and ducks. Finally they came back and pulled up by the shore. "You two gonna try it?"

"Sure," I said. "Get in, Dewey." Off we went. It was great fun paddling. After a while we decided to head back to the shore.

"I think we should take it over the dam," Chick said. "What? Are you crazy?" I said.

Dougie chimed in. "You'll wreck it if you go over the dam." "No way! It'll slide over and go down the creek, just like in the movies," Chick said, excitedly.

"I'm not going," I said.

"Me, either," Dougie said. We all looked at Dewey.

"You go first and if you live, I'll go with you the next time," he said to Chick.

"Okay. Here I go!" Chick said, and he climbed in and paddled to the pond. We ran to the bottom of the dam to watch the show, and to recover Chick's body. He paddled to the dam, lined up the kayak, paddled a few more strokes, and started over the dam. The kayak floated on the top. About five feet of it protruded before it tipped and slid down the face of the dam. There was a rounded ledge at the bottom where the kayak and Chick flew into the air and landed in the water below the dam. Chick held his paddle over his head like an Olympic champion. We cheered, not really believing that he had pulled it off.

"See, I told you," he bragged, as he came to shore. "Let's do it again. I want to go this time," Dewey said. "Okay. Help me carry it back up," Chick said.

Dougie and I stayed at the bottom of the dam. Soon we saw them paddling to the edge of the dam. Dewey was in front and Chick in back. They lined up the kayak and took a couple of strokes toward the dam. This time, the kayak immediately tipped over the edge with Dewey in the front. They flew over the dam and when they got to the ledge, going faster and with more weight in the kayak this time, the kayak hit the water and Dewey went through the bottom of it. With a boy-sized hole in the canvas, the kayak didn't float and Chick ended up going under, too.

Dewey came to the surface. Chick had bailed out. The kayak floated to the top and he grabbed it, and pulled it to shore. Dewey swam over to us, too. "Oops! Looks like the two of us were too heavy for it," he said. The canvas was torn where Dewey had gone through.

"Oh, no! We wrecked it," Chick said.

"It can be fixed," Dougie said. "It needs to be sewn and then waterproofed."

"Let's put it back where we found it and get out of here," Dewey said.

We returned the kayak to its spot. If we had had paper and a pen, we would have left a note explaining that we had wrecked it and were willing to help fix it, but we didn't have a pen or anything to write on. "Well, I guess we'll just leave it and hope for the best," Chick said.

A few days later, Dougie and I were fishing at the Mill Dam and we noticed the kayak was missing. We never did find out who owned it. Well, we were catching carp below the dam when a couple of local guys came driving up, parked, and walked over to us. "How, ya doing, guys?"

"Okay," we answered.

"Whatcha catchin'?" they asked. "Mostly carp."

"Ever get any bullheads?"

"Yeah, some. Why?"

"We're bank-poling and we need bullheads for bait." "Bank-poling?" Dougie asked.

"Yeah! You put a pole in the riverbank, attach a good-sized hook with strong line, and use a bullhead for bait. It works slick for catching those big, flathead catfish."

"Oh, sure! I know about that," I said.

"Well, we need ten bullheads a day and we'll pay a nickel apiece for them."

I looked at Dougie and his eyebrows went up. We were standing about twenty feet from millions of bullheads.

"We might be able to find some for you, Mister," he said. "Great," the man said. "Here, I'll give you my address. If you catch any, bring them over and I'll pay you. In fact, bring all you can catch. I have friends who need them, too." He handed us a piece of paper with his address and said goodbye and left.

"A nickel a bullhead?" Dougie said. "We're rich!" We were so excited that we could hardly reel in our lines fast enough. We ran to the top of the dam and threw our lines in and in a minute we each had a bullhead on the bank. "Wait a minute. What are we gonna do with them? We gotta take them back to town. They won't stay alive on the stringer."

"We'll have to take them in buckets filled with water," I said. We reeled in, put our fishing gear in our bike baskets, and set off for town. As much fun as the hill was to ride down, it was torture to climb. We usually ended up walking our bikes because our legs turned to noodles. Today, however, we were so excited about the bullhead business that we made it to the top in record time.

As we rode down the highway, I said to Dougie, "Should we let Dewey and Chick in on this?"

Dougie looked over at me. "I've been thinking about that, too.

What do you think?"

"Well, they're gonna be real mad if we don't."

He nodded his head. "Yeah! That's what I think, too. We better clue them in. Besides, they're our best friends." It was settled. We would share the millions we would make from our bullhead business with Chick and Dewey.

We stopped at Chick's house. He had been forced to help his mom move the furniture out of the house so the carpeting could be cleaned. He was annoyed because he didn't get to fish. We helped him move the stuff back into the house and got fresh cookies from his mom as a reward. Then we told him about the bullhead business. "A nickel a bullhead! A dollar for every twenty bullheads! We can catch them about as fast as we can pull them in. We're gonna be rich!" He was excited about our new business.

We got on our bikes and rode to Dewey's apartment and found him napping on the couch. "Dewey, we've got a business deal for you," I said. We told Dewey about the bullhead business and he was thrilled.

"Great! Two bullheads and I can get a bag of potato chips; five for a movie, and two for popcorn. What a deal." Good, old Dewey, always thinking about his stomach.

The day was almost shot but we decided to fix up our bikes with buckets for hauling the bullheads. We planned to head to Mill Dam early the next morning to start our new business. We had to figure out how to attach a bucket to our wire baskets. We tried a few ideas, finally settling on cutting an old inner tube into strips which would be tied to the bucket handle, then stretched around the baskets to secure them. This worked well and we were excited about the next day's business. That evening we went to our worm-digging spot and got our supply of bait. We decided to meet at eight o'clock in the morning.

The next morning we were riding merrily along to the Mill Dam. We could hardly wait to get up the hill and coast down the other side. We topped the hill and began the descent, but instead of touching the brakes a tad to slow us down, we let our bikes speed down. Normally we weren't in such a hurry. About halfway down, my front tire began to wobble. It must have been a little crooked and I hadn't noticed it because I had never gone that fast before. Soon the little wobble was a full-blown vibration and the whole bike was shaking. "I can't hold it!" I yelled, as my bike headed for the ditch. I hit the tall grass and weeds and my bike flipped over. I flew over the handlebars and landed in the bushes. My bike did a summersault and landed a short way below me. The rest of the guys couldn't stop, so they continued down the hill. They later ran back to where I was sitting.

"Are you okay?" Dougie asked.

"Yeah, I think so. My bike went nuts and I couldn't control it," I explained.

Chick and Dougie pulled my bike out of the bushes and checked it out. It seemed okay. My fishing pole was missing so we combed the tall grass and Dewey found it. It was intact. We picked up the rest of the stuff and I got on my bike and tried it. It wobbled a bit, but I could ride it. Since I was so close to the bottom and the guys were walking, I decided to walk, too.

We got our fishing gear and the buckets and headed to the pond. We caught bullheads about as fast as we could reel them in. After fishing a few hours, Dewey said, "Let's see how many we got." We agreed that we had enough for one day, so we filled the buckets with fresh water and attached them to our bikes for the ride home.

We soon realized our bikes were off balance with the sloshing water and the buckets were VERY heavy. We had to walk our bikes up the entire hill. "Whew, this isn't as much fun as going down," Dewey said.

"No kidding! Even a crash is more fun than this," I said.

They laughed at my joke.

When we got to the top, we were able to ride again and we were off toward town. We had to proceed slowly so that the water would stay level and not get us off balance. We were almost to town when Dewey lost control and ended up in the ditch. His bullheads were flopping in the grass. "Help me! Rescue my bullheads!" he yelled. We couldn't put our bikes on our kickstands because they were too heavy, so Chick and I held the three bikes while Dougie helped Dewey put the bullheads in the other three buckets.

"There. Now they'll be fine," I said.

Dewey was worried that he had lost his bullheads. "How we gonna know whose bullheads are whose?" he muttered.

"We'll split the money equally," Dougie reassured him.

"Yeah! A four-way split," Chick reiterated.

That made Dewey happy.

We found the man's house. We knocked on his door and told him we had his bullheads. He had a cattle-watering tank set up by his garage and we counted the fish as we plopped them into the tank. Final count was eighty-nine. "You guys don't fool around," the man said, smiling at the nice catch. "I'll let my friends know how expert you are at this and they'll probably want some." We were just about ready to bust. What a business; go fishing and get paid for it! The man gave us $4.45 for our bullheads and told us to bring him whatever we caught.

We rode to the cafe and sat in a booth to divide up our money. "That's a dollar and ten cents each," Dougie said. We divided the money up but there was a nickel left over.

"What should we do with the nickel?" I asked.

"Let's put it away and next time we'll add it to the pot," Dougie said. We decided that Chick should be the treasurer so he took care of the extra nickel. Then we each ordered a coke and an ice cream cone and sat down to savor our well-earned treats.

"This is the best job in the world," Dewey said.

"No kidding! We might be millionaires by the end of the summer," Chick added.

We fished the Mill Dam for the next two weeks. Word got out that we had a bullhead business and we kept the whole town supplied. One of the men we supplied was my dad's employer and one morning he knocked on our door while I was eating breakfast. There stood Carl with a catfish as big as me. "I thought you might want to see the catfish your bullhead caught," he said. I could hardly speak, let alone close my mouth.

Carl was an average-sized man and he had a big gaff hook in the catfish's lower jaw. The catfish's head was against the back of his shoulder and its tail was dragging on the sidewalk! "Oh, my gosh! Oh, my gosh!" I couldn't believe its size!

"What do you think?" he asked, laughing.

"I think I gotta call my friends and let them see this!" I said, as I ran for the phone. I called the guys and in a couple of minutes they were there, gaping at the trophy sized catfish.

"How much does it weigh?" Dewey asked.

"Where did you catch it?" inquired Chick.

"Did it pull hard?" questioned Dougie. We had lots of questions.

It turned out that he had caught it in the river, about half a mile from the Gosey. "You mean that thing was swimming in the river where we swim?" Dewey wanted to know.

"I think I'll start wearing a swimming suit," Dougie said. We all laughed at Dougie's joke.

The bank-poling season lasted another week and then the fishermen told us that they wouldn't need any more bullheads. But, they said to keep them in mind for next year.

"Well, it was fun while it lasted," I said.

"Yeah! What a way to make money," Dougie said, as we biked toward Chick's house to tell him the sad news that our business got shut down. We called Dewey and he joined us, and for the first day in almost three weeks, we didn't go to the Mill Dam.

"We made over ten dollars each. That's a lot of money," said Dougie, delightfully.

"Sure is. We can buy a lot of good stuff with that," Chick said.

"You know, I'm a little hungry for an ice cream float," Dewey added. We looked at him and laughed.

"An ice cream float does sound good," Dougie said.

"Yeah, no foolin'," I said.

Chick looked at us. "Well, count me in."

We jumped on our bikes and rode to the cafe, pockets full of money; four unemployed business tycoons.

We spent our money wisely and made it last most of the summer. It was the easiest money we had ever earned. Go fishing, and get paid; what a deal!

The Cave

"I think we've caught all the fish that are here," Chick announced.

"Yeah, no kiddin'. We haven't had a bite for an hour," Dougie said.

Dewey was sitting with his feet in the water and we three were lying in the sand watching our fishing poles which were propped up in our pole holders. A pole holder was a forked stick that was stuck into the sand. It supported the fishing pole and you could watch the tip for signs of a bite. The holder also kept the reel above the sand.

We were fishing at the river above the bridge by Snake Island.

Many years earlier there was another bridge that crossed the river and ended at a toll house. The man who owned the bridge collected money from people using the bridge. As cars and trucks became heavier, the toll bridge became inadequate. It was torn down and the new bridge was built about fifty yards downriver. The old piers that held up the toll bridge had mostly washed away with the spring floods, but the one closest to the riverbank had survived. It was a square pile of stones and pilings, and it sat about ten feet from the bank. We made a makeshift bridge of stones from the riverbank to the pier so we could walk across when the water was low. We then fished off the sandy area around the rocks.

Snakes liked the pier so we named it Snake Island.

I was definitely not a snake person. No matter what kind of snake it was, I didn't want it near me. Dewey wasn't as afraid of snakes as I was, but he also would go around them rather than be near them. Chick wasn't afraid of anything. He would pick up almost any repulsive thing, including a snake. But Dougie; he was the snake guy. He loved the things. No matter what size a snake was, he had to pick the dang thing up. If he found a little one, it went into his pocket. One time I was fishing with him at Gutweiler's and he began yelling at me to help him. I thought he had a real emergency so I took off running. There he was, kneeling on the ground by a hole, holding a snake's tail, trying to pull it out of the hole.

"Help me pull this snake out!" he begged.

"Are you nuts? Leave the thing alone. No! Wait. Let me get out of here first, and then let it go!" I said, hightailing it back a safe distance.

Suddenly he flopped backward over into the grass with about a foot of the snake's tail in his hand. T he tail was wiggling and I almost passed out when he held it up to show me. Then a long water snake came to the surface and swam off.

"You're a sick one," I said to Dougie, as he joined me by my fishing pole.

He held the snake tail out to me. "Here, wanna play with it?

It won't bite you 'cuz it ain't got a head," he said, laughing.

"I'll take a branch and beat you on the head till you ain't got no head if you come a step closer," I said, in a threatening tone.

He pretended to be scared and threw the snake tail into the water where it wriggled like a live snake until it disappeared under the surface. "You're such a girl when it comes to snakes," he teased.

"Why, thank you. That's the nicest thing you've said to me all day," I said, in a high voice.

Snakes were the only thing that I couldn't stand. Frogs, toads, turtles, lizards, and skinks were fine. But snakes, yikes! Not for me!

Skinks were similar to snakes except they had little legs. Most of the kids called them sand lizards but Dougie and I knew they were skinks. They belonged to the lizard family. They ran back and forth across the sand dunes. We tried to catch them but they were so fast that it was impossible. We wanted to capture a couple to study them, possibly adding them to our zoo. So we devised a plan to catch them. Finally I thought about making a trap. We went to Dewey's dad's restaurant and got a half dozen tomato paste and olive cans. We cut one end out and took them to the sand dunes where we dug holes and put a can in each so that the top was level with the sand. Then we filled sand in around them. Now, when a skink came running past, he would fall into the trap and we could play with it.

Dougie and I buried half a dozen cans and left them overnight. The next morning, we had two skinks. I was pleased at how well my idea had worked, and Dougie was impressed. We trapped skinks for about a week, catching six. We took them to Dougie's and put them in a discarded, leaky aquarium, and we tossed in flies and ants. They seemed happy in their new home but Dougie's dad thought we should return them to their natural habitat, so we did. I enjoyed playing with them, even if they looked like snakes.

Well, we were trying to decide what to do about the fishing situation when Dewey piped up, "Hey guys, have you ever heard of Fisherman's Point?"

"Yeah. It's upriver, isn't it?" Chick commented.

"Yeah. About five miles up, on the other side of the river. My dad says there is good fishing up there," added Dewey.

"Five miles. That's a long way to ride a bike," I said.

"Oh, come on! It's not that far. Besides, if the fish don't bite, there's a cave that we could explore."

"A cave?" we asked.

"Yeah. My dad says counterfeiters hid there long ago." That got everyone's attention, so we packed up our gear, put our poles, tackle boxes, and bait into our baskets and took off across the bridge. We rode on the highway on the north side of the river. It was narrow and had only a minimal shoulder so when cars came past they had to slow down for our bike convoy. We rode on and on and soon we arrived at Fisherman's Point.

We parked our bikes and followed a path to the river. It looked like a good fishing spot. There was an old wing dam that made a current eddy and it seemed to be the perfect place for fish to wait, and for someone to catch them. We spread out along the shore and soon we had our lines in the water. We waited and waited for a bite.

"This is just as bad as at the bridge," Chick wailed.

"Maybe they're just not biting today," Dougie commented. "Oh, really? You think?" Dewey said. Dougie threw a clod of mud at him.

Dewey stood up and looked at the hill across the highway. He stared and stared and suddenly he said, "Guys, I can see the opening to the cave." We jumped up and ran over by Dewey and looked where he was pointing. Sure enough, way up on the hillside, there was a ledge and a hole.

"Hmm. That's a long way up," Dougie said.

"Yeah! It's almost at the top of the hill," Chick said.

"What's the matter? Can't you girls climb a hill?" Dewey said.

Being compared to a girl was about the worst insult a thirteen year-old boy could tolerate.

"Okay, smart guy! Let's see who's the last one to reach the cave?" Dougie challenged, and he began to climb the trail to the highway. We stashed our fishing gear in our baskets. Each of us had a little flashlight in our tackle box for night fishing or for catching night crawlers on rainy nights, so we grabbed them and hid our bikes in the weeds.

We jumped over the fence and began the climb. Part way up we found a trail that appeared to lead to the cave. It was a good path that weaved back and forth across the hillside until it got to where the hill turned to sheer rock. Then it became very narrow and steep, and we had to continue the incline single file.

"You can sure see for a long way from here," I said.

"No foolin'. And it's a long drop to the bottom," Chick added.

"The fall doesn't scare me. It's the sudden stop at the bottom that hurts," Dougie said, making a joke. We stopped and gazed at the river valley. We could see the church steeple and the water tower in town. The sunlight looked like sparkling diamonds on the surface of the river as it flowed westward to the Mississippi. We could see its meandering path for miles as it slipped between the tree-lined banks where we fished and swam.

We kept climbing and finally we reached the ledge and the hole in the wall. It was the size of a front door of a house. We couldn't see far inside, but from what we could see, it appeared to be quite large.

"Let's go in," Chick said, always the first one to try something.

"Okay, let's go," Dougie agreed, and they walked in.

Dewey looked at me and we both shrugged; then we went in, too. We walked upright until the cave tapered off, and we had to bend over. We finally caught up to Chick and Dougie who had turned on their flashlights. They were checking out three different openings that branched off from the main cave.

"Looks like it splits here," they observed.

"We'll go left and you two take the middle passage and we'll meet back here," Chick said. We went a short distance and the cave got even smaller and we had to craw1. We continued and soon found ourselves in a good-sized room.

"This is a dead end," Dewey announced.

"Yeah, but look at this room," I said, standing up. "There've been people in here. Look at the ceiling. It's black from fire or candle smoke." There were empty food cans and broken crates and other stuff strewn around.

"Maybe this is where the counterfeiters hid," Dewey said.

"Maybe we'll find some phony money!"

"Yeah, Dewey. I'm sure we're the first ones in here since they were here."

Just then Chick and Dougie came into the room through the little doorway. "Wow, this is better than anything we found," Dougie said. "That other tunnel comes back out on the side of the hill."

"Looks like somebody lived here," Chick said.

"Dewey figures this is where the counterfeiters hung out," I said.

"I think I'd find another job rather than have to live in this place," Chick said. "Let's check out the other tunnel."

We crawled back and down the tunnel to the third cave.

Dougie and Chick led the way and Dewey and I followed. This cave also got smaller and we had to crawl on our hands and knees. The cave floor was clay and we found it to be sticky. Our knees and hands turned red as we made our way through it.

"Maybe we should go back," Dewey said.

"Why, Dewey, are you afraid you'll get your fat butt stuck?"

Dougie said.

"I might get nervous and you know what happens when I get nervous, don't you, Douglas?" Dewey warned.

"Oh, no, Dewey! Please don't do that; not in this little space," I pleaded from behind. We laughed and our laughter sounded spooky as it echoed down the cave.

"Whew, that sounds like something out of a horror movie," Dewey said. Then Dewey let one go and it sounded like a bomb going off. We laughed again, but we griped at Dewey as we headed on down the tunnel.

We crawled on and soon my flashlight began to dim. "Hey, guys! My light is almost dead," I said.

"Mine, too," Dewey said, just ahead of me.

"Well, keep up with us. Ours are okay," Chick said.

We crawled on and soon my light went completely out. I could see the light from Dewey's flashlight ahead of me and Dougie and Chick's lights ahead of that. The tunnel continued to get smaller and soon we had to crawl on our bellies. "I don't think I like it in here," Dewey said.

"We don't have much choice, Dewey. We can't back out," I said.

"Just keep going. It's gotta come out somewhere," added Chick.

Suddenly Dewey stopped and I ran smack into him. "My light went out," he said.

"Can you see the other guys?" I asked.

"Just barely," he said. "Hey, guys! Wait up. Our lights are out!" he yelled.

I couldn't really see much around Dewey but ahead there was a faint light.

"Hurry up, Dewey! We're being left behind!" I urged. Dewey started crawling and soon the faint light disappeared.

"They left us. Those dirty rats," he said. "It's REALLY dark in here."

He was right. I had never been in so much dark. Even on a cloudy night, with no moon or street lights, there's always a little light. But in here it was DARK. I held my hand up but I couldn't see a thing. "We gotta keep moving, Dewey. Just keep crawlin' and we'll find them."

"I can't see anything!" Dewey said, and I could hear panic in his voice.

"Feel ahead with your hand, and keep going. I don't like it any more than you do," I said. "I'm here with you. I won't leave you."

I could hear and feel Dewey moving forward so I began to crawl ahead. We moved slowly down the cave in complete darkness. Every so often I would get too close to Dewey and his feet would kick me in the face. The walls and roof of the cave were so close that our sides and back rubbed on them. "If this gets much smaller, I'm gonna get stuck," Dewey said. I didn't even want to think about what it would be like going backward out of this place.

"It can't get much smaller or the other guys would have got stuck," I said.

"Yeah! When we catch up to them, I'm gonna pound a knot or two on their heads for leaving us," Dewey said.

I don't know how far we crawled, but suddenly I could feel fresh air on my face. "Dewey, do you feel that air?" I asked.

"Yeah, I can. We must be almost out, thank God!" he said.

We crawled faster and we could see light ahead and smell the warm, fresh air. We reached the opening and emerged into the sunshine. It took a few minutes for our eyes to adjust to the brightness, but there sat Dougie and Chick smiling at us. They were covered with red clay.

"You rats! How come you left us?" I said.

"We thought you were behind us till we got to the end," Dougie said.

"Yeah, sure! I'm sure you did," Dewey mocked.

"We did," Chick said. "We were surprised when it took you so long to come out."

"We thought maybe Dewey had farted in there and both of you got gassed," Dougie said, laughing. We laughed and even Dewey thought it was funny.

"Well, let's climb down and go home," I said. "I've had enough cave exploring for one day." Dewey looked at me and began laughing.

"What's so funny?" I asked.

"You've got a shoe print on your face," he said, laughing like mad. The other two looked and began laughing.

"A perfect print of Dewey's shoe," Chick said.

"Well, better that than a butt print. I came close to that a couple of times," I said.

We laughed and talked all the way down the hill. It had been a good adventure but I don't think any of us was in a big hurry to explore any more caves for a while.

We got back to our bikes and began the long ride home. Cars passed us and some passengers laughed when they saw us. I suppose four boys covered with red clay looked peculiar riding along with bikes loaded down with fishing gear. We didn't care. What had begun as a boring fishing day had turned into another exciting adventure.

Treasures For Our Moms

St. John the Baptist Church had an annual summer festival. We looked forward to this time and this particular year it was going to be better because we had money to spend. Our bullhead business was financing our fun. We each made a point to save several dollars for the event and our parents usually chipped in a few bucks. We were flush with money and would be able to take in all the sights.

A major portion of the money would be used for food. In addition to the usual hotdogs and hamburgers, there was the lady who sold cotton candy, popcorn, caramel corn, and candy apples from a trailer decked with colored lights. We spent much time there. The lady was kind and we were fascinated by the strands of cotton candy that hung from her hairnet like wisps of tiny pink or blue clouds. We tried her sweet and salty treats. I especially liked the snow cones. They were served in pointed cups and a sweet syrup was drizzled over the top. I loved them in spite of the brain freezes I got from them. Chick favored the candy apples, and Dougie went for the caramel corn. Dewey loved the cotton candy and swore that the blue tasted better than the pink. He usually wore half a serving on his face and eyebrows.

We always spent money at the dunk tank. The church rented the apparatus and people were lured to sit on a board suspended over a tank of water. Game participants paid twenty-five cents for five baseballs to throw at a target on the side of the tank. If the target was hit, the person on the board dropped into the water with a big splash. It was great entertainment. We always hoped that Sister Henry or another sister would volunteer, but they never did. The closest we came to that kind of thrill was when we managed to drown a couple teachers from Dougie's school.

Then there were the games that yielded prizes. One challenge involved throwing hoops, or wooden rings, over prizes displayed on a low table in the middle of a game tent. If the ring landed around the prize and fell to the table, you won the item. How difficult could that be?

But we watched the game and noticed that no one was winning. "Hey, Mister. How do we know those rings will fit over those prizes?" Dougie inquired.

"Here, watch this," the man said, and he dropped a ring over one of the prizes and it fell to the table. "You have to do it just right," he said, smiling at us. "Six rings for a quarter. How many do you want?"

We were challenged. We huddled and decided to try to get a better deal. "How many do you get for more money?" Chick asked.

"Fifteen rings for fifty cents, or thirty-five rings for a dollar," the man answered.

"Thirty-five for a dollar! Let's pool our money and we'll have lots more chances," Chick figured out. We bamboozled the man by each giving Chick a quarter and he was then able to buy thirty-five rings. We divided them up, each getting nine, except Dougie, who settled for eight. What a deal-nine rings for a quarter!

The table had some interesting things on it. A block in the middle displayed a gold watch. Another block held a genuine leather wallet and still another had a fancy hunting knife. Around the edges of the table were blocks with lesser prizes, but we didn't care-a prize was a prize, and we intended to get lots of them.

We spread out around the tent and pushed as close to the plank as possible, took careful aim, and tossed our rings. Mine hit the edge of a block and bounced off the table onto the ground. Dougie's hit a block but hung on the edge, and Chick's fell between two blocks on the table. Dewey's ring hit a block, looped around it, and came to rest on the table. A winner! "Hey, hey! There's a prize going out to this young man!" the man announced. He picked up Dewey's ring and reached into a box under the counter and handed Dewey something that looked like an open-ended straw tube.

"What the heck is this thing?" Dewey questioned, as he turned the prize over and over in his hands.

"It's a Chinese Finger Trap," the man said. "Put a finger in each end and then you're trapped."

Dewey put his index finger in each end and then tried to pull them out. The woven straw tube contracted and his fingers were stuck. "Hey! This is cool," Dewey said, as he pulled and tugged, trying to free his fingers. We laughed at Dewey and his prize, and he finally figured out that if he pushed to loosen it, his fingers would slip out.

We took another turn and this time I got a ringer. "Hey, another prize!" the man shouted. He handed me a pair of chopsticks.

"Gee, thanks. Now if I ever go to China, I'll be able to eat," I said, looking at the crappy prize. Next round Chick got one of those finger trap things and Dougie won a whistle that unrolled like a snake when you blew, then rolled up again. Dewey got a Hawaiian necklace on the next round. We won prizes but they were just crap; all junk prizes. We had used most of our chances.

"Hey, Mister, let's see you drop a ring around the watch," Dougie said.

"What? Don't you guys trust me?" the man asked. "No," Dougie snapped.

The man took a ring out of his apron pocket and dropped it over the watch. It whirled around the block and dropped to the bottom. "See? You just need to know how to toss the ring," the man said, picking up the ring and shoving it back into his apron pocket.

"You're right," Dougie said. "I have one ring left. Would you mind trading rings with me?"

A worried look came over the man's face. "Just throw the ring, kid. They're all the same."

"Well, if they're the same, let me use that one," Dougie said.

"Hey, look guys. There's our friend Mr. Audetta, the policeman. Let's see if he thinks I should get the ring of my choice," Dougie said.

The man moved over by Dougie. "Here, kid! Take the ring.

You have to hit the target anyway, so what's the difference?" Dougie smiled. Then he took careful aim and tossed the ring. It hit the watch block and caught on the edge, rolled to the side, and then dropped over the block and landed on the table.

"Ok, I'll have the watch," Dougie said. Strangely, the man didn't announce the win, but he looked rather sick as he picked up the ring. He reached into a box under the counter and took out a little black box with a watch and handed it to Dougie.

"Here. Now beat it," were his words.

"Oh, Mister," Chick said. "I want to try Dougie's lucky ring for my last chance."

Mr. Audetta was now standing nearby and watching. The man traded rings for Chick's last toss. Chick repeated Dougie's throw and won a watch. Of course, Dewey and I weren't going to let a chance like this get by us, so we both requested the lucky ring in turn. A few minutes later the four of us were walking across the carnival grounds sporting our sparkling new; gold watches. Mr. Audetta walked with us, listening to our story about how we had figured out the man's scam. He smiled and laughed and told us to have fun as he walked toward the hot dog stand.

We were proud of ourselves, so we decided to try another game, similar to the last one, except that the table had a display of dishes. There were glasses, plates, bowls, and larger dishes. The object of the game was to throw a nickel at a dish and if it landed in the dish, you won it. That shouldn't be too tough to pull off. Others were already playing the game, so we spread out to see if we could uncover any trick. After watching for a while, we could see that it was more difficult than it looked. The glasses were small targets and if you tried for a plate, the nickel seemed to glance off and land on the table or slide off to the ground. We huddled and talked it over.

"I think putting a spin on the nickel might be the trick," Dougie said.

"Line it up so it will glance off one dish, which will slow it down, and it will land in the dish behind," Chick said.

"Aim good," Dewey said.

We got our nickels and spread out. Dougie was the first to win a dish with his spinning-nickel technique. Then I got one; then Chick, and then Dougie. Dewey got a big bowl. We were getting dishes one after another. The poor man could hardly keep up with us. He was losing prizes faster than he could count. We flipped nickels for a half hour and collected a stack of dishes.

"Our moms will be delighted," Chick said.

"No kiddin'. We'll be in good with them for months," Dougie said. The man was helpful and gave us each a box for hauling our dishes since he had many empty ones by the time we were finished.

"It wouldn't hurt my feelings if you guys didn't come back," he grumbled.

"Okay, Mister. Thanks for all the dishes," I said.

The dishes were in orange and pink hues; shiny and fancy.

Since we had won so much loot, we decided to take our prizes home before the evening events. My mom was so surprised. She stacked the dishes away in the cupboard and said she intended to use them on special occasions because they were so elaborate. I was indeed proud of myself.

We met up again at suppertime and ate hot dogs and a hamburger each, and then we topped the meal off with a candy apple and a snow cone. The playground at St. John's was packed with people and music filled the air along with the mouth-watering aromas of food and carnival treats.

"How did your mom like the dishes?" I asked the guys. "Great!" Dougie said. "She's going to use them at holidays and stuff."

"Mine, too," Chick said.

"Yeah! My mom thought they were too special for everyday use," said Dewey. "Guess they are all taking extra good care of them."

We had one last game to try. This tent had a table in the middle with a display of small glass bowls filled with water and each bowl had a goldfish swimming around. If you could toss a ping-pong ball into a bowl, you won the fish. We bargained for a good deal on balls and we had great fun winning fish for the next hour or so. By the time we ran out of money and balls, we each had a plastic bag with a half dozen goldfish.

We took our fish home and got them settled. Then we went back to St. John's and strolled around the playground, talking to our friends, and showing off our new watches. Soon it was time for the festival to close. There was a chill in the air when we headed to our bikes.

"Want to sleep out tonight?" I said.

"Yeah, let's sleep out," Dougie said.

"Sure, let's," Dewey said.

"Count me in," Chick agreed.

We rode to my house and the guys called their parents to inform them of our plan and then we crawled into the tent. Our sleeping bags were stretched out, ready to go, so we quickly settled in. It had been a long day but we had done well for ourselves.

"We really fixed that guy with the watches," Dougie laughed. "That was pretty smart of you to figure out that his ring was bigger," I said.

"Yeah, Dougie. Thanks for the new watch," Dewey said. "Yeah, thanks," we all chorused. We talked and laughed, and Dewey added a little noise to the conversation, and it wasn't long until we drifted off to sleep-four tired boys with four new watches, and four happy moms with cupboards full of fancy dishes.

It's funny though, as I think back, I don't remember my mom ever using those dishes. Maybe she thought they were too pretty to use, or maybe she forgot where she put them.

Boy Scouts

Dewey, Chick, and I were in my backyard throwing shelled corn to my chickens and pigeons when Dougie rode in, knees flying. He slammed on his brakes, throwing up a dust cloud and loose gravel. "What's your hurry?" Dewey said, fanning the dust away.

"Did you guys hear about the Boy Scout troop that's gonna start?" Dougie announced, excitedly.

"No. Are you sure?" I asked.

"Yeah! There's a meeting next week. My dad saw it in the newspaper," Dougie said, producing a folded copy from his back pocket. We gathered around, spread the paper out, and began reading.

"Local Boy Scout Troop Being Organized," the headline read. Dougie began, "There will be a meeting next Monday at the Municipal Building to organize a Boy Scout troop for the area. Local boys, ages 12 and up, are invited to attend the meeting and if there is enough interest, a new Scout troop will be formed." The article went on to explain the scouting program and it gave the time and other information.

"Wow! How cool! We would get uniforms and do all kinds of neat stuff in the Boy Scouts," Dewey said.

"Yeah! They get merit badges and stuff. Let's go," Chick said.

We agreed. That evening we talked to our parents about financing us in the Boy Scouts. Of course, what parent would say no to a boy who wanted to be a Scout?

We rode to the Municipal Building on the evening of the meeting. As we arrived, two of the town's biggest bullies rode up on their bikes. They were a year older than we were. Immediately, Roger came over and began to pester Dewey.

"Hey, fat boy! Your pants look like they're gonna fall off," he said, as he grabbed Dewey's pants and pulled them almost up to his armpits.

"Cut it out, you puke!" Dewey said.

"Oooh , I'm scared of you," Roger mocked, letting go of Dewey. Dewey adjusted his pants and then pulled the wedgie out of his backside. Then Mike, the other bully, grabbed my bike and took off with it. He rode fast, then slammed on the brakes and made a skid mark. "Cut it out! You're gonna ruin my tires!" I yelled. He laughed and continued his sport of wearing down my tires. I took off after him, yelling, just as Roger started for Dougie's bike, planning to do the same thing, when Mr. McQuillan, who was going to be the Scout leader, came out of the building.

"You guys get off those bikes!" he yelled at Mike and Roger.

They stopped and came back. "Do those bikes belong to you?" he asked.

"No, but these guys don't care if we use them," Mike said, looking at us and giving us a warning glance.

"The heck we don't," said Chick. "These boneheads think they can pick on anyone. They come on like tough guys. Let's see how tough you are," he said, walking toward Mike. Chick wasn't scared of anybody.

"Hold it! Nobody's gonna show anybody anything. Do you guys want to be Scouts, or not?" We were mad as heck but we wanted to be Scouts, so we backed down, and Mike and Roger laughed and walked into the building.

There was much interest in a scouting program so a troop was organized that night. We paid our dues and were sworn in. Mike and Roger joined, too, but I think they wanted membership just to gain access to more victims to bully.

We met every Monday evening and we soon had a fun group, with the exception of Mike and Roger, who didn't pitch in. We would work on merit badges and projects and then Mike and Roger would show up in time to share in the credit. I think Mr. McQuillan was wise to their strategy but he didn't say anything.

One Monday, Mr. McQuillan told us we were going to have a camp out at the Mill Dam. Although the four of us slept out most nights anyway, it would be great fun to camp in a big group. We gathered tents and gear and we met at the Municipal Building the following Friday afternoon. After loading our gear onto several pickup trucks, we set off for the Mill Dam. There was a picturesque flat meadow on the other side of the Mill Pond that made a great camping site. We pitched our tents, gathered rocks for a fire pit, and got our campsite organized. The canoes were brought off the trucks and a few guys paddled them across the pond so they would be ready for canoeing the next day. That evening we roasted hot dogs and had pop, chips, and S'mores. Then we sat around the campfire and told stories, laughed, and had a great time.

Typically, Mike and Roger didn't join in. They sat to the side and made smart remarks about the stories we were telling and joked about some of the kids. "Why don't you two get in your tent and shut up?" I said. Roger glared at me, but the rest of the guys backed me, and soon he and Mike walked off to their tent. Our Scout leaders decided to go to bed, too, and told us to make sure the fire was out when we turned in. ''And, don't get into trouble."

"Who, us?" we thought to ourselves.

We waited until everything quieted down and then we huddled together and spoke, ''Any of you guys sick and tired of Mike and Roger?" Chick whispered.

"Yeah! We're all sick of them," said a kid who had his S'mores "borrowed" by Mike.

"I think it is time for a lesson," I said. "What are we gonna do?" another kid asked. "Here's the idea," Dougie said.

We shared the plan that Dewey, Dougie, Chick, and I had devised upon learning of the camp out at the Mill Dam. Of course, we knew the area so well that it was easy to think of something. Everyone agreed, so we crept to Mike and Roger's tent and listened. We knew they were sleeping by their breathing. Dewey sat down, took off his shoes and socks, and then he, Chick, and two other big guys crawled into the tent. "Now!" Chick whispered, and two boys jumped on the sleeping bullies; Dewey and Chick on top of Mike, and Charlie and Ben on top of Roger. One guy shoved a sock into the mouth of each victim. By this time, their mouths were open to shout, so the socks went in easily. The rest of us then jumped into the tent and held them down. They were mad, cussing at us through the socks.

Once they were pinned down, we took rope and tied them up, like a couple of hogs, and carried them to the shore of the Mill Pond. We put them into one of the canoes and the rest of us got into the other canoes and paddled to the middle of the pond. We towed Mike and Roger's canoe behind. When we got to the middle, we stopped and Dougie stood up in his canoe.

"Mike and Roger, you guys are bullies and lazy and we don't want you in our Boy Scout troop."

The two of them, mad as heck, were trying to break free from the ropes and spit out the socks that were in their mouths.

"I now call a vote. Boy Scout troop 133 will decide if you can remain members," Dougie spoke in an official manner.

One by one, each member had his say. "It is unanimous," Dougie announced, "You are hereby voted out of the troop."

"Punishment is due!" Dewey said.

"What is the punishment for being a bully?" Dougie said.

"Drown them!" the littlest kid in the troop said.

"Any other ideas?" Dougie asked. "Okay. It seems that the troop has spoken; drowning it will be."

By now, Mike and Roger had quieted down and were looking scared. "Mo may," Mike said.

"What's that? No way?" Dougie said, and smiled evilly.

"Way."

We moved our canoes close enough to slightly tip Mike and Roger's canoe and it began to take in water. They whined and cried as they got wet and their canoe was sinking lower and lower in the water. We were silent and staring, then we tipped the canoe over, and the two bullies went into the water. We grabbed their canoe and took it with us as we paddled back.

Then, from a distance, we laughed and laughed as they sat in fifteen inches of water. Dewey, Chick, Dougie, and I knew that there was only a little water in the pond, and lots of mud, but Mike and Roger didn't know that. They thought they were going to the bottom. They began wriggling out of their ropes, trying to stand up and come after us, but they sank to their knees in the mud. The farther they came toward us, the deeper they went into the mud, and finally they were in up to their waists. Mike managed to get his hands loose and he untied Roger. They pulled the socks out of their mouths and began shouting threats of murder at us. We hurried back to our tents and pretended to be asleep. Soon their noise awakened the leaders.

Mr. McQuillan walked to the edge of the pond and shined his flashlight onto the water. By now, we all had come out of our tents, yawning, and stretching. The flashlight caught Mike and Roger, and they looked like a couple of creatures from the Black Lagoon. They were covered from head to toe with the black, stinky mud and were crawling toward the shore.

"What do you two think you're doing? You didn't have permission to go swimming," Mr. McQuillan said.

"Swimming? You think this looks like swimming?" Roger screamed.

"Those little snots tried to drown us!" Mike yelled.

We all looked at each other like we had no idea what was going on.

"You're trying to blame your foolishness on these boys? Get in here, you're confined to your tent for the night, and I'm taking you back to town first thing in the morning. You're out of the troop."

"But, they .... But, but ... " was all they could mutter.

"No excuses. You were swimming without permission. You're out of here," was the reply.

We hustled back to our tents and laughed and giggled for an hour. We could hear Mike and Roger trying to "de-mud" and cussing us for the prank we had pulled.

The next morning, we watched as Mr. McQuillan made Mike and Roger take their tent down and pack up their stuff. Everything they owned was coated in mud. Mike and Roger were still covered with the stuff but, by this time, it had dried and they made a lot of dust as they worked. They packed up and began hiking up the hill to the other side of the pond. An assistant leader was to haul them back to town. "Bye, boys," someone shouted. They didn't even turn around. Mr. McQuillan stayed with us.

"Well, gentlemen, how about breakfast?" he asked. "That sounds good! We're famished," Dewey said.

"Why so hungry? You guys just slept all night, didn't you?" he said, smiling.

"Uh, yeah, sure! We went to bed and fell asleep, immediately," Dougie said.

"That's what I thought. You know, Mike and Roger said you guys tried to drown them. What a story!" we all laughed. Yeah! What a story!

"What a story! How could they have possibly drowned in twelve inches of water?" Dougie said.

Mr. McQuillan smiled. He knew what had gone on and was probably glad to be rid of Mike and Roger, too.

Our troop was much improved after their departure and we spent many great weekends camping and working on our merit badges. Mike and Roger never bothered us again. I think they feared the whole bunch would come against them and they weren't so sure that we would dump them in shallow water next time around.

A Full Day of Fun?

Dewey came down the alley and pulled his bike up next to the picnic table where I was sorting through stuff in my new tackle box. My grandparents had visited over the weekend, and good, old gramps had brought me this as a gift. He worked at the Coast to Coast store and he always brought me the latest in fishing gear from the fishing department. I was a lucky guy because I was the first grandson. The tackle box was shiny and beautiful. Gramps had included a roll of cork sheeting which could be cut into small pieces and placed in the bottom of the various compartments to separate and protect the lures and stuff It also made my tackle box look really cool.

"Nice tackle box! Where did you get it? Your grandpa?" questioned Dewey.

"Of course. You don't think I've got money to buy something like this, do you?" I said.

"I wish my grandpa worked at a fishing store," Dewey said. "What ya gonna do today?" he asked.

"Chick and Dougie are coming over and we're gonna wash my mom's car," I said. "Then, we'll probably fish."

Just then Chick and Dougie rode into the yard. "Wow! Neat!"

Dougie said, as he examined my new treasure. "Grandpa?"

"Yup."

"Cool! Now we got all the tackle we need. We won't have to use our tackle boxes," Chick said.

"Think again. You guys aren't gonna use my stuff," I said, closing the box and latching the top.

"You guys ready to wash the car?" They were, so I went into the house and told mom we were ready to start. "I'll drive it to the backyard," I said.

"What? I don't think so," she said.

"Oh, come on! I know how to drive. It's only around the corner," I begged.

"Okay, but the rest of those outlaws can't ride with you," she instructed.

She tossed me the keys and I ran out the door.

"You guys get the hose out and put water in that pail while I drive around to the backyard," I said.

"What? You get to drive it?" the guys wondered.

"Sure. It's no big deal," I said, like it was an everyday thing.

"Just stay out of the way," I said.

"I'll be in the tree," Chick said. We all laughed at Chick's joke.

I ran to the street and got into the car. I rolled down the window, adjusted the seat, tilted the mirrors, and got situated in the seat. I turned the key and found a cool song on the radio, so I turned up the volume to a deafening level. Then I signaled, looked over my shoulder to check for traffic, and put the car into drive. I cruised about fifty feet to the corner, stopped, signaled a right turn, turned, went about fifty yards, stopped, and signaled a right turn. I went another fifty feet to our yard and stopped, and just to be safe, I signaled a right turn and drove into the backyard.

Dewey and Dougie were sitting on the picnic table watching, and Chick was gazing down from the tree. I drove up to the picnic table, put the brakes on, and put the car in park. Then I turned off the ignition and, just for good measure, I blew the horn to signal my arrival.

Dewey and Dougie gave me a good hand clapping and Chick jumped down and yelled, "Bravo!"

"That was cool," Dewey said. "You gonna drive it back to the front when we're done?"

"Probably," I said, "It's no big deal." They were real impressed with my driving abilities, and so was I.

We were washing the car and soon Chick splashed a sponge full of soapy water on Dewey. Dewey grabbed the hose and shot water at Chick, who ran behind Dougie, who ended up getting wet. "You bonehead!" Dougie yelled, as he threw a soaked sponge at Dewey. Dewey dropped the hose and ducked behind the car when he saw the sponge coming. I grabbed the hose. I sprayed Chick and chased Dewey around the yard. Chick picked up the hose, bent it in half, and cut off my water supply. There was a still a dribble of water so I swung it back and forth, splashing at least some water at him. He raised his arm to protect himself, and the metal end on the hose nailed him on the elbow.

Chick stood there looking goofy for a second and then he dropped the hose and fell over on his face. I thought he was pretending to be dead so I soaked him good with the hose. He didn't move.

"Is he hurt?" Dougie shouted. I stopped the squirting business and he still laid there in the grass, like he was dead.

"Oh man, you killed him," Dewey said. "I only hit him in the arm," I said.

We rolled Chick over. His eyes were half closed, but he was breathing.

"He's not dead. I think he's knocked out," Dougie said. "How can he be knocked out? He got hit in the arm," I said. Chick began to move and his eyes opened. "What happened to me?" he muttered.

"You got knocked out," Dewey said.

Chick moved his arm back and forth and let out a yelp. "Ow! My elbow hurts like heck." We helped him to the picnic table.

"Do you remember me hitting you in the arm?" I asked. "Yeah. Then I heard a high-pitched noise in my ears and everything went black. Did you hose me while I was knocked out?" he asked, looking at his wet clothes.

"Yeah, sorry. I thought you were pretending to be dead," I confessed.

"You must have hit a nerve and caused him to pass out," Dougie said.

"Cool! I never saw anybody pass out before," Dewey said. "Well, I'm okay now. Let's finish up but no more water fights," Chick said.

"If I remember right, you were the one that started the water fight," I said. Chick shrugged his shoulders and grinned.

We finished the car and I made a big deal over driving it back to the street in front of the house. It was a grand affair, and I parked it carefully against the curb and returned the keys to mom.

Since it was lunchtime, mom brought a tray of food to the picnic table. She had a stack of sandwiches, chips, cookies, and Kool-Aid. It didn't take long for the food to disappear and the guys left to get their fishing gear, and then we headed for the Gosey.

It was our standard practice to fish either above or below the swimming hole because we thought it wasn't a good idea to have fish hooks stuck in roots and logs in the water where we swam, especially after witnessing the incident with Johnny and the Daredevil earlier in the summer.

The remnants of an old fence stopped abruptly the edge of the river. It was easy to climb, so when we fished there, we just stepped over it. I was above the fence fishing and had caught a few nice bluegills when Dewey came up. He threw his bobber and hook but it caught in a tree. "Dang, I'm hung up," he said. He pulled and shook his pole, and finally the hook, sinker, and bobber broke off He laid his pole in the grass and climbed over the fence to replace his lost tackle. As he stepped over, the crotch of his shorts caught on the top of the fence and he ripped his pants open. "Jeez! My mom will kill me. These shorts are new," he whined. He picked up my tackle box and was carrying it back.

"Hey, why are bringing my box? Don't you have anything in your box?" I said.

"I'm out of bobbers. You'll lend me one, won't you, good buddy?" he begged.

When Dewey got to the fence, instead of stepping over like we always did, he swung out over the river at the end of the fence. He held on to the end fence post and swung around it. When he was halfway around, the arm holding my tackle box smacked against the fence post and the tackle box latch flew open. The contents hit the water and the little pieces of cork sheeting were floating on the surface.

"Yikes!" screamed Dewey.

I looked up to see my box hanging from his hand, open, and upside down. I ran over and saw the little pieces of cork floating down the river along with my bobbers and floating lures. My *Bass o Reno, Hula Popper, and Rapalas* were going down the river and the rest of my stuff was on the river bottom.

"Dewey! You idiot! You dumped all my stuff in the river!" I was ready to strangle him.

"I didn't do anything. It had a bad latch," he said, defensively and he climbed back to the other side of the fence.

Just then Dougie and Chick came running up and they took off their shoes and jumped into the river to collect the lures and cork pieces that were floating away. I looked into the water; it was pretty shallow and most of the heavy stuff was on the bottom.

"Get your shoes off and help me gather up the stuff," I said to Dewey. We worked together for about fifteen minutes. Dougie and Chick had the floating things and returned them to the tackle box.

"Whew, it looks like we got it all," Dewey said, cheerfully.

"Yeah, that's great, Dewey. Remember how nice the box looked before you put your meat hooks on it? Now look. It's a disaster!" I said.

"You're too fussy about your tackle box. Mine looks like this all the time," Dewey said.

I grabbed for him but Dougie stopped me.

"C'mon. It was an accident. I'll help you sort it out tomorrow," he promised. Good, old Dougie. He was always the peacemaker.

"Well, we might as well fish a while yet," Chick said. We took our poles and climbed the fence. We had probably scared the fish away so we needed to move upriver. Dougie cast a red and white Daredevil near a brush pile. He had turned his reel only a few turns when a good-sized fish boiled at his lure and grabbed it. "I got one!" he yelled. His drag was screaming out and he played the fish like an expert. We could see it was a big dogfish. "Oh boy! A dog," Dougie said.

Dogfish were about the ugliest fish in the river, but they were strong and fighting.

"Be careful. He's hooked loosely," I said. The hook was barely caught in the lip.

"I'll bring him in close and you grab him and toss him on the bank," Dougie said.

I stretched out on the bank and got ready. As the fish got close enough for me to reach, he made a big splash and tried for deeper water. When he pulled against the hook, it popped free and flew over my head. "Dang! He came off," I said. "It's a good thing I was lying down or I'd have that hook in my head," I said, as I got to my feet.

I turned around and looked at Dougie staring at his right forearm. The Daredevil had snapped in the air and had landed on him, and two of the three hooks were imbedded in his arm.

"Jeez, Dougie! Are you okay?" I panicked.

Dougie stared at the hooks and then looked at me. "Um, I've been better. As you can see, I have a Daredevil in my arm." He was very calm.

"Does it hurt?" I asked, awkwardly.

"Yup, like real bad."

"Hey, guys! Come here. Dougie's hooked," I yelled to Chick and Dewey.

"Wow! That must hurt," Dewey sympathized.

"No crap, Sherlock! What was your first clue?" Dougie said.

We snickered at that but it wasn't funny to see Dougie in so much pain.

"Cut the line, and let's take a look at it," Chick said. I got out my pocketknife and carefully cut the line. Dougie grimaced in pain as I touched the Daredevil.

"Whew, that's really stuck in. Maybe we should see a doctor," I said.

"Let me see," Chick said. He took Dougie's arm and carefully looked at it and touched the hook to see how deeply it was lodged. Dougie gritted his teeth but he didn't pull away.

"See if you can move the hook," Dougie said. Chick took it and pulled it backward slowly.

"It won't come out. It's in past the barb," he said. "Try pushing it all the way through," Dougie said. Chick looked at him. "Are you sure?"

"Yeah, go ahead and try it," repeated Dougie.

Dewey was turning white and wobbling around like he was going to pass out. "Sit down Dewey. We don't need you to faint and fall in the river. Then we would need a crane to haul you out."

Chick pushed the hook so you could see the points just under the skin. Dougie gasped but didn't say stop, so Chick kept pushing. The skin came up to two little points that first turned red and then white and then the points of two hooks popped through. Dougie let out his breath, and so did the rest of us. "Okay, push them till the barb is through," Dougie said. Chick began pushing again and soon the barbs were out. We all breathed again. Dougie looked at me. "Can you cut the barbs off with your pliers?" As much as I wanted to say no, I nodded my head and got the pliers from my tackle box. "Now, push them up so he can cut them," Dougie said to Chick and me. Dewey turned his head. He didn't want to look.

I put the side cutter of the pliers on the first hook point and applied pressure. I heard Dougie take a deep breath and hold it, and I squeezed the pliers and the hook point popped off. One down. We took a breather and wiped the sweat off our foreheads. I gripped the other barb and cut it off. Chick backed the hooks out of Dougie's arm.

"Whew!" we sighed simultaneously.

Dougie grinned at us. "Well, you two should be doctors."

"No way! I about puked when those hooks came through," Chick said.

"Me, either. That is the only operation I ever want to do," I said.

Dewey looked up from the ground and shook his head. "I don't think that would be a good idea for me, either, I'd probably pass out every time I saw blood." We all laughed at Dewey.

Surprisingly there wasn't much blood on Dougie's arm. Just a couple of holes with a little bleeding. He worked his fingers back and forth and all seemed to be okay. "Well, I guess I'm ready to fish again, but my Daredevil is ruined," he laughed.

"I'll lend you one of mine, but I'm not going to fish next to you," I said.

We spent another couple hours fishing and talking and laughing. It was close to suppertime and so we headed home. Chick dropped off first. "Later, guys," he said, as he turned down his street. Next came Dewey. He turned off and waved.

"See ya guys tomorrow?" and Dewey signed off.

"Yeah, Dewey. Tomorrow it is," we answered.

We came to Dougie's house. We stopped in front. "Well, thanks for fixing my arm," he said.

"No problem, pal. I don't think I could have done what you did, letting us push that hook through," I said.

"I knew you guys could do it. You're my best friends and friends do their best for each other." He punched me in the shoulder. We grinned, and I punched him back. "I'll come over and help you sort your tackle box tomorrow morning," he said, and he pulled into his yard. "See ya," and he waved.

"See ya, Dougie," I replied.

I rode the two blocks to my house feeling pretty good. What started out simple had become pretty crazy, but it all worked out in the end. With friends like Dougie, Dewey, and Chick, every day was a memorable adventure.

One Potato, Two Potatoes

I was feeding my critters as Dougie rode up. "Hey, you want a job?" he said, as he skidded to a stop.

"What job?" I asked.

"My dad was at the grocery store and heard they want to hire a few kids to sort potatoes."

"Sort potatoes?" I asked.

"Yeah! They'll pay $2.50 an hour," he stated.

"Great! At $2.50 an hour, we'd be rich in no time! You bet! Let's go," I said, eagerly.

"I've called Dewey and Chick and they're gonna meet us at the store," Dougie said, getting on his bike. I ran to the house and told my mom I was going to the grocery store to work and that I would be back later. Then Dougie and I rode uptown.

About a block from the store, I began to notice a terrible smell. "Whew, what's that?" I choked.

"Jeez, I don't know, but it smells rotten," Dougie said. We rode on and the stench became stronger. As we rounded the corner by the grocery store, we could see a semi parked at the back of the store. Dewey and Chick were standing by the truck, looking inside.

"Dewey, is that smell you?" Dougie yelled. Dougie and I began laughing at his joke.

"Not quite, Douglas, but why don't you come here and take a look?" Dewey said.

Dougie and I parked our bikes and walked over. The doors were open and the truck was piled to the ceiling with burlap bags full of potatoes. The smell was incredible; like a road-killed raccoon that had been sun-dried for a week. "We have to sort these potatoes?" I asked.

The store owner put his head out the back door. "You guys want to work?" he inquired.

"What is the job?" Chick said.

"Some of these potatoes have spoiled so we're going to dump them into several cow-watering tanks, wash and sort them, and bag up the good ones. I'll pay you $2.50 an hour," he offered.

"This whole truckload?" Dougie asked. "Yep!" he stated.

We looked at each other and Dewey spoke up. "Okay, I guess we'll do it." We nodded.

The owner left and soon came back with a pickup truck loaded with three cow tanks. We pulled them off the truck and placed them on the ground behind the semi. "We'll fill these tanks with water, then dump the potatoes in this one, sort out the good ones, and put them in the second tank. Then you guys can wash them off and put them into the third tank for rinsing before the final bagging. Any questions?" he asked.

We didn't have any, so he began filling the tanks with a hose and we climbed into the back of the semi and began to pass the bags of potatoes out the back door of the trailer. The smell was so strong, it made our eyes water. The bags of potatoes weighed 50 pounds each so we couldn't carry them; we had to drag them across the floor to the door. Not only did the sacks stink, they also oozed rotten potato juice, and soon the floor was slippery with the yucky smelling stuff.

"Whoa, I think I'm gonna puke," Dewey announced. "C'mon Dewey. This should be easy for you. You're used to rank smells," Chick said. We all laughed at Chick.

With the potatoes on the ground, we cut the strings to open the bags, then dumped the potatoes into the first tank, water and rotten potato juice splattering all over. When the tank was almost full, Dougie and I began sorting through the smelly mess, tossing good potatoes into the second tank. Dewey and Chick swished the potatoes around in that tank and then tossed them into the third tank. If one of us would get ahead, he would go to the third tank, fish out the good potatoes, and put them in clean burlap bags. These were stored against the back wall of the store for drying.

The first tank was soon filled with pungent smelling water and tons of rotten potatoes. Then we had to take a big shovel and scoop the potatoes out of the water and into the back of the pickup truck. We tipped the tank to empty it and then filled it with fresh water. The smell intensified as we worked, attracting every fly within five miles.

After several hours, our boss told us to take a break. He went into the store and returned with a bottle of pop for each of us. We sat in the shade behind the truck and sipped our pop. "This has to be the worst job in the world," Chick commented.

"It probably stinks more than any other job," Dougie said. "Yeah, except for working on the rendering truck," I said.

"Oh yeah, the gut wagon. That has to be pretty bad, too." Dewey said.

We laughed at the thought of the gut wagon, figuring that it would be worse to work with dead cows than with rotten potatoes. "Well, boys, time to get back at it," our boss said.

We had about a third of the potatoes unloaded and washed by noon. We were covered with potato juice, dirt, and mud, and not smelling good ourselves. The noon siren blew and our boss told us to take an hour off for lunch. "You guys wanna come over and have lunch at my place?" Dougie said. "My mom has hotdogs and we could grill out." That sounded like a great idea so off we went to Dougie's. Chick and Dewey got the charcoal out of Dougie's garage and they were going to light the grill while Dougie and I got the hotdogs and stuff from indoors. His mom was upstairs when we walked in. "Hey, Mom! The guys and I are gonna barbeque hotdogs for lunch, okay?"

"Sure, I'll be right down to help you," her voice trailed down from the bedroom.

We were gathering up chips, cookies, and ketchup when Dougie's mom came down the stairs. "Good God! What's that terrible smell?" she asked.

Dougie and I looked at each other.

"I don't smell anything, Mom," he said. "Me, either," I said.

She sniffed the air as she came closer to us. "My goodness, you two stink. What are you covered with?" We looked at each other and saw the dried potato juice and dirt.

"Well, it might be rotten potato juice," Dougie said, sheepishly.

"You guys get outside. You'll stink up the whole house. I'll bring the stuff out to you," she said, shooing us out the door.

Dewey and Chick had the fire going and we were soon cremating wieners and stuffing chips and cookies into our mouths until there wasn't a scrap of food left. "Yummy! That was good. Now, for a little nap, and I'll be ready to work again." Dewey said. We had about a half hour to snooze, so we stretched out in the shade. It seemed like just a few seconds until Dougie's mom came out of the house.

"You guys are late for work. Someone called from the store to ask about you," she announced. We jumped on our bikes and rode like the wind to the store. This time it didn't seem like the smell was so bad. Guess we had become accustomed to it.

The truck was about half unloaded. Chick and Dewey climbed into the trailer and began dragging sacks of potatoes to the door to dump them. It wasn't long until Dewey appeared at the door. "C'mere, guys, Chick's stuck."

Dougie and I climbed into the truck and walked to Dewey who was peering over the pile of potatoes.

"Where's Chick?" I questioned.

"I'm down here," Chick said, from behind the pile of potatoes.

"Where?" echoed Dougie. "Down here," hollered Chick.

I saw his hand projecting from the pile of potatoes. "How did you get down there?" Dougie inquired.

"I crawled on top of the pile to see how far we had to go yet and I sank between the bags of potatoes. I can't get out!"

Dougie and I crawled up and saw Chick's head sticking up out of the pile.

"Hi, Chick. What are you doing in such a nasty place?"

Dougie said, laughing.

"Real funny. Get me out of here. I can barely breathe," he gagged.

Dougie and I began pulling bags of potatoes to the edge and Dewey dragged them to the back of the truck. It took some time to reach Chick. Every time he moved, he went deeper into the potatoes. Finally, his elbows and arms were free, and by pulling, and him pushing, we freed him.

"Are you okay?" I asked.

"Yeah, I think so, but I'm sure covered with potato juice, and I've got the world's worst wedgie," Chick said.

Dougie and I started laughing at that, and while we were rolling in laughter, Chick was pulling and tugging on his underwear to get rid of his wedgie.

It was past suppertime when we finally got the last of the potatoes dumped, washed, and bagged. We cleaned up the cow tanks and used the hose to rinse the potato slime off the parking lot. When our boss paid us $20 each, we felt like kings!

"We should celebrate," Dougie said.

"Sure! Let's eat at the A & W tonight," I said. "Yeah, let's," the rest agreed.

"We need to clean up first. Let's meet there in a half hour," Dougie said. We headed home.

My mom just about fainted when I walked in. "Get out of here. You smell like a sewer," she barked.

"But Mom, I gotta clean up. We are going to eat at the A & W tonight," I argued.

"You're not coming in this house smelling like that. Take soap and a towel, and clean clothes, and go to your beloved Gosey to take your bath," she commanded. That was fine with me. Mom got everything ready for me while I waited outside. "Leave your stinky clothes in the yard when you come home. I'll find a way to clean them," she ordered.

I was as happy as a lark as I rode to the Gosey. When I got there, Dougie was already in the water with a bar of soap. "Your mom didn't like your smell?" I laughed.

"No kidding! She kicked me out of the house," he pouted. I stripped off my rotten-smelling clothes and jumped in the water. A minute later, Chick appeared with clean clothes, a towel, and soap.

"Ah, the communal bath," he laughed, as he stripped off clothes and waded in. "I wonder if Dewey's mom let him clean up at home?" I said. Just then, Dewey's bike rattled up.

"Hey guys, you bathing here, too?" We laughed and splashed and had a great time in the Gosey. Soon we loaded up our stuff and headed to the A & W.

We sat at one of the picnic tables under the awning and a carhop, a high school girl, came bouncing up to take our order. "Hi, guys. What would you like to eat tonight?" she asked, with a sweet grin. We were all agog when a pretty girl treated us nicely so we giggled and laughed but managed to come up with our order. She delivered our food and we devoured our meal, enjoying our time together. We paid up and left her a nice tip. It was a good thing to be rich.

"Well, what should we do now?" Dewey asked.

"Something restful. We worked hard today," Chick said. "Let's go to the Gosey and watch fireflies," Dougie suggested. "Good idea," I said.

We rode to the Gosey and sat on the bank. It was dusk and soon we saw the first flicker of fireflies in the shadows. We sat there talking and laughing, with our bellies full, and our backs tired. All was well.

Hobos

I lived near the west edge of town. There were houses on the other side of my street and then the woods began. My street was blacktopped, but the roads that ran off into the woods were gravel. The sleighing hill was two blocks from my house and across the street from that, in the woods, lived a couple of hobos. Now, they weren't really hobos, in the true sense. Hobos rode trains from place to place and lived off the land and from handouts. These old guys stayed put and didn't ride trains. There were three of them. Each had a little shack made of scrap lumber, tin, and tar paper. The shanties were about ten feet square and rickety, but they seemed to be good enough to make the old guys comfortable. They walked to town every day for their daily visit and to shop for a bottle of cheap wine at the liquor store. Then they ambled back to their little shanties.

Of course, our moms told us to stay clear of them because they were drinkers and weren't a good influence on thirteen year-old boys. Our only contact with them was when they walked past my house. Occasionally Chick, Dougie, Dewey, and I would sneak down to their shanty town to sort through their pile of empty bottles, looking for returnable bottles that we could sell.

One of the old guys was called Bonnie. We wondered why he had a girl's name, but we never found out. He was a hard-looking man who always scowled and growled at us if we passed him on the street. He would often sit on a bench in front of one of the taverns with the other guys and chat the day away, chewing tobacco, and spitting on the sidewalk. The men would take a strip of inner tube from their pockets to snap at flies that came to feast on the spit. Some of them would talk to us as we walked by and tell us stories, but not Bonnie. He never talked and always looked like he was mad about something. We stayed away from him.

Another old guy was Lou. He had a droopy face. The left side of his face looked like it was partly melted. He was nice enough, but scary looking. He always talked to us.

The last old guy was Fungy. He was skinny and had a sad face and a big hump on his back. He didn't say much but he seemed friendly. The kids in town made fun of him as he walked back and forth from his shanty.

One day Dougie and I were riding our bikes uptown when we met

Fungy. We pulled our bikes off the sidewalk so he could pass, and he thanked us.

"No problem, Sir," Dougie said.

Fungy stopped and looked at us. I'm sure no one had called him "sir" in a long time. His face looked kindly and he smiled and tipped his hat. We didn't think we had done anything outstanding. We got on our bikes and continued. Fungy was carrying a sack of groceries and continued towards his shanty.

We rode to Chick's house and found him painting the trim on his mom's porch. "Hey guys, I have more brushes," Chick said, cheerfully.

I looked at Dougie and we shook our heads in opposition.

"Sorry, we got something real important to do," I said. Chick began to whine but we didn't even stay to listen. Painting was not one of our favorites.

"Let's go back to my house and see what mom's got to eat," I said.

We set off and as we turned the corner, Dougie said, "Hey! What's in the street?" We checked and found a package of hot dogs.

"Where do you suppose they came from?" I said, as I picked them up.

"I'll bet Fungy dropped them," Dougie said. "He was carrying groceries."

"We should give them back to him," I said.

Dougie agreed so we rode off towards the woods. We stopped near the shanties. "Which one is his?" Dougie asked.

"I don't know," I shrugged.

"Well, I hate to just start knocking on doors. What if we meet Bonnie?" Dougie was worried about the same thing.

We didn't know what to do but we finally walked up to one of the shanties. This was a strange place. The huts were set about twenty feet apart and there were piles of bottles here and there and a place for an outdoor fire. Junk was scattered around and it looked spooky in the dim light of the woods.

"Are you boys lost?" A voice came from one of the shanties, and Dougie and I almost jumped out of our tennis shoes.

"No, we found a package of hot dogs on the street and we thought someone from here might have dropped them," I said.

The door of the middle shanty opened and Fungy walked out, all drooped over. "I was wondering about them," he said, laughing. "I thought

I was losing my mind, just dreaming that I had bought them." We laughed, too, and handed over the hot dogs.

"Here," Dougie said.

"We figured they were yours since you had a grocery bag with you earlier," we added.

"That was mighty kind of you to return them," Fungy said. "Would you boys like a cold pop?" Dougie and I looked at each other. "Sure," we said.

Fungy went into his shanty and came out with two bottles of Coke and an opener. "Don't look so shocked," he said. "I don't drink wine all the time. I like a Coke once in a while, too." We laughed and he motioned for us to sit down on the bench by the shack.

"So, you guys like to fish?" he asked.

"Yeah, we do. How d'you know?" I said.

"You've usually got poles and tackle in your bike baskets. I just figured that means you fish," Fungy laughed.

"Do you fish, Mr. Uh?" Dougie asked.

Fungy smiled. "My name is Faye, not Fungy, like you kids call me. Yeah, I fish. I used to fish a lot more till my back got so bad."

Dougie and I looked at each other. Wow! The guy fished.

"I enjoyed fishing for northerns," Faye said. "I've caught some good ones in my day, too." He looked like he was remembering long ago fishing trips.

"How did ... , I mean, what happened to your back?" I said, "...if you don't mind telling us."

"It's a spinal disease," he said. "It started when I was in the army and it kept getting worse; got so bad that I couldn't work and, well, this is where I ended up."

"You don't have a family?" Dougie asked.

"No one living, anymore," Faye said. "I get a small pension from the army that is just enough to keep me going."

Dougie and I were surprised to learn these things about Faye and also to realize that he was just an ordinary guy, similar to others, except that he had come into bad luck. We sat and talked to Faye for most of the afternoon and he told us about the army and we had a great time together. We told him about our big bass catch earlier in the summer.

"Yeah, I saw your picture in the paper," he said. "Those were some nice ones."

It was about suppertime so Dougie and I said goodbye and told Faye that we were happy that we got to know him. He told us to come back, anytime.

"Gosh, he's a nice man," Dougie said, as we headed home.

"You know, I think we should try to give him a hand; maybe help him with chores, or take him food once in a while," I said.

Dougie agreed and we both felt fortunate that we had made a new friend.

The next day the four of us were at the Gosey and we told Chick and Dewey about Faye.

"I always thought he was just a creepy guy that we should stay away from," Dewey confided.

"He's just like someone's grandpa," I said.

"If you don't look at the hump on his back, he's just a great old guy; friendly, and not a monster," Dougie elaborated.

That day we caught several catfish and a couple of bass. We decided to clean them and take a few fillets to Faye. The four of us rode to the shanties and we walked up to Faye's. I knocked on the door. He smiled from ear to ear when he saw us.

"Faye, this is Dewey and Chick. We were fishing today and got a lot of fish, so we thought you might like some for your supper," I said.

"Thanks boys. That would be great," he said, as we handed him the fish. "Could I get you a Coke, or something?"

"No, thanks," we said. "We gotta get home for supper. Maybe next time."

He thanked us again and we biked back.

"You were right," Chick said. "He's no monster."

From then on, we kept a sharp watch for stuff for Faye. We'd take him tomatoes from the garden if we had extras and carrots and potatoes as we dug them. We took him cleaned fish and managed to sneak homemade cookies and bread when we could pilfer it without getting caught. When we saw him on the street, we rode along with him and chatted and called him Faye, not Fungy. We told him about the Gosey and how we spent so much time there. He said that he swam in the Gosey when he was a kid. One day when we were fishing, Faye appeared with his fishing pole and he fished with us all afternoon. We took a swim later but he wouldn't go in the water, even though we pestered him for a half hour. He had fun just talking with us and fishing.

Sometimes we would take Cokes and chips to Faye's and sit in the shade and listen to his stories about the army and going to war, and all the other things he had done in his life. We took our own pop so we wouldn't consume his Cokes. If we took ice cream cones, we had to ride fast so his wouldn't melt. He always was happy to see us and we were happy to keep company with him.

Then one day we were headed to Faye's with half an apple pie and homemade cookies. We noticed Mr. Audetta's police car parked in the street by the shanties. We walked down the path to the shack. "What are you boys doing here?" Mr. Audetta asked.

"We came to see Faye. He's our friend. We brought pie and cookies for him," Dewey said.

A sad look came over Mr. Audetta's face. "I might have known," he said. "You guys were the friends he was talking about when he passed on."

We stood there, stunned. "Passed on?" Dougie said.

"Bonnie got me early this morning. Faye was very sick and they thought he should go to the hospital," Mr. Audetta said. "I checked and found him indeed very ill so I radioed for the ambulance. Before it got here, he was gone." The four of us just stood there staring. I could feel my eyes welling with tears but I didn't want the other guys to see. I looked away and saw the others doing the same thing.

Mr. Audetta came over and put his arms on our shoulders.

"Just before he died, Faye asked me to tell you how much he appreciated your kindness," he said. "I didn't know who he was talking about, but now, I do. Do you know how much he enjoyed your visits? You did a good thing, and made an old man very happy, right up to the minute he died."

The guys and I were speechless. We were holding sadness in and tears back and there wasn't a thing we could say that wouldn't have opened the floodgate, so we nodded our heads and walked back to our bikes. We rode to the Gosey and sat in the sand by the swimming hole. We dug our toes into the sand and stared at the river. Faye was the first person we knew well who had died. It was a new experience; one that was very hard to understand.

They buried Faye a few days later and gave him a military funeral, with a firing squad, taps, and all. They placed a flag over his casket. Bonnie, Lou, Mr. Audetta, and the four of us attended, along with other VFW guys with the firing squad, and a high school kid who played taps. It was a small funeral. When they shot the guns and played taps, we had tears streaming down our cheeks. After they buried Faye, we rode our bikes to the Gosey and sat for a long time, watching the river run, and thinking of our friend.

"He's probably fishin' in heaven," Dougie said.

"Yeah, catching huge northerns," I said, "standing straight and tall."

Big Shots

The town doctor lived across the alley from my house. His office was in the lower part of a big house and he lived upstairs. It was convenient for my family because, with three boys, there was always someone with an injury, and Dr. Klockow was great about letting us in the back door for a quick treatment. I always thought he worked too much. It seemed odd to me that he never took time off for fishing. He would go duck and pheasant hunting in the fall. Otherwise, he just worked.

He loved cars. He always had a brand new one in his driveway behind the office because every year, like clockwork, he traded cars before the old one was even broken in. I guess he could afford to do so. He also liked vintage cars. One day, while Dougie and I were feeding my critters, a flatbed trailer loaded with an old black Ford Model A pulled into the alley. Dr. Klockow came out, excited about the car, and instructed the men to put it in a shed behind his office.

"Whatcha gonna do with that old car, Doc?" I asked. "Someday I'm going to fix it up and take it for a Sunday drive," he said.

Dougie and I thought it was foolish to have a car just to drive on Sunday, but it was his money.

The car sat in the shed for many weeks and Doc, and everyone else, seemed to forget about it. But one day Dougie and I decided to get a closer look. We admitted ourselves to the shed. The outside of the car was covered with dust but inside it was clean and nice. The seats were red velvet and the side windows had little window shades. It was a four-door. The front seats had velvet backs with flower vases built into the ends. It was fancy, alright! We had thought that maybe Doc would fix it up, and then when we got old enough to drive, he would let us use it for a fishing car, but fishing cars don't have flower vases.

The next day we took Chick and Dewey to the shed to show them the car. They were admiring it and Chick suggested we see how it would be to sit in. We got in, Chick was behind the wheel, and Dougie was in the front seat with him. Dewey and I climbed in the back. We pretended that we were cruising around, waving at imaginary people, and just having a great time. We were careful not to damage anything in the few hours we fooled around.

A couple of days later, we were getting ready for a baseball game, but we had time to kill. "Hey, guys! Let's go for a drive in the old car," Dewey said. We jumped up and before long we were sitting in the car. It was Dougie's turn to drive and he shifted gears and off we went to imaginary destinations.

"Hey, guys! Look what I got from my brother!" Dewey said, producing a can of Copenhagen snuff. We looked at the little round box. "It's chew," he said. "You put a little inside your lip and it tastes good."

"Have you ever done it?" I asked.

"Not yet, but I thought it would be a good thing for a road trip," Dewey said.

None of us had ever tried chew but we had seen the old guys in town using it.

"Here," Dewey said, opening the box and holding a pinch out to me. I looked at Chick and Dougie and they nodded yes, so I took some between my first finger and thumb. "Now put it between your lower lip and teeth," Dewey said. He took a pinch and demonstrated.

Dewey passed the chew to Dougie and Chick and we all put it in our mouths at once. There was silence in the car as we got the first taste of the chew. It was hard to describe; a mint taste mixed with licorice, or something that had a strong taste. I looked at the others as they were getting their first impression, trying to figure out if they liked it or not.

"Good stuff, eh?" Dewey exclaimed.

"Yeah, good," Dougie answered.

"Yup," Chick agreed.

I just nodded. Soon my mouth began to fill with saliva.

"What do you do with all the juice?" I asked.

"Just swallow it. That's the best part," Dewey said. We nodded in agreement as if we were old hands at chewing and we began to swallow the juice. Dougie was driving and we waved at pretend people as we swallowed chew juice. Pretty soon Chick rolled down his window.

"Whew, it's getting hot in here." "No kidding," I said. "Hot as heck."

I had swallowed enough of the chew juice that my stomach felt like it had a rock in it and four or five flopping fish slapping their tails on the rock. My head was throbbing as if it could fall off my shoulders, my eyes were watering, and my ears were ringing. I looked at Dewey and he was as green as the Incredible Hulk.

"Dewey, you don't look so good," I said.

"I'm feeling pretty yucky," Dewey admitted, and he grabbed the door handle and fell to the dirt floor and threw up.

That started a chain reaction. I stuck my head out the window and blew up, too. When Dougie saw that he did the same-out the front window. Chick managed to get his door open but didn't get far enough away from Dewey and threw up all over Dewey's tennis shoes.

We got out of the car and staggered into the daylight. Dewey stopped and blew up again and so did Dougie. Chick and I both made it to the back of my chicken house before round two. The four of us weaved back and forth to the shade of our big maple tree where we stretched out on the grass, thankful for the cool breeze.

"Oh, my gosh! I think I'm gonna die," Dewey wailed.

"Great idea you had there, Dewey," Dougie said.

"Yeah! Thanks for the chew, Dewey," I added.

Chick was too weak to talk, so he just punched Dewey in the leg.

We stayed there, listening to the birds and the soothing sound of the wind, and soon we began to feel better. "What do you think, guys? Baseball time?" I asked. Everyone sat up and decided things were okay.

"Dewey, you know where you can put that chew, don't you?"

Chick asked.

"Don't worry. It's going in the trash," Dewey said. "I'm not going to show you what else I had." Of course, that heightened our interest.

"What, Dewey?" Dougie asked.

"Forget it. You'll get mad at me," Dewey said. He walked to our trashcan and threw the chew can in and then reached in his other pocket and withdrew half a pack of cigarettes. He tossed them in, too. "I think we can have fun without these," he jabbered.

We played baseball that day and continued to visit the old car for many months until one day a man came with a flatbed trailer and hauled it away. Doc never told us what happened to it. It had been a fun place to imagine adventures and it had been the place where we became introduced to chewing tobacco. The imagining had been great fun but the chew was something we never tried again. We weren't stupid. We had learned our lesson.

Mad As Hornets

The four of us were fishing above the bridge just downstream from the Gosey. Now that we were experienced river fishermen, we often fished near the bridge by the pier. The pier was left over from an old toll bridge that had been torn down long before our time. The rock pillars of the old bridge had once crossed the entire river but now most of them had been washed away by the current and ice. The one we called Snake Island-because snakes liked it there-remained. It was about fifteen feet from the shore, about twenty feet across and ten feet high.

Snake Island caused a break in the river current, creating an eddy. Fish pooled in the slack water and that was why we often fished there.

We generally used a hook, sinker, and worm and fished on the bottom, watching the tip of our pole for a bite. Sometimes we used spinners and lures, but because of their expense, we saved them for special occasions.

We were having good luck and fun-fishing, telling stories, and being teenage boys-when a man arrived on the scene and started fishing by Snake Island. He caught our attention because he looked like he had stepped off the cover of an L.L. Bean catalog. He was wearing tan chest waders, a tan shirt with those flaps

on the shoulders that made you look like you were in the army, a tan vest with about ten thousand little pockets, and a tan hat that looked like the one Sherlock Holmes wore. He was carrying a fly rod that probably cost more than all our gear put together, and that included our bikes.

"Who's that? Doctor Livingston, I presume?" Dewey said, rather loudly, and the guy looked at us.

"Shh, Dewey! That's Mr. Doctor Livingston to you," Chick laughed. We cracked up. The man continued to fish and soon he had a huge smallmouth bass making a splash behind his popping bug. He jerked back but missed the fish.

"Wow, did you see that bass?" Dougie asked. "It was huge. I hope he doesn't catch it."

We all agreed that it would be unfortunate to see a stranger catch a big bass from our river. Then the bass grabbed at his popper again. He missed it a second time. We snickered and made ourselves obnoxious. The bass smashed his popper a third time. He missed it again and this time his popper flew into the air and landed in a treetop on the bank above him. He set off up the bank to retrieve his popper. We were rolling in the sand, laughing.

I reeled in and ran up the bank to where the man had been.

I laid my pole in the grass and went in search of a frog. I spotted one and hooked him through the lips and tossed him into the current above Snake Island. As the frog made his way back to the bank, the bass grabbed him. I let the line go and waited a few seconds and then I set the hook. The bass headed upstream, jumped up out of the water, turned downstream, jumped again, and headed back toward the middle of the river. I fought the big fish like a professional and soon had him on his side next to the bank.

By that time the rest of the guys were cheering me on and when the bass came close to the bank, Dougie reached down and picked it up by the lower jaw.

"That's a good one," Chick said.

"Not bad," Dewey broke in.

The L.L. Bean guy was standing with his mouth hanging open and when Dougie held the bass up for him to see, he gave a jerk on his line, broke off his popper, and walked away. We just about split, we laughed so hard.

"Dear Chap, shall I release this little one, or will you have your picture taken with it for the cover of the next catalog?" Dougie mimicked. We roared with laughter at that, too.

"Put the little fellow back," I said, "It's not worth a photo." Dougie opened the fish's mouth and removed the hook. The frog was still hooked and although very much alive, he was probably scared to death.

Dougie took the fish and slid it back into the water and carefully unhooked the frog and let it go. It hopped up the bank along the grass until it was out of sight.

"Well, that was fun," I said, with a smirk. "I'll bet that guy never comes back here to fish."

We took up fishing again and as the afternoon wore on, it began to get real hot and humid. You could almost drink the air. Ominous thunderclouds were building in the west. "We should go to Gutweiler's Lake and fish before the rain," Dougie said. "You know how the bass and northerns bite when a storm is coming." We rolled up our lines and headed to Gutweiler's. It wasn't far from town.

We arrived and took our hooks and sinkers off and put on one of our precious northern and bass lures. My favorite and luckiest lure was my red and white *Bass 0 Reno*. Dougie had a *Bass 0 Reno*, too, but his was painted to look like a frog. Chick liked his *Johnson Silver Spoon* best and Dewey used a big *Mepps* spinner.

We cast along the shoreline, working our way down the lake.

"Whew, I'd like to take a swim," Dewey said.

"Yeah, me too. It's way too hot," Chick said.

The storm clouds were still a long way off, so we decided to take a dip to cool off. It didn't take long to get out of our shorts and shirts and soon we were in the water, splashing, and yelling, and having a great time.

"Hey, let's swim to the duck blind on the other side," Dewey said.

"Yeah, let's. I want to see it," Dougie said.

We set off across the lake to the duck blind only about a hundred yards away. It was in shallow water so when we got near it, we were able to walk through the lily pads and mud. It was a fine blind, about eight feet square, with a little place in the back to hide the hunter's boat or canoe. In the fall, it had been covered with grass, but now it was mostly chicken wire with bits of brown grass hanging here and there.

"Let's go in," Dewey said, and he climbed up the ladder into the blind. Chick went next; then Dougie; then me. As I stepped on the floor, Dewey sat down on a bench near the back. When he sat, we heard a humming noise.

"What's that?" Chick cried. Dougie and I listened. "Sounds like bees," I said.

Suddenly Dewey came running at us, screaming. Behind him were about a thousand bees buzzing and stinging and raising one heck of a noise. I was backing down the ladder and Dewey ran into me and the two of us fell into the water outside the blind. It only took about half a second for Dougie and Chick to join us. Once we were in the water, the bees began diving and landing on us, stinging us. We ran through the mud toward the deeper water and the bees followed us. When we got to deeper water, we were able to protect our bodies, but the bees kept going after our heads. We screamed and yelled and swam away as fast as we could.

Finally we had escaped the stinging monsters. We were panting and stopped to catch our breath. We had numerous stings on our faces and heads. Chick had one on his left eyelid and his eye had swollen shut. Dougie had one on his lip that made him look like a boxer that had taken a good one in the mouth. Poor Dewey had about half a dozen stings so his whole face was red and swollen out of shape. I had a couple of good ones on my right ear making it about twice its normal size.

And then the rain started. The wind picked up and we were in the middle of the lake.

"We better get out of here in case there is lightning, and we'll all get cooked," Dougie shouted over the wind. We headed for shore. It was raining so hard we could barely see ten feet in front of us. We gathered up our clothes and fishing gear and trudged back through the woods. The cool rain eased the pain of the stings, so we didn't bother to dress until we got to our bikes. Then we pulled on our drenched clothes. Dewey bent over to put his foot into his shorts and Chick began laughing. There, on Dewey's butt, were two bee stings, one in the middle of each cheek. It looked like two red eyes looking back at us. Dewey could see we were checking him out so he put his hands back to feel. "Well, it looks like I'll be riding my bike standing up," he said. We laughed like crazy and began the muddy trip to town. When we arrived, the rain had subsided and the sun was peeking through in the western sky.

"Looks like the storm is over," announced Dougie.

"Think they are still biting at the bridge?" I wondered aloud.

Dewey, Chick, and Dougie looked at each other and shrugged.

"What the heck, what else do we have to do?" Chick said. We turned toward the river and rode single file back toward the bridge. Dewey was in the lead, standing up.

Harvest Festival

The last big event of the summer was the Harvest Festival. It was like a county fair but on a smaller scale. There was a big parade and there were rides, games, and opportunity for local people to bring exhibits to the public school to be judged. Everything from jam and pies, to cattle and pigs, was awarded ribbons and cash prizes. It was an exciting time for those of us in the animal business, like Dougie and me.

The deadline for entries was fast approaching and Dougie and I were planning to enter several inhabitants of our backyard zoos. Dougie was taking pigeons and rabbits. I would take pigeons, as well as chickens and turtles. The rules stipulated one male and two females of each animal. With chickens it was easy to tell, but pigeons were more difficult, and turtles were downright impossible. I wasn't worried because I didn't think the judges would know the difference, either.

Dougie and I helped each other build little traveling cages for transporting our critters. My turtle cage had a large cake pan in the bottom for sand and water so the turtles could get wet. We spent a day preparing and then came the job of deciding which pigeons and chickens should go. We picked the prettiest ones and made certain they were clean and ready to exhibit. When it came to the turtles, I chose a large one, and two smaller ones, the same size. That way if the judge asked me which was the male, I could tell him it was the big one.

The exhibits had to be delivered on Thursday so we loaded up Dougie's dad's car and he drove us to the high school. The animals' exhibit was set up in the bus garage, so we put our animals with the others in the same class. Pigeons were in one class, while chickens were divided into regular and small birds. Of course, my Bantams were small, so I grouped them with the other little chickens. My chickens looked better than the rest and I was confident of winning. Turtles went with "Other Pets." There were hamsters, guinea pigs, gerbils, and parakeets in this class, but no other turtles, so I was feeling good about that class, too. Dougie and I had competition with our pigeons and there were many rabbits entered, but Dougie's were, by far, the prettiest and largest. We fed and watered our pets and left the area so the judges could do their job.

We paced and worried like a couple of expectant fathers while the judging was going on. They had closed the bus garage doors and the results would be kept secret until the next morning, so Dougie and I decided to get Dewey and Chick and go for a swim at the Gosey to help pass the time.

The next day the festival opened and all the rides and games and food stands were ready for business. We were waiting for the school gym and bus garage to open so we could find out who won prizes. We were not only excited about winning, we were countting on prize money to spend at the festival. We had saved up our bottle and lawn-mowing money but it wouldn't fund three days of fun, so prize money would be a lifesaver. We had decided to pool our wins and share with Dewey and Chick since they helped us with our animals, and they were our best friends.

Finally, the doors opened and in we went. There were swarms of kids and adults waiting to see the animals. We pushed our way through, running to the end of the garage where our entries were.

"First! I got first on the pigeons!" Dougie yelled at me. "What did I get?" I inquired.

"You got a third," he said.

I ran to the chicken area and there was a blue ribbon on my Bantams! "Dougie, I got a first on my chickens!" I yelled.

Dewey shouted from the "Other Pets" area. "You got a first on those stupid turtles!"

"First? That's great!" I bubbled. Obviously the judges knew quality "Other Pets" when they saw them.

Chick shouted from the rabbit area, "Hey, Dougie, You got a first on the rabbits, too."

It was better than we had hoped. We wanted to place in the top three of any of our entries. First place was worth five dollars; second place paid three dollars; and third place was awarded one dollar. Our four first places and one third place had netted us twenty-one dollars. Dewey was adding in his head. "That's twenty dollars!"

"Twenty-one dollars, Dewey. You forgot the third on pigeons," Chick said.

"Twenty-one dollars! Oh boy! Oh boy!" Dewey marveled. We could hardly believe it. With the money we had saved and this windfall, we were rich beyond belief

We ran to the high school office where the festival officials had a table set up where each winner could identify himself and claim the prize money. We stood in line for about a half hour. "Name, please?" said an old lady.

"Dewey," Dewey said. "But I don't got any critters. These guys do." The lady looked at Dougie and me and we gave our names and she handed us our envelopes of cash.

"Thanks, ma'am," we said, and raced off to count our money.

Dougie had a ten-dollar bill and I had a ten and a one.

"We're rich," Dewey said. "What should we eat first?"

We headed for the cotton candy wagon and we each got a paper tube with a huge, blue sticky cloud of cotton candy. Then we walked around the grounds looking at all the games and rides, deciding what to do next.

"Let's try that ride," Chick said. We got in line and rode the Tilt-a- Whirl. It was a wild ride and we laughed and screamed like girls as we spun and whirled around the track. Then we went on the Bullet. It was a bullet-shaped car on the end of an arm with another car on the other end. It rotated like the hands of a clock, spinning upside down and downside up. It was terrifying, but we all had a great time yelling and shouting at each other while we whirled through space. Then I heard a clinking sound.

"What's that?" I asked Dougie.

He looked around our car and suddenly he shouted. "It's money. It's the change I had in my pocket," he groaned.

Sure enough, I felt my pocket and my change was gone, too.

The ride finally stopped and the ride attendant unlocked our car and we jumped out and began searching in the grass for our money.

"Hey! You guys get out of there. You'll get hit by the ride."

"We lost our money, Mister," I said.

"Out! You can't be in here," came the reply.

Dewey and Chick got out of their car and came over to us.

"Check your pockets," Dougie said. They did and they got a sick look on their faces.

"Money gone?" I asked.

"Every dime," Chick said.

"Me, too," Dewey fumed.

"And that guy won't let us look for it," I said, pointing to the man.

"Well, we'll have to come back later," Chick said. There wasn't anything we could do about it, so we left.

"I'm hungry again," Dewey said. We went to the hot dog stand and bought a one-footer. "These are great!" Dewey said, as he squirted mustard and ketchup and piled on pickles and onions.

"Go easy on that stuff, Dewey, or you'll blow up on the next ride," Chick said. Dewey just grinned as he took a big bite.

We rode and ate all day. Late in the afternoon, Dougie and I went home for rabbit and pigeon food and corn for my chickens. I changed the water in the turtle pen and gave each of them a fish worm. Then it was time to go home. We were exhausted from the riding and eating, and it didn't take long for me to fall asleep.

I don't know what woke me up, but just past midnight, I popped awake. The full moon made a bright square of glimmering light on the wall across from my bed. I was half asleep, looking at it, when I saw a shadow of two heads. That woke me up real fast. The two heads ducked down when they heard me move in my bed. Then, slowly, they reappeared. I slipped out of bed and silently edged to the window, staying low so whoever was outside wouldn't see me. The heads disappeared again, and I raised my head. Slowly, Dewey and Chick's heads came up again. Just as they got into view, I said, "Boo!"

"Holy Jeez!" Chick said, and took off running.

Dewey fell over backwards and crawled away as fast as he could.

"What are you guys doing?" I said in an audible whisper.

Chick stopped running. "Holy crap! You almost gave me a heart attack."

"What are you two idiots doing?" I asked, again.

"We're gonna see if we can find the money we lost on the Bullet," Dewey said. "Chick is staying at my house for the night and we decided we should try to get our money back."

"Wanna come along?" Chick said.

"You got flashlights?" I asked. Chick held up three flashlights. "Wait there and be quiet. I'll sneak out." I slipped on my T- shirt and shorts. I went to the back door and picked up my tennis shoes, quietly opened the door, and stepped outside. I slid into my shoes and met the guys behind the house. "What about Dougie?" I said.

"His bedroom is on the second floor. How can we wake him?" Chick said. I didn't have an answer for that, so we walked to Dougie's house and stood in the yard below his bedroom.

"If we try to wake him up, we'll probably wake up everyone in the house," I said. "Let's find the money, and we'll clue him in tomorrow." That seemed like the best plan.

We walked the back streets to the festival grounds and climbed over the railing by the Bullet. It didn't take long to locate the coins in the grass. We picked up many coins. Actually, we found more money than we lost. We had it pretty well cleaned up and decided to check around the other rides. We found a few pennies but when we looked in the grass by the ticket booths, we found dimes and a couple of quarters.

"It's two o'clock. We'd better head home," Dewey said. "Here, you guys. Take these coins and put them with yours.

We can count money in the morning," I said, as I handed the coins to Chick. We walked past Dougie's and then I went off to

my house, and Dewey and Chick went back to Dewey's.

Mom came to wake me up at ten o'clock. "Dougie's on the phone. He says you're late and to hurry up," she said.

"Tell him I'll be there in two minutes," I said, as I ran to the bathroom to wash my face and brush my teeth. I threw on my shorts and T-shirt and grabbed my tennis shoes as I went out the door. Dewey and Chick were at Dougie's waiting for me.

"The guys tell me you had an adventure last night," Dougie said.

"Yeah, we couldn't figure out a way to wake you or we would have had you come with us," I said.

"How much did we get, Dewey?" He and Chick got smug looks on their faces.

"Well, thanks to our brilliant plan, we not only found our money. We ended up with about twice as much. We picked up seven dollars and ten cents," Dewey boasted.

"Seven dollars! No way!" Dougie said. Dewey dug into his pocket and pulled out a handful of change.

"Wow! We're rich again!" asserted Dewey.

We still had almost ten dollars remaining from our winnings.

With this new money, it was like starting over, and we hadn't spent a dime of our savings. "This is great. We've got enough money for lots of stuff and if we can sneak out again tonight, we'll have even more," Chick said.

Indeed we were riding high. We went to the festival and had a grand day: riding, eating, and acting like thirteen-year-old boys. That night we decided to sleep in the tent to make it easier to go scouting for money. We got up at midnight and made our way to the festival grounds and found almost four dollars. Apparently people were becoming more careful with their change, or they were running out of money.

The parade was on the last day of the festival. It was a grand affair with bands and floats, and fire trucks and noise. We watched from the curb and yelled and clapped at all the wonderful things that passed. We had one last afternoon at the festival. As the day came to an end, we went home and got our bikes and headed to the Gosey. We hadn't been swimming for three days and somehow we just needed to get into the river to relax. It had been a great three days.

We were basking in the water, talking about our good fortune with the animals and finding the lost money and how great the parade was.

"You know, guys," Dougie said, "there's only one week till school starts."

As much as we hated to think about it, Dougie was right. "We have to do something special to end the summer," Chick said.

"Good idea. What can we do?" I asked.

We thought for a while and suddenly Dougie said, "How about a canoe trip down the river?"

"Where are we gonna get canoes?" Dewey said.

"My dad's got one in the garage," Dougie said.

"We can find another one if we think about it," Chick chimed.

"My brother has one. He doesn't live here, but if I call him, I bet he'd let us use it," Dewey offered.

"Okay, that's it. A big end-of-summer trip! Everyone in?" Chick said.

Of course, *All fir one, and one fir all,* we cheered.

Last Hurrah

It was the last week of summer vacation. By Monday, we would be back in the classroom. We had come up with a plan for a canoe trip down the river to spend our last days of freedom in fishing, swimming, and having fun.

Although the idea was hatched on the previous weekend, it took us several days to get permission from our parents and the rest of the week to make the preparations.

On the last Monday of our freedom, we started in. "Oh, c'mon, Mom! We know how to swim, and we know the river."

"How do you know so much about the river? I thought you spent all your time at the Gosey," our mothers replied.

"Well, we, uh; we just know. We are good swimmers and we'll be careful," was our answer.

"I need to check with the other parents to see what they think and then I'll decide," was the response.

I rode to Dougie's, and we called Chick and Dewey. We compared notes, and we knew how our parents were thinking.

"My mom is giving in," Chick said. "I think if she talks to your mom, she'll agree. How about your parents, Dewey?"

"They said okay if you guys are going. They must trust you," he said, smiling.

"Of course, they trust us, Dewey," Dougie said. "We're angels."

After a half dozen phone calls, the adults finally agreed. We began to gather equipment and to figure out how to get our gear to the river. Dougie's dad gave us use of his canoe, and Dewey's brother was willing also to give us his, but he couldn't deliver it until Wednesday. That meant we couldn't leave until Thursday morning. We had two days to round up all the supplies for our four-day trip.

We decided to use Chick's tent because of its size and its ease in setting up. Our camping stuff was handy because we had used it all summer. We rounded up an ax, a small saw, and several coolers for the food. Dewey's brother was bringing us a jug for fresh water.

Then we dug enough worms for four days of fishing. Our worm-digging place was almost depleted because we had been harvesting worms all summer and the ones we had been finding were puny. But we dug and dug and managed to find a supply for the trip.

Since we had been so fortunate at the Harvest Festival, our finances were in good shape. Between us, we had over twenty dollars. We went to Mr. Kalsher's grocery store and carefully checked prices on the things we needed, such as eggs--two each for four days came to thirty-two so we got three dozen. Then we got three pounds of bacon, three pounds of butter, a bag of flour, and two bottles of oil for frying fish. We picked up two bags of potatoes and four large cans of beans. With the addition of four loaves of bread and four packages of ham and bologna, we were set with the essentials. We checked our cash and found that we had enough for Jiffy Pops popcorn, marshmallows, twelve packs of Kool-Aid, and an assortment of candy and chips. We ended up spending every penny we had.

Our moms made us sleep at home the night before our trip. I could barely close my eyes and I slept very little, waiting eagerly for the morning. Finally at six-thirty, I got up and packed my duffle bag with clothes and soap and my toothbrush. Mom made breakfast and hugged me goodbye like she wasn't ever going to see me again.

"Be a good boy, and don't do anything stupid," she called, as I flew out the door.

"Bye, Mom. See you Sunday," I echoed.

We gathered at Chick's house since he lived close to the river.

The gear was sitting in his garage and we began hauling it to the river. It took four trips each and an hour for us to cart everything to the water's edge. His mom came to see us off "Are you sure you have everything?"

"Yes, Mom," Chick said.

"Yes, Mom," the rest of us said.

His mom laughed. "You nuts be careful."

"There are whirlpools in the river that will suck you to the bottom and drown you," we chorused.

She shook her head and walked up on the riverbank. "Have fun. Remember Dougie's dad will pick you up at the last bridge before the

Mississippi. For God's sake, don't go paddling out into the Mississippi or we'll never see you again."

"Sure, Mom," we promised.

Dougie and Chick were in one canoe and Dewey and I in the other. Dougie and I shoved the canoes into the water and jumped in. We paddled into the current and slipped down the river toward the bridge. We turned and waved to Chick's mom on the bank. We were off on our great adventure.

We paddled for about a half hour. We wanted to get far away from home so no one could change their mind and spoil our trip. If we got away fast, we would be safe. We were a couple of miles from home when Dewey decided we should stop for lunch.

"Dewey, it's only ten o'clock in the morning. We just had breakfast," we protested.

"Yeah, but we're on vacation, and we don't have any place to go and no special time to be there. So, let's take it easy and have fun," Dewey said.

For once, Dewey was right. We had no schedule, no parents to set a curfew, or tell us when to eat, no teachers to correct us, and nothing to do but have fun.

"Dewey's right," Chick said. "Let's stop to fish and eat." It made sense so we looked for a sandbar with a nice drop off "I'll make sandwiches," Dewey offered.

"I'll cut pole holders," Dougie said.

"I'll unload the fishing poles and bait," Chick said.

"I'll gather firewood and make the campfire," I said.

In a short time we were sitting comfortably in the sand, feasting on bologna sandwiches and chips, and drinking grape Kool-Aid. After eating, we went to the edge of the sandbar, dangled our feet in the water, and fished.

It was sunny and warm so we peeled off our shirts, rolling over on our sides as we watched for bites, talking and laughing, just like we did at the Gosey. Dewey soon had a catfish and Chick, a bass. Then Dougie and I each had a catfish.

"This is a good fishing hole. Maybe we should stay here for the rest of the day and camp here tonight," I said. Everyone agreed, so we settled in for our first day on the river.

It was a great day. Our stringer was filled with fish so we decided to swim. We stripped off our shorts, splashed, yelled, and made a huge sand castle in the damp sand. Too soon, the sun slipped beneath the trees.

"Looks like we better set up the tent and make supper," Dougie said.

"I'll help Dewey with the fish, and you two work on the tent," I suggested. Dewey and I cleaned the fish and washed the fillets in the river. Then we stoked up the fire and placed the metal grate over it for frying the fish. Dewey was the chef and I helped him prepare the potatoes and onions. We had flour, spices, and oil for frying the fillets. I opened a can of beans and placed it on the grate and soon the sandbar area began to smell real good. Dougie and Chick came out of the tent, sniffing like a couple of coon dogs.

"Jeez! That smells good, Dewey," Chick said.

"Of course! I'm a fine chef," Dewey gloated, grinning from ear to ear.

After a few minutes, the fish and potatoes were ready, so we each took a serving while Dewey continued to fry fish. We ate and ate until we groaned, patting our full bellies. Every scrap of fish, potatoes, and beans was gone along with almost a loaf of bread.

"I think I died and went to heaven," Chick said. We laughed and kicked back to rest. We were planning the next day and anticipating the new adventures when we started to yawn.

"What d'ya think, guys?" I asked.

"I think it's time for bed," Dewey sighed.

"Yup," was one answer.

"Yeah! Me, too," came another.

"Then it's unanimous," I said.

"Unanimous? Yeah, unanimous here, too," Dougie said.

We laughed and, one by one, we wiped off our sandy feet, stripped to our underwear and climbed into our sleeping bags. We listened to the marsh sounds from across the narrow channel. There were frogs croaking, crickets singing, and an occasional hoot of an owl. It was so cool. Soon Dewey was snoring and then Chick.

"You awake, Dougie?" I whispered. "Yeah."

"This is pretty cool, huh?"

"Yeah, very cool. Night," he faded off

"Night."

I was partly awake and my mind was trying to figure out where I was when I heard Dewey roll over and fart. Soon the tent was filled with that all too-familiar smell and it roused us at once. Then, the comments of disgust: Holy cow, jeez, etc.

Chick, Dougie, and I were attempting to evacuate the tent at the same time and we almost knocked it down. Dewey was still sleeping. We escaped into the fresh morning air and dressed.

"Dewey, you stink. Go to the marsh and bury yourself," Chick yelled into the tent. Dewey rolled onto his stomach and let another one fly. We shrieked with laughter, and soon Dewey was laughing so hard, he shook the tent.

"C'mon, get up and fix us breakfast, Chef Dewey Boy R Dee," Dougie said.

We had eggs and bacon, burnt bread, and green Kool-Aid for breakfast. We seemed to lack the technique for toasting bread over an open fire, so it turned to charcoal, but we ate it anyway. We cleaned the pans, packed up our junk, and loaded the canoes. We were careful not to leave any garbage and to extinguish the fire, and we said goodbye to our first campsite.

We paddled along, not in a hurry, but not poking along, either, and soon we had passed under the bridges of the two towns downriver from us. From there, the river meandered through wooded and swampy areas, but passed no towns. We pulled up on a sandbar for lunch and then continued our trip downstream. By this time, it had become hot and we looked for a place to take a swim and then a nap. We dozed and suddenly I woke up and realized that much of the day had been spent. "Hey, guys! Wake up. We slept the afternoon away," I muttered. The guys woke up, one by one, and yawned, and stretched.

"Cripes, we slept a long time," Dougie exclaimed.

"Well, this would be a good place to spend the night," Chick suggested. "Let's make supper."

We baited up and soon we had fish for our supper. "Same thing as last night?" I asked.

"That worked for me," Dougie said. He and Chick were on the tent and wood detail and Dewey and I cleaned fish and began supper. We were getting good at this, and it wasn't long before the smell of fried potatoes with onions and fresh fish filled the air. I put a can of beans on, despite the effect they had on Dewey. After we finished eating, we stretched back in the warm sand and began our usual conversation. It didn't amount to much; just the same old stuff we talked about whenever we laid around; the stuff that made us laugh and feel good.

Because of the long afternoon nap, we were totally awake and stayed up late. Dewey decided he wanted popcorn so he got a Jiffy Pop and laid it on the fire grate.

"Don't get that too hot, Dewey, or it will burn," I instructed. "Who's the chef here?" Dewey inquired. "You gotta get it hot. Then it pops fast."

"Okay, Dewey. You know best, but don't forget there's one Jiffy Pop for each of us."

Dewey's Jiffy Pop began to sizzle, and then the corn started popping, and then ... black smoke.

"Oh, boy! Time to shake it," Dewey said, grabbing the wire handle. The handle was scorching hot and he dropped it on the grate. He grabbed his T-shirt to use as a pot holder, but all that accomplished was to set it on fire.

"Yikes! Fire! " Dewey screamed, and threw the shirt into the river where it hissed and sank. Dewey's Jiffy Pop was still smoking like a wood furnace, so he grabbed a stick to lift the cremated popcorn bag out of the fire.

The three of us were rolling in laughter as Dewey opened the foil top. Black smoke erupted and the popcorn was a charcoal gray color.

"It looks slightly overdone," Chick said. That cracked us up again.

"It's fine," Dewey said. "I like it this way. It has a smoky taste."

He took a handful of the burnt popcorn and stuffed it into his mouth. He chewed a few times and spit the stuff into the fire.

"Whew, this is really smoky," he said.

Raucous laughter, again.

Dewey waded into the river to retrieve his shirt and hung it over a tent rope to dry.

"Anyone else for popcorn?" he asked.

"Make another one, Dewey, and I'll share it with you," Dougie said. This time Dewey held the Jiffy Pop away from the fire and it popped to perfection.

One by one, we began to yawn, and finally at two o'clock in the morning, we crawled into the tent and went to sleep.

Saturday was our last full day on the river. We had about twenty miles to travel to make it easy to reach our pick-up spot on Sunday with time to spare. We were to meet Dougie's dad at noon by the last bridge before the Mississippi. We thought four or five paddling miles on Sunday morning was about right. After breakfast, we paddled steady for several hours before stopping for lunch and a swim. We rested and then pushed on before stopping to set up camp again. Dougie and I were in one canoe and Dewey and Chick in the other and we got to a long stretch of river when Chick yelled, "We'll race you to the sandbar."

"You're on!" we said, accepting the challenge.

Paddling as fast as possible, we were neck and neck for a while and then they began to pull ahead of us. We had more weight in our canoe, and they got ahead of us and won the race. "Champions of the world!" Dewey made known, raising his paddle above his head. The two of them raised their paddles and bowed to the imaginary crowds.

Dougie and I just shook our heads. Two good friends, but so insane! Such a shame!

We journeyed on and came to an area that showed signs of a wind storm some time before. Trees were uprooted and the tops were moving back and forth in the river. "Watch us do a few fancy maneuvers around those trees," Chick said.

"You guys be careful. You'll get stuck," I warned. I may as well have spoken in Japanese for all the good it did because the two canoe champions were already amidst the fallen trees.

They were looking quite impressive when they misjudged a tree and the swiftness of the current and found themselves turned sideways against the current. It didn't take but a few seconds and they were swept into the branches and then pulled down so that water spilled into the canoe. Our canoe experts were soon in the water. The current swept the canoe upside down and it popped out on the other side of the tree. Dewey and Chick were also pulled under the tree and soon popped up downriver.

"Get over there!" Dougie directed, and we paddled toward them. Dewey and Chick had survived, so we chased down the runaway canoe. Then we attempted to rescue the gear they had lost. Thankfully we had taken the precaution to put most things in plastic bags, so we were able to recover it. We paddled to a sandbar and Chick and Dewey swam over to us.

"Watch us do trick canoe," I mocked. "Oh, dry up," Dewey blurted.

We laid the stuff that had taken a drink in the sun. Their sleeping bags were soaked and Dewey's clothes were missing.

"Didn't you put them in a bag?" I chided.

"I didn't think it mattered," Dewey said, glumly.

"Well, you didn't lose much; just underwear and T-shirts," Dougie teased.

"Yeah, I've still got the burned one," Dewey blurted.

This sandbar turned out to be another good one so we fished and made camp. We were becoming expert at this, and soon we were preparing our last supper on the river.

"Dewey, I think you should become a chef," Chick said.

"Yup, I agree. Dewey, you do good cooking," I complimented.

Dewey grinned, stirred the potatoes, and ripped one.

"Except for that, Dewey. I'd hate to have you doing that around my food all the time," Dougie said. We laughed.

We ate our last supper and then studied the starry sky as we reflected on the summer.

'Jeez! It was a great summer," Chick began. "No foolin'. I can't believe it's over," I sighed.

"Yeah, baseball, and going to the Braves game ... ," Dougie said.

"And our boat and raft," Dewey said.

"And poor Johnny and that Daredevil," Chick added. We shivered at the thought of that.

"That mean Mr. Mick at the pool. We sure fixed him," Dewey said, with a hearty laugh.

"And we took care of Roger and Mike at the scout campout," I recalled.

"And then you guys abandoned us in that cave. That still makes me mad," Dewey complained.

"How about the rotten-potato job? Those things smelled worse than Dewey," Dougie broke in.

Dewey raised his leg. "Careful, Douglas. I'm loaded and ready to shoot." We laughed until tears filled our eyes.

"And our friend, Faye. I'm so glad we got to know him," I said. We became quiet when we thought of him.

"We had a full summer," Dougie concluded.

"And now, school; the fun's over," Chick lamented.

"Well, it won't be too bad," I said. "We're gonna be eighth- graders, the big boys; top dog."

"Yeah, that's right. That won't be bad," Chick said. "But Dougie's in the other school," pouted Dewey.

"So what? That doesn't mean we can't do stuff after school and on weekends," Dougie said.

"Yeah. Hey, did you hear that Hunter Safety Class starts next week?" Chick said.

''Are you guys gonna take it?" someone asked.

It was unanimous. We all intended to show up for it.

"That will be fun-shooting guns and stuff," Dewey said. "When do you think the ice will be safe for fishing?" Chick wondered.

"We can get to the good spots on Gutweiler's on the ice," I said.

"I'm wondering if my dad will let me go deer hunting," Dougie said.

On and on we talked into the night. We didn't want to stop because that would signal the end, but we eventually got tired and crawled into the tent. Two sleeping bags were still wet, so we zipped open the two dry ones and we all crawled in, warm and snug, together; and my friends drifted off to sleep.

I listened to the night sounds, the crickets chirping, frogs kathunking, and an owl hooting far away in the distance. And, there were the sounds of Dewey, Dougie, and Chick sleeping. There was no better place in the whole world, or better friends than the ones I was with. These guys were the greatest! Together we were elephant boys, the west-side baseball team, fishing mates, and sleep-over buddies. We were like brothers, maybe, closer. We were the Musketeers: Athos, Porthos, Arimis and D'Artagnan; one fir all, all fir one.

I finally drifted off with visions of new adventures that awaited us just around the next bend in our young lives.

BIG
EDNA
Back to the Gosey

Milestones

Our lives are filled with milestones. Some of these milestones are monumental events with important, life-changing consequences. Some will make a change in a person's life that you'll always remember. Others are pretty simple and basic, and they won't make a huge difference in the rest of your life.

Of course the first milestone is the day you are born. Without that one, there won't be many others. But we don't have much of a recollection of that one. We're too drowsy and worried about that next feeding to think about how important it was to get born. For many of us the second big milestone is our first day of school. This can be a very traumatic event, with which some have great difficulty. We have to leave our safe secure homes, our toys, our blankies, the smells and sounds so near and dear, and the security of our mom being there for us no matter what our problems may be. On this nerve rattling day, we have to dress in new clothes and spend half of the day with a bunch of strangers in a place called kindergarten. I can remember new jeans that seemed to be made of thin, blue boards, so I had to walk stiff legged. I remember Mom leaving me at the door, her face giving away that she felt like a traitor leaving me there. I don't remember too much about that first day and the other kids who had been abandoned by their moms, but I do remember my teacher Mrs. Saltzman and her daughter, Nancy, who was starting her first day of school, too. Nancy was my first crush. She was blond, blue eyed and gorgeous. At least she seemed so to a confused five year old. Other than nap time and Nancy, most of kindergarten was mostly a lost memory. With the exception of a large glass jar filled with tadpoles, I can't remember much else. My best recollection was the highlight of the day when we got our chocolate flavored goiter pills to chew on. In those days salt wasn't iodized so we kids had to chew up this large chocolate flavored pill so as not to get a goiter. We didn't have a clue what a goiter was, but we sure didn't want one and the pills were actually quite tasty.

The next big milestone is turning thirteen. That's one of the biggies. You are no longer a little kid, but a *for real teenager*.

Suddenly it's like the clouds part and you can see the world more clearly. Suddenly you know almost everything that is needed to be known, and adults are now really old folks who just don't understand you anymore. Overnight, you gain so much knowledge that no one can tell you anything that you don't already know. Besides—if there is actually something that you don't know, it's probably not worth learning about once you are finally a teen. It's quite an awakening.

Turning eighteen and becoming a *for real adult* is another milestone that is pretty life changing. By this age you have not only figured out all of the mysteries of life, but you also are starting to see that some adults may, occasionally, have an idea or two that makes a little sense. You've stumbled past your early teen years and if you've been lucky, you may have actually soaked up some knowledge during those years. Along with turning eighteen you gain all the rights and privileges of young adulthood which is great. The realization that you can still fall back on your parents if the going gets tough is a nice feeling.

Twenty one is the next milestone. Now you are not only a full fledged adult, but you have responsibilities and can be held accountable for things that you do. Suddenly the old idea of passing your problems on to Mom and Dad is no longer workable. Now you have to be responsible for your own actions.

The more milestones you hit the less fun they become. Turning sixty five and hitting retirement age is suppose to be something to look forward to, but I've never heard anyone yet shout for joy at the idea of getting older and older.

And then of course that last big milestone is the day you leave this world and go on to better places. Of course, no one has ever come back and told us about those places, so we have to take the word of others who say it's so, and hope that it really is.

But I skipped over one milestone. The biggie. The most important one that everyone looks forward to... at least the one that is most important to teen-aged boys. The birthday that gives us our freedom. The birthday that turns our parents' hair from brown to gray. Of course I'm talking about the day you become sixteen and can try for your driver's license. The day that the bike with its baskets that carried your fishing poles for all those years is retired to the shed. The day you start to relentlessly pester your parents for the car so you and your friends can go cruising. The day your parents take up new hobbies…. that will keep them up most of the night waiting to see their car pull into the driveway, still in one piece.

That was the milestone that my buddies and I were anticipating. One by one, during the course of a few months, we each would reach that magic age and the streets of our little town would cease to be the peaceful, tree lined boulevards they had always been.

My friends, Dewey, Chick, Dougie and I were about to turn sixteen in the approaching few months. It was what we had waited for ever since we all began hanging out together. We had spent the last few summers working together on many schemes and projects that had turned us into quite crafty businessmen. Our many ideas had supplied us with enough money for fishing tackle, food and pop, and tickets to the fair and the movies. Up until now it had been okay to walk to school or uptown, but from now on, this would no longer be suitable. Now we really had to do some thinking because if we had any luck at all, we wouldn't be riding bikes any more. We would be buying gas for a car that one of us would be driving to and from our many activities.

Dewey was the first of us to turn sixteen. Of course, we didn't have to worry about Dewey leaving us behind because he was the slowest person any of us knew. No matter what we did, no matter where we went, Dewey was the last to get ready… and the last to arrive at the meeting place.

While we complained a lot about him being late, we always had a lot of fun with Dewey. He could always come up with body noise that could turn any dull moment into one of hilarity. He was a sure thing when it came to a dull classroom or church. Leave it to good old Dewey. He could make everything a party. Dewey was one of those unlucky people who celebrated his birthday real close to Christmas. In fact, it was only one week before Christmas.

Those poor souls who are unfortunate enough to be born so near the birthday of Jesus should feel blessed, being so close to such an important birth. But in reality it is a curse that dooms them to a lifetime of getting gypped on presents.

Everyone knows that during Christmas your parents are doing all they can do to get presents for everyone on the gift list. Then that clinker comes in—an extra present for that Christmas Birthday Person. It's one present too many and it usually turns out that the birthday boy or girl gets something crappy. Or even worse, he gets an "extra good Christmas present" that covers both days. Poor Dewey was a blessed event that happened to arrive at the wrong time of the year.

Chick was next in line to turn sixteen. His birthday was about three weeks after Dewey's. Now Chick was just the opposite of Dewey—always on time, always in a hurry, and always coming up with some hair-brained idea that often got us in hot water with our parents or teachers. While he wasn't a real juvenile delinquent or a criminal, he was very near the edge quite often. His brain could come up with some of the craziest schemes, and it usually didn't take much to talk the rest of us into whatever he had dreamed up.

Chick was probably the best athlete of the four of us. At least he worked the hardest at it. We all went out for football our first year of high school but he and Dewey were the only ones who stuck it out. Dougie was pretty small and got murdered each time there was a play run in his direction, and I just couldn't resist the call of the autumn woods and squirrel hunting.

I think Chick liked football because he liked to smack into the other guys and could do it legally when playing football. Now, I'm not saying Chick was a bully or liked to fight, but he wasn't one to back down from any altercation, either. He was a tough kid and if he thought he was in the right, or he was defending one of his buddies, he was not a guy to be messed with.

Dougie's birthday was in mid-summer and of all of us, he was the most sane and steady. He loved a good prank and never backed off. But when it came right down to it, he usually had the good sense to try to convince the rest of us to stop and think before we jumped feet first into something that we would later regret.

Dougie had gone to the Public Elementary School while the rest of us were graduates from St. John the Baptist School. When he moved to our town during the summer between our seventh and eighth grades, he became the fourth member of our group. It didn't take long for us to corrupt him, and soon we had a new partner in crime.

I was the baby of the group. My birthday was the last one, and consequently, I had to suffer the indignity of being harassed about being the youngest. But as long as one of us was able to drive, I didn't really worry about when I turned sixteen.

We had spent a great summer together during the last big milestone, the summer we all became teenagers, and had since remained friends. We went from top dogs in middle school to low pegs on the totem pole in high school, and had to endure the indignity of being lowly freshmen, scorned by all the rest of the grades. But we made it through and climbed one rung up the social ladder to our sophomore year. Soon that would be over and we would rise up even further. And the addition of conveyance that had a motor and doors and a horn that we could blow at our friends as we cruised past would make our status even greater. That was our goal, that one of us would get a car, any car, once he turned sixteen.

Ice fishing season was coming up shortly after Christmas and it was degrading to think that we would have to ride our bikes to the river bottoms to fish, let alone bear the indignity of some of our classmates seeing us on bikes at our age. We *had to get a car*, and Dewey was our first chance at that goal.

We had all taken Drivers Education and were in various stages of our practice driving with our teacher. It was one of the classes that we really studied for and worked hard to pass, because it held our social future in the balance. Luckily for Mr. Anderson, our teacher, none of us had Practice Driving together. I have an idea that he arranged it that way... *for a reason.*

I did my Practice Driving with Barbie, a cute little blonde girl who I had a secret crush on. Of course, I was too embarrassed to say anything to her and surely didn't want my buddies to find out that I was interested in a *girl*. But Barbie was nice and didn't make fun of me like some of the girls did with other boys. My buddies and I had all sworn to uphold the doctrine that girls were "yucky" when we turned thirteen, but in the last year or so they were looking better. Barbie, while cute, was one of the worst drivers I've ever known.

On Tuesdays and Thursdays, she and I had Practice Driving during third period. One of us would start out behind the wheel, and half way through the class period, we'd switch and the other would drive. One day Mr. Anderson informed us that we'd be going out of town for the first time. Up until then we had just driven around town, very slowly. Driving on an actual highway instead of just on the village streets was pretty exciting for us. I drove first that day and we went out of town across the bridge, and I drove out to the Mill Dam. It was a route that I had ridden hundreds of times on my bike and I knew the road well. When we got to the Mill Dam, Mr. Anderson told me to park in the parking lot by the Mill House and shut off the car. Then I got in the back and Barbie took the wheel.

She started the car. Mr. Anderson told her to back up, turn the car around, and go back the same way we had come when I was driving. She put the car in reverse and laid her arm over the seat while she turned to watch where she was backing. As she turned, I stuck my tongue out at her and she began laughing. Instead of just backing a short way, she was giggling and backed up way too far, and the car began to go down over the bank into the Mill Creek. Mr. Anderson yelled and slammed on the brake on his side of the car. Driver's Ed cars had an extra brake pedal on the passenger side, and it was a good thing it did or we would have been swimming in the Mill Creek in a few seconds.

"What the Sam Hill are you doing?" he bellowed at Barbie. Of course, she broke into tears and began blubbering about being nervous and that he shouldn't have told her to go back because it was hard enough to go forward. It hurt her neck to look backward, and on and on. Mr. Anderson calmed her down and soon he talked her into putting the car in forward and giving it some gas. We climbed up the grassy bank and onto the parking lot again. Mr. Anderson let out a large breath and told Barbie to drive back onto the highway and back to town.

She did pretty well all the way back until we began to cross the bridge. The bridge was narrow and even though it was plenty wide for two cars, it looked much narrower. Barbie was riding the brake as we crawled across the narrow strip of pavement between the guard rails. There was a semi behind us and that made her nervous, and then about half way across the bridge, there was a pigeon sitting in the road eating spilled corn that some farmer had lost on his way to the feed mill. Barbie saw the pigeon and slammed on the brakes. The semi that was right behind us locked up his brakes and began skidding toward the rear end of the car. I, of course, was sitting in the back. I looked over my shoulder and saw the bumper of the truck coming at me. I tried to crawl over the seat to get out of the way. Mr. Anderson began yelling to go!

"But the pigeon will get killed!" Barbie said.

"It'll move! Get going!" He shouted looking over his shoulder at the semi.

It really didn't matter by then because the semi had slid across the lane and was butted up against the other side of the bridge and stopped.

Barbie let off the brake and the car moved forward. The pigeon flew up to the bridge railing and watched us go past, so it could fly back down and get some more corn. Mr. Anderson buried his face in his hands.

The next time Barbie and I were out practicing parallel parking. Barbie was driving. She pulled up next to a parked car and looked over her shoulder. She turned the wheel and then at the right moment she turned it back the other way, and we were parked. Mr. Anderson told her that she had done a good job, and to pull out into traffic and go on. Barbie checked over her left shoulder and then gave the Driver's Ed car some gas. She drove right into the back of the parked car. Mr. Anderson didn't even have time to use his brake. Barbie began crying.

"Switch places," he said to me. I got out of the back seat. As I opened her door and helped her into the back, Barbie was bawling something terrible. Mr. Anderson looked at the other car and there wasn't much wrong except a little smudge on the bumper. "Back it up," he said to me. I did and he checked the two cars some more. Then he got back in. "There's no damage," he said.

We finished the driving part of the class a few weeks later. Mr. Anderson resigned as Driver's Ed teacher that year. He transferred to Wood Shop the next year. Apparently he felt safer with kids wielding saws and hammers rather than riding with them in a car.

Barbie and I became friends—but not like girlfriend and boyfriend. We had many laughs about our Practice Driving experiences, and to this day, when I see a pigeon in the road, I think of her.

Snowballing

We were out of school for Christmas break and trying to figure out something to do. The ice was probably thick enough on the lakes for ice fishing but we didn't have a good way to get there. The streets were too slick to ride our bikes, and besides—we were all nearly sixteen, way too old for bike riding.

It began snowing first thing in the morning the day before Christmas Eve. It snowed all day long. The whole town, streets, sidewalks and houses were buried in a thick wet blanket of heavy snow. The phone rang as it began to let up in mid-afternoon.

"Hey, what we gonna do tonight?" Chick asked when I picked up the phone.

"Don't know, but this is a bummer. Why couldn't this have come when school was going, so we could get a snow day?"

"Yeah, I thought about that too. But this is too good packing snow to let it go by. Let's go out and snowball some cars tonight." Chick was our resident planner for all things slightly illegal and dangerous.

"Yeah, lets," I said eagerly. "I'll call Dougie. You call Dewey."

"Okay. What time should we meet?"

"How about seven? Let's meet up behind Cliff's."

Chick agreed and hung up. Cliff's was the local greasy spoon and hangout for the kids in town. Cliff, the owner put up with our nonsense and was pretty good about letting us have fun. There was a juke box, several pinball machines and a pool table for entertainment, and Cliff made good chili and burgers and fries. About every kid in town ended up there most Friday and Saturday nights looking for their friends or planning some excursion into the darkness for one scheme or another.

I picked up the phone, turned the crank and waited for the operator to answer. "Number Pleaaaaaazzzz," she said.

"121R, Pleaaaaaazzz," I said.

There was a pause. "If you're going to be a smart butt, you can walk over to your friend's house and give him your message," she said.

"Sorry. I was just joking," I said.

"Well, have a little respect," she said and connected me to Dougie's phone. I heard it ring three times and Dougie answered. "What are we doing?" he asked.

"How did you know it was me?"

"Psychotic," he said.

"That's psychic you moron!" I said laughing.

"I know that. I was just fooling. So what are we gonna do tonight? See all that good packing snow?"

"I talked to Chick. He's calling Dewey and we're gonna meet at Cliff's at seven and go snowball some cars."

"I'll be there."

After supper I told mom that I was going to shovel the sidewalk and then go and see if I could make some money shoveling others. She said okay and off I went. I did our walk and then stashed the snow shovel in a snow bank and went up to Cliff's. Dougie and Chick were there, and of course, Dewey was late. We sat in a booth and made plans for our ambushes and then Dewey came ambling in. "It's about time," Chick said.

"I couldn't find my heavy mittens with the plastic lining," Dewey said. "So I had to rig up some others so my hands wouldn't get all wet." He pulled off his mittens and showed us his hands which were inside two bread bags under his mittens. We all just shook our heads. There was always something, some reason why Dewey was late, and it was never his fault, so we were pretty used to it.

"Well, let's go," Chick said. We all filed out the back door. We walked across the street and went in the vacant strip of land between Walsh's Grocery store and Schwingle's Hardware. The strip of land was about twenty feet wide between the two buildings and ran the whole length of the block. The south end of the strip opened onto the highway that came into town from the west, so we figured it was a good place to hide and smack a few cars and trucks with snowballs as they went by.

It hadn't been long when a pickup truck came past. Once it was just past us we each let loose with a huge snowball and scored three hits out of four. The driver must not have even heard them hit, because he didn't even put on his brakes. We stepped back in between the buildings and each made a new snowball. Soon Chick warned us that another car was coming, so we got ready and let fly. All four of us scored that time and the driver hit his brakes and stopped. We were ready to run to the other end of the hiding place when he drove off.

"Whew! I thought he was gonna get out and look for us," Dewey said as he peeked around the corner of the building.

"All we gotta do is run to the other end if they stop and back up. They'll never see us," Chick said.

Suddenly we heard the unmistakable sound of a semi coming down the road. "Oh boy! A semi," Dougie said and began making snowballs and piling them up at his feet. We all did the same and as soon as the semi got just past us we began firing snowballs as fast as we could. I'm not sure how many hit him, but it was a bunch. He braked and then kept on going.

We all laughed and started making new snowballs. Then we heard an unusual noise and Dougie snuck a peek out around Schwingle's and ducked back quickly. "It's Vernie, in the snowplow!" he said.

Vernie was one of the guys who worked for the Village plowing snow, picking up garbage, cleaning out water mains and all sorts of stuff. He was kind of an ornery old guy and so he made a perfect target. We all got ready and soon he came past our hiding place. It was real warm that evening and Vernie had the driver's side window open with his arm resting on the window opening. "One. Two. Three!" Chick whispered and we all let fly.

Three snowballs hit the side of the truck and made loud "THUNK!" noises. The fourth snowball hit Vernie right in the shoulder and exploded all over the side of his head. He slammed on the brakes and began backing up. We all hightailed it for the other end of the hiding place.

We got to the other end, stepped behind Schwingle's and began laughing. Chick peaked around the building and jumped back quickly. "He's sitting there in the street looking down between the buildings," he said laughing. We all thought we were pretty smart and were congratulating ourselves on being so clever when we heard a loud sound coming around the corner of Schwingle's from the street side. Just as we turned to look, here came Vernie driving the snowplow right at us. He jumped the curb and started driving right down the sidewalk after us.

Of course we took off running like mad and began dashing between parked cars and light poles. Vernie had to stop because the plow was too wide to follow us any farther. "I'll get you snots!" he yelled out the window.

We were laughing crazily as we ran down the alley behind Cliff's and hid. "Jeez! Did you see that crazy old guy? He tried to kill us," Dewey said panting from the run.

"We better move our headquarters someplace else," Dougie said. He'll go tell the cop and we'll get in trouble."

"How about down at the bridge?" Chick said excitedly.

"The bridge?"

"Yeah. Right at the end of the bridge there's two small cement landings about three feet square. They're so the railing has a place to be bolted to, I think. They're low, over the bank, so if we stand on them all that will show is our shoulders and heads. We can get two of us on each side and then duck down when a car comes. When he goes by we can hit him with snowballs and he won't know where they came from. We'll just throw at people going onto the bridge, that way they won't stop, 'cause they won't want to be stopped in the middle of the bridge."

We all agreed that it was a great idea, so we took the alleys and walked down to the river. Just as he said they would be, the two small pads of cement were just perfect for two of us to hide on for an ambush.

Below the bridge there was a rock ledge and then past it was the river. The rock ledge was about four feet above the water and there was a small strip of sand on the edge of the river below the ledge. Right there where the cement pads were, there was an indentation in the sandstone wall under the ledge that went back in three or four feet, like a very shallow cave.

"If somebody does stop, all we have to do is jump down onto the edge of the sand and then hide back under there. Nobody will ever find us."

We divided up and Chick and Dougie took the west side of the bridge and Dewey and I took the east side. We made a bunch of snowballs and put them up on our cement pads, so we wouldn't have to jump down for more snow as we used up what was there. Soon we were all ready and just in time.

A milk truck was coming down the road. We ducked down and let it get just to the end of the bridge. We all stood up and slammed it with snowballs. It slowed down but then sped up and kept going. "See? This place is perfect," Chick said from the other side of the bridge.

It wasn't long before another car came by and we pelted it with snowballs. Then our favorite, a semi came rolling down the highway and we managed to each hit it twice. We were having a great time when a car started toward us. It was a pretty new looking car and was all painted up fancy like a racing car. "Who's that?" Dewey whispered.

"I don't know but that sure is a nice car."

"Maybe we should let it go past."

Dewey and I were still deciding whether or not to throw when the car got to the bridge. We both held our snowballs but Chick and Dougie each let fly and scored two hits on the car. "Why didn't you guy's throw?" Chick asked.

"We thought it was too nice a car," I said.

Just then we heard what sounded like a semi coming across the bridge. "Get ready," Chick said. A semi!"

"Yeah, but it's going the wrong way. It's coming our way from the bridge," I said.

"So what? Semi drivers won't stop for a snowball or two."

Instead of hiding we all stood up and got our arms cocked to throw. Just as the semi got to the pavement on our side of the bridge, we realized what it really was. It was the racing car going in reverse. He slid to a stop with his headlights shining right in our faces. The doors opened and two big guys wearing letter jackets from a neighboring town jumped out. "You little shits are dead!" one of them yelled.

We all jumped down off the cement pads and ran to the edge of the ledge. I jumped over and so did Dougie and Chick. "Come on Dewey, hurry up!" I urged.

"It's too far. I'm afraid I'll fall in the river," Dewey said, panic in his voice.

"Dewey, if you don't, those guys are gonna pound knots all over your head and most likely throw you in the river anyway. Get your butt down here!"

Dewey groaned and jumped. He landed with his feet in the edge of the water. We pulled him back into the shallow cave with us. Then we heard the two guys talking up on the ledge. "Where the hell did they go?"

"Looks like they jumped in the river. See those tracks?"

Dewey started to giggle and we all smacked him to quiet him down. I leaned into his ear and whispered, "Dewey, shut up or we're all gonna take a drink in the river. Got it?"

He nodded and stifled his giggle. We all sat very still, trying not to breathe too hard so they wouldn't hear us. It was crowded in the little cave but the only way the two guys would see us was if they jumped down to the sand on the bank of the river. We doubted they would try that.

The two guys finally climbed back up to the road. We heard them slam the car doors and back up and turn around. We waited for another ten minutes and then climbed out, walked down the river bank a short way and climbed back up onto the ledge where it was lower. "Wait here," Chick said. "I'll sneak up and see if they're gone."

He crawled up, peaked over the bank and ducked down again quickly. He came down to us. "They're parked down the street a little ways. I bet they think we'll come back up there."

"What are we gonna do?" Dewey asked.

"Come on. We'll go to my house and play pool for a while till they get tired of waiting for us," Chick said. We snuck up the river bank till we were in a little woody area and then cut across two yards and were at Chick's house. His mom made hot chocolate for us and we went to the basement and played pool. The time slipped by pretty fast as we laughed and talked and relived our adventures that evening. Then it was getting time to go home, so we all got our boots and coats on and thanked Chick's mom and left.

We snuck back toward the bridge but the two guys were finally gone. They must have gotten tired of waiting for us while we drank hot chocolate and played pool. We walked back up the street to town, and one by one dropped off at our houses, me being the last one home.

"You must have made a lot of money to be out so late," Mom said.

"Uh, yeah... well, I didn't charge anyone. I just did it for free."

She looked me over and smiled. "Chick's mom called to let me know you guys were there and not to worry about you."

"Ah... I see," I said.

"I bet that snow packed real well. Made some nice snowballs, did it?"

Good old Mom. You couldn't pull one over on her.

Edna

Dewey's mom took him to nearby Boscobel for his driver's license road test the Friday before Christmas. The license people were there every other Friday, and Dewey was going to be the first of our gang with a shot at gaining his driving privileges. Of course, we all wanted to go along and cheer him on, but his mom said no. So we all waited anxiously for him to return.

I ran to the phone before the ring had hardly died and it was Chick. "He got it!" he said.

"No way!"

"Yeah, he did. No kidding. He got his license."

"Did he call you?"

"No. He called Dougie and Dougie called me and I called you."

"When are we going on a road trip?"

"When one of us gets a car."

"You mean his parents won't let us use theirs?"

Chick laughed. "They just got that new car. You don't think they're gonna let us take it down through the river bottoms, do you?"

"Well, then we're not much better off than we were before," I lamented.

"Well... yeah... you're right. But at least we've made some progress."

Chick hung up and I called Dewey to congratulate him. "So... no way your parents will let us take their car for a spin?"

"When cows fly," Dewey said in his slow way of talking.

"Well... way to go anyway. Maybe we'll all have to save up and pool our money and buy a car for ourselves."

Everyone was busy for the next two days, it being Christmas Eve and Christmas Day. We all had lots of family stuff to keep us busy, so we didn't think much about the auto problem we faced.

Then the day after Christmas I was watching TV, sorting through all my Christmas loot when I heard a horn honking out in front of my house. I didn't pay much attention to it and then it began honking again. Finally, I got up and looked out the window. There was a big black car sitting across the street in front of the neighbor's house.

"Must be someone waiting for Mrs. Suda," I thought to myself. I was just turning to sit down again when I noticed the window of the car going down. My mouth dropped open. Sitting behind the wheel with a big grin on his face was Dewey! He waved to me and motioned that I should come out.

Not bothering to grab a jacket, I opened the door and ran out across the sidewalk and into the street. "Where did you get this?" I exclaimed.

"I finally got a make-up present for all those crappy ones I got for having my birthday so close to Christmas," he said.

"You mean... this is yours?"

"Yup. This is my new car."

"Dewey, you're nuts. Are you kidding me?"

"No. And if you think I'm nuts, you ought to see yourself right now."

I looked down and realized I was standing in the middle of the street in my pajamas and slippers. "Holy cow! Wait right here. I'm gonna put on some clothes and I'll be right back."

I ran to the house, threw on my clothes and brushed my teeth. I yelled to Mom that I was going with Dewey. I about broke my neck on the snow and ice as I ran across the street and climbed in the passenger door. "Holy cow! This thing is a tank!" I said looking across the seat to the back. "What is it?"

"It's a 1953 Plymouth, with Fluid Drive, 217 cubic inch, 100 horsepower, six cylinder engine." he said as if he had memorized the list.

"A 1953 Plymouth with 217 cubic inch, 100 horsepower, and six cylinder engine," I said. "How fast will it go?"

"You forgot Fluid Drive," Dewey corrected.

"What's Fluid Drive?"

"Heck if I know, but that's what it is," he said grinning and gunning the engine.

"Well, how fast will it go?" I asked again.

"I don't know. I've only drove it from my house to here. I thought we'd get Chick and Dougie and go for a road trip."

I was about ready to bust. We had a car—a 1953 Plymouth, Fluid

Drive, 217 cubic inch, 100 horsepower and it had six cylinders—and it was built like a tank. We could go anywhere we wanted in this thing.

We drove over to Dougie's and honked the horn until he looked out the window. When we saw him, Dewey rolled down the window and Dougie about fell over. He disappeared for a second and soon he was running across the street putting on his coat. "No way!" he said as he got in the back seat.

"Dewey finally got a bonus Christmas present," I said.

"Holy crap! This thing is a bus," Dougie said examining the car's interior.

"It's got Fluid Drive," I said excitedly.

"What's that mean?" Dougie asked.

"I don't know but it sounds pretty good."

We were laughing as we drove down to Chick's house.

After a lot of honking, his mom came out with a scowl on her face. She saw the three of us in the big black car, shook her head, and held up a finger signaling just a minute. She went back into the house. About ten seconds later Chick was running down the sidewalk carrying his coat and hat. "No way!" he shouted as he got in the back seat next to Dougie.

We went through all of the specifications of the car and Chick seemed impressed. "It's huge! We can push down trees and all kinds of stuff with this thing," he said. "How fast will it go?"

"We haven't taken it out on the road yet. We had to get everybody together first," Dewey said. "We have to get some gas before we go very far. The gauge is on empty."

We all dug in our pockets for money. "I've got a buck," I said.

"Ninety cents," Dougie added.

"I've only got a quarter," Chick said.

"Well, I've got a buck, too," Dewey said. "That'll get us quite a bit of gas."

We drove down to the *Phillips 66* station. Carl came out. Carl was a nice old guy who moved like Dewey—sort of in slow motion. He never got excited and always talked slow and low. Dewey rolled down the window as he walked up. "Three dollars and fifteen cents worth, please," Dewey said.

Carl pumped the gas and then opened the hood and checked the oil. "He's checking my oil," Dewey said proudly. We all were smiling.

Then Carl cleaned the windshield and walked to the driver's window. "Anything else?"

"No, thank you," Dewey said and handed him the money.

Carl looked at it and nodded his head. "Yeah, you bet. Umhm." He turned, went back into the station and sat in his barber chair.

"I wonder why he has a barber chair in his gas station?" Chick said.

"Maybe he gives haircuts when he's not pumping gas," Dougie suggested.

"Have you ever seen him cutting someone's hair?" I asked.

"No, but why else would he have that barber chair?"

"Who cares?" Chick said, "Let's go see how fast this thing goes."

We pulled out onto the highway and started down the road toward Avoca, a little town east of us. Dewey sped up and soon we were doing fifty. The huge car just soared along, hardly working. "Go faster," Chick said.

"It's pretty slick," Dewey said. "I don't want to crash it the first day."

"Oh, come on! Give her the juice."

Dewey gave the car gas and soon we were doing sixty. "That's it. I'm not going any faster," Dewey said.

The road posts were zipping by pretty fast and we were all pretty excited. I reached over and turned on the radio and soon we were all singing along with Buddy Holly and the Crickets. There was a little bridge up ahead and as we went over it, the car began to slide to the right. Instead of just wet pavement, the bridge was covered with ice. The car was sliding half way across the road, so Dewey slammed on the brakes and we spun around in a circle.

"Whoa! Hang on!" Chick said.

We spun around two or three more times and then slid backwards into the ditch. The radio was still playing full blast. We were all hanging onto arm rests and door handles for dear life. I reached over and turned off the radio. "Holy smokes! Is everybody okay?"

"Yeah," both Dougie and Chick said from the back seat.

"Dewey?" I asked looking over at him. He was still holding the steering wheel tightly and staring up at the road from the bottom of the ditch.

"I almost peed my pants," he said.

Despite the scare, we all burst out laughing. "I hope the car isn't broke."

We all got out and looked at Dewey's tank. Miraculously we hadn't hit any road posts when we went into the ditch and it didn't look like there was any damage.

"We should bolt a big piece of sewer pipe on the top and it would look just like a Sherman Tank," Dougie said as we looked the car over.

It was quite a car. It reminded me of those big cars you saw in the old newsreels of when Hitler went someplace and they drove him in a big black car with little flags on the front fenders. The only thing missing was the flags. It was even the same black paint as the Hitler cars.

"We need to think of a name for your car, Dewey," Chick said.

"It's already got a name… Fluid Drive," Dewey said.

"That's not a name. We need a name, like Titanic or The Batmobile," Chick said.

"How about Big Edna?" I offered.

"Big Edna? Why?"

"When I was a little kid, my mom used to let me go and stay with my grandma for a few days in the summer. It was great, 'cause you know how grandmas are. They buy you lots of stuff. Well, grandma took me to the Five and Dime and they had this big candy counter and she said I could get some candy. I got a bag full of jelly beans. I always loved jelly beans. They had a lady that worked behind the candy counter that was as thin as a pretzel. I always wondered how she could stay so thin with all that candy right there in front of her. Anyway, as we were walking back to grandma's house I told her thanks and that I was going to eat all the colored ones first and save the black ones, "cause they were my favorite."

"And this has *what* to do with a car?" Chick asked.

"Just wait. You'll see," I said. "So later that evening they were playing Church League softball at the park near Granny's house and we walked down to watch the game. We met one of her friends who's name was Edna. I had my jelly beans along so I could eat some while I watched the game. Grandma suggested that I offer Edna some jelly beans, so I did. Well, instead of taking a few out, she took the bag and began sorting through it and took out all the black ones. Then she handed it back to me and kept a whole handful of my black jelly beans. I didn't know what to do or say, so I just shut up and sat there. I was really pissed and I thought I was gonna cry. You gotta remember I was just a little kid. Well, anyway, pretty soon Edna and grandma began laughing and Edna put the black jelly beans back in my candy sack. Grandma had called her on the phone and they had decided to play a trick on me, to see if I'd say anything about her taking all my black jelly beans. Of course, when they thought I was about ready to cry, they gave them back. Dewey's car looks like a gigantic black jelly bean, so I thought Big Edna would be a good name for it."

The three of them stood there gawking at me. "Jeez! Sometimes I wonder what goes on in that brain of yours," Chick said.

Dougie just shook his head. Dewey grinned. "Edna. I like that."

I had to smile. Dewey liked my suggestion.

"I had a goldfish named Edna once, too," Dewey said. "But he died and we flushed him down the toilet."

"He? Dewey?"

Dewey looked confused. "Well I guess maybe he was a she. It's hard to tell with a fish. Anyways, the car is now officially *Big Edna*."

The only problem we had now was that Big Edna was sitting in the bottom of a ditch.

"Well, what are we gonna do now?" I asked.

Dougie was surveying the scene. "I wonder if we drove down this ditch to that driveway down there. Maybe we could drive back up onto the road."

We all looked and it seemed like it might be possible. "Get in and drive, Dewey, and we'll stay out here and push if you get stuck."

Dewey backed Edna down into the bottom of the ditch and started it down toward the driveway. He began to spin now and then and we pushed and kept him going. When we got about thirty yards from the driveway Dougie yelled to Dewey, "Give her some gas now and don't stop till you're on the road!"

Dewey sped up and spun snow all over us but managed to climb up the bank and onto the paved road. We all cheered, ran up and got in.

"Edna the Indestructible!" Dewey yelled.

"Edna, Edna, Edna!" we chanted.

We drove back to town at a much slower pace and then spent the rest of the day driving past our other friends' houses and blowing the horn and waving at them. We were all glad for Dewey and his new car, and of course, for ourselves, too. We had wheels!

Blizzard Warnings

The weather turned cold soon after we started back to school at the end of our Christmas break. Temperatures hovered around zero to minus five degrees during the daytime and then dropped to minus twenty during the night. Fortunately for us, we now had Big Edna. Instead of walking to school every day, we rode in style. Dewey made it his duty to get up extra early so he could pick each of us up and then we all went to school together in the giant car. We received plenty of envious looks from our friends trudging through the snow as we rumbled past in Big Edna with the radio blasting.

The school week was coming to an end and we made plans for some ice fishing on Saturday. "It's supposed to warm up, like into the teens," I said as we sat in the school cafeteria eating our lunch.

"We can take the big tent and put it up. We'll be warm inside," Chick said.

"Yeah! And we can take a charcoal grill along and cook and stuff too," Dewey added.

We assigned duties and items to bring for the great ice fishing expedition, and before we knew it, Saturday was upon us. I had all of my gear ready and was waiting for Dewey to stop and pick me up. I had been assigned a big pot of chili as my contribution to the feast. Thankfully Mom made a double batch and put it in a big pot with a tight lid. I had my ice fishing poles and bucket all ready and when Dewey pulled up in Big Edna I ran out carrying my gear and the chili. I put my stuff in the trunk and we went to Dougie's house. He brought hot dogs and buns and all the fixins. We added that to the trunk along with his fishing gear. We picked up Chick last. He was in charge of snacks—chips and cookies. He brought the small portable charcoal grill, too, and of course, the ice tent.

Actually our ice tent wasn't really an ice tent. It was our summer tent, but we figured we could put it up and all sit inside and fish and stay warm.

Dewey brought the pop, since his parents had a bar and he could get it much cheaper than we could. Most likely he got it for free, so that was even better.

We were loaded down for sure as we started out of town toward Postel's Lake, where we intended to fish. We chose Postel's because there was a road from the high bank right out across the swamp. The swamp was frozen enough that we could drive Big Edna right onto the lake ice. We wouldn't have to carry so much gear way out to where the fishing was best.

We saw that there were tracks down the swamp road that someone else had already made, so we felt pretty good about going out, too. "I'd hate to be the first on the lake, and maybe fall through," Dewey said.

"Don't worry, Dewey," Chick said. "Big Edna would just plow through the ice like a tank and take us right back up on dry ground." We all had a good laugh.

Two other cars were parked out on the ice and several fishermen who had walked out were sitting and fishing by the time we got to the lake. We drove out, parked, and started to unload Big Edna. Chick had his snow shovel and he cleared off a big rectangle on the ice where we planned to set up the tent. We laid out the tent and stood up the frame. Once we had it up we put the nylon over it and drilled some holes in each corner and part way down each side for the ropes that held it tight. We tied the ropes to wooden stakes that we put down the holes and stuck in the mud in the bottom of the lake. Then we went inside, drilled a bunch of holes to fish though, and shoveled all the ice chips outside the tent. With our buckets all situated, we started fishing.

"This is just perfect," Dougie said as he baited his pole. "No more sitting out in the cold for us."

"Ah, the good life," Chick said.

After we had fished for a while without any luck, we were getting hungry. "Let's set up the grill and get the chili hot," I suggested.

We set the grill just outside the door of the tent where we could easily keep an eye on it. Chick lit the charcoal. When the coals were nice and gray I got out the pot of chili and set it on the grill. We took turns stirring it until it was bubbling hot. I got the ladle, filled bowls with steaming chili, and we all took a break from fishing to eat. Once the chili was gone, Dougie roasted hot dogs on the grill, and we all ate dogs and drank semi-frozen pop.

We finished up dinner hour, tied the tent door closed and began fishing in earnest again. In just a little while Dougie caught a nice bluegill and just a second later, so did Chick. "Wow they're gonna bite now," I said as my bobber sunk out of sight. I lifted a big crappie up from the hole. Dewey was jigging like mad and soon Dougie got another bluegill and I got one, too. Dewey leaned off to the left of his bucket, raised his right butt cheek and let a huge fart.

"That's what I think of you guys hogging all the fish," he said laughing.

"Jeez, Dewey!" Chick said fanning the stink away from him. "Keep that up and we'll have to evacuate the tent."

Suddenly Dewey said, "Oops, oops... just a little more, just a little... Gotcha!" and he raised his rod and lifted a nice perch from the water.

From then on the fishing got better by the minute. We all were catching fish as fast as we could pull them from the holes, and we were having great time doing it. It seemed that one of us had a fish coming up from our hole all the time. There were the sounds of many fish flopping around in the bottom of our buckets.

A couple of times we heard other fishermen outside packing up their gear and walking off. "Must not be very good fishermen," I said quietly. The guys snickered.

Then we heard one of the other cars start up and drive off the ice, followed shortly after by the other. "Boy, we must be the only ones left here. I wonder why they all left so soon?" Chick said.

"Maybe they didn't bring lunch... or maybe they were cold,"

Dougie said sliding a big crappie out over the edge of his hole.

"They just didn't come as prepared as we did," I said. "Thanks to Dewey and Big Edna we can take all the gear we want and be really comfortable from now on."

The afternoon wore on and the light started to fade. It was getting harder to see our bobbers as the tent darkened. "Must be getting late," Chick said.

Dewey looked at his watch. "Cripes! It's almost five o'clock. Maybe we better get packed up. It's gonna be dark soon."

"So what?" Chick said. "Edna's got headlights."

So we fished on, and about half an hour later Dougie stood up. "I just can't wait any more. I gotta pee. I've been holding it for an hour. I hate to take time out when the fish are biting so good, but it's now or I pee my pants."

"Jeez," I said moving my bucket so he could get to the door. "Get going. We don't want to have to change your diaper."

Dougie opened the door and stepped outside. "Holy smokes! Hey guys… come out here!"

We all looked at each other and got up and crawled through the door. It was a regular blizzard and there was nearly two feet of snow piled around us and the tent. "Crimanitly! That's why all those other guys left. It's snowing!" I said.

"That's why the fish were biting so good, I bet," Dougie said. "They always bite when the weather changes."

"We better get packed up and get out of here. We've got a long way to go and the snow is deep as heck."

Dewey got in Big Edna and started her motor so she'd warm up. We took down the tent and loaded up all the gear, dumped the ashes from the grill and put it in the trunk with all our buckets of fish and poles. We picked up all of our pop cans and other trash and then we all packed ourselves into Big Edna. Dewey gave her some gas, but Edna's tires just spun. "Uh, oh," he said.

"Try rocking it back and forth," Chick said.

Dewey put Edna in reverse and gave her gas. More spinning. Then he put her in forward and the same thing happened. "Well, let's go," I said. I opened my door.

Chick, Dougie and I got behind Edna and pushed. We got her moving a bit but after just a short distance she stopped again. "Back her up in the same tracks and then go forward again," Chick suggested.

Dewey backed up and then went forward and got going pretty fast and kept moving down the lake. We ran as fast as we could to catch up. We were running along side the car trying to get the doors open so we could get in. "Slow up, Dewey!" I yelled. He slowed a little and we all jumped in, and then we slid to a stop again. "That worked good," Chick said.

We all got out again and Dewey backed up a short way and then got going again. This time we all just ran along in the tracks behind Edna as Dewey skidded across the lake. Once we got to the swamp road there was some traction beneath the snow so we were able to get in and ride the rest of the way.

We were all panting and sweating when we finally got to the highway. From there to town it was pretty easy going. "Let's clean the fish together and have a fish fry," Chick said.

"Good idea. We can clean them in my basement," Dougie said. "I'm sure Mom would be glad to cook them for us."

"I'll cook them," Dewey said. "I'm a chef in training, you know."

So we went to Dougie's house and called our parents to tell them where we were and that we'd be eating here. We spread out a bunch of newspapers and cleaned fish. When we were done we took them upstairs and Dewey started to fry them. We put some frozen French fries in the oven and Chick retrieved some left over sodas from Edna's trunk.

We were just starting to eat when Dougie's mom came in the kitchen and told us that she and his dad were going out with some friends for the evening. "Is there enough fish for your brothers, too?" she asked Dougie.

"Sure. We got lots. We're good fishermen," he said.

"Why don't you guys stay over tonight? You can have the house to yourselves. We'll be home about twelve," his mom said.

That sounded like a good idea. We all called home again and related the new plans. We ate and fed Dougie's little brothers, and then we played Monopoly and had a great time.

By about eleven o'clock everyone was yawning. We decided to go to bed. Dougie's room was way too small for us, so we all got blankets and pillows and bedded down on the living room floor. A fire blazed in the fireplace, and although we were all dozing, we were still talking.

"Not too bad a day," Chick said.

"Nope. We got our money's worth from this one," Dougie said.

"It's sure cool to have wheels to do this stuff. We never could have had this much fun if we had to ride our bikes like in the old days," I said.

"We can thank Dewey for that," Dougie said.

Dewey grinned and lifted his left leg and let a loud fart. "Thank you for your appreciation," he said giggling.

The last thing I remember as the laughter died down was my eyes getting very heavy. The last sound I heard was Dewey venting again.

El Diablo

It didn't take us long to figure out that driving around in a car was much better than riding our bikes wherever we wanted to go. The only drawback was that Dewey's car, Big Edna, was a gas hog. It was huge, like a plush limo, with all kinds of room, and an engine that drank gas at an amazing rate. Once we were accustomed to having wheels, our next mission was to keep it full of gas.

We always had pretty good luck at finding jobs and other ways of making money since we'd all become friends, so we set out to scour for every cent we could earn to keep Big Edna running.

An opportunity came up for me to earn a few bucks when my younger brother came down with the flu and asked me to do his paper route delivery for a couple of days. Of course I didn't mind. It would be easy. The paper route had been mine for several years before I reached the age when I didn't want to be seen riding a bicycle all over town, and I handed the route down to him. Now he needed me to help out. A few mornings of delivering papers would provide a few gallons of gas for Big Edna, so naturally I agreed to do it.

I asked him about any new customers, or if any old ones had stopped their papers. I was up early the next day, got my old bike out of the shed, dusted it off, and rode it uptown to load up the papers. The tires were a little squishy, so I stopped at the gas station and filled them with air. Two big wire baskets were mounted over the back fender. They were originally there to haul my tackle box and fishing gear, but they would work just fine for hauling the papers too.

I arrived at the drop off point next to the post office and found the bundle of papers that had been thrown off a truck during the early morning hours. I opened the bundle, put half of the papers in each basket and rode off into the early morning twilight.

Other than getting up so early, I had never minded the paper route. One thing about getting up early is the opportunity to see a lot of cool stuff. Often in the spring and summer, a flock of geese would be leaving the marsh, honking and sailing over me like gray ghosts through the first rays of sun, heading to a field somewhere to feed. Most mornings a few sand hill cranes sailed over the town uttering their cry that sounded like a rusty screen door hinge.

Once I found a set of false teeth in a puddle of vomit in front of one of the local bars. In the street or along the sidewalk I'd frequently find a few coins dropped by folks who had indulged in too many adult beverages the night before.

Every morning I had an appointment with my friend, Delta, who worked at one of the local cafes. She must have gone to work in the middle of the night, because by the time I got there each morning after loading up my papers, she would have a big pan of hot cinnamon rolls ready for her early customers. She always gave me the biggest cinnamon roll from the batch and a small carton of milk for a quarter. I ate it as I rode to my first stop.

This morning was quite the same as the mornings of past. A small flock of geese sailed over as I pulled away from the post office, and several sand hills soared in the thermals rising above the town warmed by the early morning sun. I stopped and chatted with Delta a few minutes and told her about Dewey's car. Then I got my cinnamon roll and rode off down the street to my first stop.

Some of the paper customers had on their porch steps a little box, or a brick to put on the paper so it wouldn't blow away. At others I had to get off my bike, open the screen door, and put the paper between the screen and door. But at most houses I could just ride up and toss the paper onto the porch without getting off the bike. Those were the easy ones, and I liked them the best.

There were many customers with dogs, but I didn't mind any of them except the two places that had Chihuahuas. One guy had a huge police dog that was always waiting for me so I could scratch his ears. Another had a golden retriever that took the paper in her mouth and delivered it to the house. One even had a Basset hound that snuffed at me each morning as if it were saying hello. But the two I hated to go near were the houses with the yappers.

Now, I don't mean to offend anyone who is a Chihuahua owner. I understand that people have different tastes in dogs, or pets in general, for that matter. I know a guy who has a Tarantula for a pet.

Now that strikes me as something rather unusual. You can't take them for a walk; they can't play ball; and who'd want to pet them? I guess it's a matter of choice. For me, a Chihuahua would be lower on the pet scale than a snake or a Tarantula... my very last pet choice.

Chihuahuas aren't good for *anything*. They're too small to carry a dead duck. They're too noisy to hunt for squirrels, and a good sized squirrel would probably take them to the cleaners anyway. They shiver and their eyes bug out and look like they might shoot out of their heads like peeled grapes at any second. And they bark! No, that's wrong... they *yap,* and yap and yap. Often their yap is so high-pitched that only other dogs can hear them. As far as I'm concerned, they're just a waste of good dog material. Take three or four Chihuahuas and put all that material into one good beagle. You'd be a lot further ahead.

Two of the paper customers had these little shivering screamers. The next house had two of the darn things. About the time I turned the corner I could hear them yapping. Every morning they sat on the back of the couch in the north side window, watching for the paper boy. They started their high pitched yapping as soon as my brother or I came into sight. As I came closer to the house the yapping moved from the north side to the west side. I could see them jumping up and down on the back of a chair. Then as I reached the front door they burst out of one of those little pet doors onto the porch and the yapping continued, up close and personal.

It always amazed me how such a little dog could make so much noise. They jumped up and down and shivered and yapped while their eyes threatened to shoot out at me at any second. And this was a house where I had to put a brick on the paper on the top porch step. I hurried to put the paper down because the yappers were always at the screen just about making me deaf. As I rode away they ran back into the house, and then I could see them jumping up and down at a window on the south side of the house, still yapping.

Every morning it was the same. I suppose it kind of made their day. I was glad that they couldn't get out and come after me... not that they could hurt me very much, but the vision of them chasing me down the street was rather embarrassing. They probably felt pretty proud of themselves chasing away a big, full grown human every morning, like they were some kind of hero guard dogs.

About ten houses later I came to yapper number two. This one was a single, at least, and he did the same thing—followed me from window to window and yapped constantly. His name was *Senior Julio.* I always thought the name was a bit of overkill for a dog that weighed in at about five pounds.

At this house I just rode my bike up to the back porch and tossed the paper onto the landing. Then I'd walk the bike backwards down the sidewalk and go on to the next house. Of course *Senior Julio* would serenade me with his yapping all the while I was there. He'd stand on the back of the sofa with his little pointed ears standing straight up, his fangs bared and his bulbous eyes bulging. I could see the resemblance to Satan—the ears like horns, the fangs, the bulging eyes. It always looked like his head was about to explode. So I re-named him *El Diablo*.

I came down the street expecting *El Diablo* to start his yapping. Surprisingly, I was greeted by silence. Hmm, that was strange. Maybe the little bugger died... and my brother forgot to tell me. I doubted that, though, because we shared the same opinion of yappers. I'm sure he would have informed me of the joyous event, had the little monster met an untimely end. Anyway, I rode up to the all quiet house.

I turned down the sidewalk to the back porch, rode up and tossed the paper onto the landing. Just then I saw a flash out of the corner of my eye; *Senior Julio* flew out from under the bushes. He was so fast that I didn't have time to react. He latched onto my shin with his needle-like teeth. Instinctively I kicked almost immediately. It was like when you go to the doctor and he hits your knee with one of those little rubber hammers, and your leg flies up. Something like that.

Well, *Senior Julio* had sunk his teeth into my leg, and I kicked in response to the attack. Next thing I knew, *Senior Julio* was just about at roof level, sailing through the air like a shivering, bug eyed, wingless bird. He came down in the top of the arborvitae.

He squirmed around as if he were coming back for another bite. I backed the bike down the sidewalk as fast as I could. Then Mrs. Rusk opened the door! "*Julio!* My baby! Are you okay?" She stooped over and picked up *Julio* who immediately put on his injured dog act, whimpering and shivering. Of course, the shivering was standard fare for him. "Oh, you poor little thing," she crooned to the whimpering dog.

"I'm sorry," I said. "He startled me and he bit me."

"Are you sure? He's such a sweet dog. He never bit anyone before."

I pulled up my pants leg. There were four little puncture marks with blood streaming from them. "See? He sunk his little needle teeth right into my leg," I said.

She held the dog up and looked at him. "*Julio!* You are a bad little dog!" Then she spanked him on his scrawny butt with a little slap that wasn't much more than a pat.

"I'm sorry. I'll be sure to keep him in the house from now on."

I said "thanks" and off I went down the street. I finished the paper route and went home to tell my brother about *Senior Julio's* flight to the roof. He thought it was hilarious.

The next day when I came to Mrs. Rusk's house, *Senior Julio* was peeking out of the window. I bared my teeth at him and he disappeared from the back of the sofa in a flash. I could hear him yapping from somewhere in the house, but he wasn't brave enough to come for another flying lesson. From then on, *Senior Julio* wasn't a problem for my brother, or for later paper boys. Most of the time, all you'd see of him was the tips of his horns… or ears… whichever you chose to call them.

Back to the Gosey

Spring had finally arrived and my buddies and I were ready for some open water fishing. Although we enjoyed ice fishing, it just wasn't quite the same as summer fishing. Ever since that summer that we all turned thirteen, we spent most of our free time at the Gosey, (Pronounced Go Zee) fishing, swimming and just hanging out. Most people have a favorite hideaway, or a meeting place, and the Gosey was ours. A lot of the kids in town hung out at Cliff's Cafe. A nice old guy who put up with kids quite well ran the place. He served up lots of *Cokes* and malts and greasy fries. Others hung out at the swimming pool or in the park, but we always had the Gosey as our special place.

The Wisconsin River is flanked by sloughs that look like a lot of dead water surrounded by mushy ground and puddles of water. But those sloughs—small lakes to us—are actually slow moving water that flows from east to west just as the river does. The river has a very fast current, but the current running through the sloughs is slow and steady. The stream that runs out of the sloughs follows along the high bank of the river, and where it joins the main channel is a place called the Gosey, and because the current is very slow, it's a great place for fishing and swimming.

Over the years there have been times when the river cut a channel into the arm of land that keeps the Gosey separate from the river. A fast current scoured out the sand bottom and made the Gosey very deep. But as happens in most rivers, things change. The current was obstructed and the Gosey got shallower until it became a sluggish side channel. But it was still our favorite place to go.

A stone foundation still marked the steep bank where a lead smelting business had operated over a hundred years earlier. The rest of the building was long gone. The legend is that a young guy from France worked there. He was called Gosey the Frenchman, because the local people couldn't pronounce his name. One day he fell into the river and drowned, and from then on the place was known as the Gosey Hole.

There was a big maple tree on the bank above the swimming hole, and we had tied a long hay rope to it the year we all turned thirteen. We used it to swing out over the water and then dive or jump from the rope into the Gosey. During a spring flood, the bank had been undercut and had caved into the river, leaving a nice sloping sandy beach just below the swing. We couldn't have asked for a better place to spend our free time.

The first really warm weekend day, the four of us were driving around in Big Edna with the windows down, radio playing as loud as it would go, looking for something to do. "Hey! Let's go down to the Gosey and see how it looks," Dougie suggested.

"What? Do you think it will have changed?" I asked.

"No, but we haven't been down there in a long time," he said. "I kinda miss it."

So Dewey steered Big Edna down the sand road to the Gosey and parked her. We had never driven down the road in a car; we had always ridden our bikes. So it seemed pretty strange parking Big Edna at the swing tree. "Looks pretty good," Chick said. "All the ice is gone."

"I wonder how cold the water is," Dewey said.

"I bet it's colder than what you want to get your butt into," Chick said.

We all got out and walked down the sand beach to the water. Dewey dipped his fingers in. "Whew! Way cold," he said. "No swimming today."

We sat in a row at the edge of the water and just talked about some of the things we wanted to do during the upcoming summer. Now that we had wheels, there was no end to the possibilities. The warmth of the sun soon heated up our backs, so we took off our shirts and shoes and socks and sat in the sand barefoot and shirtless, dreaming of the summer ahead.

"I wonder if the fish would bite yet," Dougie said.

"The water's pretty cold," Chick said. "Maybe a walleye, but I doubt that any bass would."

"You know," I said. "Trout season opens next Saturday."

"Yeah, but we're not trout fishermen," Dewey said. "We only fish the river and sloughs."

"I know. But all that kept us from trout fishing before was that we couldn't get to a trout stream on our bikes. Now that we have Big Edna, we can go anyplace we want."

"Hey! That's right," Chick said excitedly. "Why don't we try it?"

We made lists of gear that we needed, and it wasn't long before we had our first great trout fishing expedition planned. The season opened the following Saturday at midnight. We planned to be on the stream for the opening minute, and we'd take our sleeping bags and food. We'd make a night of it, camping and fishing… *all* night. All we had to do now was convince our parents, get some food rounded up, and fill Big Edna with gas.

The week went quickly by. Saturday evening we gathered all our stuff in my back yard. Dewey was bringing Big Edna over at 8 o'clock so we could load her up and head to the trout stream that we had decided to fish. Dewey must have been excited about our first fishing trip of the year—he was actually about five minutes early. The rest of us were nearly struck dumb by that, and Dewey could barely keep the smirk off his face. "See," he said. "I'm not always late."

"Yeah, Dewey," Chick said good naturedly. "On time once in three years is a pretty good average."

We loaded up and off we went to the trout stream, about fifteen miles from town. When we got to the place we had picked to fish, we were surprised to see about a dozen other cars already parked at the bridge that crossed the stream. "Holy cow!" I said. "I didn't think there'd be anybody else out here in the middle of the night."

"What's wrong with these people?" Dewey asked. "Don't they have something to do besides screw up our fishing?"

"Well, we'll have to make the best of it and share the stream with them."

We unloaded our gear, made a little campfire at the edge of a gravel parking lot, cooked some wieners and ate chips and cookies. We just sat there. Then we noticed that other fishermen were getting their gear ready and heading for the stream. I looked at my watch. "It's only eleven. Why are they going so early?"

"They probably want to get the best spots," Dougie said.

"Well then," Chick said. "We'd better go and get some good spots, too."

We pulled off our tennis shoes, slipped on our hip boots and got our fishing rods from the trunk. We each had a small plastic tackle box with a few hooks and sinkers, so we didn't have to carry a lot of gear, a small can of worms and a plastic bag to carry our fish.

We decided that Dougie and I would stay on this side of the stream, and Dewey and Chick would cross the bridge and fish from the other side. We all headed upstream.

As we walked through the darkness we came upon other fishermen standing along the bank below ripples, or where there was a bend in the creek that held a deep pool. "I see what kind of water we're looking for," I said. Dougie agreed.

After some distance we came to a ripple that was vacant. I stopped and Dougie kept walking up the stream. A few minutes later Chick and Dewey came along. Chick stopped on the other side of the stream. "You think two of us can fish this ripple?"

"I don't see why not. Dougie is upstream just a little ways. One of you stop here, and the other go up with him."

Dewey stayed with me and Chick walked up around the corner to find Dougie. "What time is it?" Dewey asked.

I held my watch up toward the stars; I could see that it was almost midnight. "About three minutes to midnight," I said.

We waited a little while and then I cast my worm into the stream. "I think it's time," I said.

Dewey cast in too. We held our rods in the dark, waiting for a trout to eat our night crawlers. We waited… and waited…. and then I felt a little tic on my line. "I've got a bite," I whispered to Dewey.

I raised my rod and felt carefully. There soon came another tic, tic. I almost jerked, but decided to wait for one more bite. Then it came—tic, tic, tic. Bam! I set the hook and the fight was on! The fish ran downstream and then turned back up into the ripples.

"Hang on!" Dewey shouted over at me.

I played the fish until it came to the edge of the water. I reached down and picked it up. "Aw, phewy," I said. "It's a sucker."

Dewey giggled. "Sucker boy. Sucker boy."

I unhooked the fish, took careful aim and threw. It hit Dewey right in the head. The fish flopped around in the grass at the edge of the stream for a couple of seconds and then flipped into the water. "Hey! That wasn't very nice," Dewey said, wiping sucker slime off the side of his head.

"Just thought you'd like to see it up close," I chuckled.

I baited my hook again and cast out. Soon I felt a little movement on my line and tightened it up. I raised my rod and felt a pretty good pull. I reared back and set the hook.

"I got one!" Dewey yelled.

"Me too!"

We both began fighting our fish and soon it became obvious that we had each other's lines.

"Dewey, you've got my line, you idiot," I said.

"You've got *MY* line," he yelled back.

"Let it loose and I'll get them untangled."

I reeled up our lines and in the dim light of the stars I could see that we had trouble. "Oh boy. A rat's nest," I said.

"Can you untangle them?"

"Not without a light. They're really tangled up."

Just then we heard the brush crackling. Dougie and Chick came down the stream on either side. "You guys get any?"

"I got a sucker and a big whale fish," I said, showing Dougie our tangled lines.

"I'm all tangled up, too. So is Chick. We should'a brought flashlights."

"Let's go back to the car and see if we can fix them," Chick said.

I bit off my line. Dewey reeled up both lines and we walked back to Big Edna. Dewey turned on the lights. We cut our tangled lines and re-tied new hooks and sinkers. "I don't know about this trout fishing," I said.

"Me either," Dougie said. "I'd rather catch bass or northern."

"Hey! I know a bass pond where we can go," Dewey said.

"A pond? Where?"

"Up on Jerry Johnson's farm. He's my dad's friend and he has this pond that's full of big bass. I bet we could catch a bunch of them."

"Would he care if we fished there?"

"Well, I don't know. But if we went right now, he'd never know."

We looked at each other, and we all smiled. This sounded like something that we could pull off with a little luck... and some danger... and come home with a bunch of big bass to boot.

"Let's go!" Chick said.

We loaded up and Dewey headed Big Edna down the road. We drove about ten miles, and then he slowed down near a farm house. "The pond is across the road from the house... up that hill," Dewey said pointing across the pasture. "We have to be quiet and keep the lights off or he'll see us."

We were all excited and urged Dewey to get going. He turned off the lights and drove down a dirt road that went across the pasture and up the hill. The road was quite steep and wasn't much more than a path cut into the side of the hill by a bulldozer. There were big rocks and lots of dirt with tractor tire tracks showing in the center.

Dewey drove slowly and when we reached the top of the hill, there it was—the pond glistening in the moonlight. We got out of Big Edna, quietly shut the doors, walked along the earthen dam and spread out to start fishing. It wasn't long when Dewey whispered that he had a fish on his line, and he drug a nice bass up onto the bank. Then Chick got one, and soon Dougie and I each had one. Then it started to rain.

We didn't pay much attention to the rain because we were catching fish. But the little shower soon turned into a downpour. In a few minutes, there were little rivers of muddy water gushing down the dirt road and we were getting soaked. "We better get out of here," I said. "The road's getting muddy."

"Yeah, let's go," Dougie said. "I'm cold, too."

We put our gear and the fish in the trunk, and then we all got into Big Edna. "Take those shoes off!" Dewey ordered. So we all took off our shoes and socks and carefully piled them on the floor mat where Chick was sitting. Dewey turned Big Edna around and started down the road. Just a little ways down the hill Edna slid sideways and Dewey was frantically trying to keep the big tank of a car going straight. “There’s no traction! It’s like snot!” he yelled.

Dewey managed to get us going straight again, but that lasted for only a few seconds before we were sliding out of control again. But the worst was yet to come as we slid into the ditch and came to a sudden stop. Big Edna’s doors on Dewey’s side were right in the bottom of the ditch. Chick and I had thrown over to the other side on top of our seatmates.

Dewey spun the tires but it was no use. “We’re stuck!” he said glumly.

“No foolin’,” Chick said. “Nice driving, by the way.”

“I’d like to see you do any better,” Dewey said bristling. “And *by the way*, get off me and sit on your own side!”

Chick grabbed the arm rest and pulled himself over to the other side but had to put his feet up on the seat against Dewey to keep from sliding back down. I climbed across the seat, too, and had to do the same to Dougie to keep from sliding back down on top of him. “Well, this is something,” I said. “What do we do now?”

Rain was coming down in buckets, lightning flashed and the water ran down the road like a rapids. “What time is it?”

I looked at my watch. “Dewey. Turn on the inside light for a second.” Then I could see the watch. “Three fifteen,” I said.

“I think we should wait till daylight and see if we can get it out then,” Dougie said.

We all agreed that was the best plan, so we tried to get comfortable and catch a little sleep. I lay on the seat and held onto the arm rest so I wouldn’t slide down to the other side.

The next thing I knew, I found that I was piled up against Dougie on the down side of the back seat. He was still sleeping, and so were Dewey and Chick similarly situated in the front seat. I heard a motor running, and I sat up and looked out the back window. There was a man coming up the road on a tractor!

“Oh no!” I said to myself. “Hey guys! Wake up! There’s a guy coming up here.”

Everyone stirred as the sound of the tractor got louder. We all looked out of the side window. "It's Mr. Johnson," Dewey said. "Oh boy."

Mr. Johnson got off the tractor and walked over to the car. I rolled down the window. "Mornin' boys," he said.

"Morning," we all answered.

"Looks like you got a little stuck," he said.

"Uh, yeah. We must have made a wrong turn and thought this was a road," I said.

"That right?"

"Hello, Mr. Johnson. You remember me?" Dewey said.

Mr. Johnson looked in the window. "Ah, Dewey... is that you?"

"Yes sir. And how are you today?"

Mr. Johnson tried to suppress a grin. "I'm a might bit better off than you boys are, I'd think."

"We do seem to have a problem," Dewey said. "I got this car for my birthday and Christmas combined. Pretty nice, isn't it?"

"Yes, it certainly is. Large, too. Reminds me of a tank I drove in the army."

We all burst out laughing.

"Mr. Johnson," Dougie said. "We have a confession to make."

"And what might that be?"

"You see, we went trout fishing last night, and well, we're not very good trout fishermen. We fish at the river all the time and catch bass and northern. Well, Dewey mentioned that you had this bass pond, so we thought we'd come up and maybe catch a bass or two. That's why we're stuck here."

"I see. Did you have any luck?"

"Um, yeah. We got a few," I said.

"You know, if you guys wanted to fish here, all you had to do was ask. I'd have said okay."

Well, that made us all feel really bad.

"Let's see if I can pull this tank out with the tractor."

We all got out and did what we could to help get a chain hooked to Big Edna. In no time at all Mr. Johnson was hauling her down the hill behind his tractor. We all walked along barefoot in the mud until we got to the grassy pasture where he stopped and unhooked the car.

"There you go, boys. Good as new 'cept it's got a bit of mud on it."

We all stood there feeling pretty crappy. "Thanks, sir. And we're sorry about going to your pond without asking," I said.

Everyone nodded and agreed. "Forget it boys. I've got lots of bass, and I don't expect it'll hurt anything for them to get thinned out now and then. Come on up anytime and fish. Just stop at the house first and let us know."

We all thanked him again and shook his hand. Then we piled into Big Edna and drove toward home. We were quite a sight. The left side of Big Edna was covered with mud up to the windows. Our feet and legs were mud covered and our shoes in the trunk were coated with it. And we had slept less than three hours. We were quite a bedraggled looking lot.

As we pulled into town Dewey turned toward the Gosey where we washed the mud from our feet and legs, and cleaned our shoes. Then we got a bucket from the trunk and washed off Big Edna. We cleaned our fish and drove home. Dewey dropped each of us off and we made plans to meet later for a fish fry. But first, we all needed a shower and a good nap.

Odd Jobs

We were at the Gosey fishing for the first time of spring. It was a nice, warm, sunny day, so we all were barefoot and wearing shorts for the first time of summer. We were doing a lot more fishing than catching.

"It's a little too early," I said. "I don't think they'll bite yet."

"Yeah, but it's better sitting here than someplace else," Chick said. We all agreed with him.

"Oh, hey! I forgot to tell you guys," Dewey said. "Mr. Johnson called me and asked if we wanted a job for a day."

"Mr. Johnson? From the bass pond?"

"Yeah. He said he has some pens or sheds of some kind that need cleaning out after the winter and wanted to know if we wanted to do it for him."

"Because he caught us fishing in his pond?"

"No, I don't think so," Dewey said. "He said he'd pay us for the work."

"Cleaning out what? Old furniture and stuff?"

"I don't know. He just said cleaning out some pens and sheds."

We agreed we would do it. Our funds were pretty thin and Big Edna kept us scratching for money to keep her filled with gas. Dewey said he'd call Mr. Johnson back and set up a day for us to work. We lay back in the warm sand and although we didn't get any fish, we had an enjoyable day at our favorite place.

Dewey picked us all up the following Saturday and we headed out to Johnson's farm. When we got there Mr. Johnson met us in the yard. "You guys didn't bring any boots?"

"Boots? Why do we need boots?"

"The pig shit is a foot deep in the pens. You sure don't want to be wading in it in your tennis shoes, do you?"

"Pig shit! Is that what we're cleaning?" Dewey asked.

"Yeah. That shed over there. The stalls were full of pigs all winter. I want you guys to shovel it out into the manure spreader and then I'll take it out and spread it."

We all glared at Dewey. "I didn't know," he said.

"I've got some chore boots in the barn. I think there are enough for all of you," Mr. Johnson said, and we all followed him into the barn.

There was a whole box of boots. We dug through them to find some that might fit. Dougie was the only one who couldn't find some that were close to the right size. He had the smallest feet of all of us and his boots were about three sizes too big, so they flopped when he walked. "Just walk careful and you'll be okay," I said to him.

When we were all booted up, we followed Mr. Johnson to a large low shed. He opened the door and stepped inside. We followed him in and the second we were inside the smell hit us. It was like all of the worst farts of the world had been stored there all winter.

"Holy crap!" Chick said gagging.

"We gotta shovel where?" I said holding my nose.

"See all these pens?" Mr. Johnson said pointing to about twenty small wooden enclosures, each about ten feet square. "They had pigs in them all winter. Two of you can work together in one pen. Start at that end and shovel it out into wheel barrows, and then wheel it over there," he said pointing to a door. "Dump it in the spreader. When it's full, you guys can take a break while I spread it in the fields. Then we'll move on to the next pen till they're all cleaned out."

We were all stunned. There must have been tons of pig poop in the shed.

"I'll give you each $1.25 per hour."

Suddenly we all perked up. With four of us working, we were earning $5 per hour. That was a lot of gas for Big Edna.

"Ok," I said. "Who wants to work together?"

As it turned out, Chick and I went to one stall and Dougie and Dewey started in the one across the aisle from it. When we opened the gate to the pen we found the poop was the consistency of wet cement. We waded into it and began shoveling it into our wheel barrow. Once the sticky stuff was disturbed, the smell got even worse. "Oh man. This is making my eyes water," I said.

"I'm sorry, guys," Dewey said from his pen on the other side of the aisle. "I didn't know it was going to be this bad."

"That's okay Dewey. We'll live through it. It wasn't your fault," Dougie said. "Shit!"

"What's wrong, Dougie?" I asked.

"My boot came off. I lifted my foot and this big boot just stayed in the poop. Now my foot is full of pig poop!"

We all laughed at poor Dougie's predicament. But Dewey came to his rescue and retrieved his boot. Dewey helped Dougie as he hopped down the aisle to the door and out into the yard where he found a hose and washed off his foot. His sock was ruined so he took it off and put the boot back on his bare foot.

We worked until the spreader was filled. Dewey walked up to the house to tell Mr. Johnson. In a short time the farmer took the load out to the fields while we sat outside breathing fresh air. But in about fifteen minutes he was back, and we started again.

The day passed and we were finishing in the last two pens. By that time the smell had seemed to lessen and it didn't bother us too much any more. When we finished, Mr. Johnson was waiting for us as we walked out. "You guys did a good job," he said. "Just leave the boots over by the hose. I'll clean them up and put them away."

We took off the boots and put on our tennis shoes. Mr. Johnson looked at his watch and did some figuring in his head. "You guys worked for six hours. Do you each want to get paid or can I just write one check and you can divide it later?"

"Just one is good," Dewey said.

Mr. Johnson got out his check book, wrote a check, and handed it to Dewey. "That's for one extra hour. You guys did a good job, so I'm giving you a bonus."

We all thanked him, got into Big Edna and off we went down the road. "Let me see that check," I said. Dewey passed it over the seat to me. "Holy cow! Thirty five dollars!" I said.

"We can fill Edna with gas for a long time with that," Dougie said.

"No foolin," Chick said. "And a little left over for pop and movies and other stuff, too."

We all felt pretty smug with our newfound wealth. We made plans to go to the movies later that night, and then Dewey dropped us off at each of our houses. I walked into the house, took off my shoes and started for my room. "What is that smell?" my mom asked.

"What smell?"

"That stink!" she said coming closer to me, sniffing like someone had farted. "It's you! What have you been doing?"

"We worked for Jerry Johnson today. We cleaned his pig shed."

"Out!"

"What?"

"Get outside. You're stinking up the whole house!"

"I can't smell anything."

"Out! Hurry up! The whole house will smell like pig manure."

She started pushing me out the door. "But how am I supposed to take a shower?"

"Take your clothes off outside."

"Ma! I'm not going to get naked outside in front of the neighbors."

"Well, you're not coming in my house with that stink on you!"

I didn't know what to do. "Can you give me some clean clothes and some soap and shampoo? I'll go to the Gosey and take my bath."

"Gladly."

I stood there feeling like an outcast, and shortly she came to the door with a bag full of clothes and my bath items. "When you get home, leave those clothes in the yard. I'll figure out what to do with them later," she said.

I went to the shed, got my bike out, put the clothes in the baskets and rode down to the Gosey. I wasn't too surprised to see Dougie's bike lying in the sand above the swimming hole. "You got kicked out too?" I yelled as I rode up.

Dougie grinned up at me from the water. "My Ma about had a stroke when I walked in."

"Mine too," I said. "How's the water?"

"It's not too bad once you're in, but it's a little cool at first."

Just then I heard a rattle and saw Chick biking down the sand road. "You too?"

"I thought my mom was going to shoot me," he said. "I couldn't even smell anything."

Chick and I stripped out of our clothes and waded into the water. It was cool but not too bad. Soon the three of us were all soaped up and washing off the pig stink. "Listen," Chick said.

We heard the sound of a car coming down the sand road. "Betcha it's Dewey," Dougie said.

Sure enough, Dewey drove up, grinning. "I thought I'd find you guys here. Jeez! My ma just about had the big one when I walked into the kitchen in the bar."

We all laughed and soon Dewey was in the water with us. We all scrubbed to make doubly sure all of the smell was gone. When we were clean we got out of the water, dried off and dressed. As we sat there cleaning the sand off our feet so we could put on our shoes and socks, Dewey said, "Uh, I hate to even bring this up, but we got another job offer today."

We all stopped in mid-socking and looked at Dewey. "No more farm work, I hope," Chick said.

"No, this is different. You know Mrs. Foley?"

"Over by my house?"

"Yeah. She's friends with my mom. She asked if we would want to take off some wall paper for her."

"Wallpaper? Like in a living room?"

"Yeah, I guess. She's going to paint the walls, and needs somebody to take the wallpaper off first."

"How hard could that be?" I asked.

"I don't think it's hard. But you know... she's an old lady... probably at least 40. So she needs somebody to do it for her."

We talked it over and decided it was okay, so we told Dewey to let her know that we'd do it. Then we all went home, put our bikes away, and Dewey picked us up. We filled Big Edna with gas and cruised for a few hours.

The next Saturday we met at Mrs. Foley's house. "I want the wallpaper steamed off this room," she said as we walked into a large living room.

"Steamed?" I said.

"Yes. There are several layers... maybe seven or eight. I've rented a steamer. You can loosen it up with that and then scrape it off with putty knives."

Well that didn't seem too bad. "Okay," Chick said. "Just show us how this thing works and we'll get started."

At the end of the hose coming from the steamer there was a flat, rectangular thing that looked like a clothes iron, except about three times bigger. It had holes in the bottom so steam could be applied to the wallpaper to loosen the glue. It seemed like a pretty simple job.

"Fasten those tarps over the doorways, so the steam will stay in the room," Mrs. Foley said. "It will help loosen some of the paper while you're working in other areas."

That made sense. In a little while we had the machine fired up and the steam was pouring out of the iron rectangle. The room got really hot in just a short time. We all were sweating and our clothes were sticking to us. "Whew! This is like a sauna," I said.

"You ever been in a sauna?" Chick asked.

"No. But I've seen them in movies."

"Me too. And you're right. It sure looks like one, except the people in the movies just sit and have a towel wrapped around them. They're not scraping wallpaper."

When the steam head was held up against the wall, not only steam came out. Super hot water dripped out, too, and if you weren't careful you got a hot drip on your hand, or worse, on your back or head. We started the steaming process, and then one of us would scrape off the paper with a putty knife. But there was layer upon layer of the stuff, and each layer had to be steamed. We finally got to bare plaster on one spot after removing nine layers of wallpaper. "This is going to take all day," I said.

After nearly four hours, we were about done in, soaked to the skin and our hair hung down like we'd been out in a rainstorm. Being in that heat and humidity for so long, we felt like we'd been running a marathon all day. Each of us had ugly looking red spots on our arms and elsewhere from the dripping hot water. But the walls were clear of wallpaper. Dewey shut off the steam machine. We took down the tarps and let some fresh air in. "Ah, that feels great," Dougie said as a cool breeze came through the window.

Mrs. Foley came in and inspected the room. She was very pleased. "Nice job, boys. Very nice. You look like you're kind of tired."

"We're lots tired," Chick said.

Mrs. Foley got out her pocket book and handed Dewey a twenty dollar bill. "That's for four hours at $1.25 per hour each. Is that right?"

"Yes ma'am," Dewey said. "That's what we agreed on."

We thanked Mrs. Foley, drug ourselves out to Big Edna and slumped down in our seats. "Let's get some food, go to the Gosey and take the rest of the day off," I said.

Everyone agreed. We stopped at the grocery store and bought a bunch of hot dogs, buns, all the fixins, pop and chips. Off we went to the Gosey. First thing we did was strip off our wet, sweaty clothes, rinsed them out in the river and hung them in tree branches to dry. Then we swam naked for a while to cool off.

We built a fire and cut some sticks for roasting hot dogs. By that time our underwear was dry enough to put on. We sat in the sand feasting, having a great time.

"Well, we've got our gas money and then some for a while," I said.

"Yeah," Dougie said. "We've had some pretty good luck getting jobs so far this summer."

School would be out soon, and that meant we would be looking for summertime jobs. But that was a few weeks off, so for the time being we decided to just take it easy and enjoy the fruits of our labor. We finished off the food, took another swim and then stretched out in the sand for a nap. Life is good when you're wealthy.

Bridging The Gap

With the end of the school year in sight, we were looking forward to a summer of fun, and hopefully some part time jobs. Now that we were in the automobile age, we needed to make money to keep Big Edna's thirst quenched, or we'd be back riding our bikes. And we weren't about to let that happen.

Chick turned sixteen and got his license on the first try, just as Dewey had. Dougie's birthday was coming up in a few weeks. I was the last one to turn sixteen and wouldn't be able to try for my license until after school was out. But as long as we had at least one licensed driver—and Big Edna—we were in good shape.

The weather forecast predicted a warm spring weekend, so we planned on spending some time fishing. Even though we could now go anyplace we wanted, we still gravitated toward the river and the Gosey. These places had been our favorites for years, so it was no surprise that we found ourselves sitting on the riverbank above the bridge on that first glorious sunny day of spring.

"Boy, what a day," Chick said as he stuck his pole holder into the sand.

"No foolin'. If the water was a little warmer we could even go for a swim," Dougie said sticking his hand into the water. "You know, it's not too bad. Try it."

I stuck my hand into the water and although it was cool, it *wasn't* too bad. "We should try to get across to Snake Island. I bet we can get some walleyes if we got out there in that current."

Snake Island was not really an island, but an old bridge pier that was left from the first bridge ever built across the Wisconsin at our town. Somehow, they drove big wooden pilings down into the bottom of the river until they reached bedrock. Then after they had a base of pilings, they built stone piers over them with rocks from the size of a shoe box to huge boulders half as big as a refrigerator. They were all cemented together to form a pier for building the bridge. The piers stuck out of the water about ten or twelve feet, and wooden deck was then built on top of them. Horses and wagons could cross on the wooden bridge, and the man who owned it charged a toll.

Apparently there were a lot of piers. When the water was low in the summer time, little piles of rocks sticking up could still be seen all the way across the river. Most of them were eroded away by the floods and all that was left of them was the tops of the pilings and some of the larger rocks. But one was still mostly intact, the one closest to shore where we fished. It still stood up out of the water ten feet high, or so. It had survived all the floods and high water. Somehow, a tree seed had found a crack on top of the rock pier where it took root, and it was now a pretty good sized tree. Something else that lived on the pier was snakes, thus, the name, Snake Island.

Actually, there probably weren't any more snakes on Snake Island than there were in the rocks along the shore, but someone named it that and the name stuck. Between it and the shore was a fairly deep little channel about twelve feet wide with very swift running water. We often caught fish that lay in that channel when we would first arrive at the shore to fish. But after we had been fooling around there for a while, the fish moved farther out, away from all of our noise.

On the other side of Snake Island, there was another deep channel between it and what was left of the next pier. It was a great place to fish, but it was just far enough out in the river to be out of range for us to cast our baits. And there was a snag in that channel that had gobbled up dozens of our lures and hooks over the years.

"You know," Dewey said. "If we could get out there we'd be able to get to that snag, I bet."

"Yeah, probably so," I said. "But we can't get there."

"How about a bridge?"

"What do you mean?"

"There's tons of rocks here. Let's carry some over and put them in the channel on this side of Snake Island, and then we can walk across."

We all looked at each other like the secret of the Atom Bomb had just been shown to us.

"Of course! We can build a stone bridge!" Chick said as he headed toward the new bridge where the builders had dumped tons of large rocks. The whole shore under the new bridge was piled high with all sizes of rocks to protect the bank and keep the water from washing out the new bridge piers.

Working quickly, nearly running back and forth, we carried rocks from the new bridge to the channel at Snake Island. After almost an hour we stopped for a break. "We didn't make much of a dent in the thing, did we?" Dewey said.

All we could see were a few rocks near the shore that we had dropped in. "I wonder if they're washing out with all that current." I said.

"Maybe we need some real big ones for the bottom," Dougie suggested.

We all agreed that Dougie had the right idea, so we started hauling rocks that took two of us to carry. Several pinched fingers and bruised knuckles later we had a bit of a start on the bridge. Our rocks were now staying put when we dropped them in, and our rock bridge was out about four feet into the channel.

"I say we take a break for lunch," Dewey said, looking over a skinned thumb.

"Yeah. We don't have to finish this in one day," I said.

We picked up our poles and gear and headed up the bank to Big Edna. We drove down to the grocery store and bought a bunch of hot dogs, bread, pop and chips. Then we went to the Gosey to cook and eat. When we had filled our bellies we decided to have a little rest. We were soon all napping in the warm sun.

After our nap we had run out of ambition so we just sat and talked and laughed until it was time to go home for supper. The next day Dewey picked us up and we drove down to work on the bridge again. When we got to the river there were some bikes lying on the bank above Snake Island. We walked down over the bank and there were some kids, probably Middle School kids, about 12 or 13, hauling rocks and working on our bridge. "Hey, what do you guys think you're doing" Chick asked.

"We're making a bridge out to Snake Island," one of the kids said. "Somebody started one and we're helping."

We all looked at each other. "I guess it's a free river," I said. "We started it but you guys are welcome to help."

They all seemed pleased to work with guys who had a car, so we all pitched in and soon we had quite an operation in motion.. By late afternoon the bridge was complete, narrow and just barely above water. But if you walked slowly and carefully, you could cross to Snake Island.

We all crossed and stood there looking at the river from a new vantage point. "This is gonna be great," one of the kids said. "The fish out here have never been caught yet." We all agreed it would be a big improvement in our fishing success.

All the while we talked, Dewey stared down into the fast current between Snake Island and the next rock pile. "That snag is right down there," he said pointing to the swift water. "I'm gonna get it. You wait and see."

We spent the next five days in school and the following Saturday we planned to spend the day fishing from Snake Island. We gathered food and Dewey picked us up. When we were getting our stuff from the trunk at the river, Dewey pulled out a fishing pole that looked like a pool cue with guides on it. "What is that thing?" I said.

"My brother let me use this. It's his Musky pole."

"Dewey, I hate to tell you this, but there aren't any Muskies in the river."

"I know that. I'm gonna catch that snag with it and winch it up out of there."

We all were pretty impressed with Dewey's idea, so we filed down the river bank, crossed to Snake Island, and began fishing. "This has eighty pound test on it," Dewey said. "I'm gonna put on a big treble hook and a sinker, and just try to get snagged. Then we'll get that thing out of there."

We watched as Dewey cast out and drag the hook across the bottom. He reeled it back slowly and then tossed it out again. He reeled it in *again* and tossed it back out. "Sure! If I had a brand new *Rapala* on here, I'd be snagged in a minute. But now that I'm ready for it, I can't find the darn thing," he lamented. Suddenly his line tightened and he began to grin. "Got it!"

He pulled on the rod and it barely bent. It was super heavy duty, and the reel was so huge you could probably pull a car with it. Dewey pulled and groaned and moaned, but he wasn't making any headway. "Help me here," he said.

Chick took hold of the rod a little above Dewey and they both pulled. They seemed to gain a little. "It moved," Chick said excitedly.

Just then we heard the rattle of bikes as the three kids who had helped us build the bridge pulled up on the shore. "Hey! What you got?" one hollered.

"I got that big snag. We're trying to pull it up," Dewey yelled back.

"Can we help?"

"Sure. Come on down."

Dougie and I were standing close but there wasn't much we could do except watch. Then Chick and Dewey moved the snag a little more. "It's coming," Chick said.

By now the three kids were standing barefoot at the edge of the water looking down, trying to see the snag. Chick and Dewey moved the thing a little closer.

We could see the water swirling around something that they were pulling closer to Snake Island. "I can see it!" Dougie said. "Holy cow! It's huge!"

Just then I saw it, too. It appeared about the size of a basketball—a huge gob of line—a giant bird nest of line, hooks, sinkers, lures and spinners. "Crimenitly! It's a whole tackle store!" I shouted.

Chick and Dewey were pulling with all their might, but it wasn't budging. "It's stuck," Dewey panted.

Dougie and I exchanged glances. We both had the same idea at once. We sat down in the sand, took off our shoes and socks, slipped off our pants and then waded out into the current. The three young kids were right behind us. It was really hard keeping our balance, but we managed to get close enough to the snag to get hold of it. "Be careful," I said to Dougie. "It's full of hooks."

We both were up to our waists in the water; we pulled on the snag. The three kids stayed closer to Snake Island because they were much shorter, but they shouted encouragement. Suddenly something gave way and we both fell over backwards in the water. I came to the top first and saw Dougie struggling to hold onto the snag and get his head up. I lifted on my side of the snag and he managed to get above the water. "Thanks," he said as he gasped for breath. We gained our footing and waded back toward Snake Island. By then Dewey and Chick had their shoes and pants off and were wading toward us to help bring in the snag. Offering their help, the three kids carefully grabbed hold of the thing, too.

We got the thing to the shore and could barely lift it up onto the sand. "Holy smokes! There's a ton of lead sinkers and stuff on this," I said.

We all stood there staring at the snag, amazed at what it had turned out to be. Nearly round, it consisted of miles of line of every imaginable color and size. All tangled and snarled, some broken off right at the snag, others trailed out into the water, and hanging from them were hundreds of hooks, sinkers, swivels, and dozens of jigs, crank baits, spoons, and spinners.

"Dewey, you'll never have to buy another lure for the rest of your life," I said shaking my head.

Dewey had a grin a mile wide. "See? I told you it was a good idea to get that thing. See?"

"You did good Dewey," Chick said.

The three kids were dumbstruck when they saw the tackle we had recovered. In fact, we were all out of the mood for fishing, now with this treasure before us. "Let's take it up to the car. We can start cutting this stuff off."

"Jeez! You guys won't have to buy hooks for the rest of your lives," one of the kids said.

We picked up our shoes and put on our pants. Chick and Dewey carried the snag and Dougie and I carried the rest of the stuff. We put the ball of line in the trunk and bid our young friends farewell. We decided to go to Dewey's parent's restaurant to get some empty cans for sorting the stuff from the snag. Then we all got our knives and a piece of rope. We poked a hole through the ball and strung it up on the rope over the branch of our swinging tree at the Gosey.

With the cans placed around us, we sat in the sand, shirtless and barefoot, cutting off lures and hooks and putting them in their assigned cans. After a while we ate our usual hot dogs and chips, and then continued until we had the entire ball of line stripped of goodies. At the center, we found a small root, which was probably the first snag. Someone got caught on it and lost some line with a hook, and that caught someone else's hook. Eventually, the single little root was a huge ball of snarled line.

When all was said and done, we had an enormous amount of fishing tackle. Many of the hooks were rusty, but we still managed to keep nearly a hundred good ones. We ended up with three large coffee cans full of good sinkers, seventy-one *Rapalas,* one hundred six other crank baits, forty-six *Mepps* spinners, fifty-eight spoons, and nearly two hundred jigs.

We bought some new hooks and split rings to replace some of the rusted ones on the spoons and *Rapalas.* Good old Dewey shared all of it with us equally, and we even shared the sinker bonanza with the kids who had helped with the bridge.

Our bridge out to Snake Island has lasted quite well and is still used. We spent many great hours out there, and eventually we lost most of that recovered tackle back to the river. But it was an adventure we'd always remember, and we sure had a lot of fun with all that free stuff.

Fetch'er In

Dougie and I were sitting at the picnic table in his back yard when Dewey and Chick drove into the alley in Big Edna. "Hey! Want a job?" Chick asked through the open window.

"What job?" I asked.

"Look here," Chick said handing me the local newspaper as he got out of Big Edna.

Dougie and I opened the paper and spread it out on the table. "Right here," Dewey said pointing to an advertisement.

"Wanted: High school kids to trim Christmas trees," Dougie read. "Must be at least fifteen years old and five feet tall. Apply in person at the Railroad Depot, Monday the 14th between 8 am and noon."

"Christmas trees, like all of those in those fields out of town?" I asked.

"I suppose so. I guess that's why they look like Christmas trees and not just regular trees. I never thought about it before, but of course, we weren't old enough before, anyway."

"We can make money for fishing and gas for Edna," Dewey said.

"Yeah. It sounds like a good idea to me," I said.

"Too bad Dougie won't be able to do it," Chick said grinning.

"What do you mean? I'm same age as you," Dougie replied.

"Yeah, but you're not five feet tall, are you?" Chick said laughing.

Dougie jumped to his feet; Chick took off running across the yard with Dougie in hot pursuit. "I'll show you who's five feet," Dougie yelled. Dewey and I laughed at them. Dougie was the shortest of the four of us and we always gave him static about being a dwarf, so he was used to it, but he liked to act like he was mad. They quickly tired of running around the house and joined us at the picnic table again.

"Well, let's do it, huh?" Chick panted.

"Yeah, sounds like a good idea," we all agreed.

The following Monday morning we pulled up to the old depot in Big Edna. Many of the other kids rode bikes, but we were past that *kiddy* stage now. We all gathered around a man who told us about the job. We would be hauled to the fields of trees in an old school bus, and we should each bring a lunch. We'd start at seven in the morning and work until mid-afternoon, so we'd be working in the cooler part of the day. The pay was $1.25 per hour, and if we worked the whole season we got ten cents per hour bonus at the end. Normally it took about three or four weeks to trim all of the trees.

We all were pretty excited about getting hired. We filled out the papers and were told to report to the depot at seven the next morning. That evening I asked Mom to make me some sandwiches and she put them in a little cooler in the refrigerator. The next morning Dewey and the guys picked me up and we drove up to the depot to get on the bus with about twenty five other kids from town.

We rode out of town to the sand prairies where fields of trees were planted in rows. Some of the fields were half a mile across. When we got to the first field, foreman Cecil Piper stood up and instructed us to get off the bus and line up so he could show us how to do the job.

Cecil was an old guy, kind of short and squat, wearing a pale blue cotton button up shirt under bib overalls. He had about a weeks worth of whiskers and a dribble of brown tobacco juice streaking his chin. "Hurry up! Get in a line here!" he shouted.

We all stood in a line and Cecil showed us the tools of the trade. "Now a few of you guys, the tallest ones, will use these shears," he said holding up a big clipper that was like an oversized scissors. "You'll take two rows of trees and just clip the top of each tree." He walked over to a tree near the edge of the field. "Now, look here," he said taking the top of the tree in his hand. "See these light colored parts here?" We all nodded. "That is what is called the candle. It's the new growth this year." We all acknowledged that we understood. "Now you toppers will choose the best of the candles and just clip off the very tip of it. Then you clip off the other three or four candles about half way down." We all nodded again. "That will make this candle the leader and it will be the main stem of the tree. Wherever you cut these candles, there will be a scab that will heal over and it will sprout three or four new buds that will be candles next year. That's why these trees get sheared each year. Shearing makes them thicker and fuller. Got that?"

We all nodded again.

"Now, the rest of you will take these," he said reaching into a box and pulling out a machete with a blade about 18 inches long. You go behind the toppers and just slice all the candles off about half way of their growth, all the way down to the bottom of the tree. You just walk around the tree and whack them off, and then move on to the next tree. Be sure to fetch 'em in at the bottom, too. Don't leave them gangly at the bottom!"

Everyone was looking at the box of machetes, hoping to get one of them instead of the shears.

"Okay, you and you and you," Cecil walked down the row and chose the tallest people for toppers. I tried to stand shorter but sure as heck, I was chosen. He repeated that we each had to do two rows and to keep ahead of the trimmers, and then he told us to start.

We all were pretty careful for the first few trees, and then it became a bit easier as we developed the technique. Now we were off and clipping into the field. We could hear Cecil giving orders to the rest, and the blades pinging as they sliced off the side candles.

It was cool and pretty easy work, and once we the toppers had the technique under control, we were chatting as we moved along ahead of our trimmers. We worked across the field and when we got to the other end we moved over several rows and started back. As I began working back I came by Dewey and Chick who were whacking off the sides of the trees. "This isn't so bad," I said.

"Nope. Not bad at all," Chick said.

"Where's Dougie?"

"He's over there," he said pointing toward the west. "Cecil is hollering at him about not "Fetchin 'em in at the bottom!"

I laughed but I had to keep going or my trimmers would be catching up, so on we went. As the sun climbed higher in the sky, the temperature rose to hot and the deer flies came out. You'd be working along and one of those darn deer flies would land on you and bite. You didn't have time to swat them; once they landed you were bit. And they hurt! They'd take a little bit of hide with them, and then next time, they'd go right back and bite you there again. They were like miniature vampires.

When we got back across the field Cecil told us to take a water break. They had a big metal water can with a spigot and a couple of tin cups. We lined up and drank and soon the trimmers were there with us taking a break too.

"How's it going?" I asked Dougie.

"Fetch 'em in at the bottom!" he said. "I'd like to fetch him in at his stupid bottom."

Chick and I laughed. "Cecil picking on you?"

"He must think since I'm short, he can get on me," Dougie said. "But I'll be okay. I'm ignoring him."

A short time later Cecil came to the water can and started yelling at us to get back to work. "Get back in a row, Combat," he said to Dougie.

We all snickered and started off into our rows of trees, working back across the field. The sun rose higher and so did the temperature. By mid-morning we had out shirts off and wishing we had worn shorts. Finally it was noon and time for lunch. The four of us gathered in what little shade we could find and sat down to eat. "Boy, I don't know if I can take three weeks of this or not," Dougie said.

"It wasn't so bad when it was cooler, but now it's mega hot," I said.

"Well, we'll probably just go across and back once more. They said we'd only work till mid-afternoon," Chick offered.

"I hope so. I'm about ready for a swim," Dewey said.

That was on all our minds as we trudged across the field, sweat running down our backs and deer flies biting at will. Finally Cecil told us to put our tools back in the wooden boxes and we all loaded into the bus and rode back to town. We were all full of pine pitch from the trees, so we were careful when we got into Big Edna. We stopped off at each of our houses and got soap, shampoo, towel and clean clothes and then went to the Gosey. Dougie brought a can of paint thinner and an old rag. It worked quite well to get the pine pitch off. Then we stripped and took our bath in the Gosey. We were all lying in the sand resting afterward when Dougie said, "I don't think Cecil likes me."

"Why do you think that?"

"He doesn't pick on anyone else… just me."

"Well, if he keeps it up, we'll have to make him sorry he's doing it," I said.

Everyone looked at me and grinned. We didn't have a plan, but we could easily figure out something if Cecil kept picking on our buddy.

Next day we finished the field we started the first day, and then moved a few miles farther down the road to another smaller field. The day went along pretty well, until Cecil came up to the toppers and started ranting and raving about skipping dogs. "See these bad trees? They ain't no good… no shape to them. Just skip them. They're dogs. You're wasting time with them. Ain't never gonna make a tree."

"How are we supposed to know?" I asked.

"Use your judgment. You guys are smarty pants high school kids, ain't you?"

Off Cecil went, yelling at someone else, and the rest of the toppers and I kept working. A while later I came upon a nasty looking tree and just skipped it. Then later Cecil came up my row. "You skipped one!" he yelled at me.

"It was ugly, so I didn't waste time on it… just like you said."

He stood there a few seconds, and then turned and walked away. I shook my head. The old fool was getting sunstroke or something.

At break time, we were getting a drink when Cecil came up to us. "Combat, you keepin' up today?"

Dougie ignored him. "Hey, Combat! You go deaf?"

Dougie reached out his hand, took the cup from me and filled it.

"Combat! I'm talkin to you!"

Dougie threw the cup of water over his shoulder right into Cecil's face.

"Hey! You snot. What you doin?"

Dougie turned and looked surprised. "Were you talking to me?"

"Darn right, I was. What's wrong with you?"

"Nothing's wrong with me, and my name isn't Combat. It's Doug, Dougie, or Douglas, whichever you like. But don't call me Combat! Okay?" Dougie was nose to nose with Cecil.

Cecil just stood there, tobacco juice ru nning down his chin. He opened his mouth as if to say something, and then turned and walked away. We all cheered and patted Dougie on the back.

"Whew!" Dougie said. "If you ever have to get that close to him, don't. Boy, does he stink!"

We all laughed and soon Cecil yelled to get back to work.

We had our first week of work in and took the weekend off for fishing and swimming. When we reported for work Monday morning, Chick noticed that Cecil was wearing the exact same clothes he had worn the entire week before. "He hasn't changed all week!"

"I told you not to get too close to him," Dougie said. "I about passed out when he breathed on me."

About mid-day that day, Chick found an arrowhead as he trimmed a tree. It was a beauty and we all gathered around him as he showed it off. From then on we kept one eye to the ground looking for more of them. We were getting pretty good at our jobs and could trim a field of trees in a lot less time than the first week, and before we knew it, the second week was over. Cecil announced that we had about three or four days of work left, and then we'd get our bonus for staying on the whole time. Many of the kids had left after just a few days, but we stuck it out despite the heat getting worse each day and the deer flies nearly eating us alive.

Next to the last day of work, we were eating our lunch, and Dougie was doing an impression of Cecil. He walked around bowlegged, let some spit run down his chin and yelled, "Fetch'er in, fetch'er in, Goddamit! Fetch'er in at the bottom!" As he ranted, we laughed like mad, and suddenly there stood Cecil.

I tried to get Dougie's attention, but Dougie continued. "Combat! Fetch'er in!" he yelled. "Skip those dogs, you idiots. Can't you tell a dog when you see it?" Then he lifted his arm and pretended to smell his armpit. He rolled his head from side to side and pretended to faint.

He laughed as he sat up and then he noticed that none of us were laughing. "What's...?" He turned around and saw Cecil, about ready to explode.

"Think yer pretty funny there, Combat? Well, that little stunt just got you fired. Go to the bus and the driver will take you back to town."

"But, if I don't work tomorrow I won't get my bonus," Dougie said.

"Tough. That'll teach ya to be a smart ass."

"Wait a minute!" Chick said. "Dougie's worked hard for three weeks. That's not fair."

"You can go with him. You're fired, too."

Dewey looked at me and I grinned. We walked over to Cecil and handed him our tools. "You fire them, you fire us, too," Dewey said.

"Good! Yer all fired," said Cecil.

The four of us gathered up our lunch pails and just as we started for the bus, Dewey stopped and walked back to Cecil. "Just wanted to tell you, this is what I think of you." Then he let a tremendous fart. The four of us doubled over with laughter and so did all of the other kids. Cecil's mouth dropped open but he didn't know what to say.

"I know you won't smell it," Dewey said, "'Cause you stink so bad. That probably smells like o'de'cologne."

The driver grinned at us when we got on the bus. "I don't know how you guys put up with that stinkin' old man this long," he said.

He started the bus and we headed back to town. Of course, when we got to Big Edna we all piled in and went back to the Gosey. We had kept the paint thinner, soap and shampoo in the trunk, and soon we were in the water getting cleaned off. "Hey guys. Thanks for sticking up for me," Dougie said.

"No problem, Combat," Chick said.

I'd never seen Dougie move so fast. He put some kind of wrestling hold on Chick and they went under. Chick came up sputtering and laughing. "Not bad for a little guy," he said as he was pulled under again.

"Okay! Okay! Truce!" Chick said as they came up the second time.

We all laughed and moved up onto the sandy beach to lay down. "Sorry I cost us the bonus," Dougie said.

"Ah, who cares? It was worth it to see the look on Cecil's face when he saw you making fun of him... and when Dewey farted on him! That was worth *at least* five dollars."

We may have lost a few dollars, but we were rich in friendship, beyond our imagination.

Oysters Rockefeller?

Despite his habitual gas attacks and sometimes lax manners, Dewey was a pretty good cook. He had become our official chef on our camping trips and cookouts. He got his skills working for his parents who owned a restaurant and bar. Many times we were the beneficiaries of Dewey's job, getting leftovers from the restaurant. Of course, we were always happy to help out by eating up chicken, deep fried fish, French fries, and other goodies, just to keep them from going to waste.

When we planned camping trips, Dewey often brought some delicious things that we'd never, ever get if it was up to the rest of us to provide the food. Most of the time his mom was more than generous, knowing that the food surely wouldn't go to waste. Once, he came with a large container of prime rib. To us it looked like some leftover roast beef, but his mom about had a heart attack when she found out that we had eaten nearly ten pounds of very expensive meat that she could have served in the restaurant on sandwiches. She was a little peeved over that one, but normally it was no problem for us to feast on her leftovers.

Of course, we were always available to help out if she needed something done at the restaurant. Dewey helped on weekends, and we would often help him with his chores, which made his mom happy.

Friday evening was fish fry night. Dewey worked on the deep fryer, taking care of the fish orders, while another cook did the potatoes, steak, and chicken. We usually tried to show up about the time the restaurant closed, hoping for some fish and fries that would go to waste. We filed into the kitchen about the time Dewey was done. "Hey, you guys hungry?" Dewey asked.

"Of course. Why do you think we're here?" I replied.

Dewey dumped a big fry basket of fries onto a plate and tossed a half dozen pieces of fish with them. "We almost sold out all the fish tonight. Sorry, but that's all we've got left."

"No problem," Chick said.

Dewey was putting things away as we stuffed the fish and fries into our mouths. He turned and set a large can on the work table next to us. "Here, try one of these," he said dipping his fingers into the liquid in the can. He fished around a little and then he lifted an oyster out of the can. It looked like the clams we used to catch catfish on the river. Dewey held up the oyster and a long string of snotty liquid dripped off.

"Oh my gawd! That's gross," Dougie said.

Dewey let the oyster drip again and then held it over his mouth and dropped it in. He chewed a couple of times and swallowed!

"Arrgh. That's sick," I said, gagging.

"Dewey, are you crazy?" Chick said with a horrified look.

"They're good," Dewey said dipping his hand into the can and lifting out another oyster. "Here. Try one."

He held the oyster toward us and just then it dripped a big splash of snot onto the plate of fries. We all backed up like he was pointing a loaded gun at us. "Get that thing away," Chick said as he backed into the wall. Dewey just laughed, tipped his head back and dropped the slimy thing down his throat. "You guys don't know what you're missing."

"I don't eat bait," I said.

"Yeah. That's bait, not food," Chick added.

"That's just plain gross!" Dougie exclaimed, gagging.

Dewey just chuckled. We finished our fries, carefully avoiding those that had oyster snot on them. Dewey went upstairs to change clothes so we could go out cruising in Big Edna.

We drove down to the Root Beer stand and got cold root beers. While we were sitting there talking, Dewey said, "Hey, we're having a game feed at the restaurant tomorrow night. Want to come?"

"A game feed? What do you mean?"

"The Sportsman's club is having it and we're cooking it for them. It's all wild game—deer, moose, bear, beaver—you know... strange stuff like that."

"Hmm. Is it okay that we come?"

"Just come to the kitchen. I'll get plenty of food and we can eat in there together."

Being guys who never turned down free food, we agreed. We

spent the rest of the night just cruising, and the next day went by without much happening. Dewey had to go to work early in the afternoon and told us to show up about 8 o'clock.

We trooped into the kitchen at the appointed time. The restaurant was full of people who were eating and drinking and having a good time. There were long tables with roasters full of food, and people were just filing past loading up their plates. "I'll get us some food," Dewey said, and headed out to the dining room.

We pulled stools up to the work table and sat down. Dewey came back with two plates full of meat and set them on the table. "This one is Moose," he said pointing to a plate of meat that looked like beef roast, "And this one is Bear." We each got a plate and put some of the meat on them. One by one we tasted the meat and all agreed it was very good. "Never thought I'd eat a bear," Dougie said.

Next Dewey brought in a plate of pheasant that tasted like chicken and a plate of elk, which was very good. "One more to try," Dewey said and went to get the last plate.

He came back with a plate of small chunks of meat in brown gravy and small pieces of carrot and potato mixed in. "Try this and see how you like it," Dewey said.

We all took some of the meat and tasted it. "Mmm. This is the best yet," Chick said. "Tastes like pork."

"Yeah, this *is* good," I said. "Really tender and the gravy is great."

"Really good, Dewey. What is it?" Dougie asked.

"Oysters," Dewey said.

"Oysters! No way."

"Well, that's what they call it. Actually they call it *Rocky Mountain Oysters."*

I was puzzled. *"Rocky Mountain?* How do they have oysters in the Rocky Mountains? There's no ocean there."

"Yeah, Dewey. What's going on? These aren't oysters," Chick said.

"I didn't say they *were oysters.* I said they *call them oysters.* Don't you recognize what they look like?

We all sat there looking at the small ovals of meat.

"Slide two of them together, so the flat sides are together."

We all pushed the pieces of meat as Dewey said. They made a

little oval shaped chunk that looked something like an egg. "Okay, Dewey. What are we suppose to be seeing here," I said.

Dewey couldn't keep the grin from his face. "What do you have that looks like that?"

We were completely baffled. What did we have that is shaped like an egg?

Suddenly Dougie got a look on his face that was something between horror and stomach flu. "Dewey, are these…?"

"Pig nuts. Yup."

"Pig what?"

"Pig nuts. You know… testicles, the family jewels," Dewey said.

Suddenly we knew what Dewey was saying and our faces drained all color. "Dewey, you're kidding. Tell me you're kidding," Chick said.

Dewey shook his head. "Nope. That's what they are. But they're good, don't you think?"

"Good? Dewey, they're testicles! Are you crazy?"

"You thought they were good until you knew what they were," Dewey said.

We were flummoxed. We didn't have a good answer for him. "Yeah… but they're… testicles," I said.

I looked to the Dougie and Chick for support but they were grinning. "He's right. We thought they were good until we knew what they were," Dougie said.

I thought it over, and I guess it did make sense. I looked at Dewey and he was grinning. "See, I'm trying to teach you guys about gourmet food. Now, who's going to try an oyster—one of those real ones?"

Chick looked across the table at Dewey. "You got us on this one, Dewey, but I still don't eat bait."

"Well, eat up your pig jewels and I'll get you some more, then."

For some reason we had lost our appetites. Even though the Rocky Mountain oysters had been delicious, somehow they didn't taste quite as good now.

Clamming

We were out of work much too early in the summer. After our short-lived careers as Christmas tree trimmers, we had about a week off with nothing to do. Chick, Dewey and I were sitting down at the Gosey fishing when Dougie came riding down the sand road on his bike.

"Hey, I thought you had to go to your Grandma's today," I said as he slid to a stop, throwing up a cloud of dust.

"I found this," he said waving the newspaper at us, "and my parents said I could stay home."

We all gathered around Dougie as he opened the paper. There was a picture of a kid about our age standing next to a huge pile of clams. Behind him was a steaming tank. The caption below the photo told about the summer business that had sprung up in southeastern Wisconsin.

Dougie read the story that accompanied the picture: *"Little did anyone suspect that the streams of the area held so many clams. They were found by accident by a turtle trapper who was trying to drive a stake into the stream bed and couldn't find an open space between all the clams. Once he talked to the right people, he found that there was a thriving market for clam shells in Japan, where they are cut into small cubes and inserted into oysters as the catalyst to cause the oyster to form a pearl."* Dougie continued reading the story about the man and his son, and that they would begin hiring crews to harvest the clams.

"Holy smokes! We could do that!" I said excitedly.

"No kidding. We know all about clams. We use them for bait all the time," Chick said.

We all babbled about how rich we would be. It didn't take long for us to put Dougie's bike in Big Edna's trunk and head to our homes to seek permission to go on this new quest. We started with Chick's mom, and although she was skeptical, she said it would be okay with her if the rest of our parents agreed. It took most of the morning but we finally had permission from all of them, so we started making plans for our trip.

"We'd better go right away tomorrow, so they don't hire a bunch of other people and we'd get there too late for a job," Dewey said.

We all agreed with that.

"Where are we going to stay?" Chick asked.

"How much money do we have left in our treasury?" Dougie inquired of Chick.

Chick was our treasurer. Whenever we worked at jobs that paid us in one lump sum, he put the money away, and it was there when we needed it for a big purchase or trip. "I think with the pig pen cleaning and the wallpaper job and tree trimming we've probably got about ninety dollars," he said.

"And we've each got some money of our own, too," I said.

"Yeah. So we're good on money so far."

"Okay. Let's get some clothes together and go down there and see what it's like. We'll take our treasury money; if it's a good deal, we'll find a place to stay and work this week; if it's not, we'll come home. We'll only be out a little gas and food money." This seemed to be okay with everyone, so we decided to leave first thing in the morning.

We each packed some clothes and essential things. Dewey picked us up the next morning, and then we stopped at Carl's to fill the gas tank. Carl was used to us getting eighty one cents, or so, at a time, so he almost tipped over when we spent such a huge amount of money. "Yeah, you bet. Um hmm," he said as he walked slowly back toward his barber chair with a large amount of our money in his hand.

Off we went toward Monroe. "Do you know where we apply?" Chick asked Dougie.

Dougie opened the now quite crumpled paper, carefully read the whole article, and then re-read it. He looked confused. "Well, it really doesn't say. It talks about the Sugar River, the Pecatonica River, and the Rock River. It does mention two towns in the story—Monroe and Albany."

"So we don't know where to go?" I asked.

"Well, I guess we'll just have to get down there and ask somebody if they know where this place is," Dougie said pointing to the picture of the pile of clams and the kid.

It was a beautiful day. We rolled down Big Edna's windows and tuned in the radio to one of our favorites, *WLS*, and listened to all the new tunes with the volume as high as it would go. After a couple of pit stops for snacks and pop, we pulled into Monroe. "Where should we ask?" Dewey said as we pulled up to a stop sign.

We looked around and then Dougie pointed to a gas station down the street. "Let's pull in there and ask. We can go to the bathroom and get some more snacks at the same time."

We did as Dougie suggested. While we took turns peeing, I went to the counter and asked the man about the story. He looked at the paper but shook his head. "Sorry. Don't know nothing 'bout this." I started for the door when he said, "Why don't you stop at the Sheriff's office? They'd probably know."

"Good idea. Where is that?" I asked.

While the man gave me directions, the rest of the guys came in. Chick got out the Bank and paid for some snacks and pops. We followed the directions to the Sheriff's office and pulled into the parking lot amid several squad cars. A couple officers were coming out the door and said hi to us. Dewey asked them about the clammers.

One deputy looked confused, but the second one knew what we were talking about. "Yeah, I was down that way on patrol a couple days ago," he said. "You boys looking for work there?"

"Yeah. We read about it in the newspaper and thought it might be a good summer job," Dougie said holding up the newspaper.

"Well, they seem to be decent people," he said. "You know how to get to the Pec?"

We looked at him, not knowing what a Pec was. "The Pecatonica River," he said when he realized we were confused. "That's what we call it here... the Pec."

We told him we didn't know our way around, that this was our first time in the area. He gave us directions and Chick wrote them down on the back of a paper bag that had held our pop.

"Where are you boys going to live while you work here?" the officer asked.

We shrugged our shoulders. "We thought we'd see about a job

first, and then worry about a place to sleep," Chick said.

"Well, the hotel here in Monroe is pretty cheap and the rooms are clean. If you get the jobs, that might be a place to look," he said.

We thanked him for all the information, got in Big Edna and pulled out onto the street. Chick read the directions and soon we were headed out of town down a gravel road. We made a turn here and there and then we found a blue school bus and a couple of pickup trucks parked at the edge of a farm pasture. We pulled off the road and found an old man stirring the very tank that was in the photo over a gas burner. We walked up to see what was going on. The tank was filled with clams and boiling water. Thick steam rose up and the smell was something between fish and swamp mud.

"Hi mister," Dougie said. "Are you the boss here?"

"Nope. I'm the clam cooker. The boss and crew are out on the river clammin'," the old man said. He wore bib overalls and a button-up cotton shirt that had once been white. About five days of whiskers adorned his face and a floppy straw hat sat on his head barely covering snow white hair, and shading his twinkling blue eyes. He grinned at us with a smile that was missing all four middle front teeth. "You guys lookin' for work?" he asked.

"Yeah. We saw the story in the newspaper, and we were hoping to get jobs," I said.

"Well, take this road down that way a piece," he said nodding. You'll see a boat landing. That's where they put in today. They've got two big flatbottoms. They were gonna work downstream from there. If you wait till about noon, they'll come up to the landing for lunch. Then you can talk to him... Rooney... Buster Rooney."

We thanked the old man, got back in Big Edna and drove until we found the boat landing. Just as he said, there were two pickups and two empty boat trailers parked there. We backed Big Edna into the shade, sat back and waited for noon. We had enough junk food to keep us busy, and it didn't seem long when we heard the sound of outboard motors coming up the river. We walked down to the edge of the river and watched the two boats pull in.

The kid in the newspaper picture was sat in the front of the first boat and a man that looked like his father was driving it. Two kids about our age were in the second boat driven by another older man. When we helped them pull the boats up on shore we saw many clams in the bottom of both boats.

"Hello. Is one of you Mr. Rooney?" Chick asked.

"That's me," the man in back of the first boat said. "You guys looking for work?"

"Yes sir. We saw the story in the newspaper and thought we'd like to give it a try."

By now the whole crew was on the river bank and had opened coolers from the pickups and they were eating their lunch. "You guys aren't city boys are you?" Mr. Rooney asked.

"No sir. We live in a small town on the Wisconsin River—Muscoda," Dougie said. "We spend all of our time fishing and hunting and swimming. And when we can find jobs, we work hard, too."

"Not afraid of hard work?"

"So far this summer, we cleaned out twenty pig pens, steamed off a house full of wall paper, and trimmed Christmas trees, so I guess we're not afraid to work," I said.

Mr. Rooney smiled. "You don't mind getting wet and a little dirty, then?"

"Nope," Chick said. "Wet and dirty are okay with us."

"Okay. You've got a job. I pay twenty dollars a day and expect a full day's work. We get on the river at eight a.m., take an hour break at noon, and then work till five in the afternoon. When we get back to the cook site, I expect you to help unload the clams and then your day is done. Any problems with that?"

Twenty dollars a day! We all shook our heads no at the same time. "That sounds great to us, sir."

Mr. Rooney grinned. "A couple of things. One, don't call me sir. Call me Rooney. Two, I'll pay a fair day's wage for a fair day's work, so don't try to screw me or you'll be on your way back to Muscratville in a flash."

"That's Muscoda, and don't worry, Rooney, you'll get your money's worth from us," Dougie said. "When can we start?"

"Be here first thing in the morning ready to go," Rooney said.

"What do we need to bring?"

"Just you. Wear shorts or a swimming suit. You'll be in the water most of the day."

We thanked Rooney and piled into Big Edna, excited about the job and the pay. As we pulled out onto the road back to Monroe we could hardly control our excitement. "Holy smokes! Twenty dollars a day! I about pooped when he said that," Chick said.

"If he only knew we've been working for about a dollar an hour all our lives," Dougie said.

Talking a mile a minute, we were soon back in Monroe. "Let's find that hotel and see how much it costs," Chick suggested.

We drove downtown and easily found the hotel, the biggest building in town. We parked on the street and went inside. It was old but it looked well cared for. We walked up to the desk and a man came out of an office behind the desk. "May I help you?"

"We were wondering about getting a room," Dougie said.

"One room for all of you?"

"How much are the rooms?"

"A single with one double bed is sixteen dollars. A double with two double beds is twenty dollars."

We looked at each other. "Just a minute, please, sir," Chick said. We stepped back from the counter a ways and huddled.

"Twenty bucks a day. That's pretty expensive." Chick said.

"Yeah, but if he would let all of us in one room for twenty bucks that wouldn't be so bad," Dougie said.

"If we're making twenty bucks each per day, we can afford it for a while. Maybe we can stay here this week, and then drive home over the weekend and get our tent. Then we'll find a place to camp next week and save the cost of the room," I suggested.

Everyone thought that was a good idea. We walked up the desk again. "Um, sir, could we all stay in one of the twenty dollar rooms?" Chick asked.

"What are you doing here in Monroe? If you don't mind my asking."

"We saw the story in the newspaper about the clamming, and we drove down here all the way from Muscoda to try to get jobs."

He looked us over. "Can I expect you to act like gentlemen? No loud noise and no disturbing the other guests?"

"Of course, sir," Dewey said. "We're very quiet and courteous." I heard Chick snicker behind me.

The man smiled at us. "Okay. That's pretty admirable to come all this way to find work, so I'll take a chance on you. But... one complaint from another guest and out you go."

"Don't worry, sir. We'll be good. We promise."

"Okay. How many nights do you plan to stay?"

We huddled again. "If we pay for two nights," Chick said, "we'll still have enough money for food and gas. Then if we can get paid, we can pay for a couple more until we get a day off to go home for the tent."

We walked back up. "Can we pay for two nights now?" I asked. "Then once we get paid, we'll have money to pay for the other nights?"

"That will be fine. One of you sign the register and put down all of your names. That will be forty dollars. I'll have the maid take some extra towels up to room twenty-two. The shower and bathroom is at the end of the hall. Your beds will be made and clean towels brought in each morning after you've left. Here is your key," he said handing us a big heavy key. Attached to it was a piece of leather engraved with the number twenty-two.

Chick got out the Bank. Actually, the Bank was a wool sock that had lost its mate, tied shut with an old leather shoe string. Our fortune was in that sock. He counted out forty dollars and handed it to the man.

"You can park you vehicle in back if you like," the man said.

We thanked him, and walked out to Big Edna and drove around to the parking lot in back of the hotel. With our clothes, the left-over pops and snacks, we climbed the stairs to our room. Chick unlocked the door and we went in. It was nice; nothing special but it was clean and the beds looked soft. There was a closet and a dresser, so we unpacked our clothes and put everything away. "I'm going to test out the pooper," Dewey said, and then ambled off down the hallway to the bathroom.

We lay on the beds and tested them out. Then Dougie got up and looked out the windows. "What are we going to do the rest of the day? Too bad we didn't bring our fishing poles. We could go fishing."

That had been an oversight, but we would correct it on the next trip to Monroe. Then Dewey came back. "There's two bathrooms and two rooms with showers and bath tubs," he reported.

"Which one did you go in Dewey?" Dougie asked.

"Why?"

"'Cause I gotta go and I don't want to go in the same one. It probably stinks in there."

We all had a good laugh, Dougie left for the bathroom, and Dewey tested out the beds. Getting bored just sitting in the room Chick said, "I'm going down and ask that guy if there's any good sightseeing here."

Dougie came back and Chick walked in right behind him. "Hey! They've got a brewery here. The guy said you can take a tour of it for free. That sounds like a good thing to do."

We were all excited about that, so we locked up the room and followed Chick's directions to the Huber Brewery. A sign on a door said the tours started every hour on the hour. It was about fifteen minutes until the next tour so we went inside and sat in what looked like an old-time beer hall. A lady asked us if we'd like something to drink. We all said "of course." Much to our disappointment, she served us big mugs of root beer, smiling as she set them on our table. "We give the older folks the Real stuff."

A college kid in leather shorts, suspenders, knee socks, white shirt and a goofy little hat with a feather in the side came and told us the history of the brewery, and then he took us through the place. It was really cool to look down into the huge copper kettles as the hops and all the other ingredients were mixed and cooked. Then we went into a big cellar where huge tanks of beer were aging. Then it was on to the canning and bottling part of the brewery. Finally we came back to the beer hall and were treated to big baskets of pretzels and more root beer. "Where'd you get those fancy leather britches?" Dewey asked the guide.

"These are Lederhosen. They're what people in Germany wear in the summer time," he said.

"Wouldn't be very good for swimming," Dewey said. They'd get all hard and cracked if they were in the river as much as we are most of the summer."

Our guide wished us a fine day, and then he went off with another group to show them the brewery. We ate all the pretzels, drank our root beers, and thanked the lady for her hospitality. As we walked out into the late afternoon sun, we decided to take a little nap, and then we'd find a place for supper before our first night in a hotel.

By suppertime we were starved, so we drove around until we found an *A&W* root beer stand. A girl on roller skates came rolling up and took our order. We were really hungry, and we ordered so much food and drink that when it was ready, it took two girls on roller skates to bring it to us. Three of those little metal trays hung from Big Edna's windows. After our grand dining experience, we drove around Monroe for a while, and then decided it was time to go back to the hotel to get some sleep.

Chick and Dougie were first in the bathroom, and when they got back Dewey and I took our turn. When I got back to the room, Chick and Dougie were in one bed and Dewey was lying in the other, grinning. "Who decided where we were gonna sleep?" I asked.

"What? Don't you want to sleep with me?" Dewey asked acting offended.

"It's nothing against you, Dewey. It's your butt and those awful noises and smells that come from it."

"Oh, come on. I'll be good," Dewey said laughing.

I turned off the light and went to my side of the bed. When I pulled back the covers to get in, the most awful stink rose up from the bed. Dewey was giggling like a middle school girl. "Jeez, Dewey! You did it all ready," I said fanning the stink away.

"It was an orphan fart," Dewey said.

"Orphan?"

Dewey was giggling so hard he could hardly talk. "Yeah. An orphan. No pop."

We all broke out laughing.

I swatted Dewey with my pillow. "No more now. You go to the

bathroom if you have to do that again," I said as sternly as I could manage.

"Yes, Mom," Dewey said.

I settled into my side of the bed, and I was just drifting off when I heard another blast from Dewey. "Oops. Slipped," he said.

An hour later, we finally went to sleep. It didn't seem like very long afterward that the alarm clock rang. We all got up, went to the bathroom, and dressed in tee shirts, shorts and tennis shoes. We had given ourselves an extra hour so we had time to stop at a truck stop for a good breakfast. We asked the waitress there for some sandwiches and apples to go. We'd have that for our lunch break at noon.

Everyone was waiting for us when we got to the boat landing. Rooney introduced us to the other guys. Eric, the kid from the newspaper article was Rooney's son, as we had guessed. The older guy was Fred, and the two kids our age were Billy and Tom from Monroe. We all got into the boats and headed down the narrow river. "This isn't what we call a river back home," Dewey said to Eric. "We live on the Wisconsin. It's twenty times wider than this. We call something like this a creek."

We motored quite a long way, and then the two older men piloting the boats stopped the motors. Eric and Billy slipped off their shoes, stepped into the river and set out an anchor for each boat. Rooney and Fred stayed in the boats while Tom and the rest of us took off our shoes and stepped out into the thigh deep water. Rooney handed each of us a round metal basket like the ones used to gather eggs. "Eric, show the boys how to do it."

Eric walked a little ways below the boat and sat down in the river, water up to mid-chest. With the basket between his legs, he began feeling with his hands to the sides and in front of him. He came up with a clam and dropped it into the basket. Then he picked one from the other side, and he was soon dropping them in quite regularly. Once in a while he'd pick one up and toss it back into the water off to the side.

"Bring a Mucket and those good ones so they can see," Rooney said to his son.

Eric stood, picked up his basket and brought it next to the boat. Rooney took a clam from his hand. "See this one here? See how smooth it is? These are no good. Their shells are too thin. We call them Muckets. Throw them back... we don't want them."

We looked at the clam and Dewey said, "We've got lots of those at home. We use them for catfish bait."

"They're good for that, but not much else," Eric said.

Then Rooney picked up a clam that had a scalloped shell. "This one is called a Three Ridger... see these ridges? This is a good one. We keep these." He sorted through the basket and picked up another small compact clam with little bumps on the shell. "This one is a Warty Back. These are good, too," he said handing the clam to us.

Just then Tom tossed a large flat clam into the boat. "Show them that one, Rooney," he said.

The clam was very large but thin and sharp on the edges. "This one is an Elephant Ear, or another name is Heel Splitter. See how sharp this shell is? You got to be careful walking or these can cut your foot, or split your heel."

We all examined the clam and then Rooney tossed it into the boat. "That's all there is to it. We keep Elephant Ears, Warty Backs and Three Ridgers. The others go back. Sit just far enough apart so you can cover the entire bottom, and then move along and pick 'em up. When your basket is full, dump it in the boat. When one guy goes to dump, the others next to him stay put so he can come back to the same spot to start again. Fred and I will keep the boats just above you so you don't have to walk a long way. Any questions?"

We had none, so the seven of us young guys sat down across the river and began clamming. Before long Billy had his basket full, so we stopped while he dumped it, and then mine was full. On we went, clamming, dumping and then more clamming, and the morning slipped away much faster than I had ever expected it would. We filled Fred's boat and he had left to take it up to the landing to start unloading. Rooney's boat was nearly full, so Eric tied a handkerchief to a tree branch to mark the spot. We climbed into the boat with Rooney and rode back to the landing.

Our measly few sandwiches and apples didn't begin to fill us up.

We were famished! Billy and Tom had a whole loaf of bread and a big package of cold meat. They offered us an extra sandwich… that we gladly accepted. Eric had a whole package of chocolate chip cookies, and we got a few of those, too. We were quite thankful that we had the good fortune to find some really good guys to work with.

Fred took us back downriver while Rooney unloaded the other boat. He showed up again later, and it was a good thing, because Fred's boat was nearly full. We began filling Rooney's boat the second time, and then the sun was getting low in the west.

My basket was just about full when I felt a clam with my right hand. I could tell that it was open, so I figured it was one that had died and the meat was gone. We found empty ones now and then, so I didn't think much about it. I was just lifting my hand from the water to drop the Warty Back into my basket when a large crawfish poked its head out of the open clam. An instant later its claw came out and clamped onto my finger. "Yeeooow!" I yelled, shaking my hand trying to get rid of the crawfish. Everyone was laughing. Eric jumped up and grabbed the crawfish behind its head. He tossed it into the boat.

"That big boy will make some good eating," he said grinning.

Our first day was finished and so were we. While it wasn't hard work, it was a long time to sit in the water. We helped unload the boats, and then the pickups at the cooking site. Old grandpa with the toothless grin was there stirring clams and scooping the cooked ones out of the vat. "What do you do with all that clam meat?" Dewey asked.

"Don't get any ideas Dewey," Chick said.

Rooney looked at us wondering what the joke was. "A farmer up the road feeds it to his hogs. They love it. It doesn't go to waste."

"Ever find any pearls in it?" Dougie asked.

Fred opened a little leather purse that he took from his pocket. He dumped out about a dozen small pearls. Most of them weren't very smooth, but kind of lumpy and not real round. There was one quite large one that was very nice and smooth. "That one will be worth a quite a bit, but most of them aren't too good from these clams," he said.

"You guys are welcome to sort through the meat before the farmer comes," Rooney said.

I stared at the huge mound of smelly dead clams and turned to the guys. They all shook their heads. "Guess not. We're gonna get cleaned up and find some food."

"Can you get along until tomorrow after work to get paid? A buyer is coming in the morning, and then I'll have plenty of money to pay you for today and tomorrow."

"No problem," Dougie said. "We've got enough for supper tonight."

"Well, okay," Rooney said. "You guys did a good days work. I'll see you in the morning."

We said good-bye to the rest of our new friends and drove back to Monroe. That evening we ate a huge meal at the same truck stop where we'd had breakfast. Then on the way back to the hotel, we bought a small cooler, several packages of cold meat, cheese, two loaves of bread, cookies and apples. We made sure it was all packed for the next day.

We clammed the Pec for the rest of that week. Then on Sunday we drove home to get our big tent, blankets and other camping stuff. After a brief visit with our parents, we met the rest of the crew near Argyle where we'd be clamming on the Sugar River. We set up our tent in a small park. The local policeman told us he'd keep an eye on our stuff while we were working.

We worked all that week and then took off Sunday for a day of rest. We invited Eric, Billy, and Tom to our campsite and we had a grand picnic with lots of hot dogs and food. We had become good friends, and it was nice to just sit and get to know them. It turned out that Tom shared with Dewey the talent of passing gas and before the night was over, they were demonstrating lighting farts with a match. When Tom told us about it, we had our doubts, but when he laid back, lifted his legs up over his head and then let one go over a lit match, we all just about had a heart attack from laughing.

Of course, Dewey had to try that, too, and he almost set the tent on fire with the dragon's tongue of fire that shot out. It was a great lot of fun.

The next week, we clammed every day, and on Saturday Rooney paid us. "Well, guys, my buyer is full. He has all the clams he can sell to Japan for this season, so this is our last day."

Although we were a little disappointed that it hadn't lasted a little longer, we knew it had to come to an end. But our great adventure had not only made us a lot of money, we had made some great new friends, too. Eric, Billy and Tom came to helped us clean up our campsite and load Big Edna. We all promised to keep in touch, but I suppose, in our hearts, we knew we'd never see them again.

When all was said and done, after all of our expenses were paid, we each cleared almost two hundred dollars. We each put twenty five dollars in the Bank sock, and Chick took it back to its hiding spot for a rainy day.

We hadn't been at the Gosey for a long time, and it was good to get back to our favorite spot for a few hours of fishing. After a while we decided to take a swim. We were goofing around when Dewey stopped. A serious expression came to his face like he was concentrating. "What are you doing, Dewey?" I said.

He grinned as he reached down. "I felt a clam with my toes, and I got it," he said, lifting the clam from the water.

We all stared at it. "Mucket," Dougie said.

Dewey tossed it back into the water. From then on, clams had much more meaning to us. Now we looked them over a lot closer than we ever had in all the years before our summer of clamming.

The Winds of War

I can see it in my mind. A Neanderthal family is resting by the fire; Mom and Dad, two teenage boys and a twelve year old girl watch as a Brontosaurus roast blackens on the spit. Then one of the boys leans over on his side and passes gas. The other boy begins to laugh crazily while Dad hides his face and chuckles. Mom and daughter hurl insulting grunts at the offending teen.

This is the way it has been for all time. Men and boys think farting is a hilarious event. Women and girls think all men are pigs.

Of course, my buddies, Dewey, Chick, Dougie and I were of the manly persuasion, and had taken fart art to a much higher plane.

During the summer that we had all turned thirteen and began camping out most of the summer, we had been entertained by Dewey and his vocal rear end almost every night. Of course, the rest of us had our days, too, but good old Dewey was always on deck to let one go. It always livened up the party, and over the years we developed passing gas into an Olympic-like event.

We re-named the act Krepetating, so as not to sound so boorish by talking about farts all the time. We also developed a decorum and point system whereby the participants could earn a score. It all came about after we had watched Olympic diving on TV. When a contestant finished his dive, the judges each held up score cards indicating the points they were awarding for form and perfection. We thought that could be adapted to farting, so we set out to develop a scoring system.

We rated each other by sound, loudness and smell. The first score of 1 was issued for a SBD fart. (Silent-But-Deadly). These were very small, quiet events that were sometimes called Orphan Farts. (No Pop.) Often the participant who let one of these didn't even ask for a rating.

Next were the Freeps. A Freep was a small snappy sounding fart. Tone quality was of the utmost importance. Bonus points were awarded for smell along with the Freep Points which were two, and possibly three with an adequate loudness and smell factor.

Getting into the more important farts, we next had the Flutter

Blast. This one was much more noticeable, usually one that would resound through the whole Church or upset a classroom. They were usually fairly long and had a mid range of loudness. As usual, bonus points were awarded for smell. Flutter Blasts were three pointers.

A Thrill Blow was a four pointer. This was a major fart. It often consisted of multiple tones and duration of several seconds. Its volume had to be loud enough to be heard by people at least twenty feet away. With bonus points for smell, this fart could be up to a six pointer.

At the top of the list was the show stopper—the Bazooka Blast. It was not often achieved because it took a lot of planning and pressure control. Occasionally when someone attempted a Bazooka Blast, he Frocked. Of course, a Frock was the emitting of Finesse Debris, or... well, you can guess. A Frock disqualified a person from that day's scoring, and meant one had to run home and change his undies, so we were very careful when attempting a Bazooka Blast.

The smell points were rather complicated. One point was awarded for those sweet ones that smell like bread dough; two points were for those that made the smeller fan the stink away; three points were awarded for one that caused the windows to get rolled down in a vehicle or made people run for cover; and a four pointer was one that caused the smeller to gag.

Though they very seldom were achieved, five points were awarded if the smeller actually hurled. Dewey was the only one to ever achieve that status. Once, while we were playing volley ball down at the park, he let one loose that drifted across the net, and the center on the other team lost his lunch on the court. Of course, that halted the game for a clean-up.

Once we got all the rules ironed out, it was not unusual for one of us let one go and then call for a "Courtesy Sniff" if we thought it merited a smell bonus point or two. We'd be at school in Phys. Ed. and Dewey would yell out, "Courtesy Sniff." The rest of us would waft a sample and then lift the number of fingers we had awarded to the effort. The girls would just shake their heads.

About the middle of the summer when we were fourteen, our farting game took a decidedly wonderful turn. We were in our tent at Dougie's house, had turned off the lantern and bedded down. A short time later, Dewey stumbled around looking for something. "Dewey, you oaf," Chick grumbled. "You stepped on my hand!"

"Where are those matches?" Dewey asked.

I could hear Dougie rummaging around. "Here," he said, apparently handing the book of matches to Dewey.

Dewey lay back down and then I saw him strike a match. I looked up from my pillow. He was holding it down near his butt. "Dewey, what the heck are you—"

There was a loud blast… at least a Thrill Blow… maybe a Flutter Blast, and a tongue of flame shot out of Dewey's butt and across the tent like from a flame thrower. The rest of us just about died laughing, and we were all soon calling for the matches as our attempts at pyrotechnics filled the tent with both sound and fire.

For the rest of that night and for many nights after, we burned farts. At first we did it like Dewey had done, by holding the match next to our butt and hoping for the best. That technique was, at best, kind of haphazard. Often you were too far away for ignition, and sometimes you got too close and almost set your undies on fire. So after a few miss-fires, we took turns lighting each others efforts.

Lighting technique also evolved after Dougie got the hair on his hand and arm burned off by a particularly violent blast from Chick. He had been holding the match above the flash point and the fire rose up and singed him. After that we always held the match below the opening. We also learned that wooden kitchen matches worked better than paper matches, and gave the holder more length to make the lighting a little safer.

We added three more bonus scores: Little pops of gas that just flashed were called Puffs—worth one point. A flame that extended six inches or more was considered a Flash—worth two points. The biggie—a flame that shot at least a foot—was called a Dragon Tongue. That was a three point bonus.

We had come a long way from "pull my finger". The girls and some of our male friends thought we were a bunch of complete pigs, but we really didn't care. We had a lot of fun with our little game. Dewey was the only one to ever achieve a perfect score of thirteen.

We were at a birthday party for one of the girls in our class. It was a real snooze. Everyone was bored stiff, and of course, good old Dewey was always primed and had one in the launch tube, so we talked him into lying back in a patio chair and lighting one. All of the adults were in the house, so Dewey laid back, lifted his legs over his head and got ready. Chick lit a birthday candle and held it in place. Dewey shut his eyes, his face turned red and he took a deep breath. Then he let go.

The blast was so loud that the adults in the house quit talking and looked out the windows toward the sky, thinking it was a sonic boom. The flame shot out and singed the hair on the girl's poodle who was watching with great interest. It was much too close to Dewey's backside, and when the thing went off, the poodle nearly got cooked. It took off like it had been shot, and wasn't found until two days later under the woodpile behind the garage. The girl's older brother who was home from college began laughing so hard that he threw up. Bonus points were sometimes awarded for exceptional stink that caused an onlooker to puke, but this time we awarded them anyway for the brother's upchuck.

It was the time of the Cold War with Russia. We heard later that NORAD had detected the blast and had launched bombers, but that was all just hearsay.

That one was as close to perfection as we had ever been. And I guarantee it sure turned a boring party into an event that no one would ever forget.

A Little Down Time

After our careers as clammers had ended, we decided to take some time for relaxation instead of finding more jobs for the summer. We all had a pretty good amount of money saved, and our community Bank was nice and full, so we felt that a few days of fishing and swimming would be justified.

Dewey picked us up and we drove out to our worm digging spot to dig some worms for a day of fishing. The worms were nice and fat and plentiful, since we hadn't been digging there for a long time. In just a short while we had enough for a good day or so of fishing.

"While we're out here, why don't we borrow a melon, too?" Chick suggested.

"Borrow a melon?" I asked grinning.

Chick chuckled. "Well, okay then. Let's sneak one and eat it."

Hundreds of watermelons, if not thousands of them, lay in a farm field just over the rise from our worm spot. We couldn't see any harm in taking *one* now and then. After all, the farmer had lots more than he could use.

"Dougie and I'll go," Chick said.

"I'll go too," Dewey said.

"No. You stay here," Chick said. "You'll make too much noise or fart so loud that the farmer will hear you."

Dewey protested, but he and I stayed behind. There was no need for all of us to go to take just one melon. Before long, Chick and Dougie ran down the dry creek bed toward us, Dougie carrying a large melon. "This one is perfect," he said. "I thumped it and it's ready for eating."

We gathered up our worms and shovels and loaded everything in Big Edna. A few minutes later we were sitting at the edge of the water at the Gosey with our bare feet soaking, and our lines baited. The water was low, it being the middle of the summer, and the fish weren't biting worth a hoot.

After an hour of fishing, we decided to strip off our clothes and wade out to a sandbar above the bridge. "We better leave our underwear on," Dougie said. "That sandbar is pretty close to the bridge. We don't want to get arrested for indecent exposure."

So we carried our poles and worms and the watermelon out to the edge of the river current. I took Dougie's pole, he took the melon, and we swam to the sandbar. Chick and Dewey followed with their poles and the worms. Soon we had our lines out and were relaxing in the cool water. We started to catch fish right away, and in no time we had several nice catfish and a couple of walleyes on our stringer.

It was getting quite hot and we were getting thirsty, so we busted open the melon on a log that was lying on the sandbar. We each took a fourth and began eating the warm melon. Of course, it was runny, and in no time we were all covered with watermelon juice from our chins to our shins. "This is the way to eat melon," Dewey said, slurping a big bite of melon. "You can just let it drip, and then when you're done you can jump in the river and wash it all off."

Then we had a seed spitting contest that resulted in spitting seeds all over each other. It was great fun, and when we had washed the melon juice off, we settled down to fishing again. Late in the afternoon we swam back to the Gosey, dressed in our shorts and tee shirts, and carried our wet underwear home.

The next day we decided to go back to the sandbar and fish some more, so Dewey came to pick us all up. When he got to my place, I ran out, put my fishing pole in the trunk and got in Big Edna. A Springer Spaniel sat on the seat. "Who's is this?" I asked Dewey as I made the dog move over.

"My uncle Mike's. He's here visiting. He said we could take Mike fishing with us."

I was confused. "Who's Mike?"

Dewey looked at me as if I was completely stupid. "The dog is Mike."

"I thought you said your uncle's name was Mike."

"It is."

I thought I must be missing something here. "So your uncle is Mike and he has a dog named Mike, too?"

"Of course."

How could I be so stupid? Didn't everyone name their dogs the same as themselves?

We picked up Dougie and went through the same routine, and again with Chick. They both thought it was strange way to name your dog, but Dewey thought it was perfectly normal.

"So, what can he do?" Chick asked after he had been briefed on the dog situation.

"Who?" Dewey asked.

"Mike."

"Mike the dog? Or Mike the uncle?"

It was going to be a long day.

"He can smile," Dewey said.

"No foolin?"

Dewey looked at Mike. "Mike... smile for the boys."

Mike looked at us and raised his upper lip in a big smile. We just about cracked up laughing.

We swam out to the sandbar. Dewey had to swim along with Mike, because he was a little afraid of the current. Then, when we were ready to fish, I cast out my hook and sinker. Mike jumped in, swam out and tried to retrieve it. "Oh, yeah. This is going to work real well," I said.

We finally got Mike settled down and did some serious fishing. After a while we swam, and then we dug a shallow pit and buried Dewey with just his head showing. Of course, we put some big boobies on the sand man (and some other body parts that shall not be named). We were laughing at how funny it looked when Mike walked over to Dewey, raised his leg and peed on the back of Dewey's head.

Chick, Dougie and I almost had a heart attack, we laughed so hard. Dewey felt the hot pee on his head and tried to get up from the sand, but we had him buried pretty well. Finally, he managed to get out, ran to the river and jumped in to wash off his head. Mike jumped in with him, thinking it was great fun.

We had a great day of fishing and swimming, and then bid farewell to Mike the dog. He was going back home with Mike the uncle. We were glad that craziness was behind us.

The next day we all spent a day at home, doing chores that our parents had been harping about for a while. We all got our lawns mowed and did other little chores so on the following day we could fish again. We dug worms, "borrowed" another melon, and when we got to our sandbar, we were surprised to see tiny plants growing all over it.

There were little watermelon plants everywhere. "Holy cow! We'll have our own melons in a few weeks," Dougie said.

We spent the next couple of weeks making sure our watermelon crop was safe. Every day, or so, we'd swim out and water them with river water. They were growing like mad, becoming vines that stretched across the sandbar. But about two weeks later, the river started to raise, the current cutting away our sandbar. In another three days, most of it was washed away, and with it, our fortunes as watermelon czars.

We hadn't really expected to make any money on the melons, but it was fun watching them grow. It would have been cool to get some melons from them, and then maybe one day we could have snuck up to our farmer's field and left a few extra for him... to replace all those we'd "borrowed" over the years.

Foursome

"Hey, you want to go golfing?"

"Golfing? You mean playing golf?"

"Yeah," Chick said sounding exasperated. "What do you think I meant?"

"Well, I guess that's what I thought, but since when did you become a golf player?" I answered.

"It's called a golfer, and I've been one since my brother gave me his old golf clubs. I already talked to Dougie and Dewey, and they're up for it. Dewey's on his way over to pick you up."

Just then I heard Big Edna's horn honking in the street. I looked out the window. "He's here right now. I'll see you in a minute." As I ran out the front door I shouted, "Mom? I'm going golfing with the guys."

Dougie was riding shotgun and Dewey had the radio tuned to WLS as usual. "What's all this golfing stuff?" I said as I got in the back seat.

"I don't know. Chick called and said we were going golfing. I've never golfed. Have you?"

"Cripes, no! That's a sissy game... chasing a little white ball all over the place. I've read about it in the newspaper, but I never tried it."

"I played mini-golf once when we were on vacation," Dewey said. "I hit my ball into the alligator's mouth and I was all done for the day."

"That's different. This is for real golf," I said.

Just then we pulled up in front of Chick's house and he came out carrying a bag of golf clubs. "Dewey, open the trunk," he said as he got to the car.

Dewey shut off Big Edna and we all got out to look at Chick's golf clubs. "So, your brother gave you these?" Dougie asked.

"Yeah. He got a new set and thought we'd like to have the old ones," Chick said handing us each a club. We began swinging them and chopping holes in his front yard. "Jeez! Quit that or my mom will come out here and shoot you!" he said, trying to cover up the holes.

The golf clubs were okay... as far as golf clubs go. Of course, we didn't have much to compare them to. Had they been fishing poles, we'd have been much more impressed.

Chick's brother was a cool guy. He was about five years older than Chick and had always been nice to us. And he had the coolest car—a red Corvette. We always were glad to see him and he always let us sit in the car and pretend we were driving. So, if he was a golfer, it might not be such a bad thing after all.

We piled into Big Edna and headed for Richland Center. "The country club has a junior membership that allows members under eighteen years old to play on Tuesdays, Thursdays and Saturday morning," Chick reported. "My mom got me a membership so now I can invite guests."

We were mildly impressed but still not convinced that precious fishing time should be squandered on something non-water related like golf. We pulled into the parking lot of the country club. Chick went in to the desk and signed us up for nine holes of golf. We followed him to the blast off place which he said was called the first tee. We stood and watched as two men and two women got ready to play.

They put their ball on a little wooden spike and then went through a lot of preparation before they took their swing and actually hit it. They did a lot of practice swinging, and looked down the golf course at the flag on some really nice green grass. The first guy got all set and smacked the ball. It landed off in the trees to the right. We all clapped and cheered, thinking it was a pretty good hit. The man turned around and looked at us like we had been swearing at him. "Please! Quiet is mandatory!" he said.

We quit cheering and just stood there, not knowing if he was kidding. Then a lady got up and hit her ball. It didn't fly as far as the man's did, but it stayed on the mowed grass in front of the hitting place. We were very quiet, not wanting to make the man angry again.

We waited until all four of them had hit their balls, and then watched as they each went to their ball and hit it again toward the flag that was quite a long way down the mowed area.

"Okay," Chick said. "Now we can hit. "I've got a ball for each of us, and this is called a tee."

He set his ball on one of the little wooden spikes, lined it up, swung back and smacked it. It went way up high and straight down toward the flag, but not too far, since it went so high. It bounced on the grass and Chick stepped back from the hitting spot. "Who's next?"

Dewey said he'd go next. He stuck the little wooden spike in the grass and set his ball on it. Then he lined up, took a heck of a swing and his ball took off like it had been shot out of a cannon. "Holy smokes, Dewey!" Chick said. Dewey's ball was still climbing into the air and was going a little off to the right. "Holy crap! Fore! Fore!" Chick yelled.

The first man whose ball had gone into the trees on the right looked up and then ran off the mowed grass quickly as Dewey's ball smacked into the ground almost at the same place where he had been standing. He gave us a nasty stare and then hit his ball toward the flag.

"Cripes, Dewey! That was a heck of a hit!" I said. "What's that *Fore* stuff about?"

"That's what you say when somebody's out there in front of you. You yell *Fore*, and then they know to look out."

"Why not just yell, *Watch Out?"* Dougie asked.

"I don't know. Somebody decided you should yell *Fore,* so that's what you yell."

Well, that seemed kind of silly, but like a good player, I stepped up next, lined up my ball, yelled *"Fore,"* and smacked it. I must have done something wrong because instead of flying through the air, my ball bounced along the grass for a ways, and then stopped in a big hole full of sand.

"That wasn't very good," Chick said. "You're supposed to *not* hit into the sand."

"Thanks for telling me now," I said. "I thought you got extra points for hitting a sand hole."

Dougie blasted off and his ball went straight but not as far as

Dewey's. Then Chick picked up the golf bag and we walked down the grass toward my ball. "Here," Chick said. "Take this club... it's a sand wedge."

I looked at the club. It had a metal head that was angled back a lot. "Try to get under the ball and smack it up out of the sand toward that flag," Chick said.

I crawled down into the hole, lined up my ball and smacked it. About ten pounds of sand flew up onto the grass... and my ball rolled farther down into the hole.

"Nice shot," Dewey laughed.

I lined it up again and really smacked it. This time it flew out of the hole and landed about ten feet from me.

"That was better," Chick said. We all took another shot, and then we were getting close to the nice green grass with the flag on it. I shot again since I was still the farthest from the flag. This time I got a good hit. My ball came down pretty close to the flag. The four people ahead of us gave me a dirty look when my ball landed. I remembered that I was supposed to yell, so I yelled, *"Fore!"*

By the time we got to Chick, Dougie and Dewey, the other people were gone to the next hitting place. We all got our balls on the place called the green. It was pretty cool, like a green carpet. The grass was really fine and thick and cut really short. In the middle the flag was sticking in a metal hole. Chick took a club he called a putter and carefully hit his ball toward the cup. It rolled across the green carpet and just missed the hole. Then Dewey hit his and it went way past the hole. Then it was Dougie's turn and his ball rolled up to the hole, stopped at the edge and then dropped in. We all cheered for Dougie. My turn came next and I hit mine too hard. It rolled off the green and into a sand hole on the other side. "Oh boy! This is fun," I said.

Another four impatient guys waiting behind us asked if they could play through as we fooled around trying to get our balls into the hole. I looked at Chick. "What's that mean?"

"I think they want to go ahead of us, 'cause we're kinda slow," he said.

"You want to go ahead of us?" I asked them.

"Yeah, we would like to play through," one said.

"Okay. Why didn't you just ask if you could go ahead?" I said.

The guys just shook their heads, hit their balls up on the green, and then each took one hit to get them in the hole.

"Must be professionals," Dewey whispered to me.

We sat on a little bench while the guys got ready to hit off. There was a metal bucket-like thing for washing off your ball, so we all had to put our ball in it and pump it up and down. We talked about our scores and how my score of eleven wasn't the best. "In golf," Chick laughed, "you go for the lowest score."

Just then one of the guys looked at us. "Could you guys please be quiet? We're about to tee off."

We all looked surprised. Tee off?

One of them got up and smacked his ball down the grass, and then the others congratulated him on a good tee shot.

"Tee off. Cripes! That's what they mean," Dougie said laughing. "I thought he was *teed off*... like mad."

The men gave us another nasty stare. Oops! We were having fun and talking. A no-no in golf... apparently.

We let the guys get far enough ahead so we wouldn't hit them with our tee shots, now that we knew what they were called. We smacked our balls down toward the next flag. Mine bounced along and disappeared over a little knoll into a ditch. When I got to the place I thought it had gone, I found a little stream running at the bottom of the ditch. "Hey! There's a trout stream over here," I yelled to Dewey.

He came over and we walked down into the ditch. "I bet your ball went into the water," he said.

I was sure of it, and was already sitting down to take off my shoes. Dewey took his shoes off, too, and soon we were both wading in the stream looking for my ball. A few minutes later Dougie and Chick were in the water with us. Then Dougie came up with a ball. "Here it is," he said. "Oh, no. This ain't it. This one has somebody's name printed on it."

"Let me see," Chick said. He looked at the ball. "This is somebody else's ball, but it's ours now," he said slipping it in his pocket. Then Dewey found a ball, and then I found two just under the grass hanging over the bank. Before long we were scattered out along the whole length of the stream hunting for golf balls.

Another three golfers came to the edge of the stream and asked us if they could play through. "Go ahead," we told them, and kept searching for balls.

After three or four more groups went past us we finally decided that we had found all the balls in the stream. Our pockets were full of them. We climbed up on the flat ground, emptied our pockets, and Chick began sorting and counting the balls. "Holy crap! We found forty one balls, and here's the one you lost, so we have forty extras."

"What are we going to do with them?" I asked.

We were standing there talking it over when a man drove up on a golf cart. "What are you guys doing?" he asked.

"Playing golf," Chick said.

"I've been getting complaints that you're impeding play of others."

"Impeding play? You mean those people who asked to play through? Cripes, we told them to go ahead. Why are they complaining?" I asked.

"It's not proper golf etiquette to impede others. I have to ask you to leave the course."

We looked at each other. "I don't think I like this game very much," Dougie said.

"Me either. And I don't like these snooty people, either," I said.

Dewey farted. "Oops. Not proper etiquette," he said. We laughed like mad.

Chick began picking up the balls and put them into the golf bag. "Where did you get those balls?" the man asked.

"We found them in the creek," I said.

"They're members' balls. They have names on them," he said.

"So what? They were in the creek. They're ours now," Chick said.

"If you find another member's ball, you're supposed to turn it in to the clubhouse," the man said.

"Well, these guys aren't members, so they don't have to follow your stupid rules. And I was a member until about three minutes ago when I was told I had no proper etiquette. If you want them, we'll be glad to sell them back to you for... um... what do you guys think" We all thought, then huddled. We agreed on a price.

"You can have them all for ten bucks," Dewey said.

"Ten bucks? Are you crazy?"

"Fine. Then we'll take them with us and hit them into the river on our way home," I said.

"I'll give you five," the man said.

"Eight."

"Six."

"Seven."

He pulled out his wallet and handed me seven one-dollar bills. Chick picked up the golf bag and dumped the balls out onto the ground. "Nice doing business with you," he said.

We picked up the clubs and our shoes and walked across the grass back to the first hitting off spot, and then to the parking lot and climbed into Big Edna. "Let's get something to eat with our profit from the golf ball sale... and then go fishing," Dougie said. We all thought that was a good idea.

As we left the parking lot, the two men and two women that had been ahead of us at the beginning were on the final green trying to put their balls into the hole. One of the men was carefully lining up his shot. Just as he swung his putter, Chick yelled out Big Edna's window. *"Fore!"* The man smacked the ball three times harder than he should have. It flew off the green into the parking lot, and then it rolled across the lot into the ditch.

He was waving his putter at us as we drove off down the road with the radio blasting and laughing like mad.

Otter Slide

The fish weren't cooperating very well at the Gosey. "I think we need to find some new places to fish," Dougie said. "We've caught all the fish here."

"At least all the dumb ones," Chick said.

"Hey! Why don't we go over to the Mississippi?" Dewey asked.

"That's a long way to go just to fish," I said.

"Yeah, but we could drive there and stay over. My dad and mom bought a little cabin over there a few weeks ago. They spent the weekend there and said the fishing was really good."

"Is there a boat for us to use?"

"Yeah. There's a boat chained up at the cabin."

Suddenly this sounded like a good idea. We started making plans for a trip to the Mississippi. Of course, the first thing on our list of important items was food. Dewey thought he could get some stuff from the restaurant, and we could go grocery shopping for the rest. We'd have to dig a lot of worms and get our parents' permission. We weren't too worried about that, since we'd talked them into the clamming enterprise earlier in the summer.

We were soon all at home working on our trip. After some arm twisting we all had permission, and through about a dozen phone calls, we decided to leave first thing the next morning.

I was waiting in the living room watching the street when Dewey pulled up in Big Edna. Dougie was already with him. I shouted "goodbye" to my mom, picked up my tackle box, fishing pole, and a duffle bag with extra clothes, toothbrush and other stuff. Dougie had kept our worms in their cool basement, so I didn't have to worry about bait.

I put my stuff in the trunk and off we went to pick up Chick. He had about the same gear as I did, and we stored it in the trunk with the rest of the stuff. Dewey had a big silver cooler in the back seat between Chick and me. I opened it as we drove down the highway toward the Mississippi. "What did you get for us?" I asked.

"I cleaned out the refrigerator in the kitchen. There's leftover salads, baked beans, and some more of that prime rib like we had one other time. I found some deviled eggs and other stuff. I think we'll have enough for tonight. Maybe tomorrow we'll have to go grocery shopping."

We were all excited. It didn't seem to take long at all until we reached one of the Mississippi bluffs. Just as we came over the rise, we saw the river down in the valley. Dewey began singing *Old Man River.*

We all laughed and joined in with the singing as we wound down the road toward the big river. Because it was a nice warm day, the windows were wide open with a nice breeze blowing through the car. We were singing at the top of our lungs when Dewey suddenly started jumping around in the front seat. The car swung back and forth across the steep, winding road, and we yelled at him to quit fooling around or he'd kill us. He was stomping on the brakes and desperately trying to get his shirt off.

"DEWEY! YOU IDIOT! YOU'RE GONNA CRASH US!" Dougie yelled as he grabbed the steering wheel.

"BEE! I got a BEE!" Dewey yelled.

Up ahead there was a sharp curve to the right. If we didn't turn we'd go over the bank, and it looked like about a quarter-mile to the bottom. "DEWEY! PUT ON THE BRAKES!" I yelled from the back seat.

Dewey was determined to take off his button-up shirt by pulling it over his head. He was stomping on the brakes but Dougie was steering. As Dougie steered us into the ditch on the right side of the road, we slowed down and finally stopped. Dewey put the car in park and jumped out, running in circles still trying to get his shirt off.

"BEE! BEE!" he yelled.

He finally got his shirt over his head and threw it on the ground. By then we had all gotten out of the car, kind of wobbly after almost going over the cliff. "What the heck are you doing, Dewey?" Chick yelled.

"There's a big bumble bee in my shirt! It flew up the sleeve when I was driving. I had to get it off or get stung!" Dewey answered, obviously a little peeved at Chick.

Dougie cautiously picked up Dewey's shirt from the middle of the road. He shook it and sure enough, a big bumble bee about the size of a hickory nut flew out. We all stepped back as the bee flew around for a few seconds and then took off up the hill.

"See? I wasn't lying. Did you see the size of that thing?" Dewey yelled at us.

We all started laughing, and then Dewey joined in, too. "I about pooped when that thing went up my sleeve," he said. We all doubled over with laughter.

When we finally got our senses back and piled into poor old Edna, parked half in and half out of the ditch, I said, "Jeez. We just about drove Edna over the cliff."

"That wouldn't have been good for Edna... or us," Chick said laughing.

We carefully proceeded the rest of the way down the hill and then drove along the Mississippi until we came to the cabin. Dewey knew right where to turn. We pulled into a little valley off the main highway where there were ten small cabins. Dewey pointed to the first cabin on the right. "That's ours," he said.

The cabin up on the bank wasn't very big—one or two small rooms with a front screen porch. We carried the cooler and our duffle bags up stairs built into the side of the hill and deposited them in the cabin.

Inside, there was a small bedroom with bunk beds, and a couch that opened to a bed in the living room/kitchen. There was another couch on the front porch that opened to a bed. "One can sleep out here," Dewey said motioning to the porch, two can use the bunk beds, and I'll sleep on the couch in the living room."

"I'll take the porch unless somebody else wants it," I said.

"That's fine. We'll take the bunks, won't we?" Chick said to Dougie.

"Fine with me," Dougie said.

We put our duffle bags in their respective places and then put the food from the cooler into the refrigerator. "Well, let's go and get the boat and go fishing," Dewey said.

The boat was on a trailer chained to a tree down by the road where we had parked Big Edna. It was a sixteen foot long flat bottom with a twenty-five horse *Evinrude* motor. "You know how to run that thing?" Chick asked.

"Sure. There's nothing to it," Dewey said.

Dewey unlocked the padlock on the boat, hooked it to the hitch on the back of Big Edna, and then we tooled down the road pulling the boat. When we arrived at the boat landing just a mile or so from Dewey's cabin, we all got out to watch Dewey attempting to back the boat trailer down to the landing. First he went too far to the left, then straightened it up, and went way too far off to the right. Back and forth he went, with us shouting instructions. With a little chaos and a lot of laughing, we managed to get the boat backed down to the water and then launched. Dewey pulled the trailer out of the water and parked it and Big Edna in the parking lot. We were just standing there waiting for him when he came trotting down the gravel landing. "What the heck?" he said. We didn't know what meant, until we turned to look at the boat.

It was about half full of water and sinking fast. "Whoa! We forgot to put the plug in," Dewey yelled.

We all ran to the boat, trying to pull it up farther onto the gravel. Of course, since it was half full of water it was very heavy, so it was quite difficult to move very far. Chick and I took off our shoes, waded in and began pushing water over the side. Dougie and Dewey pulled again, and it slid up a little farther. Chick and I bailed more water, and slowly but surely we managed to get enough out so we could pull the boat all the way up, and the remaining water drained out.

"Well, we're off to a good start," Chick said.

When the boat was empty we put the plug in and then pushed it back into the water. Dewey got in first, went to the back so he could run the motor, and then the rest of us piled in. Dewey pulled on the starter cord a few times and soon we were putting down the river, the wind in our hair, on our way to a fishing adventure.

We spent the rest of the day fishing several different spots. The end result was a nice stringer of crappies, bluegills and a couple of white bass. We were pretty satisfied with our catch as we pulled back into the landing. Dewey's boat trailer backing success wasn't much better than earlier in the day, but with the trailer empty, the three of us just slid it one way or the other as needed to keep it going straight. It didn't take long to get the boat loaded onto the trailer. When we got back to the cabin, Dougie and Chick took the fish down to a community fish cleaning shack. Dewey and I began getting the food ready. We got put out a pan to fry fish, and several of the leftovers to go with it. Dewey was soon frying the fish that Chick and Dougie had cleaned.

We feasted on our great meal and had a crazy time laughing and goofing around. We all tasted most everything Dewey had brought. One container was full of spinach and we let Dewey have all of that. "This is good," he said dipping his fingers into the container and dropping a wad of the stuff down his gullet.

"It looks like that junk that gets under the lawn mower when the grass is too wet," Dougie said.

We shuddered as Dewey ate the whole container of the stuff. Then when we were all done, he finished off the entire container of baked beans too. "Jeez, Dewey. You're gonna stink up the whole place with all that stuff you ate," I said. Dewey just laughed and lifted his leg and let one go.

"Oops. slipped," he giggled.

After we cleaned up the supper mess, we decided to play cards for a while. Of course, Dewey's beans and spinach was making him a human gas pump and about every three minutes he'd stick his hand out and say, "Pull my finger."

Of course, one of us *would* pull one of his fingers and he'd let out a blast. For some reason, the more we did it, the funnier it seemed to be.

Finally we all were getting tired so we got ready for bed. There wasn't a bathroom in the cabin. "Anybody got to go potty, you got to do it down there," Dewey said pointing out the window to an outhouse a little ways down the hillside.

Nobody had to go. We turned out the lights and everyone went to bed. As tired as we were, it didn't take any of us very long to get to sleep.

The sun was just peeking up over the hill shining in my eyes, waking me from my slumber. I stretched and yawned and decided I needed to go down the hill to the little house. I slipped on my shorts and tee shirt and walked barefoot onto the wet grass. I walked down to the outhouse, did my business, and as I sauntered back toward the cabin I noticed a smear going down over the side of the hill. I stopped to look at it, but I couldn't figure out what it was.

It looked like an otter had been sliding down the bank. We'd seen places like that in the river bottoms at home. Otter love to play; they find a place where they can slide on the river bank, and then they do it over and over.

I was trying to figure out where the mud had come from when Dougie, in shorts, tee shirt and barefoot, came walking out of the cabin. "Morning," he said.

"Hi. How did you sleep?"

"Like a rock. But Dewey… jeez… he was banging around out in the living room all night long. Cripes. It stinks like a sewer in there, too."

"He's probably been farting all night. It's no wonder, with all those beans and stuff he ate."

Dougie went to the outhouse and in a little while he joined me on the hillside. "What do you suppose made that?" I said pointing to the mud slide.

He shook his head. "Looks like an otter slide, but not up here on dry ground."

We didn't worry too much more about it and went back to the

cabin. I made my bed back into a couch and then went into the living room/kitchen. Whew! Dougie was right. It smelled like the outhouse in there. Just then Chick came out of the little bedroom on his way to the outhouse. "Cripes! It stinks in here," he said.

"Dewey! What did you do? It smells like shit in here?"

Dewey was all rolled up in his covers. He rolled over and then we saw dark brown stains on the sheets and blankets. I looked at Chick. He and I turned toward the trash can. It was full of paper towels, all covered with brown stuff.

"Dewey! What the heck is all this?" I asked.

"Well... I think I might have pooped my pants last night," he said.

Just then Dougie came from the bedroom and heard what Dewey had said. He looked at Dewey's bed and the paper towels, and made a mad dash for the door. Chick and I were right behind him.

"Now I know what that otter slide is," Dougie said.

We walked over by the brown streak that went through the grass, down over the hill. Sure enough, it was the same color as the brown inside the cabin. "Oh no. Dewey pooped himself."

We heard the screen door slam, and Dewey came waddling down the path toward the outhouse in his underwear. "Dewey. What the hell happened?"

Dewey stopped, scratched his behind and looked over the hillside at the brown trail. "Well... I had to poop pretty bad during the night, so I got up and was walking down to the outhouse, but I kinda got off the trail in the dark. My feet slipped out from under me. When I hit the ground, I kinda pooped, and it slid up the back of my shorts, and I slid down the hill in it."

By the time Dewey finished his story, the three of us were as close to a heart attack from laughter as I've ever been. I could just picture Dewey sliding down the hill on his backside, lubricated by his own poop.

When we finally got back to our senses, Dewey stood there, grinning. "Well, guess I'll go to the outhouse." He turned and we couldn't help laughing again. His entire back was brown, covered in dried poop.

When Dewey got back from the outhouse, we made him go in the cabin and pick up all the wads of paper towel that he had used last trying to clean off his back. Of course, he didn't get it all, and the whole bed was dirty, too. He pumped a pail of water, heated it, and then washed himself. He wanted one of us to help with his back, so Chick wrapped a towel around a broom, dipped it into the warm water and scrubbed his back.

Then we put all the bedding in the trunk of Big Edna, went across the river to Iowa and found a laundry. When the bedding was put into a washer, we went to a diner for breakfast. Somehow it didn't seem too appetizing to cook back in the cabin. By the time the bedding was dry and we returned to the cabin, half the day was shot. We decided to fish the same places we had fished the day before. Then we'd go out to eat... someplace that didn't serve beans.

It's Good Deep Fried

Dewey managed not to blow up the next night at the cabin, so our morning was off to a much better start. We got up, made breakfast and got ready for our last day of fishing. We had told our parents that we'd be back in three days, so we would stay over one more night, and drive home the next morning.

"Let's go down and fish below the dam," Dewey said as we were getting ready.

"You think we can catch fish there?" I asked.

"Yeah. There's walleyes, catfish, sheep's head, and lots of other fish there. With the boat we can move around and find them, and then we should be able to really catch a bunch."

That sounded good to us, so we loaded up Big Edna, hooked onto the boat, and then headed down the highway to the boat landing that was about a mile below the dam. We managed to unload and launch the boat without sinking it, and soon were motoring up the river.

"Let's try over by that wing dam," Chick suggested.

We all nodded rather than trying to speak over the noise of the motor. Dewey pulled in near the shore just above the wing dam.

A wing dam is a pile of rocks that extends out from the bank toward the middle of the river. It's there to keep the current in the middle, where the channel is, where the big barges navigate. If the wing dams weren't there, the channel could just run anywhere, and it would be impossible for the huge barges to get up or down the river. A bonus of the wing dams was that they attracted fish as a place to rest and to feed away from the current. The rocks attracted lots of insects which attracted small fish, and the small fish attracted bigger fish. It was like a diner for all the fish in the area.

We all started jigging along the bottom as Dewey maneuvered the boat along the end of the wing dam. It wasn't long until Dougie snapped his pole up and set the hook into a fish. We all watched him fight the fish, and then a nice walleye popped up on the surface. Chick netted it, put it in the live basket and hung it over the side.

Chick hooked a sauger, and then I got another walleye. By then we had drifted past the wing dam. Dewey told us to reel in our lines.

We motored upriver again, and then did the same drift past the end of the rocks. This time it was Dewey who hooked into a fish. "Whoa! This one is a big one!" he said holding onto his pole for dear life.

"Are you sure it's a fish? Maybe you're hooked on the rocks," I said.

Dewey carefully tried to lift his rod. The rod suddenly throbbed and pulled down toward the water. "It's a fish… and it's a whale!" Dewey said.

The rest of us rolled up our lines and I got the net ready. We drifted along as Dewey fought the fish, gaining line and then watching as his drag spun on the reel and all the line he had gained was pulled out again. "What the heck can it be?" Chick wondered.

"It must be a big catfish, or maybe a sturgeon," I said.

By now we were a quarter of a mile below the wing dam, nearing the boat landing. Dewey did a good job of fighting the fish; the next time it came near the surface we got a glimpse of its tail as it bulldogged to the bottom. "Holy smokes! Did you see that?" Dougie yelled.

"It was almost a foot across!" Chick said.

"What the heck *is* that? Dewey… take it easy. This might be a world record fish of some kind."

We drifted on, and on went the battle. We finally saw what it was the next time Dewey raised the fish to the top and it flopped over on its side. It was the biggest sheepshead any of us had ever seen. "Holy smokes! Look at that thing!" Dewey said, sweat running down his face. The fish made another dive but it wasn't nearly as far as before and Dewey soon had it up on top again. "Get the net under it!" he said, panting from exertion.

I slid the net under the fish and there was no way it would fit in. "It's too big! It won't fit!" I exclaimed.

"Get its head in. We'll get hold of it and lift it over the side," Chick said as he and Dougie knelt at the edge of the boat. I slid the net over the fish's head and lifted as they each grabbed hold of a part of the body and suddenly we had the biggest sheepshead any of us could imagine, thrashing around in the bottom of the boat with us.

The fish was tangled in the net, rolling around and slapping its tail. It slammed into my open tackle box. Instantly my lures were getting tangled in the net and being launched through the air. "Holy smokes! Hold that thing down! It's wrecking my tackle box!" I yelled.

We finally got the fish calmed down and out of the net. It was immense. I pulled the tape measure out of the end of my Deliar. The thirty-inch long tape wasn't nearly as long as the fish. "See how much it weighs," Dewey said.

I hooked the Deliar to the fish's lip and lifted. The Deliar weighed up to 28 pounds and it was bottomed out. "It's more than 28 pounds," I said gritting my teeth as I tried to hold the fish.

I lowered the fish back to the bottom of the boat. We all sat down and just looked at it. "I didn't know they got that big," Dougie said.

"Me either. This one makes those little twelve inch ones we catch look kind of puny, doesn't it?"

"What we gonna do with it?"

"Let's let it go," Dewey said.

I looked at the other guys and we all nodded. "If this thing's been in the river long enough to grow this big, it deserves to live a while longer," Chick said.

Dougie and I got hold of the fish and lifted it over the side of the boat. We held it with its head pointing upriver and let it rest and get some fresh water through its gills. Then it began to move its tail back and forth and was trying to swim. We let it go and it disappeared into the depth of the river. "Well, Dewey. You da man!" Chick said.

We all high-fived Dewey and then we looked around to see that we were about a mile below the boat landing. "Holy smokes! We drifted a long way catching that fish," I said.

On the way back upriver I picked up all my lures and put them back in their little compartments in my tackle box. We passed the wing dam and kept going until we were at the dam, where Dewey pulled into an area next to the big gates. "This is the Safety Lock," he said. "My dad told me it's a good place to fish."

We put out the anchor, and we were soon catching one fish after another—walleyes, catfish and sheepshead, though nothing like our last sheepshead. It *was* a great place to fish. One of us was pulling in a fish almost all the time.

I noticed that we were getting closer to the end of the wall between the Safety Lock and the dam. "Dewey... check that anchor. We're slipping out toward the dam," I said.

"Yeah. Just a minute," Dewey said as he fought a fish on his line.

By now Dougie and Chick had noticed us moving, too, and they both looked worried. "Dewey! Hurry up! Were getting close to the end of the wall," Chick said.

Dewey was farting around with a catfish, taking it off his hook. The boat began to slip around the end of the wall toward the big gate, where water was rushing under the gate and boiling up on the lower side like a giant surfing wave. The wave rushed back toward the dam, and the boat was about to get caught in the wave and be pushed up against the gate. It was not the place for us to be, and the three of us shouted at Dewey to start the motor and get us out of there.

Dewey looked up and saw where we were. His eyes suddenly got as big as saucers. He dropped his catfish and grabbed the pull cord on the motor. It started on the first pull. He pushed the shift lever into reverse and gunned the motor. We began moving back away from the tidal wave. I was kneeling down in the bottom of the boat holding onto the side. I saw that my tackle box was still open. I reached down, closed the cover and latched it. At least if we went over, my tackle wouldn't spill.

In only a few seconds we were safely back around the wall into the calm water of the Safety Lock. "Holy cow, Dewey! You almost got us killed!" Chick said.

"I was busy. Why didn't you tell me we were getting so close?" Dewey whined.

"What did you think we were yelling about?" I said.

Dewey grinned. "I just thought you were being funny."

"Let's go fish someplace else," Dougie said. "This place is too scary."

We all agreed. Dewey started the motor and we moved to the end of the long wall of the lock. There was slack water behind the wall that was very similar to the Safety Lock, except there wasn't a big deep tidal wave by it. All we had to watch out for here was a boat coming out of the lock, and we could get out of the way of that pretty easily.

The fishing was good here, too. We caught lots of fish and had great fun. I felt a tic on my line and set the hook into a good fighting fish. It bulldogged down toward the bottom and I worked on it until it came up next to the surface. Just as it began to pull down toward the bottom again, I got a glimpse of its head. "Catfish," I said.

"Looks like a good one," Dougie said. "It's putting up a good fight."

"It must just think it's big. Its head was pretty small," I replied.

I fought the fish to the top again where I could see it. "Holy crap! What the heck is that?" I shouted.

There on the surface was a critter that had a head that looked like a catfish, but its body looked like a snake.

"That's an eel," Dougie said.

"Like one of those blood sucker things?"

"No. this is a jawed eel. They're cool."

Dougie had always been one who liked slithery things. He was always picking up snakes and other slippery things, so this was right up his alley. "Get it in here. Let's look at it," he said.

The eel was wriggling around and wrapping itself around my line, so I didn't have much choice but to lift it into the boat. I managed to get it on the other side of the middle seat, away from where I was sitting. We all looked down at it. "Cripes!" Chick said. "That thing is creepy."

"I think it's cool," Dougie said picking up the line and holding the slithering thing up so he could get a better look. "Do you guys know where these things come from?"

None of us did, so Dougie told us. "They're born in the Sargasso Sea, down near Bermuda... like in the Bermuda Triangle. The Sargasso Sea is a huge weed bed out in the middle of the ocean. After they're born, they migrate up the same river that their parents came from and live in the fresh water river. Once they're adults they migrate down the river, swim out to the Sargasso Sea and mate. Then they go back up the same river, and so do their babies."

"Holy smokes. You mean that thing was born in the ocean?"

"Yup. Pretty cool, huh?"

"Yeah, I guess so. But I'm still not interested in touching it."

Dougie looked it over and shook his head. "Okay if I cut the line and let him have the hook?"

"By all means. I've got lots of hooks."

Dougie took out his pocket knife, cut the line, and the eel dropped over the side into the river. "Well, that was something we don't see much of at home, either," he said.

"Good!" I said.

We fished for another hour, ate lunch and then decided to take a nap. After our nap we loaded the boat and chained it up back at the cabin. We cleaned our fish, had a good supper and went to bed early. Next morning we loaded up all the trash—including Dewey's paper towels—and headed home.

Just as we came over the last hill and our Wisconsin river valley came into view Chick said, "That was a pretty good trip."

"Yeah, no kidding. The world champion sheepshead, a traveling eel, and the biggest otter in all of Wisconsin," Dougie said. We all laughed.

Before Dewey dropped us off at our homes, we decided to call each other the next day, not too early, and we'd decide then what we wanted to do. It would surely be something that we'd do together... there was never any doubt about that.

Twist and Shout

Our fishing trip to Dewey's cabin had been quite a couple of days. It felt good sleeping in our own beds again, so we all slept in the next morning. The phone rang about ten o'clock. Chick wondered what we were going to do with the day ahead. I told him I'd call Dewey, and that he should call Dougie, and we'd all get together.

Surprisingly, Dewey was already up and moving around when I called. He said he'd pick me up, and that he wanted us to help him clean up Big Edna, since she was looking kind of dirty after our trip. I put on shorts, tee shirt and tennis shoes and sat on the curb waiting for him. A few minutes later he rolled up, and then we picked up Dougie and Chick.

Dewey had buckets, sponges and soap in the trunk. It was time to give Edna a bath. First we cleaned out all the empty pop cans, candy bar wrappers, and other debris from the floor and under the seats. Then Chick had a brilliant idea. "Why don't we drive Edna out onto the flat rock below the boat landing and wash her in the river?"

That sounded like lots more fun than doing it in Chick's back yard, so we piled in and drove to the river. Just below the Gosey there was a boat landing by a small campground and park. A rock shelf extended out into the river for about thirty or forty yards, and about a hundred yards or so long from the lower part of the boat landing. The water was only about a foot deep during the summer. We waded on it many times and walked along the edge and fished in the deeper water next to it.

At the park Dewey drove down a little road that wasn't really a road right out onto the flat rock. We knew just how far we could go so we weren't in any danger, but many cars coming across the bridge stopped to stare at the crazy people driving their car *in the river.* At the middle of the flat rock we all took off our shirts and shoes and started washing Edna. Dewey left the radio blaring as we soaped up the big tank of a car, and then rinsed her off with buckets of river water.

We were just about to wipe off the excess water with towels

when a song came over the radio that stopped us in our aquatic tracks.

A guitar playing very loudly went: *Da da da dum de de da da dum, da da da dum de de da da dum.* Then came the lyrics: *Well shake it up baybeee now.... Shake it up Baybee....... Twist and Shout... Twist and Shout, C'mon, c'mon, c'mon, c'mon baybee now.... c'mon baybee, C'mon and Work it on out!.... Work it on out! Wooooo.*

We all stood there with our mouths hanging open at the marvelous new song. We gathered around the open window like a bunch of June Bugs next to a candle, kind of dancing around, listening to the song. Suddenly it was over. "That was the Beatles from England with their new release, *Twist and Shout,"* said the announcer.

"The Beatles?" We were all very excited about this new music and this new group. "Holy cow! That was the coolest song I've ever heard," I said.

"No kidding," Chick added.

We finished Edna and drove to the Root Beer stand for some refreshments. While we were waiting in the car for our root beers and hot dogs, the guy on the radio said he was going to play *Twist and Shout* again because he had so many requests for it. "Turn to *WLS,* we shouted to our friends in other cars, and before long, the whole parking lot was blasting the Beatles.

In the next few weeks, everyone was listening to more Beatles songs. *I Want to Hold Your Hand, I Saw Her Standing There, Please Please Me.* We were hearing new ones all the time... and they were all great. We started buying their records. Excitement was in the air when we heard they were going to be on the *Ed Sullivan Show* Sunday night.

We all gathered at my house and watched plate jugglers, an opera singer, Topo Gigo, Senior Wenchis, (who we liked a lot with his little hand puppet, Jani, and the head in the box that said "So Right!") There was other boring stuff, and then, when there was only ten minutes left, Ed Sullivan came out and introduced: THE BEATLES! The place went NUTS! There they were. We had never seen anything like them, with hair clear down to their jacket collars, high pointy boots, slim ties, and matching suits. The girls in the audience went absolutely ape nuts, screaming so loud that you could hardly hear the song, jumping up and down, crying, and some even fainted. We just sat there, stunned.

You couldn't hear Ed Sullivan at all as he tried to talk to the Beatles when they finished the song, because there was so much noise from the screaming girls. So they got back in their places and started to play and sing *I Want to Hold Your Hand.*

By the time it was over it was like an asylum in the TV studio.

We were just speechless.

My mom was watching with us and she wasn't impressed. "Sounds like a lot of silly noise to me... and their hair, good God! What kind of mother would let her son have a girl's haircut?"

Tens of thousands of moms all across the US would find out in the next few weeks and months that there were tens of thousands of teenaged boys intent on just that very thing... a Beatles haircut.

Until the Beatles, we hadn't been really hot for any one singer or group. There were some that we listened to, and Elvis had already been a big deal for a while. We didn't like Elvis too much. I think it was something about how all the girls ran to him. It kind of gave teen boys an inferiority complex. We just didn't see what the girls saw in him, but the Beatles were different. They changed everything.

The guys and I had a run at Beatle haircuts, but we didn't get too far. We did let our hair grow a bit, but we never convinced our parents of the necessity of letting it get to *Beatle* length. We did manage to get some narrow ties, Beatle boots, (which just about killed my feet) and we bought every record they made.

The world of music changed that day when we heard those first guitar chords, and it was never the same for us again. It was never the same for millions of others, either. To this very day, when I'm listening to my favorite Oldies-but-Goodies station and I hear *Da da da dum de de da da dum...* I think back to that day, standing in the river next to Big Edna with my best friends, and I feel like a kid again.

Camp Indianola

Dougie and I were sorting tackle in his back yard when Chick and Dewey drove into the alley in Big Edna, parked on the grass, and left the windows open so we could listen to the radio.

"Hey, you guys want another job?" Chick asked.

"What job?"

"My mom heard about this camp in Madison on one of the lakes. They're looking for kitchen help. It's a three week job."

"No kidding? How much does it pay?"

"You get a room, food, and three hundred dollars for the whole time," he answered.

"A hundred bucks a week? And food, too? That's not too bad. When does it start?" Dougie asked.

"The camp opens a week from Saturday. They want the help there three days earlier to clean up the place before the kids get there," Chick said.

We discussed it for a while and decided it sounded like a good deal. Chick said he'd have his mom call and see if they would have jobs for all four of us.

Chick and Dewey left and Dougie and I kept sorting tackle. In a little while they returned with the good news: the camp would take all of us and we could start in five days. We all went home to tell our parents and to start packing up clothes and stuff for the three week stay. Of course, we all packed a fishing pole and tackle, too, since Chick told us there was a good fishing dock at the camp.

The next Tuesday morning we drove towards Madison with a map that Chick had received in the mail from the camp director. We had never driven in a big city, so it was pretty exciting as we cruised down the highway amongst all the other cars and busses and trucks. We followed the map and took a road that went around Lake Mendota, and then we saw the sign for Camp Indianola. An arrow pointed down a road that went through the woods. down that road a ways we saw cabins, and then some long buildings that looked like barracks. All the buildings were painted white with green trim and green roofs. Near the lake we found the main office, kitchen and dining hall.

A tall, bald man wearing shorts and a tee shirt came out as we drove up. His face was long with a big nose, and his legs looked like chicken legs sticking out of his shorts. We parked and got out of the car.

"I'm Haskell Woldenberg," he said as he shook hands with each of us. "I own the camp." We introduced ourselves. "You can call me 'Chief.' That's my official name here at camp," he said.

Just then a lady walked out. "This is my wife. You can call her 'Miss Chief,'" he said. Then we went into the office to fill out the papers for working there. Inside was another lady—a female version of Chief. "This is my sister, Muriel. You can call her 'Miss Mur,'" Chief said. "She runs the camp and I just do what she tells me," he said smiling. Miss Mur nodded her head.

Chief took us around and showed us the camp. The cabins we had seen earlier were for the older campers, kids about our age. They each held eight campers. The barracks were for the younger kids, from about six to twelve years old. There would be a counselor staying in each of the barracks, as well as in each cabin.

Then he showed us around the kitchen and dining hall. "The cooks will be here tomorrow," Chief told us. "So today we want to get the kitchen all cleaned up for them."

There was nothing special about our rooms he showed us above the kitchen. We each had a bed and we all shared a bathroom, but that was about all we needed. He told us to unpack and that he'd meet us in the kitchen in an hour. We pulled Big Edna up to the steps leading to our rooms and unloaded our stuff.

At noon we went down the steps to the kitchen, only to find that Chief had laid out a bunch of cold meat, bread and chips for our lunch. We ate, and then the cleaning began. Dougie and Chick moved all the tables and chairs to one side of the dining room so they could clean the floor on that side, and then moved them over and cleaned the other side.

Dewey and I stayed in the kitchen and Chief showed Dewey how to work the dishwashing machine. He started washing all of the hundreds of dishes. I was shown to the pot room where there were dozens of pots and pans that all needed to be washed, too.

Dewey and I put on big plastic aprons, turned on a radio that was there on a shelf, and had a pretty good afternoon washing things. Later that day three more boys our age arrived to work with us. One was a very tall boy, Bob Opal, who we were told to call Opie. He was six feet nine inches tall, and I doubt that he weighed more than a hundred and fifty pounds. His legs were nearly as long as Dougie was tall. His arms were long and thin, and he walked partially bent over, I suppose because he had hit his head so many times in the past, he didn't take any more chances.

Another kid named Will was from Opie's town, and the other one named Gary was from some other town. They seemed like good guys. They pitched in and by the end of the day we had the kitchen all ready for the cooks to arrive.

That evening, Chief cooked hamburgers for us, and after we ate we walked down to the dock extending out into the lake. It was a really long dock, about eighty yards long, and at the end it formed a T. Sailboats, canoes, and other small boats were tied up to the dock. Chief told us that we could use them when we were not working, if the campers were not using them. We all thought that was a fine idea.

We decided to paddle out into the lake in canoes. Gary, who was kind of quiet, decided he didn't want to go, so Chick and Dougie took one canoe, Opie and Will took another, and Dewey and I got in another. We were soon a long way out in the lake paddling along, talking back and forth, getting to know Opie and Will.

After a while, Chick suggested we race, and off we went. We were all pretty tightly grouped, and the water was really getting riled up by all the paddles when Dewey and I began to lose our balance. "Keep in the middle, Dewey!" I shouted.

Two seconds later we tipped over. The others kept going, still racing. We weren't scared because we were both good swimmers, and we didn't have anything with us that would sink, like a fishing pole. We laughed and I splashed water at Dewey, cussing him for tipping us over. "Let's get under the canoe and flip it up so we can get back in," I said.

We went under water and came up under the upside-down canoe. We took hold of the sides, lifted it up out of the water and tossed it to the side. It landed right side up, nearly empty of water. "Hold it while I climb in," I said. Dewey steadied the canoe as I slid up over the side and sat down on my seat. "Okay," I said. "Climb in."

Well, Dewey pulled on the side of the canoe and tried to climb up, looking like one of those big walruses when they climb out onto a rock. He wallowed around, and about half way up he tipped the canoe over again. I went back into the lake. "Jeez, Dewey! You're about as graceful as a cow!" I said.

"Let me get in first this time, then," he said.

We flipped up the canoe again. I held onto the side as Dewey floundered around and finally got up across the canoe. When he tried to turn to get in, he fell head first off the other side into the lake again. He came up to the top, and pulled himself up again. This time he made it into the canoe, but when he tried to sit down he lost his balance and flopped over the side again, tipping over the canoe.

By then I was getting a little tired of treading water. "Dewey, we're gonna need a crane to get you up in this thing," I said.

"You got to hold it better," he said.

Chick, Dougie, Opie and Will had paddled back and were enjoying the show. "Maybe we should just tie a rope on Dewey and tow him back to shore," Chick said.

Dewey lifted his hand in a one finger salute to Chick.

"Let's try to both get up at once," I said. "I'll go on the right side. You come up on the left. We'll do it at the same time and maybe balance each other out."

I swam around to the other side of the canoe, counted to three, and then we both jumped up onto the side of the canoe. We teetered there, got our balance, and then we both moved up a little more. One more stop to settle, and we slid into the canoe. "Wait for me to sit," I said. I carefully climbed up onto the seat and then told Dewey to get onto his seat. Of course, he tried to stand up and tipped us over again.

By now I was getting tired, and I know Dewey was too, because he was huffing and puffing. "You guys gotta help us," I said. "We're not gonna be able to get in by ourselves."

The others paddled over and positioned their canoes along our canoe, which we now had upright and empty of water… again. Chick and Dougie were on one side, and Opie and Will on the other. They all hung onto our canoe and made kind of a big platform of the three canoes. Then Dewey climbed up onto Chick's canoe and I climbed up onto Opie's, and when we were settled, we both climbed over into our canoe held firmly by the others. When we sat on our seats, they gave a cheer. "I thought we'd have to get a Coast Guard boat out here to get you guys," Chick said.

"We'd have been all right if one of us wasn't so heavy and uncoordinated," I said.

Dewey lifted his leg and farted. "Oops. Sorry. It slipped."

By the time we got back to the dock it was almost dark. It didn't take us long to get ready for bed, especially Dewey and me. We were very tired.

It seemed like I had just lain down when I heard a voice say, "Whe's my helpas? Is they some helpas up here?"

I opened my eyes; standing in the doorway of our room was the biggest black lady I had ever seen. She was wearing a white uniform and a hairnet. "Uh, hello," I said.

"Monin.' Is you boys the kitchen helpers?"

"Yes, ma'am, I guess that's us. There's others in the other rooms, too," I said. Dewey just laid there staring at the lady.

"Well, we's about to start breakfast and you boys c'mon down and give us a hand?"

"Yes, ma'am. We'll get right down," I said.

She stood there for a minute as if she expected us to jump out of bed right then. We were only wearing our underwear, and neither of us was brave enough to get up almost naked in front of this very large black lady. "Um, we'll be down in a few minutes," I said again.

She grinned, turned and left. We heard her stop at the other rooms, talking to the others, too. In a short time all of us were up and dressed. We filed down to the kitchen.

When we walked in, we were surprised to see two more black ladies. One was much younger and very pretty. The other was older, with that kindly grandma look. The big lady was obviously the boss as she was giving the others orders.

Just then Chief came in. "Ah, good everyone's up and ready for breakfast," he said. "Boys, I want to introduce our camp cooks." He walked up to the big lady. "This is Essie. She is the head cook." Essie looked like the lady on the bottle of *Aunt Jemimah* pancake syrup. "This is Jimmee," he said pointing to the younger lady. "And this is Ruthie," he said as the older lady gave us a big smile. "These ladies are the cooks for one of the fraternities at the University. They have some time off while the students are on summer break, so we're lucky to have them as our cooks. They will tell you what to do, and I expect you to do it for them. Any questions?" We had none, so Essie took over.

"Okay. I need a couple of you to set this here table in the kitchen. We's gonna eat here, not in the dinin' room. That's for the rich payin' customers. One of you help Ruthie with the oatmeal; one help Jimmee with the eggs. One of you get that toaster going and make a bunch of toast, and one of you get yo mamma Essie an iced tea." We all got busy and in no time we had the breakfast ready.

We all sat down to eat, Essie talking nonstop. "Too bad we don't have a little bacon with these eggs," Dewey said. The three ladies and Chief stopped eating and looked at Dewey like he had just farted.

"We don't have bacon here... ever," Chief said.

"Don't like bacon?" Chick asked.

"This is a camp for Jewish boys. Jews don't eat bacon, or anything else that comes from a pig," Chief said.

"Jewish boys?" Dougie said. "That's all that comes here?"

"Yes. I thought you guys knew that," Chief said.

"Nope. Nobody told us," I said.

"Does it matter?" Chief asked.

We all looked at each other. "I don't guess it does," I said. "I don't think we've ever met anybody who is Jewish, so I don't see why it would matter. At home most everyone is either Catholic or Lutheran, and we all get along good, so I think we'll be fine with Jews, too."

"But no bacon for three weeks?" Dewey asked.

"We'll get you some nice smoked brisket," Chief said laughing.

After breakfast Chief asked me if I knew how to drive. Of course, I told him I did. He didn't ask me if I had my license, so I didn't bother to tell him. He took me down behind the barracks and showed me a big oven used to burn all the trash from the camp. An old blue pickup truck was there, too, for hauling the trash. He told me I would be in charge of that job, besides washing pots and pans and kitchen help. I thought that was great. I got to drive the truck around the camp every day, and that was a big deal for me.

We had cleaned every building in the camp spotless. Saturday came and the kids started to arrive. The parade of Cadillacs, Lincolns and chauffer driven limos was endless. Often a limo from the airport drove up with two or three kids inside. Some of the parents brought their own kids, and it was quite a parade of expensive-looking clothes and jewels.

By dinner time all of the kids were there. We were helping Essie and the other ladies with the meal. Everyone was running here and there, scrambling to get this and that done as Essie barked out orders. Occasionally, she stirred a pot or tasted something, but mostly she sat on a stool and directed traffic. Every once in a while she'd call out to one of us to "Get yo mamma some iced tea."

The guys who were designated as waiters soon began carrying out the food and things quieted down in the kitchen. It didn't seem long at all until the dining room was empty, the campers all filled up, heading back to their cabins. Then the waiters brought in dishes and Dewey and I started washing. We had eaten before the campers arrived, so once everything was cleaned up and ready for breakfast, we had the rest of the evening off. We were tired after a long day, so we all just went up to our rooms and turned in early.

The next morning we began a routine that had us up early enough to get breakfast ready for the campers. Then after the clean-up, we had a few hours off before we helped get lunch ready. After lunch we had a few hours again until the dinner preparation began. It wasn't a bad job, and the ladies and we boys quickly became friends.

Essie was everyone's mom. She fussed over us and although she was boss, she made sure that "her boys" got plenty of the best food at each meal. She demanded lots of hugs... and she was an armful to hug.

Jimmee was quieter, but she was very nice. Very efficient in the kitchen, she showed us many little tricks to make things easier. She always wore a big smile, and she sang quietly as she worked.

Ruthie was small and quiet. Of course, with Essie around, there wasn't much room for anyone else to say much. Ruthie was the pastry cook. She could make the most wonderful cakes, cookies and pies that any of us had ever tasted. She, too, made sure that we got more than our share of all the sweets that she made.

And so our strange little "family" settled into the days of work and the evenings of rest. We got to know many of the campers, too, especially the ones that were close to our age. Some were kind of "rich" acting, but many were just kids like us. After a few days, when the kids were coming to lunch or dinner, they would often ask Dewey or me what was on the menu. One day one of the kids asked Dewey; he looked up and said, "Pork chops." The kid's mouth dropped open and Dewey just about laughed his head off. From then on every time someone asked what was for lunch, it was pork chops, bacon lettuce and tomato, ham sandwiches, or some other non-Jewish food. The kids enjoyed seeing what Dewey would come up with next.

Although we missed ham and bacon, we learned to eat brisket, matza balls, and many other Jewish foods. Then one day Chief came to the kitchen and with him was a rabbi. He was doing some religious thing to the kitchen to make it kosher. After he did his thing he chatted with us. "So, this kosher stuff... how does that work?" I asked.

"Well, to be kosher, things must be done to meat and poultry. A rabbi must use a special ceremony when the animal is killed to make it kosher."

We all nodded that we understood, and then Dewey, good old Dewey asked, "So, how do you get kosher pickles? You gotta kill them, too?"

The rabbi laughed. "No. I just walk through the pickle factory and bless them," he said. At least he had a good sense of humor.

Each Saturday night they had a big camp fire. All the campers dressed up like Indians, and Chief wore buckskins and a big headdress. He looked pretty goofy. They sang songs and danced, and it was kind of fun to watch. The first night of these campfires was especially fun. Some of the older campers and Chief took canoes out into the lake at dusk. The campers were dressed in loincloths, and their faces and bodies were painted. Chief was in his chief outfit. Then at dark, they lit torches and paddled into the camp at the fire pit. It was pretty dramatic, and even though it was kind of corny, we had a good time, as did all the other campers. We were treated to everything that the paying customers had, so it was a pretty good deal for us.

About half-way through the last week, Dewey, Dougie, Chick and I decided to fish for a while out at the end of the dock. The kids had been swimming, but now they were in their cabins, so we thought we'd fish until dark.

With just worms and bobbers, we sat with our feet in the water, talking, when I got a bite. I pulled in a huge perch. I put it on my stringer, and before I had it back in the water Dougie had its twin. I put his on the stringer, too, and then Chick and Dewey both pulled up perch just like it.

From then on things went nuts. A school of perch must have moved in below the docks, because as soon as our bobbers hit the water they went down. In no time we had all our stringers filled, and the fish were still biting like mad. Dougie ran up to the kitchen and grabbed a cardboard box, and as we caught fish we threw them into the box. It was crazy for about a half-hour and just as quickly as it had started, it was over. The school of fish had moved on. When the fish quit biting, we had perch everywhere. "Holy smokes! I never caught fish that fast," Chick said. "What are we gonna do with all of these?"

We gathered up our gear, the stringers and box of fish, and headed to the kitchen. Chief was just coming from the camp fire and we showed him our catch. "What are you going to do with all of them?" he asked.

"If we had a place to clean them, we could put them in the refrigerator and cook them for supper tomorrow," Dewey said.

Chief thought that was a grand idea, so we spent the next two hours filleting the fish. "We must have close to a hundred and fifty," Dewey said. "That should feed the whole camp."

The next evening Chef Dewey was in charge of frying fish, and it was the Dinner-of-the-Year at camp. Essie turned over "her" kitchen and fussed over Dewey as he expertly fried the fish. All of the campers clapped when it was over, and Dewey had to go in the dining room to take a bow.

The last weekend was Parents' Weekend. They came to get their kids, or sent drivers for them. Most of the kids' parents did arrive and we fed them with the kids. Many stopped and talked to us and told us how their kids had enjoyed their time at camp. Even better, most of them tipped us. When it was all said and done, we all had a pocketful of ones and fives.

As the kids loaded up to leave, many stopped and said good-bye to us. It was kind of sad to see them leaving, but it was also good to think we'd soon be home, sleeping in our own beds again. The day after the kids left, we cleaned up everything one last time, and then packed up to leave. Dewey drove Big Edna down next to the kitchen and we loaded up all our stuff. Essie, Jimmee and Ruthie were there to see us off with lots of hugs and tears. It was hard saying good-bye to our new friends.

Chief paid us and told us that if we were looking for jobs next summer to let him know. We thanked him, and then drove out of Camp Indianola for the last time. On the highway we talked about what we wanted to do when we got home. Of course, a stop at the Gosey for a little swim was first on our agenda.

It had been a good summer job. We made lots of new friends, eaten foods we'd never even heard of, and we made a pocketful of money.

Camp Indianola operated for a few more years, but then one summer a tornado destroyed almost all of the buildings. Chief was getting too old to rebuild, so he sold the lakefront land to the State. A State Park occupies the land now, and all traces of the camp are gone. I occasionally drive past it now, and I can still remember the white buildings with the green roofs and trim. I think back to that summer, and I can picture the kids playing ball, canoeing, and a camp fire with Chief in his headdress. I see Essie, Jimmee, and Ruthie. It makes me smile.

Up North… On the Road

Dewey's parents didn't get away much because they ran a restaurant, but they owned a share in a cabin in the northern part of the state where they spent a long weekend a couple of times a year. Dewey invited Chick, Dougie and me to go with him and his parents, his brothers and sister and their families for the weekend "up north." Of course, we were all for a trip, and started gathering up our fishing gear. There was no sense in going all the way up north to a lake without fishing poles.

His family planned to leave on Thursday after they closed the restaurant. Dewey and the three of us would stay behind and help with the Friday night Fish Fry. It was always a busy night and with the four of us helping the regular staff, there would be plenty of help. Then, after we had finished the work, we'd start off on the trip north, and camp out somewhere along the way to the cabin. Then we'd drive the rest of the way on Saturday morning, spend the rest of the weekend there, and then return home on Monday.

We were happy to help Dewey at the restaurant. Plus, by working in the kitchen, we'd get lots of free food to boot.

Dewey packed two Army surplus pup tents in Big Edna's trunk, a fishing pole for each of us, and a couple of tackle boxes. We each brought a sleeping bag, extra clothes, and a tooth brush. There were towels and all the other things we'd need at the cabin.

We met at Dougie's house, walked up to the restaurant and found Dewey in the kitchen getting things ready for the fish fry. "One of you can grind up that cabbage for coleslaw, and one can unwrap these packages of fish and cut them up into pieces," he said. I grabbed the fish and Chick started shoving cabbage into a big grinder.

"Dougie, you can start washing those potatoes," Dewey said, pointing to a huge bag of potatoes on the floor. "Then put about fifty pounds of them in those big kettles. We'll boil them for hash browns."

We all pitched in and the kitchen was buzzing with activity. The two ladies that usually worked on Friday nights showed up a little while later. They were happily surprised to see much of their preparation work already done. The time passed quickly and then the waitresses arrived, and in no time they began bringing back orders for food.

Dewey was cooking the fish and a lady named Alice was in charge of hash browns. Dewey put me in charge of dropping handfuls of frozen French fries into the fryer when an order called for it. The other lady, Alma, took care of other non-fish orders, and Chick and Dougie dished up the coleslaw and other sides. The kitchen hummed right along and the orders flew out into the dining room. Every once in a while I'd drop too many French fries into the oil and Dewey would put in a few too many pieces of fish, and we'd have to eat our mistakes. We made a lot of mistakes, and we all got full as ticks while we worked.

Since we were so busy, the time flew by, and it was nearly ten o'clock and time to close down the kitchen. We helped clean up, and a short time later we were ready to head out on the long road north.

Smelling like fried food, we piled into Big Edna and started off into the night. We were all pumped up from the excitement of the kitchen, and for the first hour we talked about how we should open our own restaurant when we got a little older, since we were so good at running a kitchen.

We drove until about midnight. Everyone was getting tired; there were a lot of yawns. "Let's find a place to put up the tents and get some sleep," Dougie suggested.

"Yeah, I'm getting real tired," Dewey said. "I'm gonna drive us into a ditch if we don't stop pretty soon."

"Are we gonna find a campground?" Chick asked.

"Heck, no! That costs money. Let's just pull off someplace and put up the tents," I said.

We were just coming into a little town. I saw a sign for a boat landing. "Hey! Pull down that road... we can camp at the landing," I said.

Dewey drove down the road until we found the parking lot next to a little lake. There was a nice grassy place on the lower side of the parking lot next to the water. "That looks good," I said.

We pulled the two pup tents out of the trunk. "Where are the tent poles, Dewey?" Chick asked.

"Poles?"

"Yeah. The things that hold up the tent!"

"Oops. I bet that was what was in those two long canvass bags," Dewey said shrugging his shoulders.

"Oh, great!" Dougie said. "How are we gonna put up these tents?"

We looked around for some sticks to use instead of the poles. Suddenly Dewey shouted, "Hey look!" He was pointing at a bunch of small trees near the edge of the lake.

"Yeah? So what? Those are trees."

"We can tie some of that bailer twine to the top ends of the tents and stretch it between two of those trees. Then we don't need any poles."

We all broke out in smiles. "Dewey, you're a genius," Chick said.

We lit our flashlights and rigged up a piece of twine on each end of each tent, pulled it tight and tied it around two trees. It worked like a charm. "Well, who's going to sleep with who?" Chick asked.

"I don't care," I said. "I'm so tired I'll even sleep with Dewey."

"Gee, thanks," Dewey said.

We pulled our sleeping bags from Big Edna, paired off and crawled into the little tents. There was barely enough room to lie down, let alone sit up to get undressed. So we crawled back out, took off our shoes, socks and jeans, and then crawled back in and slid into our sleeping bags. It didn't take me long to fall asleep despite a couple of loud blasts from Dewey's backside.

It was pitch black when I opened my eyes. I could hear drops of rain falling on the tent. I looked over at Dewey but I couldn't see if he was asleep. "Dewey," I whispered. "You asleep?"

"I was," he answered.

"It's raining."

"So what?"

"Are these things waterproof?"

"I think so."

"Okay. Just checking."

I closed my eyes again and tried to get back to sleep. But the few drops of rain had turned into many drops as the storm passed right over us. Several flashes of lightning lit up the sky, and through the tent material it made the inside of the tent look like it was full of green light. Those were followed by cracking thunder and heavier rain. Soon it was a downpour.

"Dewey!"

"What?"

"You sure about this tent?"

"Turn on your flashlight and see if it's leaking," he said. "I don't feel any water dripping on me."

I turned on my flashlight and much to my surprise, the top of the tent was only about three inches from my face. "Dewey! The tent's sagging. That twine must be stretching."

Dewey turned on his flashlight. "You're right. I hope it doesn't get any lower."

Just then we heard Chick yell from his tent. "Hey! Is your tent sagging?"

"Yeah," I yelled back.

"Ours is just about on our faces," Dougie said with a worried sound in his voice.

"Ours, too."

Dewey pulled his arms up out of his sleeping bag and put his finger up toward the tent fabric.

"Dewey! Don't touch it!" I said excitedly.

"Why not?"

"If you touch it, it'll start leaking."

He turned and looked at me. "What?"

"No foolin.' If you touch wet tents they leak."

He shook his head. "Where'd you hear that?"

"I don't know, but I heard it."

He shined his light up on the canvas and then touched the tent with his finger... right over my face. He pulled his finger back and grinned. "See? No leak."

He had just said the words when a drop of water formed on the canvas right where his finger had touched. It grew larger, and larger, and then dropped onto my forehead. As soon as that drop hit me, another formed and soon it dropped, too. "See! I told you!" I yelled.

"It's a good thing I touched it on your side, then," Dewey said laughing like a fool.

The drops became a steady little stream of cold rain water running onto my face. "Move over!" I said, and tried to get nearer to Dewey's side of the tent.

"I can't move much more, or I'll be touching the tent, and then you know what will happen," Dewey said.

I turned and looked at him; he was grinning like a madman. "Oh, you're real funny, you are," I said.

The rain was coming down in sheets. The thunder and lightning was deafening. Suddenly Dewey was squirming. "I'm getting wet. The water's coming in under the tent!"

He tried to move back towards me and in all the commotion, we both bumped into the tent above us and two more leaks rained down on us. Just then we heard Dougie and Chick yelling that their tent was getting flooded. "Time to abandon the tent!" I yelled.

It must have been quite a sight. As the lightning flashed I got glimpses of four boys clad in only our underwear, trying to pull down the two tents and gather our sopping wet clothes as water from the parking lot flooded upon us like a river. The ground turned to slick, black mud and was sucking at our feet as we tried to carry our clothes, sleeping bags and soaked tents to Big Edna's trunk.

I don't know how long it took, but by the time we had everything loaded, we were covered with mud and freezing cold. Dewey started Edna and turned on the defroster and heater. Then he turned on the headlights and moved the car so we could see if we had missed anything. Sure enough, one tennis shoe stuck up from a mud puddle. I got out, ran over to retrieve it, and then jumped back into Big Edna. The heater had warmed the inside and the windshield was clearing up. Chick looked at his watch. "Holy cow! It's 2 AM!"

"What are we gonna do now?" Dougie asked.

"We've got enough money," I said. "Let's find a motel and get a room."

Everyone agreed that it was a good idea. We pulled out of the boat landing parking lot and back on the highway. It wasn't long until we saw a small motel. We pulled in and stopped in front of the office. "We have to get some money from the trunk, and then someone has to get a room," I said. Dougie and I got out, opened the trunk, and sorted through the soaked gear. We found Chick's wallet and mine, closed the trunk, hurried over to the office door and rang the buzzer.

We were standing there shivering when a man came into the room wearing a bathrobe. He turned on a light and came to the door. His eyes got big as he looked out at us. "What do you want?" he asked.

"Hello, sir. Uh, could we get a room, please?" Dougie asked.

He looked us up and down. Of course, we were in our soaked underwear, and covered with mud. "What happened to you?"

Just then I realized we must have looked like a couple of crazy people, out in such a storm… in our underwear. "We were camping and got washed out by a flood," I said. "That's why we're all wet and muddy. We'll be real careful not to get your room all dirty. Promise."

The man sighed and unlocked the door. He opened it just a little and handed us a key. "Here… room 8 is a big double. Try not to make a huge mess. Come back in the morning and we'll settle up for the room." Then he closed the door and walked off into the back shaking his head.

We turned and held up the key triumphantly, motioning for Dewey to follow us. We walked down the parking lot to room 8. Dewey parked, and he and Chick got out. "Get our duffle bags with our dry clothes. We can pay in the morning," Dougie instructed.

Dougie opened the door and I turned on the lights. The room was pretty big with two double beds. "You get in the shower first," I said to Dougie. He didn't argue and tiptoed into the bathroom. Just then Chick and Dewey came hustling in with our extra clothes that had been in Big Edna's trunk and were still dry. "Hey, nice room!"

We all took hot showers and washed the mud off. By that time it was nearly 3 AM. We crawled into the beds and turned off the light. We settled in, safe and dry.

The next morning we showered again to get the mud off that we had missed the night before. Dewey went in first and we heard some unpleasant noises coming from the bathroom soon after he closed the door. "Dewey," Chick yelled through the door. "Make sure the exhaust fan is on… on high!" A while later Dewey came out, wrapped in his towel, his hair standing up and still wet. I noticed a strong smell that reminded me of my great aunt Gertrude.

"Whew! Dewey! What's that smell?"

"You like it?"

"No. It smells like an old lady who fell into a bottle of perfume."

"I think it's nice," he said reaching back into the bathroom, picking up a bottle of purple liquid. "It's Lilac Vegital. I got it at the drug store before we left. It's aftershave," he said, handing the bottle to me. I took the cap off and the stuff was so strong it almost made my eyes water.

"Holy cow, Dewey! That stuff stinks. Are you sure it's for men?"

"I didn't see anything on it that said it was for one or the other, so I figured it was unisex," he said spilling another handful of the stuff into his hand and rubbing it over his chest. I think it's nice. I bet the girls will like it."

Chick and Dougie stood there open mouthed listening to us. Chick reached out, took the bottle and smelled it. "Wow! About all that's good for would be to cover up skunk spray!"

Dougie smelled it and just shivered. He handed it back to Dewey. "You guys just don't know good stuff when you smell it," Dewey said. "And it was a real bargain. It only cost $2.50… and it's a big bottle."

"Yeah… that's real top shelf stuff at $2.50 a pint. It's got to be imported from France or someplace," Dougie laughed.

Dewey smelled the stuff again and then completely surprised us. He tipped up the bottle and drank some of the purple stuff. He shut his eyes and grimaced. "Whew. It doesn't taste nearly as good as it smells." We laughed until I thought we'd all be sick.

The rest of us showered, and then we cleaned up the room as well as we could. A few muddy footprints were still on the floor, but otherwise it wasn't too bad. We organized the wet stuff in the trunk and went to pay the man for the room. He was very understanding about the mud, and we left an extra $5 in the room for the extra cleaning.

The motel man told us about a coin laundry up the road, so we stopped and washed our sleeping bags and muddy clothes. We did one load with all the tennis shoes in it. They made quite a lot of noise clanging around when we put them in the dryer. Then after a quick stop for breakfast, we were on our way north. We left the windows wide open to keep the scent of Lilac Vegital from putting us in a coma. If the rest of the weekend was as much of an adventure as the trip, it was going to be a lot of fun.

Up North... At the Lake

We turned down the sand road to Pigeon Lake just before lunch time. Dewey had been at the cabin many times and knew the way, even though it was the first time he had driven to the lake himself. We parked next to the other cars belonging to Dewey's relatives and went inside.

Five families owned the cabin and each summer they took turns using it. A typical north woods log cabin with a big screen porch, it was divided into two rooms: the big front room was the kitchen, living room and part-time bedroom, and the other half was one large bedroom with three sets of double bunk beds. And with three couches that opened to beds in the living room and two more on the screen porch, the place could sleep about two dozen people. It had an indoor bathroom, but if it was in use and you had to go in a hurry, there was an outhouse, too.

The kitchen took up half of the front room with a huge table that looked about twenty feet long in the middle. It was like a picnic table with about ten four- or five-foot-long benches to sit on. Dewey's mom and his sisters-in-law were loading up platters and bowls with food. We were all invited to sit and eat, and soon there was a table full of people talking and laughing and stuffing their faces.

Chick, Dougie and I knew Dewey's family, so we weren't bashful, but we were pretty surprised when Dewey's older brother leaned forward and farted. Everyone laughed like it was an every day thing. Then we heard another blast from farther down the table. No one took credit for that one. We were still laughing about the farts when Dewey raised his right leg and let one blast at his little sister sitting right next to him. She slugged him in the arm and fanned the air. It looked like it was a normal thing that happened every day. Several blasts had given everyone a good laugh. Apparently Dewey's family was not up tight about farting.

We decided to go water skiing, so the four of us, Dewey's brothers, and some of their sons went into the bedroom and changed into our swimming suits. While the women changed, we walked down to the lake and gassed up the boats. Two of Dewey's brothers had big ski boats and one had brought his fishing boat. The four of us piled in with Dewey's oldest brother and his two boys and off we went.

The boat was fitted with two tow ropes, so Dewey's nephews dropped over the side with skis. We circled around and brought the ropes up next to them. When they were situated with the rope handles, they nodded their heads. Dewey's brother pushed up the throttle and we shot forward. The two boys popped up out of the water and flew along behind the boat, jumping the waves and skiing like professionals. We went around the lake a few times and then Dewey's brother motioned for them to drop off.

"Two of you guys get ready," his brother said. "We'll drop you off and pick them up." Chick and Dougie volunteered to go next. We stopped next to Dewey's nephews in the water and they climbed up onto a little platform at the rear of the boat. Dougie and Chick jumped over the side and put on the skis. We moved the boat forward and the ropes slid through the water until the handles got to them. They got situated and nodded their heads. "Hit it!" Dewey yelled, and the boat shot forward.

Dougie and Chick popped up onto the skis and went about twenty yards, looking pretty good until Chick lost his balance and crashed. Dougie held on as we went in a big circle and came back alongside Chick with his rope. When we got next to Chick, Dougie settled down into the lake and was pulled along slowly until he was next to Chick.

They got set again and off we went. This time they both got up and stayed up. We went around the lake three times and Dewey motioned to them to drop off. "We're next," he said to me.

"Have you done this before?" I asked Dewey as we put on the ski vests.

"Yeah... a few times, but I have trouble getting up most of the time."

I had *never* been on skis, so I was a little nervous, but I hoped that Dewey wouldn't be any better at it than I was, so I wouldn't look too stupid. Dougie and Chick climbed onto the boat and we jumped in the water. I had to adjust Dougie's skis because my feet were bigger than his. When I got them on, Dewey was ready, too. The ropes slid through our hands until the wooden handles came to us. We took hold of the handles and were slowly towed through the water as the ropes straightened out and tightened. "You ready?" Dewey asked.

"As ready as I'll ever be," I said nervously.

Dewey nodded his head and suddenly we were being pulled through the water. "Pull back on the rope and raise yourself out of the water," Dewey shouted. I pulled back and up I came onto the skis. Dewey was still down in the water, and the boat was struggling to get him up. I suddenly had a lot of slack in my rope and in no time I was falling back into the water. I crashed into Dewey as I lost my balance and fell, and we both went under.

When we came up, Dewey spit water out of his mouth and burped. "That wasn't quite right," he said.

"I got up. You pulled me back down, lard ass!" I said.

"Hey! I told you I have trouble getting up," he said grinning.

On about the seventh or eighth try, I was about to let go to keep my arms from being ripped from their sockets, when Dewey managed to rise up out of the water next to me. That took some of the pressure off, and I popped up on the skis, too. I was delighted that we were up. I turned my head to congratulate Dewey. That's when I saw his swimming trunks around his knees. Apparently the force of him rising up had been too much for the weak elastic, and they had slid down when he stood up on the skis. I laughed so hard that I swerved over at Dewey, we crashed into each other and went into the lake head over heals. "Cripes! We were up, you maniac!" Dewey yelled as he came to the surface.

I could barely talk I was laughing so hard. "Your big hinder was about to terrify everyone on the lake," I laughed. Dewey grinned.

To make a long story short, Dewey's brother came around about a dozen times and hooked us up. And about a dozen times we got up, or nearly up, and then crashed. One time Dewey let loose of his rope while I was up on the skis. I was so surprised with suddenly going very fast that I got a little carried away and did a nose dive over the front of the skis. That did it for me!

"That's it! I give up!" I yelled to the boat. Apparently Chick and Dougie and Dewey's nephews thought it was very humorous because they were laughing quite raucously. Dewey swam over by me. "Well, I guess we won't be in the *Tommy Bartlett Ski Extravaganza* after all," he said laughing.

"No foolin,'" I said. "Boats should be for fishing anyway. This is kind of stupid if you ask me."

They picked us up and when I got into the boat I realized how tired I was from being drug through the water so many times. My arms ached and my shoulders felt like they had been dislocated.

After our ski adventure, we went back to the cabin and we all took a nap. Later in the afternoon we took the fishing boat out and had a grand time catching bluegills and walleyes. This was my way of thinking when it came to water sports.

That evening we grilled out and had a wonderful supper of steaks, baked potatoes, and corn on the cob. One thing about going someplace with Dewey's family: you always ate well. We had a fun evening playing cards and games and then Dewey suggested we drive down to the dump to see if there were any bears. That was right up our alley, so the four of us and Dewey's two nephews piled into Big Edna. Off we went down a forest road toward the dump. Of course, Dewey knew right were it was, but we turned down two wrong roads before we found the correct one. We pulled into an open area where there were piles of garbage, trees and branches. Dewey shut off Edna and we sat there, looking for bears.

"Sometimes they leave when a car comes in," Dewey whispered.

"They'll come back if we just sit quiet."

Suddenly Dougie grabbed my arm. "Look there!" he whispered, pointing to my right. Sure enough, there was a bear coming across the bare ground toward the piles of garbage. "See him, Chick?" Dougie asked.

"Yeah. There… there's another one, too!" Chick said.

There were soon five bears climbing around on the pile of garbage, tearing bags apart and finding things that seemed to make them happy. They were having a good time sorting through the garbage and eating, and after a while they had worked their way around the end of the pile so we couldn't see them any more. "Let's walk around the end and see some more," Dougie said.

"What? Go over there?" I asked.

"Sure. They're not interested in us. They're eating."

"Yeah. Lets go," Chick said.

I looked at Dewey. "What do you think, Dewey?"

"I don't know. Have you ever seen a bear run? They can go pretty fast. I think faster than I can run," he said.

"Oh, come on, girls," Chick said.

Well, of course, that did it. We all got out of the car, walked very quietly down along the pile of garbage, and carefully edged our way around the end where the bears were about half-way down the pile. Dougie got his camera out of his pocket and took a picture of them. When the flash went off the bears looked our way, but then went back to eating. We edged closer, watched them, and took more pictures. As we watched, the bears climbed up the garbage pile and were soon going down the front side.

"Let's get back to the car," Dewey said urgently.

When we came around the end of the garbage pile, there were the bears, standing right next to Big Edna! One of the smaller ones was standing with his paws on the bumper, licking dead bugs off the hood. "Oh, this is bad," Dewey said.

"What are we gonna do now?" I asked.

"Well, I guess we wait till they leave," Chick said.

We squatted down and watched as the bears climbed around on Big Edna. One even stuck his head into the car through the open window. "We'd have really got a good close look if we'd have stayed in Edna," Dougie said.

Finally the bears must have gotten tired of looking over Edna and they ambled off into the woods. We snuck back to the car. There were bear footprints all over the hood and sides. "Well, let's go back," Dewey said. "But don't tell my mom we got out of the car. She'll have our heads if she finds out."

We drove back; the rest of the family was just getting ready for bed. It was all one big happy family as everyone undressed and climbed into one of the many beds. The four of us took the beds on the porch. After a full day, we dropped off to sleep quickly.

Just as I was dozing off, I thought I heard a bear roar. It may have been partly my imagination. It was only a blast from Dewey.

Up North…
Time for Church

A beam of morning sun was shining in my eyes when I felt Dewey shaking my shoulder. I turned over in the pull-out bed to see what he wanted. He leaned in close to me and whispered, "Let's sneak out and go fishing. Otherwise, Ma will make us go to church with them."

I nodded and sat up in the bed. Immediately I felt the ache in my arms and shoulders from the beating I had taken the day before while learning to water ski. I groaned as I moved my arms. "Shhh," Dewey whispered. "Ma's got ears like radar. Be quiet."

Dewey got up, moved to the other bed, woke Dougie and Chick and whispered to them our plans. They both got up quietly and slipped on their shorts and t-shirts. Dewey snuck into the cabin, grabbed a sack of donuts and a quart of milk, and we all snuck out of the porch, careful not to let the door slam behind us.

Our fishing poles and tackle boxes were still in the boat. All we had to do was pick up some night crawlers from a cooler on the dock and we were ready to go fishing. Dewey got in the boat and untied the back rope and Dougie and I climbed in while Chick untied the front rope. We used the oars to push off, not wanting to start the motor that would wake Dewey's mom. We were about ten feet from the dock when we heard the screen door on the porch slam.

"You will be back in time for church, I expect."

Dewey's shoulders drooped. "Yeah, Ma. We'll be back."

Dang! Busted!

We started the motor and headed out onto the lake. We baited our poles, sat back and ate the whole bag of donuts and shared the quart of milk. The bluegills were biting, and Dougie caught a huge Dogfish that gave us a lot of thrills as we tried to get it into the boat. We were laughing and having a great time when Chick suddenly looked at his watch. "What time is church?" he asked Dewey.

"Ten o'clock. What time is it now?"

"Nine thirty… well, almost nine forty."

"Holy cow! We gotta get going. If we're late Ma won't let us go fishing this afternoon."

We all reeled up our lines and flew down the lake as fast as the twenty-five horsepower Johnson motor would push us. We were going a little too fast when we roared into the boat dock and hit it pretty hard. We tied up the boat, put the fish basket in the lake so the fish would stay alive while we were gone, and ran for the cabin.

It was like a tornado on the porch as we all threw off shorts and t-shirts and put on jeans and nicer shirts, shoes and socks. Even Dewey was hurrying which was something that hardly ever happened. It took us about four minutes to change, and in the next minute we were flying down the dirt road toward the highway to the church.

Big Edna was purring right along and I was bent over tying my tennis shoes when Dewey said, "Hey! Look! There's a little bear in the road."

I looked up from the back seat. Up ahead was a small, black animal standing next to the road. "That's the smallest bear I've ever seen," I said.

Just as we came even with the little bear, it turned and we saw the white stripe down its back. "That's not a bear," Chick yelled, rolling up his window. "That's a skunk!" I reached for the crank for my window and cranked like crazy. Just a nano-second later the skunk gave us a blast, all along the side of Edna. The caustic odor of Eau-De-Peppe-LePew filled the car immediately. "Arrgh! We got blasted!" Dougie yelled.

We coughed and gagged and rolled down the windows trying to get rid of the stink. Fresh air helped, but we could still smell the stink as we continued on down the road. "Whew. That was too close. I think he got Edna," Dewey said.

"We'll wash her down when we get back," Chick said leaning out the window to look. "I think I see a streak of stuff on the side."

We pulled up to the church just as the bells were ringing. We parked Edna, trotted up to the door and walked in. Dewey's family was in a pew a few rows up so we slid into the end beside them. Suddenly everyone in the church began looking around and sniffing the air. Dewey's mom looked at us with horror on her face. "Did you guys get sprayed by a skunk?" she whispered to Dewey.

"Yeah. But he just got the car, not us."

"It's all saturated into you guys. You stink terrible," she said, getting a hanky from her purse and holding it to her nose.

"Well, we can go back to the cabin if we stink too bad," Dewey said with a hopeful lilt in his voice.

"Not on your life. You stay here and pray. You guys need it if anyone does."

The church people must have been getting used to the skunk stink because they quit looking around and fanning themselves. The priest started the Mass and soon we were listening to the sermon. Dewey was sitting next to me. Suddenly I felt the pew vibrate. I looked at him. He was trying not to laugh. I leaned over to him. "Did you just blast one?" I whispered.

He nodded. I began to laugh. Chick was next to me. "Did Dewey just explode" he whispered. I began to snicker and soon the four of us were laughing, trying not to be too obvious. Dewey's mom shot us a look of death rays. We settled down.

A little while later Dewey did it again, but this time it made a little noise, kind of like a far off outboard motor. We all began laughing again and the harder we tried to stop, the more we laughed. Dewey's mom shushed us and we tried to stop laughing, but there was no stopping.

The sermon was over and everyone stood to sing. Poor Dewey's mom was so embarrassed that she grabbed his arm with a grip like a professional wrestler, and told him to get out of the church and take his heathen friends with him. We were all happy to get out of church early and laughed all the way back to the cabin.

"Let's make some sandwiches and go fishing," Dewey said. "I don't want to be here when Ma gets back. If we're fishing she might cool off by the time we come in later."

We made a sack of sandwiches, put some pop in a cooler and took off for the lake. We stayed out all day, and when we came in, we went to the fish cleaning shack and cleaned our catch. At the cabin everyone was visiting and playing cards. We showed them our catch; it was decided to have a fish fry for supper. That seemed to get us off the hook for our foolish deeds in church.

The rest of the family was leaving for home after supper. But the four of us didn't have anything special to do the next day, so we decided to stay that night, and then head home the next morning.

We took a boat ride and caught a few fish that we released, since we didn't want to clean any more fish. We tied up the boat and sat on the edge of the dock with our bare feet hanging in the water as dusk settled on the lake. "Well, this was a fun weekend," Dewey said.

"Yeah. No foolin.' This was cool," I said.

"Kind of like the Gosey, but a lot more water... and we've got a boat here," Chick said.

Just then a loon made its eerie call across the lake. The lonesome call rose and fell, leaving the lake in silence. "Now that's something we don't hear at the Gosey," Dougie said.

"Yeah," I said. "But the Gosey has its own sounds that we like pretty well." Everyone agreed.

We walked barefoot across the yard to the cabin... four tired friends, with the faint smell of Peppe-Le-Pew still lingering like a faint aftershave.

Last Hurrah: Hatching the Plan

After our trip to Pigeon Lake with Dewey's family, we kind of took it easy for a few days. School was quickly sneaking up on us, and we would soon have to suffer the indignity of going shopping for school clothes with our moms. To our way of thinking, we were much too old to have a mom pick out what we would wear for the next school year. Of course, if it were up to us, we'd all have a half-dozen tee shirts, a couple pairs of shorts for the warmer weather, and a couple pairs of jeans. There wasn't much else that we ever wore, but our moms had different ideas about our school attire.

Dougie and I were at the Gosey half-heartedly fishing when Dewey drove up in Edna amid a huge cloud of dust. "How they bitin'?" he yelled out the window.

"Not too great, but we get a nibble now and then," Dougie answered.

Dewey got out of the car and took his pole from the back seat where it was sticking out the side window. He ambled down to us. "Got a worm for me?" he asked as he plunked down in the sand next to us.

I passed him the worm can; he baited the hook and threw out his line. "So... you guys got all your new school clothes yet?"

"Yeah," I said. "Jeez! My mom about drove me crazy trying on all these geek shirts and dweeby pants. I finally ended up with pretty much what I wanted, but it took a lot of whining."

"Me too, but my mom made me get a couple of really ugly shirts in addition to the good stuff," Dougie added.

"I got most of my stuff," Dewey said grinning. "My mom was really pissed at the guy in the store. When we asked about jeans, he directed us to the "Husky" section. That made Ma mad, and then I was trying on a shirt and it had such a small neck hole that I couldn't get it over my head. The sales guy said there was nothing wrong with the shirt, that I just had an abnormally huge head."

"Holy cow. What did your mom say?"

"Well, I hate to repeat it, being a good Catholic boy. But she wasn't very happy. She told the guy where to put his stuff and we walked out. I let a huge fart just before I walked through the door and Ma stopped and looked back and said, 'There… my son just left a kiss for you.' I about pooped my pants laughing."

We had a good laugh—we could just picture Dewey's mom doing that. She was a tiny lady and very sweet, but we'd seen her in action a few times when she got mad, and you didn't want to be on the receiving end of one of her mads.

Then Chick came ambling down the river bank with his fishing pole in hand. "I thought I'd find you guys here. I called everyone, and they said you left with your poles, so I figured you'd be here. Are they biting?"

"Not so good," Dewey said. "But we're enjoying it anyway."

Chick baited his line and sat down. He took off his shoes and socks and put his feet in the water next to ours. "Well, summer is almost over," he said.

"Yeah. Football practice starts in two weeks," Dewey said.

"You guys going out this year?"

I looked at Dougie and shook my head. "I'm not. I'd rather go squirrel hunting after school."

"Me neither. My ears are still ringing from getting murdered when we were freshmen. I think I'll do some squirrel hunting, too."

"You know," Chick said. "We ought to take one last trip before practice starts. Once that gets going, Dewey and I aren't going to be able to go anywhere until about the end of October."

"We've got plenty of money saved up, don't we?" Dewey asked.

"Yeah. We're full of money. We could go all the way to Canada if we wanted," Chick replied.

"Hey! Why not?" I said.

"Why not what?"

"Why not go to Canada?"

"Do you think your mom will say, 'Sure, go off on a trip to a foreign country with your brain-damaged buddies? I'm all for it'?" Dougie said.

"Well, I guess you're right. Where can we go that would be

something new and different?"

"How about we go up to Lake Superior?" Chick said. "They have huge lake trout and salmon and some pretty big fish that we've never caught."

"Wow! Yeah! That sounds good, and it's almost to Canada," I replied.

"Yeah. If we can go up there and back this summer, maybe next year we really *could* talk them into letting us go to Canada," Dougie suggested.

From that instant on, we talked about organizing our trip to Lake Superior. The more we talked, the more excited we got about it. A couple of hours later we had everything planned. We loaded up into Big Edna to go home to start pestering our moms about letting us go.

Surprisingly, my mom agreed to the plan rather quickly. I guess we had proven—so far during the summer—that we could travel without killing ourselves, so she said I could go if the rest could. Half a dozen phone calls later we all had permission. We arranged to meet the next morning to start gathering up all the gear we would need for the trip.

Dewey pulled up in front of my house at *almost the agreed time* towing his brother's boat, a big sixteen foot flat bottom with a 35- hp motor. We thought that since we'd be on such a big lake, we should take a big boat. It also worked well for hauling a lot of the gear we wanted to take. I jumped into Edna and we picked up Dougie and Chick. At Chick's house we loaded up a big cooler, camping lanterns and a portable stove for cooking. Chick added his sleeping bag, clothes and fishing gear.

At Dougie's we gathered up another cooler and four army cots that his dad had said we could take. They were made of wood and canvass and were all folded up in to four bundles. "They open up about three feet wide and six feet long," Dougie said. "It'll be a lot better than sleeping on the ground." We were going in style.

I added a bunch of cooking gear, pots and pans. We were almost ready for take off. The only thing left to do was grocery shopping.

We drove to the grocery store and then pushed a cart up and down the aisles, picking out all sorts of good things for the trip.

Since Dewey was such a good cook, we bought stuff for making real food instead of junk food. At the check-out we had almost $70 worth of food. "Wow! That's a lot. But I guess it'll feed us for a long time, too," Chick said as he paid the bill.

We packed the coolers with the cold food and ice blocks. We packed the rest into boxes, and then went home for one last night in our own beds. Blast off time was 8 o'clock the next morning.

Dewey pulled up in front of my house at three minutes to eight. I could hardly believe it. Maybe all the verbal abuse he had taken over the years was finally sinking in, and he was actually trying to be on time. "Did you notice what time it is?" he asked as I slid into the front seat of Edna.

"Yes, I did, Dewey. And I must say I'm impressed."

He just grinned, gave Edna some gas, lifted his left leg and let a blast. "Oops. Slipped," he laughed.

It was going to be a long drive.

Last Hurrah:
On the Road

The trunk was full, and the boat was filled to the brim. By the time we were safely settled into Big Edna, it was mid-morning and we were pretty excited to get going.

"Hurry up and get us out of town," Chick said as we pulled out of Carl's gas station with a full tank.

"What's your hurry?" Dewey asked.

"I just want to get out of town before someone's mom finds us and something goes wrong so we can't go on this trip," Chick said, looking down the street as if he expected to see our moms trooping toward us en mass.

As we crossed the bridge I noticed that all of us glanced upriver toward the Gosey. "It'll still be here when we get back," I said.

I guess we all had the same idea. Everyone grinned. We turned up the radio to a nearly deafening volume and sang along with the songs as we steadily drove north. After a couple of hours, the hills and valleys we were accustomed to seeing began to flatten out. "Looking kind of Norther up here," Chick said.

"Yeah... lots Norther. Pretty flat isn't it?" Dougie said.

The road was lined with birches, poplars and spruce trees, and very few maples, elms, and oaks we normally saw around home. The terrain was nearly flat, with very small rises, like baby roller coasters.

"You know what these little rises are called?" Dougie asked.

None of us did, so of course, professor Dougie told us. "They're called drumlins. They're left over from the glacier as it melted. They were rocks and dirt that had been embedded in the ice and when it melted, they were left behind."

I turned and looked over at Dougie. "Sometimes you scare me with the stuff you know," I said. Dougie just grinned.

We were tooling along at a little over the speed limit when we came up on a farm stand beside the road. There was a sign offering melons and sweet corn for sale. We weren't paying much attention to it until we got right even with the stand. "Holy smokes! Look at that!" Chick yelled.

We all looked. Two girls, both blond, both wearing swim suits, were lying on a couple of lounge chairs next to the farm stand. We almost went in the ditch as Dewey gawked over his shoulder.

"Cripes, Dewey! Keep your eyes on the road! You'll kill us!" I yelled, holding onto the armrest for dear life.

"Did you see those girls?" Dougie asked.

"Yeah. Do you think I'm blind?"

"Maybe we should go back and get some corn. It would be really good for supper tonight," Dewey suggested.

We all seemed to be of the same opinion, so we looked ahead for a place to turn around. Of course, since we had the boat behind us, we needed a pretty big place for a turn. A few miles up the road we found a place, did a U-turn and headed back. We pulled off the road by the farm stand and sauntered across the road, trying to look casual. The two girls got up from their lounge chairs and smiled.

"Hi, boys," One of them said grinning. "You looking for some melons?"

Well, our usually glib bunch was rather speechless. We all kind of nodded and stammered, and we soon had three melons and two dozen ears of corn. The girls weren't shy at all, and once we got over the initial shock, we had fun flirting with them. Finally we couldn't think of much else to do or say to stretch out our little encounter, so we loaded up and started off down the road... the wrong way.

We had to drive a few miles to find another turn around, and then headed back north. As we passed the farm stand again, the girls waved and blew us kisses.

We were all sort of worked up after our little produce stop. A few minutes later Chick said, "You remember back when we were thirteen and we kind of took a vow that we'd never like any yucky girls?"

We all nodded. "I think it's time to re-think that," Dougie said.

Indeed we might just have to alter our little agreement about hating girls for the rest of our lives, especially if they looked like our two farm girls.

We drove until noon and stopped at a drive in for some burgers. Then we got right back on the road and drove until about 6 o'clock, when we were at the front gate of Copper Falls State Park. Chick, our navigator, had seen the park on the map and that had been our destination for the night. We paid the park fee, got a campsite, and the ranger gave us a map of the park. We found our site, backed the boat into it and piled out of the car.

"Let's get the tent up first, and then we can cook supper," I said.

The tent was in the bottom of the boat. We unpacked coolers and a bunch of other stuff to get to it. It was huge! A pole ten feet long was supposed to go in the center. Then there were six other poles, each five feet long, a box full of wooden tent pegs, and finally the canvas, rolled up into a big sausage-looking bag. "Holy crap, Dewey! Did you bring some elephants and lions, too? This thing looks like a circus tent."

"Well, you remember the last time when we used those little tents and got all wet? My brother had this one and it's big enough so we can all sleep on comfortable cots, and still have lots of room. Once we set it up a time or two, we'll be just fine."

It took both Dougie and me to haul the canvas over to the flat ground where we decided to erect our Big Top. Chick and Dewey carried the poles and stakes, and a big maul to pound them into the ground. Dewey had set up the tent before, so he directed us. To put it mildly, it was a chore. First one of us had to take the top end of the long pole inside the canvas and find the hole in the top that it stuck up through. That job went to Dougie. He crawled in and cussed up a storm working his way through the hot canvas. He finally got the pole in place and we all worked to stand it up. When it was up,

Dougie and I held it while Chick and Dewey pulled the tent out from the middle and drove in some stakes to hold it temporarily. After about fifteen minutes of grunting and groaning, we got the thing to stand up on its own. Then we had to put all of the six shorter poles in their places around the outside, pound in more stakes for ropes that held up the shorter poles, and then re-position most of the original stakes as we stretched out the tent. It took about half an hour, but when we were done, we had us a Big Top, about sixteen feet across, ten feet high in the middle and five feet high along the sides. It was HUGE!

We looked around the campground at our neighbors. They all had nice compact nylon tents with aluminum poles holding them up. About three of their normal tents would fit inside our giant. Many of them were looking our way, chuckling.

We were all sweaty and dusty from the work. "Let's put up the cots and get the stuff inside, and then go down to the falls for a swim before supper," Chick suggested.

We did just that. We splashed and cooled off in the roaring water below Copper Falls. We walked back to our campsite and Dewey started making supper—fried potatoes and *minute steaks.* We put a big pot of water on the stove and cooked a dozen ears of our farm girl corn, too.

We sat at our campsite picnic table and ate a delicious supper. The corn was really excellent, and after we finished all the food, we cut open one of the watermelons. "I think this is the first watermelon I've ever eaten that I paid for," Chick said. We all laughed and began spitting seeds at each other.

After we cleaned up the cooking utensils, we sat around the campfire talking. It was pretty much the same kind of conversation we always had:

"You sure you're not going out for football?" Dougie asked.

"Nope. Interferes with my squirrel hunting," I said.

"Did you see Ed Sullivan the other night? Topo Gigo was on again."

"Topo Gigo is stupid!"

"I wonder where those elephants we made friends with a few

years ago are now."

"Probably wishing they had us to get them some melons again."

"Charlie McCarthy was on Ed Sullivan, too."

"He gives me the creeps. He's got weird eyes."

"He's a dummy, dummy."

"I know, but I can't stand those wooden dummies. Yuck. They give me nightmares."

"I wonder if those girls have boyfriends."

"Did you hear the new Beatles song?"

And so it went. We talked and talked until the fire was just embers. Then without anyone saying anything, we all got up and walked into our tent to get ready for bed. The four cots were set out against the sides of the tent and our clothes and other stuff was piled in the middle. We all undressed and climbed into our sleeping bags. Dewey turned off the lantern, and as he walked past my cot he farted right in my face. "Oops. Slipped," he said laughing.

"Dewey... someday... you just wait."

For the next half hour, Dewey vented about once every half minute, one right after another until the tent smelled like the sewer plant. "Jeez, Dewey," Chick scowled. "Go down the road to the outhouse and take care of that!"

"I don't gotta go. It's just a little indigestion." Dewey giggled.

Fifteen farts later we heard Dewey suddenly snoring. "Jeez! He can go from a human fart machine to a chain saw in about ten seconds," Dougie said.

The longer he snored, the louder he snored. Soon the whole tent was vibrating. Then about every five minutes he farted in his sleep, too. "Oh, man. This is gonna be a long night," I said.

"Wake him up, so he'll quit," Chick said sleepily.

"He won't wake up. He's like he's dead when he sleeps," I said.

"I've got an idea," Dougie whispered.

"What?"

"You got a flashlight?"

"Yeah."

"Bring it over here."

I got out of my bag and tiptoed over to Dewey's cot where Dougie and Chick were waiting. "Shine it so we can see his head, but not in his eyes," Dougie whispered.

I pointed the light to illuminate Dewey's head. Dougie leaned forward. I saw his hunting knife in his hand. "Holy cow! Don't kill him!" I whispered excitedly.

"I'm not… I'm going to shave off his eyebrow."

Chick and I about exploded trying not to laugh out loud and wake up Dewey. Dougie's knife was razor sharp, and he carefully began shaving Dewey's right eyebrow off. In just a little while it was as smooth as a baby's butt. "Are you going to do both of them?" I giggled.

"Nope. Just one," Dougie said grinning.

We all climbed back into our sleeping bags, laughing so hard we could hardly breathe.

"Don't say anything in the morning," Dougie said. "Let's see how long it takes him to notice it."

Oh boy! I could hardly wait for breakfast.

Last Hurrah:
Clam Lake

The sun was beating down on the side of the tent, and in no time it was quite hot inside. I rolled over and unzipped my sleeping bag. Then I noticed that Dougie was already awake, lying on top of his bag, too. "Getting hot in here," I whispered.

"Yeah. Let's get up and start breakfast."

We got up, put on our shorts and tee shirts and walked barefoot out into our campsite. Just as we emerged we saw a couple of little kids about 8 or 9 snickering, and backing off our site. "You guys want something?" I asked.

They stopped, but they were still giggling. "We were just wondering when the elephants and clowns were going to come out of that circus tent," the blond kid said laughing.

"Do you have a trapeze hanging in there, too?" the dark-haired kid snickered.

Dougie and I laughed. "You guys making fun of our tent?" I asked.

"Well, you gotta admit… it's a little larger than most of them in this campground. Everyone here was walking by last night wondering if a band of gypsies had moved in," the first kid said.

"Hey, it's really comfortable in there," I said. "We've got cots and lots of room."

"We need lots of room," Dougie added. "We've got one guy who farts all night, so we need to keep away from him."

The kids laughed. "You should hear Andy," he said poking the other kid. "He can toot with the best of them."

One of the kids turned and listened. "That's my mom bellowing. We gotta go. Nice talking to you." They scampered off down the road toward their campsites.

Dougie filled a big pot with water and set it on the stove to heat, while I found the makings for breakfast. Then Chick came out of the tent snickering. "Jeez, Dewey looks hilarious," he whispered. "He doesn't have a clue about his eyebrow."

Just then Dewey backed out of the tent butt first and let out a blast. "That's a morning kiss for you guys," he chuckled.

Dougie and I had all we could do to keep from busting out laughing. Where Dewey's right eyebrow used to be was white in contrast to his tanned face, like it had a spotlight on it. He didn't have a clue.

The water was hot so we washed up and brushed our teeth. When Dewey was finished he began frying bacon. We had a little wire holder to toast bread over the fire. I started toasting bread while Chick and Dougie set the table. The bacon was done and Dewey had just cracked some eggs into the pan when a pickup with a National Forest Service sticker on the side pulled up at our campsite. A guy wearing a uniform got out and came up to the picnic table. "Morning, guys. I'm collecting camping fees," he said. Then he noticed Dewey's missing eyebrow. "I… uh, I…"

Chick stepped up to the guy, winked and shook his head 'no' very discretely. The warden grinned and nodded. "Are you guys staying for another night?"

"Nope. We're on our way to Lake Superior," I said. "How much do we owe for one night?"

"One night of camping is eight dollars," he said, still glancing at Dewey every few seconds.

"You like to stay for breakfast?" Dewey asked as he dished up a plate of eggs and bacon.

The warden grinned. "No, but thanks for the invite," he said. "I'd better be going. You guys have fun." He walked toward his truck and we could see his shoulders shaking as he laughed.

"Seemed like a nice fella," Dewey said as he put a platter filled with eggs and bacon on the picnic table.

We all sat down and did our best to eat without choking from laughter. After breakfast we packed up our camp and took off northbound up the road. After driving for three and a half hours, we were all beginning to feel a little hungry again. "Let's stop someplace and get some burgers," Chick suggested.

We saw a diner up ahead, pulled into the parking lot, and went in. It was pretty crowded, so we figured it must have pretty good food. We slid into an open booth, Dougie and I on one side, and Chick and Dewey on the other. There were menus in a little holder, so we each grabbed one, looking to see what they offered. A lady wearing a pink waitress uniform and a bee hive hairdo came to the table. She cracked her gum as she looked us over. "So what'll you young studs have today?" she asked winking at us.

Dougie and I ordered burgers and chili; Chick ordered a barbeque and fries. Dewey was still looking at his menu lying on the table. "How about you, hon?"

When Dewey looked up, the waitress's mouth dropped open and her gum fell on the table. "I think I'll have a fish sandwich and a bowl of chili and an order of baked beans," he said.

The waitress stared at Dewey's missing eyebrow, and then finally came to her senses. "Uh, fish, chili and beans," she stammered. She looked at me and I winked. Then her face split in a wide grin and off she went.

We watched her as she went behind the counter and whispered to two other waitresses. They looked over to us, snickering. Then she told the cook and a couple of customers, and soon the whole place was sneaking a glance our way.

"I think that waitress thought I was pretty studly," Dewey said. "Did you see the way she looked at me?"

"Yeah, Dewey," I said. "Too bad she's older than your mother.

We ate our lunch and paid amidst lots of giggles from the

waitresses and patrons. I stopped in the restroom on the way out, and Chick and Dougie went to Big Edna. Dewey came into the restroom just as I was washing my hands. "Yeah, that waitress likes me," he said. "She just winked at me."

Dewey came to the sink. He got his hands wet, started to scrub, and looked up in the mirror. He looked back down into the sink again, and then slowly looked up at the mirror a second time. His mouth dropped open and his hand went up to his missing eyebrow. "What the hell?" I laughed so hard, I thought I would fall onto the dingy floor.

"Which one of you guys did this?" Dewey said, looking closely in the mirror, as if his eyebrow might suddenly reappear if he looked hard enough. "I don't know, Dewey," I stammered. "I think someone snuck into the tent and pulled a prank on you."

"Someone my butt! It was one of you guys!"

Dewey and I left the restaurant and walked toward Edna. Dougie and Chick were sitting on the fenders, waiting. When they saw the look on Dewey's face they knew the jig was up. "Which one of you guys is going to die?" Dewey said.

Chick began laughing. Dougie jumped down from the fender and ran to the back of Edna. "So it was you Douglas... you *will* pay!" Dewey bellowed.

"How do you know it was me?" Dougie asked, keeping Edna between him and Dewey.

"Why did you run?"

"Oh, crap."

The three of us were laughing crazily. Finally, Dewey began laughing, too. He looked in the rear view mirror at his missing eyebrow again and shook his head. "I'd hate to be you when my ma sees this," he said.

Dougie looked scared to death.

We pulled out onto the road, heading north again. By late afternoon we were deep in the Chequamegon National Forest, following a road to a lake with a campground. The road wasn't much more than a track through the woods. When we had driven for what seemed like many miles and an eternity I said, "I think this is the wrong road."

"This is GG," Chick said. "The map says it will take us to the lake." Being the official navigator, we decided to listen to him. Just a few minutes later we saw another sign that said CLAM LAKE. It pointed to a trail t into the woods.

We followed the trail and soon came to a nice campground on a small lake. There weren't any other campers, so we had our choice of sites. a sign told us to put our camping fee in an envelope and to deposit it in a locked box attached to a fence post. It also said the water from the pump was safe to drink, that we should take all garbage with us, and last, to *Be Careful of Bears.*

"Be careful of bears!" I said. "What does that mean?"

"I think it means to keep our food in the car... not in the tent with us," Dougie said.

We set up the Big Top and arranged our cots and sleeping bags. Then we backed Edna down to the lake and slid the boat into the water. We all got in the boat and went out for an evening of fishing. It was a really nice little lake. We found a spot that was full of bluegills, fished until we had enough for supper, and then went in, as we were getting hungry.

Chick and I cleaned the fish while Dewey and Dougie got the other stuff ready. They had potatoes and beans already cooking when we brought the fillets to the campsite. Then, while they cooked the fish, Chick and I took the fish heads and guts out in the boat and dumped them way out in the lake, far from the campsite.

The food was ready by the time we got back and we feasted. The fish and fresh potatoes tasted amazing. We all had full bellies when we were finished. We washed up all the dishes and put everything edible in Edna. Then we built a fire in our rock circle and sat back for the evening.

"I wonder how the Braves did today."

"Don't know, but have you noticed how good a hitter Henry Aaron is getting to be?"

"I heard Warren Spahn is going to be a guest star on Combat this fall."

"I heard The Beatles are gonna have a new album."

"Something about Sergeant Pepper."

"I wonder if they have fire flies up here."

"Anybody know when squirrel season starts?"

And on it went. As we talked, moonlight flooded the campsite. We were yawning and someone suggested bed. We all walked off to the edge of the light from the fire, watered the bushes, and then went into the tent. Dewey lit a lantern and we undressed and crawled into our sleeping bags. Once we were all settled, Dewey put out the light. "I think I heard a bear," he said.

"Really?"

"Yeah. Listen close." FRRRRRRRRRRRRTTTT!

We all laughed like we'd never heard a fart before. "Good one, Dewey," Chick laughed.

We all settled down and then I heard everyone's breathing getting slower. I was just about to drift off when there came a sound from the lake that I had never heard before—a loud whistle, starting on a low note and getting higher and louder until it died off going lower and softer. The hair on the back of my neck stood up. I raised my head to listen again. The sound came again, making me think of what a banshee must sound like as he comes to take your soul. My arms were covered with goose bumps.

"What the hell was that?" Chick whispered. "Did you guys hear that?"

"We're not deaf?" Dougie whispered.

"Somebody go out and see what it is," Dewey whispered.

"If you're so curious, why don't you go?" I said.

Just then the sound came again, and it was answered by another on the other side of the lake. "Holy crap! There's two of them!"

By then we were all sitting up on our cots listening very intently when there came a scratching sound on the side of the tent. "Holy shit! It's a bear!" Dewey yelled.

We all jumped up and ran to the side of the tent away from the scratching, but Chick stayed behind. He chuckled and reached over, scratching the tent *again*. "You wise ass," Dougie said. "You almost gave me a stroke."

"Jeez! It's like camping with a bunch of girls," Chick laughed.

"Let's go out and see what's making the noise."

"Are you crazy? Out there?"

"Well, that's where the noise is. If we want to see what it is, we have to go out there."

"I'll go," Dougie said.

"Dewey? You coming? Or are you a chicken, too?"

"Okay, I'll go."

Well, I sat there, not liking this turn of events very much. "Wait a minute. If you all go out there, I'll be in here all by myself."

"Come on. Let's go," Chick said. He got up from his cot. Dougie and Dewey followed him, and as they went through the door, I jumped up and went with them. There was lots of light from the moon. We all walked, very close together, down to the edge of the lake. We were all in our underwear and barefoot, and it was just a little chilly, so it was just a matter of time until we were all shivering, partly from the cold, partly from being a little scared.

Then the wailing sound came again. Chick pointed. "Look! It's one of those loons."

Sure enough there was a loon sitting on the water, its head up in the air, making the sound we had heard. Seconds later another one answered it from down the lake. "Well, now, that's not so scary," I said.

We watched for a little while longer, and then we realized that we were getting very cold. We hustled back up to the tent, wiped off our feet and climbed into our sleeping bags. A little while later, when we were all quiet again, I heard Dougie snoring. "Is Douglas sleeping?" Dewey whispered.

"Sounds like it," Chick said.

"Yeah... why?" I asked.

I could hear Dewey's cot creaking as he got up. He snuck over to Dougie. I heard a click as he lit the lighter we used for the stove. Dougie was on his back, his mouth hanging open, dead to the world.

Dewey turned around, backed up to Dougie's head and held the lighter next to his butt. FFFRRRRRRRRRTTT! A tongue of flame shot out like dragon's breath and engulfed Dougie's head. He shot up to a sitting position, slapping his face with his hands.

The other three of us were crippled with laughter, Chick and I in our beds and Dewey on the floor, tears streaming down his face. "What the hell was that?" Dougie shouted.

The smell of burnt hair hung in the tent. I grabbed my flashlight and shined it on Dougie. His eyebrows and hair in the front were singed. It wasn't gone, but all curly on the ends. "Dewey blasted you with a fire fart," I laughed.

Dougie sat there, looking kind of stunned for a minute, and then he laughed, too. "Jeez! It smells like somebody's singing chickens."

Dewey returned to his bed, gratified by the avenging deed, and we all settled down again. One by one, my friends dozed off. Dang, we sure could have a good time with not too much effort. Looking forward to the adventures of the next day, I drifted off.

Last Hurrah: The Big Lake

Since there weren't any showers at the Clam Lake campgrounds, and we were the only ones camping there, we took our morning bath in the lake. The water wasn't icy cold but it was cold enough to get our attention when we waded into it.

Dougie's eyebrows and the front of his hair looked a little funny, but all the little curly ends had washed off in the lake. Now he just looked like he had trimmed eyebrows. He complained about how Dewey tried to incinerate him; we all had a good laugh. "At least you've got both of yours," Dewey lamented. "I look like a freak with only one."

"Come on over here, Dewey," Dougie said brandishing his razor sharp hunting knife. "I'll take the other one off so you match."

We had breakfast, loaded up the gear, and off we went back to the main road that would take us to Lake Superior. Our destination was the Red Cliff Indian Reservation at the northernmost tip of the state, near the Apostle Islands. We figured there'd be good fishing around the islands. At home we liked fishing near islands on the river. There always seemed to be fish around them.

After several more hours of driving we noticed the air getting cooler. Then we came over a rise and there it was. "Holy smokes!" Chick said. "That's an ocean, not a lake!"

Dewey pulled Edna over to the side of the road. We all got out and walked in front of the car gawking at the big water. It stretched all the way across the horizon and was so wide we couldn't see the other side. "We're going fishing on *that?*" Dougie said unbelievingly.

"I didn't think it was going to be so big," I said.

"What did you think? It was going to be like Gutweilers?" Dewey asked.

"Well, no... but I didn't think it was this big."

Chick checked the map. "We've got a ways to go to get to the Indian Reservation. Maybe it's not so far across up there by those islands."

We piled back into Edna and continued toward the huge lake. We came to Ashland a while later, and stopped at a cafe for lunch. Of course, Dewey's missing eyebrow got us a lot of looks and grins. When the waitress brought our food, Dewey saw her staring at his missing brow. "Birth defect," he said.

After lunch we headed for Bayfield. It was a cool little town with a bunch of fishing boats at the docks. Trouble was, all the boats were ten times bigger than ours, and there wasn't a flat bottom in the bunch. These were big fishing boats with high sides and inboard engines. An old grizzly looking man sat on the dock fishing and looked at us. "You guys going out on the lake in that flat bottom?" he asked.

"Yeah, we figured to," Chick said.

He shook his head sadly. "Been nice meetin' ya."

"Why? Don't you think that boat is big enough to go on this lake?"

"The lake is dead calm right now," he answered. "Once a breeze comes up, she'll get choppy, and if the breeze gets a bit heavier she'll get downright bumpy. You need a boat that will cut into the waves, not some flat nosed scow like that. You'll take a wave over the bow and be in the water before you know it. Go down there and stick yer big toes in that water and then tell me if you think you'd like to be swimming in it for a few hours... cause that's what will happen if you capsize that there river boat of yours."

Well, that didn't sound like much fun. We all kind of looked at each other and Chick shrugged. "Well, we're here and we don't have much choice, do we?"

We thanked the man for the information, wishing in the back of our minds that we'd never walked down next to him. We got back into Edna and drove on north to the Reservation.

We came to a sign that stated we were now on Tribal Lands and subject to Tribal Law. We didn't know for sure what that meant, but we decided to be really careful not to break any laws. Then we came to a gate and a small building next to it. We stopped. A young woman with dark skin and shiny black hair, wearing a Tribal Warden uniform came out to the car. "Will you be camping on the Reservation?" she asked pleasantly.

"Yeah, if that's okay," Dewey said.

"Of course. We welcome visitors. How many nights will you be here?"

"We plan on staying four nights," Chick said getting the Bank out. "How much is it?"

She told us it was eight dollars a night to camp. Then she gave us a map and showed us a campsite that we could use right next to the water. She circled the site's number, 113. We paid her; she turned to go, and then stopped to look at Dewey.

"Birth defect," he said, and we drove away.

We followed the road through the Reservation past many other campers with nice nylon tents with aluminum poles, and finally we found our site. It was great, on a high point with the lake a stone's throw away from where we planned to set up the Big Top. We unloaded our gear and started to erect the tent.

We had the tent almost up when a couple of Indian kids rode past on bikes. They stopped and snickered at our tent. "The elephants will be here soon," Chick said. "They're in a truck with the clowns and the band."

The kids looked at each other and then took off on their bikes riding as fast as they could go, kicking up a cloud of dust.

"They'll probably be back with every kid on the Reservation now," I said laughing.

The map showed a boat landing a short distance from the campsite. Dewey and Dougie went to put the boat into the water. A while later, Dougie came driving the boat down the lake, and ran it up on the beach in front of the tent. Dewey came down the road in Edna pulling the empty trailer and backed it off to the side, out of the way.

"Boy! The water is so clear you can see the rocks on the bottom," he said.

"Did you see any fish?"

"Nope. Just rocks."

It was almost suppertime, so we got everything ready and Dewey cooked. There was a ring of rocks at the campsite but we didn't have any firewood and no trees around to get dead branches from, so we just used the stove. As we ate, a couple of kids drove up in an old jeep. "Need any firewood?" one of them asked.

"How much?" Chick asked.

"Two bucks for a big armload."

We looked at each other and nodded. "Cool. We'll take some."

They got out of the Jeep. One held out his arms and the other loaded him up with wood. The one doing the carrying had a hard time to manage the big armload of wood. He staggered to the fire ring and dropped it close by. "That's an extra big armload," he said smiling.

Chick gave him two bucks and we invited them to sit down and have a pop with us. They sat and the one that had carried the wood introduced himself. "I'm Alex, and this is Tim," he said nodding to the other kid. They were both about our age and size with very dark skin, like an end of summer tan, and shiny black hair, cut about like ours. They wore tee shirts and cutoffs. One had tennis shoes and the other, sandals.

We introduced ourselves. They looked curiously at Dewey. "Dewey was the subject of a little prank," I said laughing. They both laughed and Alex said, "My brother, Tom, did that to one of his buddies, too, once when they were camping. The guy was farting up a storm, so they got even with him."

We all cracked up when we heard that. "That's exactly why Dewey got the same treatment," Dougie laughed.

Dewey leaned back, raised his left leg and let go a blast. Alex and Tim doubled over laughing.

"I'm kind of surprised that you have regular names," Chick said. "I expected you to be Little Deer or Lone Wolf."

Alex laughed. "Our grandmas have names like that for us, but we use just regular names."

We built a campfire and we were soon sharing stories with our new friends. It turned out that they were both going to be Juniors at Bayfield High School. Alex was a football player, and Tim, who was a little smaller and more wiry, was a wrestler. Then the conversation turned to fishing.

"You planning on going out in that flat boat?" Alex asked.

"Not a good idea?" I asked.

"You haven't seen the lake when it gets rough, have you?"

We shook our heads. "Sometimes there are six and eight foot waves. I don't think that boat will stand waves like that."

"That's about the only kind of boat anyone uses where we live," I said.

"Those are river boats... not good for a big lake like this."

We were disappointed. "Well," Dougie said. "Looks like we came a long way to fish in Lake Superior and it's a waste of time."

Alex and Tim exchanged glances and Alex nodded. "My dad has a charter boat... takes people out fishing. He charges them, but when he doesn't have clients, he lets Tim and me take it out. You guys want to go out with us?"

"How much does it cost?"

"Nothing... if you go with us. All we have to do is pay for the gas we use. If you chip in for that, it won't cost any more."

Well, now we were getting someplace. "Wow! That sounds like a good time," I said. "When can we go?"

"I don't think Dad has a charter for the next couple of days, so unless somebody called this evening, we can go tomorrow."

We were excited and began asking questions about many things like what kind of bait to take. Alex explained that we needed big rigs with four or five hundred yards of line on them, and that they had all the gear on the boat. "Those little sunfish poles you guys have aren't heavy enough for the fish out there. No offense, but just leave them here at your campsite. We'll provide the gear, and all you have to bring is lunch."

Well, this was getting better all the time. We agreed that we'd meet them in the morning. They drove off in their jeep to sell more firewood around the campground. We enjoyed the campfire for a couple more hours and then filed into the Big Top to bed down, visions of huge lake trout in our dreams.

The next morning we were all just waking up, listening to Dewey serenade us with a medley of morning farts when we heard the jeep pull up. Then there was a scratching on the tent. "Come on in," Dougie said.

The flap opened and there were our two new friends grinning at us. "Jeez! You guys sleep late. There are trout to be caught... whew, it stinks in here!" Alex said backing from the tent. We all laughed crazily as we dressed and walked out into a beautiful morning.

"We got time for breakfast?" I asked.

"Sure. We don't have any time schedule, but I usually like to get on the lake early. It usually gets windy in the afternoons and then we like to get off the lake, before it gets too rough."

Dewey fired up the stove and whipped up scrambled eggs while Dougie made toast. We set six places at the table, and soon we were shoveling two dozen scrambled eggs into our faces. While Dougie and Dewey cleaned up the breakfast pans and plates, Chick and I and our two new buddies made sandwiches and filled the cooler with pop. We took a couple of big bags of chips, too, and piled everything in Edna. Alex and Tim rode with us to Bayfield where the boat was moored at the marina.

"Geez! This thing is like a tank!" Tim exclaimed as we roared down the dusty road.

As we walked down the dock we passed the old guy we had talked to the previous day. "Ah, my advice is heeded," he said as we passed. "Now we won't have to search for bodies."

"Don't mind him," Alex said. "He does that to everybody."

The boat was a beauty. Alex told us it was 26 feet long, powered by an eight cylinder Chrysler engine. A little doorway led down under the bow where there were a couple of bunks if someone wanted to take a nap. The steering wheel was on a covered deck, and behind that was an open deck. Several rod holders were bolted to the top of the sides, and some kind of contraptions with wire cable and small cannon balls hanging from them.

"Those are downriggers," Alex explained. "The lake trout are just off the bottom, so we clip our line with the lures on it into this release," he said showing us the little clip. "Then we lower the cannon ball down to just off the bottom and troll. When a trout hits, the clip lets the line go and we fight the fish on the rod and reel."

"How do you know how deep it is?" Dewey asked.

"See that graph on the dash? Once we get on the lake, you'll see.

It shows the bottom and how deep it is, plus it shows fish."

"No foolin'? Jeez! That's really cool!" Chick said.

We were impressed with the boat and all the gear. "This is a little more high tech than our usual fishing," Dougie said. "We put a forked stick in the ground and wait for a bite."

We cast off and roared down the lake to some hot spots that the boys knew. After a run of several miles we slowed down and Chick took over steering the boat while Tim and Alex rigged the rods. They put down four downriggers and then set out two other lines, one out each side on a thing that looked like a ski. They explained that they were called ski boards and took the lines out away from the boat. These lines were rigged for rainbow and brown trout that liked to stay in shallower water near the surface. In fifteen minutes we had six lures dragging along behind the boat. We took turns steering as Alex and Tim gave instructions as to where to go.

"Now we wait for a strike," Alex said. The words had no more than come from his mouth when a downrigger line popped to the surface. "Fish on!" he yelled and grabbed the rod from the holder. He turned and offered it to Dewey, but he backed off. "Let somebody else do it first," he said.

Dougie stepped up and grabbed the rod. "Just keep the line tight and pump it, raise it and then reel down," Tim instructed.

"I *have* caught a fish before," Dougie said.

"Sorry. We get a lot of first timers out here, and some don't know crap," Alex said laughing. "We call them dumpers."

"Dumpers?"

"Yeah. They manage to dump more fish off the line than they catch."

"Like Dewey," I added.

Dewey lifted his leg and the usual noise followed. Dougie pumped on the fish and gained line. "Jeez! It pulls like a ten pound catfish," he panted.

We were all watching over the side when Tim yelled, "There it is." He was pointing, and we could see the silver flash of the fish behind the boat. Alex got ready with a huge net with about a twelve foot long handle. "Lift him once more, and then when he gets to the top, walk backwards toward the front of the boat," he said to Dougie. Dougie did just as instructed and Alex netted the Laker.

It was a dandy, as far as we were concerned. Alex and Tim said it probably weighed about eight or nine pounds—a fine fish in our eyes. We took it off the line and put it in a cooler, and they re-rigged the rod and set it back into the holder. "There, number one… the beginnings of a fish boil," Tim said grinning.

Ten minutes later we had another fish on and Dewey hauled it in. It was a twin to the first one, and as we took it off, one of the outside lines tripped. I grabbed that rod and began fighting a fish that jumped from the water like a porpoise. "Rainbow!" Tim shouted.

Just then another downrigger popped and Chick grabbed the rod. As he began reeling, the downrigger next to it popped and there was another fish on. Tim grabbed that one and Alex began reeling up the other two downriggers. "We'll have a hell-of-a mess if they get tangled in the other cables," he said as he reeled. Take that other outrigger in too," he said to Dewey.

Dewey pulled the rod from the holder, snapped the line free and started reeling. He had only gone ten feet when there was a smashing strike on the line. "Holy smokes! I've got one, too!"

Well, the next few minutes were pretty much chaos. There was a lot of shifting of positions as the fish fought back and forth and a lot of shouting as we tried to keep the lines from crossing. The two rainbows ran from side to side jumping and thrashing and threatening to tangle all the lines together. The two Lake Trout on the downriggers bulldogged to the bottom like a catfish, so they stayed out of the way. Alex and Dougie were left with the tasks of driving the boat and netting the fish.

Chick's fish came to the boat first and Alex netted it with one swipe. He was working furiously to get it off the hook so he could get the net free. Dougie grabbed the thrashing fish and tossed it into the cooler and then ran back to make sure we kept going straight. Dewey's rainbow was getting close to the boat, so Alex netted it and swung it aboard. He took the hook out just as my fish jumped at the side of the boat. "Hurry up! Mine's right here!"

Alex lifted the net over the side with Dewey's fish still in it and made a swipe at my fish, getting it in the net, too. Then they worked fast to get them both out and he turned to Tim who had been keeping the fish on his line just below the boat. Alex lifted Tim's fish into the boat and we all began yelling and high-fiving. "Jeez! That was amazing," Chick laughed. "I'd have bet we'd never get them all in. That was *so* cool."

We were all panting and worn out from the madness, and all the lines were now laying in the bottom of the boat, so it seemed a good time for a break. We drove over next to a large island and dropped anchor. We had six nice fish in the cooler. Tim said that was just enough for a good fish boil. We ate our sandwiches, and then we all laid back and had a little nap. About half an hour later I woke when I heard a loud splash. Tim and Alex weren't anywhere to be seen, so I stood up and looked over the side. They splashed water at me and laughed. "Come on in. The water's great."

I saw their clothes lying in piles on the deck and knew they were skinny dipping, so I slipped my clothes off, climbed up on the rail of the boat and cannon balled into the lake. *Great* wasn't what I'd call the water temperature. *Cold* was more like it! "Jeez! This is freezing," I said as I came to the surface.

"Oh, don't be a sissy. This is good. Just wait a minute… it'll be just fine," Alex said grinning.

Within a minute the rest of the guys were in the water with us. We had a great time swimming and goofing around in the crystal clear water. There was a little platform with a ladder on the back of the boat; we'd climb out of the water onto that, and then cannon ball off the side. We swam for half an hour and then climbed up the little ladder into the back of the boat. Alex grabbed towels from the bunk room under the deck and we all dried off and dressed.

"Well, how about we go in?" Tim asked. "We'll have an authentic fish boil for supper."

That sounded like a plan. We started up the motor and took turns driving in toward the marina. The lake was much rougher, now that the wind had come up, so we hit some pretty big waves as we sailed toward land.

In the harbor we pulled the boat up to a floating gas station at the dock. Tim filled the tank; the gas came to a little over $14. Chick pulled $15 from the Bank and gave it to him. "Tim and I can pay part," Alex said.

"No way. This is fine. Just pay the guy," I said.

Tim paid the attendant; we motored to their stall at the marina and tied up the boat. We loaded the fish into a plastic tote and hauled them up to a fish cleaning shack. Tim and Alex gutted them, took off the heads and then cut them into about two inch steaks. It didn't take them long to get the fish cleaned, washed, and ready to eat. We stopped at a grocery store and bought a bag of potatoes, carrots, onions, a dozen ears of sweet corn, two loaves of hard bread and a pound of butter. "We brought the fish boil bucket with us this morning, just in case we got some fish. It's in the jeep," Tim said.

Back at our campsite we built a nice fire in the fire pit. Then Tim and Alex set a metal tripod over the fire and brought the huge bucket to the picnic table. We washed the red potatoes, cleaned the carrots, peeled the onions and corn and they dumped all of it into the huge bucket. Then they filled it with water and hung it from a chain over the fire. Half an hour later, the water boiled, and when the vegetables had been cooking for 15 minutes, they dumped in the chunks of fish. "Ten minutes more… and we eat," Tim said smiling.

Table set and everything ready, our stomachs growled at the thought of all that food. When the ten minutes were up, Tim took a canning jar full of some liquid and walked to the fire. "Stand back," he warned, and he dumped the liquid onto the fire. The liquid in the jar was gas, and the fire bellowed up causing the water in the bucket to boil over.

"Jeez! That's pretty dramatic," Chick said.

"It makes all the oil from the fish boil over, so it's not greasy, and it's kind of a crowd pleaser, too," Tim said grinning.

Alex and Tim grabbed a couple of heavy gloves and took the big bucket from the tripod. They poured the contents of the bucket into a big metal pan with a drain in one end hanging over the end of the picnic table. There, before my eyes, was one of the most beautiful sights I had ever seen—chunks of snowy white fish, boiled potatoes, carrots, steaming ears of corn, and whole onions. The aroma was incredible.

Tim produced a large, shovel like spatula and handed it to Dougie. "Dig in," he said.

We had melted the pound of butter on the stove; the pan was sitting in the middle of the table. We all filled our plates with the food, broke off a large chunk of the hard bread, poured melted butter over the food and began eating. "Oh my gosh," Dougie said, his mouth full of fish. "This is amazing."

We congratulated our new friends on the food. They smiled from ear to ear. We chomped, slurped and munched for nearly an hour. The entire pan of food was consumed. We were all so stuffed that we could hardly wiggle. "I'll never forget that meal for the rest of my life," I said raising my pop can in a toast. "To our new friends, thank you for a memorable day."

We sat around the campfire talking and laughing. It was nearly midnight when Alex and Tim decided they better get home or their moms would be out looking for them. We made plans to meet them in the morning and take a trip to Ashland to see the sights. The boat was chartered for the day, so this would give us something to do, and Alex and Tim were glad to get a little road trip in with us.

The four of us ambled into the tent. Our heads had hardly hit our pillows when we were all soundly asleep. It had been a big day.

Last Hurrah: The End of an Era

"This thing is like a bedroom on wheels," Alex laughed as we drove down the road toward Ashland.

"Yeah. The back seat is as comfortable as my bed," I said. "In fact, I've slept back here a couple of times... once when we were sitting sideways in a ditch."

Our two new friends looked at us questioningly, so we explained about the night we snuck into Jerry Johnson's bass pond and got stuck. "That must have been pretty embarrassing, when he came to pull you out," Tim laughed.

"He was real nice about it, actually," Dewey said over his shoulder.

When we arrived at Ashland, we drove down by the docks and saw the big ships loading with grain that would be transported to Europe. Then we went to a marine museum that told all about the Great Lakes. After that we went to a café, ate lunch, and then walked down the street and saw a movie. We toured around the town for a while longer and then stopped at a nice restaurant on the way back to Bayfield for a good supper. Chick paid the bill for all of us from our Bank. Alex and Tim wanted to pay for their own, but we felt it was the least we could do to thank them for the greatest fishing trip we'd had.

We returned to our campsite just at dusk, built a campfire, and sat there drinking pop. With two new friends, the conversation took a delightedly new twist:

"You guys got girlfriends at home?" Alex asked.

"No, not really," Chick replied. "We swore a pact a few years ago that we'd never like girls, but I think we're all kind of thinking that was a bad idea."

Alex laughed. "Tim and I did the same thing, but they're not so bad now as they used to be, right Tim?" Tim blushed. "Tim has his eye on a little cutie from Bayfield," Alex teased.

We talked about fishing for a long time, and then ice fishing.

"Does this lake freeze over enough to walk out and fish?" I asked.

"Freeze over! They drive cars out to Madeline Island in the winter. They make a road across the ice and mark it with Christmas trees."

"Holy cow! They drive all that way?"

"Yeah. It's nice for the people who live there. They don't have to take the ferry in the winter. We don't ice fish much. If we ice fish, it's on some of the smaller lakes around here. It would take a lot of line to get to the bottom here."

We talked about movies and school and sports; and then I had a thought. I motioned for Chick to come with me to the tent. "You've got your *Muscoda Indians* tee shirt, don't you?"

"Yeah, but it's dirty. I wore it on the way up here."

"I've got mine, too. It's not dirty, but I don't think it would be any problem that yours had been worn. What do you think about giving them to Alex and Tim?"

"That's a good idea… something to remember us by. But, do you think they might be offended by the Indian logo?"

I thought about it, but I just don't think they are the type to let it bother them. "Let's give the shirts to them, and if they are, we can apologize and take them back."

We dug in our duffle bags, found the two maroon-and-white tee shirts, and walked out to the fire ring. "Hey guys. We'd like to give you something to remember us by, and the only things we have from our part of the world are these two tee shirts from our school." I handed them to Alex and Tim. "They're not brand new and that one was already worn this week, but if you wash it, it'll be okay."

They held up the shirts and grinned. "Wow! Thanks. They're great," Alex exclaimed.

"Yeah," Tim added. "We'll be the only ones in our school with *Muscoda Indians* tee shirts."

"You're not offended by the Indian?" Dougie asked.

"Crap, no! That's stupid. Some people make such a big deal about those things. How do you choose a mascot for a team? You choose something that you admire, something brave and strong. I don't see what some of those gripers are talking about, but for me, this is an honor and I'm proud to wear it." Alex stripped off his own tee and put on mine.

"Me too," Tim said, doing the same.

"Well, good. I hope you'll think of us when you wear them," Dougie said.

We talked for a long time after that. The moon rose and cast a silver beam across the lake that illuminated everything in its glow. "We better get going home," Alex said yawning. "So, we're gonna fish again tomorrow?"

"It's okay with your dad?"

"Yup. No charter, so we can have the boat."

We were all for that. "We'll have breakfast ready at seven," Dewey said.

"Why don't you guys bring sleeping bags and stay with us tomorrow night?" I asked. "We don't have any extra cots, but you could bring a couple of air mattresses."

"Good idea," Alex said. "We won't have to worry about our moms sending out a search party for us."

Alex and Tim drove off in their jeep and we got ready for bed. "That was nice of you to give them your tee shirts," Dougie said.

"I wish it had been something better, but that's about all we had," Chick said.

"You know, we really should be starting home tomorrow afternoon," Dougie said. "You guys have football practice in two days."

"If we fish tomorrow, we'll just get up real early the next day and drive all day to get home," I said. "We probably won't have a chance to fish like this again for a long, long time."

We all agreed, and we were soon dreaming of giant lake trout.

The next morning I woke to the sound of pans rattling on the stove. I was surprised to see that Dewey was already up. I staggered out into the bright sunshine. Dewey was standing at the stove in his tee shirt and underwear frying bacon.

"Better be careful, Dewey," I said. "If that bacon grease splatters, you might get a terrible burn on your most sensitive place."

"It wouldn't be much of a burn," Chick said as he walked out of the tent.

"Oh, very funny," Dewey said grinning. "Make fun of the fat guy's wiener."

Then Dougie came out. We all pitched in and got the breakfast ready. Then Alex and Tim drove up, both wearing their Muscoda tee shirts and shorts. Tim was carrying a white paper bag filled with donuts and rolls from a bakery where they stopped on the way.

Alex was carrying a handful of leather thongs with carved clam shell amulets hanging from them. "We brought you guys something to remember us by," he said. He handed each of us one of the amulets. They were beautifully carved with Indian symbols from mother of pearl clams.

"This is the sign of our tribe," Tim said pointing to one side of the amulet. "This makes you honorary members. On the other side is the Indian symbol for brother, so you are now our new brothers."

We were all very touched. We put the amulets around our necks and shook hands with both of them. Then I thought better and hugged each of them. The rest followed my lead. When everyone had hugged, we all felt a little embarrassed, but glad that we had done it.

"We'll keep these and be proud to be members of your tribe and your brothers," Chick said.

We all sat down to eat, chattering about the upcoming fishing trip. After we finished breakfast we drove to the marina and off we went to the big lake. The fishing was as good as the previous trip, and by mid-afternoon we had seven fish in the cooler. The wind was coming up and Dewey was looking a little green around the gills. The boat was rolling on the big swells, so you had to hang on to the side, or walk like you were drunk. "You gonna blow, Dewey?" Alex asked.

"I'm feeling a little poorly," Dewey answered.

"Stay close to the rail, so if you do it goes over the side," Chick said.

We fished for another half hour. It was getting to be work just to stand upright, so we went in, made the boat ship shape, and then cleaned the fish. We stopped for more groceries, and by the time we got back to our campsite, Dewey was looking pretty good again. We all pitched in and had another fish boil that could have fed about a dozen people. We were all stuffed, so we made a bonfire and sat and talked late into the night.

Alex and Tim had brought their sleeping bags and air mattresses as planned. It was fun for us to camp with them, and they could help us tear down the camp in the morning. We had told them about getting on the road early, and they wanted to see us off.

It turned out that Tim and Alex could hold their own in the fartfest that ensued in the tent that night. They competed with Dewey, and even he had to admit, they were quite talented. We laughed ourselves to sleep.

The next morning we cooked everything we had left in the cooler. It was a smorgasbord breakfast with everything from hot dogs to pancakes to prime rib. After breakfast, Alex drove the flat bottom to the landing while Dewey backed the boat trailer down to the water. They loaded up the boat and came back just as we finished taking down the Big Top. We loaded up everything. We were ready for the road.

We stood there feeling kind of awkward. Finally Alex came forward and hugged Dewey, then Chick, Dougie and me. Tim did the same. "We sure had a good time with you guys," they said.

"Same here. You guys made our trip for us."

"You gotta promise to come to Muscoda next summer, so we can show you all our good places to fish," Dewey said.

"We'll try. I promise," Alex said.

We got into Edna and started down the dusty road. Alex and Tim were still watching us, waving, as we topped a little rise and then they disappeared. We were all strangely quiet for a long time. If the other guys felt like I did, they had a little lump in their throats, and it just felt good to sit and think of how lucky we were to have such good new friends.

We drove steadily on, stopping only for gas and fast food. The miles piled up. After several hours, Chick took over driving while Dewey had a nap. The flatness and pine trees of the north gradually disappeared. Small hills and an occasional oak or maple was visible along the road. It was just getting dusk when we entered into our own familiar terrain. The hills and valleys lay out in front of us and the familiar sights of home were there, right outside the windows.

It was dark when we crossed over the Wisconsin River Bridge that led into Muscoda. As we got about half way across we all just naturally looked upriver to the Gosey. "Holy smokes! Look!" Dougie said. "There's a campfire up at the Gosey!"

"We better see what's going on," Chick said.

We turned down the sand road to the Gosey and saw the campfire ahead of us. Four bikes lay in the sand along the road, and four kids were lying on sleeping bags around a campfire in *our* fire pit. As we pulled up the kids shielded their eyes against the glare of the headlights. We stopped the car, got out and walked over toward them.

"Hey," one of the kids said, kind of like he was scared.

"Hey," I said. "Gonna camp here tonight?"

"Yeah. We thought we would. Is that okay?"

"Sure," Dougie said. "It's public land."

"We were fishing down at the bridge today and wandered up here. And here was this cool place," another kid said, "So we thought it would be a good place to camp."

"There's a rope swing on that big tree, too," the other one said.

The first kid sat up on his bag and moved over to one end. "Wanna sit?"

We said yes and each of us sat down with one of the kids. One was the younger brother of one of our friends, but I didn't know the rest. Two were just average kids, one was a little smaller and one was a little chunky. Chick and I sat with the average kids, Dougie with the smaller kid, and Dewey plopped down next to the chunky kid. "I'm Andy. I think you guys know my brother," the kid next to me said. "That's Chuck, and that little guy is Denny. The lardass over there is Arthur, but we call him Boomer."

Just as he said it, Boomer lifted his leg and blasted a good fart.

We all laughed and Dewey patted him on the back. "Nice tone," he said.

Boomer produced a big paper bag full of popcorn and passed it around. Then we began chatting with them about the Gosey and fishing and lots of other stuff. We found out that they were all just 13 that summer.

"You guys ever come down here much?" Andy asked.

"Yeah, you could say that," I said. "We've kinda had this place as ours for quite a few years now."

"Oh, sorry. We don't want to barge in," Denny said.

"No problem. We've been out of town a lot this summer, so we haven't been here as much as usual."

"So what did you call this place?" Boomer asked Dewey.

"It's the Gosey," Dewey said.

"Why's it called that?"

Dewey began to tell the story of the Gosey just as he had told it to us in a dark tent in my back yard several years earlier. The kids were wide eyed when he told about the guy drowning and that he was buried somewhere down there on the shore.

"Wow! That's kind of spooky," Denny said. "You guys ever have anything weird happen when you camped here?"

"Nothing more than Dewey making horrid noises with his butt," Chick laughed.

It was getting late and everyone was starting to yawn, so we decided to let the kids get some sleep.

"You guys take good care of this place," Chick said. "We've watched over it for a long time. Now it's up to you."

"We will. Promise," Boomer said. "We'll keep it clean and take good care of it. If you guys want to, you can come down here any time."

We all smiled to ourselves as we walked back to Edna.

We waved good-bye to the kids and drove down the road. "Kind of reminds me of us a few years ago," Dougie said.

"Yeah, like a set of younger us's." I said. "Weird."

We stopped at Chick's house first and he got out. "Kinda like the end of an era isn't it?" he said. He tapped the roof of the car and turned and walked into his house.

Dewey stopped at Dougie's house next. I got out there, too, since my house was just a block away. We agreed to meet at noon the next day and put away all our camping gear. We bid Dewey a good night.

Dougie and I sat down on his front porch steps and watched Edna disappear down the street. "Well," he said, "it's been quite a summer, hasn't it?"

"It's been quite a summer... *and* quite a few years of the four of us being together."

"Yeah, that's for sure. Do you think it's over now?"

I thought for a second. "No, not over, but I think it'll be different. We're getting older, and we have new interests. We're bound to see less of each other."

"Do you think we'll still be friends?"

"I think we'll still be friends when we're old men... like when we're 40, even."

"I hope so. We've sure had a bunch of fun together," he said quietly.

I put my arm around his shoulders and gave him a squeeze. "Don't worry... friends don't just forget each other. We've had too many good memories to do that. Good friends are forever."

I got up, started down the sidewalk and Dougie said, "Night... see ya tomorrow." I turned and waved as he got up and climbed the porch steps.

When I got home I woke Mom and let her know that I was still alive and that all my extremities were still intact. Then I washed up and climbed into my bed for the first time in a long, long time. I thought of those kids down at the Gosey, so much like we had been a few years ago, on the verge of so many new discoveries and fun times. I thought of the many times we had lain right in that very spot, our sleeping bags circling the fire, talking, laughing and finally drifting off to sleep. I remembered the sounds of the night that we listened to: the bullfrogs ka-thunking off in the marsh; the owls in the river bottoms calling "Who cooks for you? Who cooks for you?"

There were the sounds of mice scurrying through the grass and leaves, scrounging for a fallen bit of potato chip or a crumb of bread.

I remembered the smell of smoke from a wood fire as it drifted up toward the black sky, filled with a billion tiny pinpricks of light from the stars. I remembered the fun of watching the green lights of fireflies as they flittered through the darkness, turning their lights on and off. I remembered how we watched the fire die to glowing red coals that heated up the front side of our sleeping bags.

How many nights had we slept on that river bank? How many times had we laughed… hundreds, maybe thousands?

I envied those kids just starting out as friends, so much like we did, just a few years ago. I envied them for all the fun that was waiting for them. I wondered if we'd still have times like that, now that we were getting older, and would soon be finished with high school and off to college and jobs.

But I was excited about the upcoming school year, too. This year we would finally be *upper classmen.* In another year we'd be the rulers of the school. In our senior year, those kids who were down at the Gosey would be freshmen. Would they remember us then?

I was picturing the embers of the campfire as they turned gray and began to die, and the *new* residents of the Gosey snuggled in their sleeping bags… when I drifted off to sleep.

Good Friends ARE Forever!

Several years ago when I had the idea for *The Gosey,* the first book about my friends Dewey, Dougie and Chick, I called each of them and told them what I had in mind. I explained that if it was alright with them, I was going to use them as characters in the book, and that I might—just might—embarrass them a little. Good guys that they are, they all told me to go ahead.

As is with all fiction, some of the things an author writes are true, and some made up. Often a story needs to be embellished a little to make it better, but sometimes the story was crazy enough to be told just the way it really happened. I told some pretty good tales about these three guys, and hoped that they didn't take offense.

When *The Gosey* was published, I contacted each of them and we arranged to meet for dinner. I wanted to give them each a copy of the book and see what they thought of it.

Chick, real name Craig Chicker lives in Richland Center, Wisconsin and spent the bulk of his career as a policeman and chief of police in Richland Center. He's still an avid hunter and fisherman and we see each other often.

Dewey, real name Duane Froh lives near DeSoto, Wisconsin and is retired from Dairyland Power. For several years after graduation he was a chef. We, too, see each other now and then.

Dougie, real name Doug Stamm lives in Sauk City, Wisconsin and is an outdoor photographer. His job takes him all over the country taking pictures that he sells to outdoor publications.

The day came for our dinner. It was one of those events that you would like to go on forever. When we met at the restaurant, we quickly figured out that, although we had seen each other many times over the years, our meeting that day was the first time in 35 years that all four of us had been together at the same time. There was no awkwardness, no wondering what to say. Three minutes after we all said hello, we were reliving adventures from nearly a lifetime ago. The phrase, "Remember the time—?" was repeated over and over.

I sat there listening and laughing. I looked across the table and saw Dewey, Chick and Dougie, the same three kids I grew up with—not old guys with gray hair or no hair—not soon-to-be elderly guys, but three grinning, laughing kids. It was an evening I'll long remember.

It confirmed my belief... *Good friends ARE Forever!*

ABOUT THE AUTHOR

Dan Bomkamp has made his home in the Wisconsin River valley all his life with the exception of his college years in La Crosse. He has been an avid hunter and fisherman his whole life. For many years he was in the sporting goods industry and began writing in the 80s for outdoor magazines. He is active in the Foreign Exchange Student program having hosted 33 boys from 13 countries over the years. Golden Retrievers have also been a big part of his life. He had at least one Golden sharing his home for 33 years. He lives in Muscoda with his cat, Tigger and his Boston Terrier, Buster.

E-mail: Danbomkamp@live.com
Website: www.Danbomkamp.com

Other books by Dan Bomkamp

The Adventures of Thunderfoot
More Adventures of Thunderfoot
Thanks, Thunderfoot
Voyageur
Lost Flight
Tag
Whiteout
Spirit
The Lost Treasure of Bogus Bluff
November Gales
Bringing Ethan Home
The Boy Who Fell From the Sky

Non-Fiction
River of Mystery

www.ingramcontent.com/pod-product-compliance
Lightning Source LLC
Chambersburg PA
CBHW070311030726
47505CB00004B/977

* 9 7 8 0 6 9 2 5 3 3 3 0 7 *